Cambiare

AVERY AMES

Cambiare

AVERY AMES

Az
AZULINE
PUBLISHING

First Edition

ISBN-13: 978-1-7332122-0-5

Cover illustration by D.C. McNaughton.
🐦 @DCMcNaughton

For Nathan

Your encouragement and support made my dream a reality.
I couldn't have done this without you.

Prologue

THE MOONS WERE BICKERING TONIGHT.

Shara had fled the sky completely, a hollow black spot occupying her place in the heavens. Her sister, Resa, was a mere sliver, leaving only the stars to illuminate the world below.

Orwe's head broke the water's surface and took in the bare starlight glinting off the inky black waves. *Perfect lighting for a task like this,* he thought as the sea crashed and frothed against the slick wall of the nearby cliff.

He squinted at the immense building atop it. The Unseelie Palace. Impenetrable.

Unless Ellian was right after all. Orwe ducked back under the water, diving deep. A long gulp forced the brine over his gills. He shuddered at the feel of the thick saltwater. *Just this one mission,* he promised himself. Soon enough, he'd be back home in his sweet river.

The cliff wall came into focus as he swam closer, a maiden discarding her veil of silty seawater. His fingertips brushed the cold rock. White as bone, it ran for miles along the coast. If Ellian's theory was to be believed, there might be an opening somewhere above the waterline. The palace's garbage had to go somewhere, and the ocean was the likeliest candidate.

A way out also meant a way *in*.

Orwe wrapped a webbed hand around the necklace at his throat, the sea serpent's tooth that had belonged to his grandfather and his grandfather before him. *Please help me find it*, he asked them silently.

In the depths below him, a flash of obsidian glittered.

Sealurk.

Orwe's pulse quickened and the water roared against his ears. He would never stand a chance against the giant predator's deadly teeth. Panic pounded a frantic rhythm inside his ribcage as he scrabbled along the rocky surface of the cliff.

A flurry of movement swirled the water beneath. The creature had seen him. Its scales flashed as it undulated upward, its maw opening.

A silent scream caught in Orwe's throat. *This is how it ends.*

Frantically, he surfaced and cast about for something, anything. There. An outcropping of stone just above the waterline. Orwe kicked his way to it while the sealurk closed in.

He hauled himself over the edge as the creature's enormous teeth closed around his foot. Orwe shrieked when the beast sheared half his foot off in one snap. Despite the pain, he dragged himself further away from the water's edge, out of the sealurk's reach.

The harsh air scraped his skin and his lungs. A jagged agony consumed him, and his blood smeared a grisly line across the pearlescent stone. Where the lower half of his foot should have been, there was only a bloody, jagged bone.

The sealurk's head broke the surface, teeth gnashing, but Orwe was too far from the water's edge.

He huddled over his foot, muttering prayer after prayer to

his ancestors as blood continued to pool beneath him. *What now?* He couldn't swim like this, and the sealurk prowled the edge of the outcropping. Orwe was trapped. His flimsy seaweed garments would not be enough to bandage this.

I'm going to die here. Would Ellian mourn him, or the others? A sob broke free. *Osra, I'm so sorry.*

Orwe curled into a ball as each beat of his heart poured his life out onto the stone. He closed his eyes and waited for death, to sink into the everlasting river forever.

He was not to be granted such peace. A sudden, invisible grip wrapped itself around Orwe's wrist and yanked. He was hauled upward along the tall cliff, struggling against the force that grasped him.

The unseen thing pulled him over the precipice to collapse onto more hard stone. His eyes met the vibrant gaze of a sidhe, and Orwe's guts turned to jelly. The faerie did not hold Orwe with a physical grip, but with a gesture of one hand. Sidhe magic, wrapping about him strong as any chains.

Still Orwe continued to bleed. Dizziness washed over him.

The sidhe dragged Orwe closer with the flick of a wrist. The invisible bonds tightened, drawing Orwe's hands and ankles together behind him despite his flailing resistance. His wound shrieked at him every moment, and Orwe gritted his teeth against the pain.

The stranger frowned as if he'd found a weevil among his grain. "And why, do tell, is a little nacken creeping about the edges of the palace?" His lips curled into a smile that was more savage than pleasant. For a moment, the sidhe's eyes flicked toward the trail of blood Orwe had left, at the gruesome remnants of his foot.

A small sigh slipped from the sidhe. "I do suppose you'll refuse to talk, won't you?"

Orwe trembled now, every limb shaking as he sucked in gasps of dry air. To breathe above the waves would not kill him, but the sidhe standing before him certainly would. Terror gripped him in its sharp, rending teeth.

He met the sidhe's cruel gaze without a word, his jaw clenched shut. The edges of the world had gone dark, and sparks wavered in his vision. Nausea roiled in his guts.

The sidhe's wicked little grin widened. "Oh, I was so hoping you'd be a difficult one. We're going to have a marvelous time getting to know one another." With a small gesture of his hand, those invisible ropes circled Orwe's throat. He choked and gasped as even the arid breath of air abandoned him. His chest heaved futilely. A second pain erupted inside his chest, and the world went black.

Chapter One

"*The fae can be enchanting, no doubt, and painfully charming. However, they hold not to human morals. Even their pleasures are cruel and cut deeper than knives.*"

- Scholar Atra Vae, <u>In Dealing with the Sidhe</u>

CIRELLE RAN HER FINGERTIPS over the faded ink of the ancient book, reading Scholar Vae's words once more and savoring the little thrill that shimmered through her.

Faeries.

Charming. Beautiful. Dangerous.

Forbidden.

The mantel clock interrupted her musings with its tinny chime. Cirelle spat out a word that should not be part of a princess's vocabulary and scrambled from her chair. Aidan would be insufferable if she were late again. She slammed the book shut and locked it away with her other faerie contraband before dashing out of her room.

Stupid. Cirelle shouldn't have tried to sneak in reading before her appointment, but her handmaiden Rainah was too skillful at her tasks. The girl had applied Cirelle's cosmetics and elegantly coiffed her hair a full hour early, leaving the princess with dangerous idle time to indulge in her forbidden hobby.

She'd grossly miscalculated her time. Again.

Cirelle held up her voluminous skirts, ruffled and trimmed in fine lace, to hurry past a cluster of courtiers whispering in hushed tones. She knew what they would be gossiping about. Only two salacious topics floated around the palace these days. The pox—and whether it truly encroached on the capital—and Cirelle herself.

Since the nobles' mouths clicked shut as she dashed by, Cirelle could surmise which one they discussed.

No time to put them in their place now. She tossed them all a vicious, beaming smile and kept running, her fine slippers softly thumping on the polished marble floors. Cirelle turned a corner and crashed headlong into someone. She stumbled back a step, but steady hands grasped her shoulders.

The princess blinked. Who would dare be so familiar with a royal? When she caught sight of the woman's face, her expression softened. "Lydia."

The guard was wearing her uniform, her thin lips caught in a grimace, her brow pinched. Lydia's hands slipped from Cirelle's shoulders and she dipped into a bow. Cirelle smiled at her old friend, her chosen bodyguard when one was needed. *Dutiful as always.* Lydia could easily have skipped the bow, but never did, not in public.

The soldier tugged on her own blond ponytail as her eyes took in Cirelle's freshly-dyed hair. "Oh. Your Highness...please tell me that's just a very convincing wig."

Cirelle interrupted before Lydia could chide her, sidling around to make her escape. "Sorry, I'm going to be late again and I don't want to endure another lecture from my brother. See you later!"

She left Lydia behind and hurried to the parlor where Aidan awaited, steeling herself for the inevitable scolding. As Cirelle's fingertips brushed the doorknob, the first pang of nervousness slithered down her spine. When he saw her...

No. No regrets. It was too late to turn back now, anyway.

A deep breath, a straightening of her shoulders, and she swept into the parlor with a swish of taffeta. She flipped an elegantly-curled tendril of her hair over one shoulder.

"Good evening." There. Her voice didn't quaver at all.

"Evening," her brother murmured around the easel, his attention focused on the palette where he mixed his paints. Cirelle would have been disappointed at Aidan's lack of reaction, if not for the viscountess, Briere, gawking in the corner, slack-jawed.

Cirelle collapsed into the plush, powder-blue chair with a grin until Briere found her tongue. The woman coughed as she fought back a smile. "Your Highness! What did you do?"

That made Aidan glance up. His palette teetered. "Red? Really?"

"What?" Cirelle plucked her lap harp from the nearby table and tilted her head so the late afternoon sunlight would emphasize her hair's new crimson hue. She'd dyed it herself, much to the dismay of her handmaiden. When poor Rainah had seen the blotches around Cirelle's hairline this morning, she'd nearly fainted. Several washes had resulted only in red-stained water and hair no less scarlet.

Red. An unholy color to followers of Ordrae. Like the oh-so-pious Beddig.

Briere cleared her throat, her hands returning to the embroidery in her lap. A tiny blanket, just the right size for an infant. Cirelle's gut tightened, as it always did when she looked at her friend's rapidly-swelling belly, a painful and ever-present reminder of Briere's new life. Even if her husband was currently away on diplomatic matters, the ghost of his presence still hung in the air.

As if sensing Cirelle's distress, Briere set aside her needlework and stood to help pose Cirelle for the portrait. She arranged the loose curls that framed Cirelle's face, her fingertips warm and gentle. Cirelle thanked the gods for the cosmetics that would hide her blush.

The viscountess' gaze also held a bittersweet tenderness that only increased the knots in Cirelle's stomach. Briere's touch was feather-light, hands trembling. She pursed her lips with a faint shake of her head, a blink of her eyes, and then withdrew.

"There," Briere said, her voice only a tiny bit hoarse.

Luckily, Aidan took little notice of anything save his work. He cast Cirelle a weary glare. "Well, I'm leaving your hair brown in the painting." His golden skin was pale, and dark circles hung beneath his eyes. He'd been growing more haggard as of late. It must be hard, running a kingdom while Mother and Father were away.

Cirelle's pity was quickly swallowed by frustration. It wasn't her fault he was stuck with the important work. If she'd been born first, she'd be the one running the place, and Aidan would be sent to the coast to cement an alliance instead.

She frowned and pointed at the painting. "At least fix my mouth. It's the wrong shape. *And* you made me too skinny. I look like a starving waif."

Briere let loose a small snort as she settled back into her seat, tucking a loose lock of hair back into place. A shame that her lovely copper hair was braided and pinned tightly now, prim and proper as any married woman. No more loose curls tumbling about her face like the reckless maiden she'd once been.

The viscountess leaned over to peer at the painting from her seat. "She's right, you know."

Aidan grimaced. "She doesn't need your encouragement, Lady Briere." Aidan met Cirelle's eyes and continued, "This is for your future husband, not you. The coastal kingdoms like their women slender."

Cirelle's harp twanged a discordant note. "Well, if Beddig thinks I'm a fat Arravene cow, then he can search somewhere else for a bride. Rhine likes how I look." She shifted in her seat, smoothing her skirt. A sudden pang of remorse made her eyes flicker toward Briere, but the viscountess resolutely peered down at her needle and thread.

Aidan sighed as he dabbed a cautious bit of paint onto the canvas. His pensive expression softened, taking on the small smile he wore while he created something beautiful. When he volunteered to do her portrait, Cirelle had urged her parents to let him. Aidan had so little time now to practice his art.

Did he miss it the same way she would miss music, were it stolen from her? With a sigh, Cirelle settled back into the seat as her fingers danced over the harp strings.

"Please sit still." Aidan rinsed his brush, then frowned at her. "Mother and Father have let a lot of your antics slide—"

"The ones they know about," she pointed out. Out of the corner of her eye, she caught Briere's silent smile. An old familiar grin, the impish one. Cirelle's heart stuttered for a moment.

Aidan rolled his eyes, oblivious. "—but you're well past the age of wild fancies and idle rebellions." Harsh words, but his tone was sympathetic.

Too old, indeed. To hear the courtiers' gossip, you'd think she was withered and dead to reach nineteen unmarried. Not that her reprieve would last much longer, now that the coastal kingdoms had finally reached consensus on a treaty.

All that remained was for her parents to decide which would claim her. Then all parties would sign the document and peace would settle once more. All it took was her lifetime pledged away in return. She sighed. "But do I have to live with him? I can't move to the coast. I just can't. It's cold and wet all the time. And they eat pickled fish *for breakfast*."

"You'll adjust."

Cirelle's mood darkened, one of her familiar and sudden spells of bleakness. Her next words were almost a plea, and she hated how pitiful she sounded. "Why can't Rhine come here? He's only the third eldest." Rhine, with the crystal-clear blue eyes and those lovely dark eyelashes.

"You don't even know if it'll be Rhine yet."

"Well, it had better be."

"You just like him because he's pretty."

With a guilty glance at Briere, Cirelle retorted, "I like him because he doesn't step on my feet when we dance or simper at me. Beddig gives me that creepy, puppy-dog stare all the time." Truthfully, being easy on the eyes didn't hurt Rhine's case. Nor did his casual charm that filled a room when he walked into it, or the way he merely laughed off Cirelle's fits of temper before silencing her with a stolen kiss.

But she couldn't leave Arraven, her home. Not forever.

Aidan fell quiet for a time and Cirelle's fingers went rigid and still on her harp. Only the scrape of the knife on the palette and the soft hiss of the brush on canvas broke the silence.

When her brother next spoke, his question was a weary one. "Where did you even get the dye?"

"I had a runner bring it from the city," she lied.

Aidan bit his lip. "No more runners. If you need something, it has to come from within the palace walls." His piercing gray eyes made Cirelle shift in her seat. Did he know of her trips outside? "I'll be shutting down the palace gates due to the pox."

A shudder trickled down Cirelle's spine. Briere frowned and brushed a loving hand over the swell of her belly. "Lady Hestia told me it's come to Palace City. Is that true?"

Aidan nodded, his face grim. "It seems to be. No one in the palace is to leave without my express permission until the King and Queen return."

"Hypocrite," Cirelle spat. "You go to the City every other day."

He ignored the insult. "And you're to be confined to your rooms until we can fix your hair. I'll speak with the seamstress today and see if she has anything dark enough to cover that red." He sighed, pinching his brow. A flush crept into his cheeks.

"You can't do that!"

His tone grew firmer, his back straightening, but regret lingered in his eyes. "Yes, I can. I'm your King until Mother and Father get back." He chewed his lip, then set it into a thin, hard line.

"You know, you were a lot more fun before you were almost a king."

Briere's hands froze, her gaze pointed down at her lap while her face reddened at overhearing this private argument.

Aidan's sympathetic eyes met Cirelle's. "We all have to grow up sometime." But all the pity in the world wouldn't change his demands.

"It seems an awful lot like 'growing up' just means doing whatever you and Father tell me to."

Her brother stared down at his paints, his eyes unfocused and far away, his hand gone still.

"Are you even listening to me?"

Aidan didn't respond. Without warning, his eyes rolled back

and he collapsed bonelessly to the floor in a splatter of paint. The easel fell, the clatter unbearably loud. Paint flew everywhere, blood reds and sickly greens and jarringly vibrant yellows.

"Aidan!" All Cirelle's anger fled, and her stomach twisted in horror. She stood and darted over to him, heedless of the messy oils staining her favorite blue gown or how her slippered feet smeared the mess all over the imported rug.

Briere reached him first. She nudged the prince, but he flopped limply. "Your Highness?" Her voice rose a notch. "Prince Aidan?"

The same moment Briere gasped, Cirelle saw them. The telltale red blotches on Aidan's neck. The viscountess yanked her hand away as if she'd touched a hot stove, then stared in horror at her hands before she began wiping them frantically on her paint-smeared gown.

Cirelle rushed forward, but Briere threw up a hand. "No!" Her voice cracked. "Stay back. You...you can't touch us."

Balling her hands into fists in her fine skirts, Cirelle slumped to the floor. "No." Tears sprang to her eyes as Briere shouted for help.

Soon, a flurry of servants descended upon the room, shrieking and sobbing at the signs of the pox. Among the crowd was Lydia, her sharp, pale features a welcome comfort. The guard took one glance at Cirelle and ushered her into a chair. Lydia knelt before the princess, taking both of Cirelle's hands in her own. Few servants could touch a royal so casually, but no one dared scold Cirelle's favored guard.

"Aidan," Cirelle whimpered. "Briere." Both of them stricken in a single moment. Briere wasn't sick yet, but if she'd touched Aidan's rash, she soon would be.

Though Cirelle had just argued with her brother, only pleasant memories of him consumed her now. Like the time Aidan had let her cry on his shoulder for a full hour when she found out she'd have to leave Arraven, abandoning her beloved decadent sweets and sunny summers for seafood and gray, cloudy skies. Or the way he would laugh through his scowl when she took his final piece in a game of fox-and-hounds, challenging her to a rematch with a defiant glimmer in his eyes. How, weary after a long day, he would come to her music salon and sit down with his sketches while she played.

Today's bickering seemed so stupid now, and lying there unconscious, Aidan couldn't even hear her mumbling, disjointed apologies.

And Briere. The emotions that swarmed Cirelle's mind as she locked gazes with the woman across the room were too much to bear. Her heart swelled and ruptured with them:

The viscountess's hand rested on her belly as tears drew shimmering lines down her cheeks. There was the possibility the disease would bypass her, but her hands brushing Aidan's pox-ridden skin made that a slim chance.

"The healer is on his way," Lydia interrupted Cirelle's agony. She gave Cirelle's hands a small squeeze. "Look at me, Your Highness."

Cirelle blinked, tearing her gaze from Briere to meet Lydia's hazel eyes, steadied by the grip of her callused hands.

The soldier gave a wan smile. "It's going to be okay." A lie, and they both knew it.

The healer arrived and ordered Aidan hauled away on a stretcher, into quarantine in the healer's hut. Briere was ushered off behind him, to be shut away as well.

"Your Highness!" The healer snapped at Cirelle. He shoved Lydia aside, ignoring the soldier's glare.

Cirelle's brain buzzed like a hive of bees, her vision gone gray.

The healer scowled. "Did you touch either of them?"

"No." She said it again, as if to convince herself, "No."

He reluctantly let her go, but demanded she stay in her room for three days and call for him immediately if she felt any shakiness or fever. The royal advisors would manage the kingdom until the King and Queen returned. Cirelle just nodded until the healer finally left.

Lydia somberly walked her back to her rooms. When they reached the door to Cirelle's quarters, she asked, "Do you...do you need company?" Loyal as ever, despite the danger of the plague.

"No." Cirelle shook her head. Everything had gone numb, sounds muffled as if her ears were stuffed with cotton.

An awkward pause held, Lydia's eyes full of sympathy. Finally, she nodded and turned away.

Cirelle shut the door firmly with trembling hands. Alone at last, she could think.

No one knew of the illegal books stacked in that locked chest in her room, stolen from the deepest, darkest corner of the treasury. She'd also snatched a small stone that kept her tea hot if she dropped it into the pot, and a fragrant sachet with a scent that matched her mood and never faded.

Forbidden faerie artifacts, they'd been locked up for decades. But since the first time Cirelle held one of those enchanted objects in her hands and felt the warm tingle of magic, she'd been unable to stay away. She'd devoured every book on the fae that her father had hidden away, tucking each neatly back into place once it was done.

Now she would save Aidan and Briere with the knowledge that lay in those pages.

She retrieved a set of clothing she'd secreted in a back drawer and shucked off her paint-stained gown. Without a servant, she was forced to tear the dress to remove it, but the oil paints had stained it anyway. The trousers she donned afterward were a bit small, clinging too tightly to her legs. She'd hidden these nearly two years ago, when she and Briere had entertained fantasies of running away together. The foolish dreams of children.

Cirelle fought back the rising tide of despair that began to seep into her mind. An old, familiar enemy, this sorrow, but she could not let it claim her. Not now. Aidan and Briere needed her, as did the small life growing in Briere's belly.

She hid away all her faerie artifacts in her chest—save the ones she needed tonight—then jotted a hasty letter and dusted it. The note was sealed with her crest and set atop her desk for her handmaiden to find if Cirelle didn't return.

She prayed it wouldn't be needed.

With everything stowed into a small pack, she threw the hood of her cloak over her head. Heart in her throat, Cirelle opened her door a crack and peered out into the hall. Empty. She darted out and down to the kitchens.

A few servants bustled about, preparing food for the next day. A tension hung in the air, hushed gossip whispered back and forth. Cirelle caught her brother's name and blinked back tears. She slipped past a plate of glazed berry scones and surreptitiously snatched one along with a napkin to wrap it.

None of the servants took much note. Guardsmen would often sneak into the kitchens to filch a snack at the end of their shift, and she kept her hood up. The warmth of the room was stifling, dizzying. She carried on, slipping through corridors. The main gate would be guarded. The gesture was more for propriety than anything else, but it was still an obstacle. It was a good thing Cirelle knew every inch of this castle and every possible way to slip out of it unnoticed. Along the west wall, a third-floor window brushed right up against a giant, gnarled arrowleaf. If Palace Arraven had been intended as a fortress, it would have been inexcusable, but this luxury estate rested far from any border.

It had been years since Cirelle climbed a tree, and the experience was rather more heart-stopping than she remembered. A sudden spring shower doused her as she scrambled downward. The bark was both rough and slick, rain-damp and coarse under her hands. Her booted feet slipped more than once, threatening to spill her to the ground below. *For Aidan, for Briere.* She repeated the mantra to herself as she made her way down to the base.

When her boots squished into the damp earth, Cirelle said a silent prayer of thanks, casting her gaze up to the sky in gratitude. She shouldered her pack and lifted a pendant from where it hung around her neck.

The smooth oval of moonstone glowed in the fading twilight. It pulled to the side as if an invisible hand tugged on it. Squaring her shoulders, Cirelle set out in the direction the pendant indicated.

A mile in the distance, the dark tree line of the forest beckoned, far more ominous in the moonless night than the bright sunshine. Still, she swallowed back her fear and began walking. A few steps later, a voice spoke from behind her.

"Your Highness," it called, barely more than a whisper, almost lost to the patter of the rain.

Heartbeat roaring in her ears, Cirelle turned. Her face flushed with humiliation and anger. Had one of the guards at the gate seen her creeping away from the palace?

A familiar face greeted her instead. Lydia's hands balled into fists at her sides and her mouth a thin line. The rain soaked her through, her normally golden hair turning dark in its warrior's tail. She hadn't even bothered to grab a cloak.

"Go back, Lydia. Please."

"Your Highness, you're headed out into the dark alone."

Lydia's voice was firm, steady with resolve. "You're doing something to help Prince Aidan and Lady Briere, aren't you? I swore to protect your family and this kingdom. Let me help."

Cirelle took in Lydia's belligerent posture, the set of her jaw. There would be no budging her, and every moment Aidan spent in pain felt like a century. "Fine." Cirelle huffed out a sigh. "There's no time to waste arguing."

Lydia's face broke out in a tenuous smile. "So, what are we doing?"

Cirelle held up the compass pendant. "We're summoning a faerie."

Chapter Two

THE FOREST WHISPERED TO CIRELLE.

She ignored it, of course. Only a fool would respond to the distant hissing of her name, the half-heard snatches of melody. Though the susurrus of voices was nothing new, a lump of dread still knotted her stomach. Cirelle had never been to the forest after dark, nor had she ever left the safety of the enchanted paths.

Until now.

Her hands shook as she carefully arranged the offerings before her: a delicate music box and an ancient statuette that tingled with faerie magic, its enchantment long since lost to human memory. On the stolen napkin, the scone rested beside the latest bottle of expensive brandy Cirelle had pilfered from the palace's cellar. A cut crystal glass scattered the faint starlight.

She twisted Briere's ring on her finger. It was a simple thing, a band of silver with a small, glossy oval of polished amber. Something that wouldn't attract too much attention. Cirelle's heart ached as she slipped it from her finger. The stone was the color of Briere's eyes in sunlight, the color of honey. A nameday gift, the last one exchanged between them before Briere's marriage.

Faerie rules demanded a sacrifice for the summoning, an object of emotional importance.

"I'm sorry, Briere," she murmured softly.

Cirelle placed the ring on the corner of the napkin and stood, scrubbing her itchy, watery eyes. Toadstools encircled her, the ground still damp from the brief spring shower. The air smelled of loam and earth and moss. She tilted her head back and her eyes sought out Marya's constellation through a hole in the canopy. The Diplomat.

Divine Marya, if you're up there, if you're watching, please help this work.

Cirelle looked to her guard. Lydia stood at the edge of the clearing, eyes scanning the trees with every strange rustle or far-off giggle.

"I must ask," Cirelle said, "why did you come out here instead of dragging me back into the palace?"

Lydia shifted her weight from one leg to the other. "Your Highness... do you remember that I had a cousin in Greenriver?"

A small tremor of dread shivered in Cirelle's stomach. Greenriver was a mid-sized city along the border to the southern coastal kingdom of Asheir, a center of trade along the river. It was also where the plague had first come to Arraven.

"She was a chandler," Lydia continued. "Had a wife and a son. They always asked me to come visit, but I was too busy here." Her voice hitched. "They were gone before I knew they were sick." Lydia's voice was a hoarse murmur. "It has to stop, Your Highness. Even if this is a fool's errand, we need to try."

Tears stung Cirelle's eyes. "I'm sorry." There was little more to add to that, and it was time. Straightening her shoulders, she called softly to the night sky. "Ellian, I summon thee. Ellian, I summon thee." She paused, taking a deep breath before the third repetition. "Ellian, I summon thee."

Cirelle bit her lip as her heart thudded in her ears like heavy drumbeats. Ellian, a sidhe. Her books had mentioned his name as a faerie willing to bargain with humans. Her fingers and toes tingled. She couldn't decide whether she wanted to cower or toss her head back and laugh at the thrill of it.

Metal scraped as Lydia readied a blade.

"No," Cirelle chided her gently. "We don't want to give offense." If a human insulted a faerie, retaliation was certain.

"Yes, Your Highness." A soft click sounded as the blade's hilt settled against the sheath.

"Good advice," a husky, rumbling voice said.

Cirelle startled and turned toward the sound. *Stars, it actually worked.*

The faerie's movements were too fluid to be human. He was tall and long-limbed in elegant lines that reminded her of fine-boned racehorses. A sidhe, one of the more humanlike races of the fae, but still wondrously strange. A great weight of magic clung to him, making the air heavy and close. Her skin prickled all over.

She lifted her chin to meet his silver eyes. Two dark brows swept over them like a hawk's outspread wings. He could have been a sculpture carved of cool gray stone, all sharpness and edges, softened only by the curve of his full mouth. His skin bore the colorless hue of damp ashes. Pointed ears peeked out from long, dark curls, with shining silver hoops at their tips.

The faerie stepped over the toadstools to stand within the ring. Cirelle was forced to crane her neck upward to look him in the eye or else stare at his improperly exposed chest, his open shirt barely covering half of it. His tall boots were strangest of all, the dark leather barely visible beneath a network of filigreed silver metal pieces that made a soft tinkling noise like bells.

He regarded her for a few heartbeats, then knelt in one smooth motion to examine the array of bribes.

"Lord Ellian, I have brought these offerings to open negotiations between us." Cirelle tried not to let her voice tremble. *Steady now. Just pretend you're meeting a foreign ambassador.* Never mind that she'd skipped or failed most of her lessons on diplomacy. "For the sake of hearing my plea and entertaining my request, they are yours."

The faerie's mouth quirked upward on one side. He picked up Briere's ring, turning it about to admire the gemstone. "Who gave this to you?"

Cirelle cast a guilty glance at Lydia before she admitted, "My first beloved." Her deepest secret, one she'd never dared utter aloud.

The faerie peered into the amber, then nodded. Though his hands were already laden with an assortment of rings, he slipped the new one onto the first knuckle of a finger and returned to the rest of the items.

His hands danced over the other offerings before plucking up the tiny carved figure. Made of yellowed stone, the small woman spun merrily, her skirts whirling. He slipped the figurine into a pouch on his belt, then selected the music box and turned the crank. His eyes closed, and he tilted his head to enjoy the lilting melody that emerged in bright, silvery tones. With a nod, this piece went into the pouch as well. In a liquid movement, he folded his legs and settled himself down on the forest floor.

"I shall hear your request," he said, his voice low and cultured, the timbre of it like velvet brushed the wrong way. He poured the brandy into the glass and held it in one hand while picking up the scone with the other.

It seemed odd to stand while Ellian sat and ate, but he had

not motioned her to take a seat. So, Cirelle remained where she was. "My people are dying."

"An unfortunate consequence of mortality," he pointed out before she could continue. He took a dainty bite of the scone.

Anger spiked. Cirelle bit her lip to hold back a retort. She went on, continuing the speech she'd cobbled together since they'd slipped from the palace a scant hour or so ago. "A plague threatens our land. I ask for a cure, a way to stop the pox from driving my kingdom to ruin."

"*Your* kingdom?" Ellian sipped the brandy. "Who are you, to make this claim?"

She straightened. "I am Cirelle telArraven, princess of the kingdom of Arraven. These are my people, and I come prepared to strike the bargain that will save them." *And save both Aidan and Briere.* The thought of two people she loved lying in quarantine, feverish and hurting, left her knees weak.

The faerie arched an eyebrow, but otherwise did not startle. His eyes raked up and down Cirelle's body, and she was suddenly all too conscious of her trousers snagged with burrs, the plain woolen cloak, the heavy boots. Doubt was written clearly on his face, and his voice dripped with skepticism. "Truly?"

"On my honor, I swear it." Cirelle lifted her chin, glaring down into those unsettling metallic eyes without flinching. She may have looked a mess, but the disdainful note on his voice pricked her pride nonetheless. A sharp note entered her voice. "If you wished me to greet you in silks and a tiara, then perhaps you shouldn't require a summons in the middle of the woods."

Contrary to taking offense, a shadow of a smile flickered across his lips. "Indeed. A princess... It seems I could ask a hefty price, if the weight of a kingdom's treasury is prepared to bargain with me."

She stiffened.

Ellian delicately licked the last of the sticky honey glaze from his fingers. He took his time about it while he met her gaze with darkened eyes. Something uneasy fluttered in her stomach. When he was done, the faerie sipped the brandy. "You brought quality gifts to open the bargaining. So yes, I do possess what you request." His free hand pulled something from his pouch. A glimmering spike, perhaps as thick as Cirelle's thumb at the base and tapering to a fine point at the tip. It shimmered opalescent white in the faint starlight, a spiral of ridges curling around its surface. There was no possible way its length could have fit in the pouch on his belt.

"Is that...?"

"A unicorn's horn. Dip this into water and anyone who drinks it will be cured of illness."

Cirelle's heart pounded heavily in her chest. This was the key. It could save them all, including Aidan.

Her breath hitched on her response. "What do you ask in return?" It could bankrupt her kingdom if he asked for gold. In some stories, fae requested firstborn children in exchange for a bargain. Could she give him that, a future prince or princess to be raised by faeries?

"I assume you read and write well enough in the human Trade tongue?" He swirled the brandy in the glass. The question was asked in flawless, unaccented Trade, though he'd been speaking Arravene this entire time.

Fear and frustration warred within her. "Yes," she responded in Trade. Her courtesy slipped again beneath the pressure of her familiar, infamous temper. "What does this have to do with anything? Tell me, what do you want in exchange for the horn?"

His lips curled into a thin smile. "You." He took another sip of the brandy. "I think a princess would do nicely for the bargain."

"What?" Cirelle's blood ran cold.

"No," Lydia said at the same time.

"One year of your life, to be precise. I find myself soon to be bereft of my personal servant, and I rather enjoy the idea of a human princess for a new one." He tossed her a languid grin. "If you consent to return to Faerie with me and reside there until one year of your life has passed, I will give this unicorn horn to your guard. You will go with me tonight, immediately."

Cirelle swallowed hard.

How would this affect her betrothal? *Will Rhine wait for me?* He'd promised her his love, after all, in soft whispers on moonlit walks. A year was a long time. Would she lose him forever if his family gave up on her and forged another alliance elsewhere?

Part of her ached for the fledgling thing that had begun to grow between them, snuffed out before it could truly begin.

Were Aidan and Briere's lives worth it? Or stopping the plague?

Yes. Even if it meant abandoning her world for a year.

Faerie. A world drenched in mystery and magic, inhabited with beings as beautiful as they were deadly.

Enticingly forbidden.

A frisson trickled down her spine. A shudder of fear or a spike of excitement? The thrill of danger had always sung to her, a whispering voice that pushed her to take risks a princess shouldn't. And this would be the greatest one.

She spoke carefully. "The unicorn horn is to be given to my guard, Lydia. In exchange, I offer one year of my servitude."

"Your Highness." Lydia's plea sliced through the air. "You can't do this. It's madness." She paused, her voice fading to a near-whisper. "Let me go instead."

"I didn't ask for you," the faerie told Lydia. Those eyes met Cirelle's, deadly serious and painfully piercing. "It's the princess or nothing."

Cirelle swallowed. "I'm sorry, Lydia. I have to. You said it yourself. This plague has to stop." Before her courage could falter, she nodded to the faerie. "Agreed." A small shiver rippled through the air, as if a bell had been rung.

"No!" Lydia exclaimed behind her, but the deed was already done. The faerie nodded and tossed the horn in the woman's direction. It fell into the grass at Lydia's feet with a soft thud. The guard bent to pick it up, fist clenched tightly around the shimmering spiral. Her eyes met Cirelle's with tears glimmering in a grim, determined stare.

Ellian was just finishing off the last of the brandy bottle. That much alcohol—especially in such a short time—would have left Cirelle swaying on her feet, but he seemed no less sober than when they'd first met. He tossed back the last swallow of amber liquid and slipped the crystal glass into his pouch where he'd placed the other gifts. It, too, didn't make a bulge in the bag.

He stood in a single graceful movement, like a marionette pulled upward on strings, and extended a hand to her.

"No," Lydia growled, holding the horn in one hand and drawing a blade with the other. "The price is too high." She advanced a step.

Panic sparked. "Lydia!" Cirelle snapped. "Would you let your prince die? Or so many of our people?"

The soldier's voice cracked. "I should never have let you come out here, Your Highness." She took a step forward, tracks of tears painting silvery lines on her cheeks. Lydia was going to get herself killed or cursed.

Cirelle gritted her teeth and took the faerie's hand, ignoring the frantic pounding in her chest. *Don't think, don't think, don't think. Just go.* "Let's go. I'm ready." A lie.

Ellian hadn't even flinched at Lydia's approaching threat.

Cirelle gripped his hand so tightly she could feel the bones beneath his skin.

The soldier lifted her blades and charged.

"No!" Cirelle shouted as the faerie raised his free hand before him. One of his rings, set with a vibrant emerald, bathed his hand in an eerie green glow.

Lydia screamed, collapsed to the forest floor, and vanished. Gone in the blink of an eye, along with the horn that would save Arraven.

Cirelle dropped the faerie's hand as if it burned her. "No!" The word tore its way from her throat as she rushed forward to the spot where Lydia had been, only to find emptiness. Anger and horror roiled in her gut, and tears spilled free. "What did you do?" she snapped at the sidhe. "Is she—" her tongue tangled on the word, coming out thick. "Is she dead?"

"She drew a blade on me. I defended myself."

Grief and terror washed over Cirelle in drowning waves. She barely felt it when the faerie strode toward her and snatched her hand. "I gave her the horn, as promised. Our bargain holds."

Cirelle felt raw, numb, just as she had when Aidan had collapsed. She wanted to claw bloody furrows into the faerie's skin, to scratch out his eyes. But then she'd be blinked out of existence in a moment, too.

Lydia. She hiccupped out a sob.

What did the disappearance of the cure mean for Aidan? For Briere and her child?

The faerie's skin burned hot, his long, slim fingers tightening about Cirelle's. Her heart thudded wildly against her ribs.

"Hold tightly," Ellian admonished her. The forest dimmed, shapes swirling into fog, and they left her world behind.

Chapter Three

THE MIST SETTLED and a light flared to life in the deepening night. Cirelle tried to yank her hand free, but Ellian held it in an iron grip. "Don't let go yet, Princess." His voice cut through the silent forest in warning. "There are dangers among these trees."

"Dangers other than you?" A small challenge, that. She tilted her chin up despite the terror that inched up another notch. Her skin crawled where they touched, but she didn't withdraw her hand.

Those silvery eyes met hers, and the faerie's thumb brushed lightly across her knuckles, back and forth. "All of Faerie is dangerous." A faint tremor danced across her skin.

"Lydia..." She choked out the words, the tears finally spilling free. "What you did to her..." In a single moment, he'd murdered Cirelle's oldest friend, doomed both her brother and Briere, and signed the death warrant for so many of her people left to fall to the plague.

The faerie's eyes were dark, unfathomable. Cirelle tore her gaze free of his unsettlingly sharp stare.

"She drew steel on a faerie. We are not to be trifled with, Princess."

Cirelle swallowed hard and didn't reply. After a heavy moment of silence, Ellian held up his free hand, another ring giving off a steady white glow.

It was quiet here, unnaturally so. Cirelle hadn't realized how accustomed she'd become to the soft chirring of insects, the rustling of leaves, and even the insidious whispers. Here, not a trace of noise shattered the calm, the air as still as if it held an indrawn breath.

The trees extended high above, their branches weaving together so thickly the night sky was obscured. The grass beneath her feet had taken on a blue tint and brushed the tops of her boots. An unfamiliar scent hung in the air, heady, damp, and sweet.

Ellian led her along a winding path in the woods. In the heavy silence, the chiming of his strange boots was terribly loud. The trees grew impossibly immense as they walked. Some of them were as wide around as houses. Indeed, a carved door and windows glowing softly in the bark of a massive old oak indicated they were used for such a purpose.

They walked through a field of lights, like brilliant fireflies in every color she could imagine. They flitted about, dancing in the moonlight.

Wait, moonlight? The night had been moonless when they left Arraven.

A gap in the canopy overhead revealed a patch of sky. Not one, but two moons hung above her.

The forest thinned into gently rolling hills. Too beautiful a place for the dangers that lurked here. For the danger that held her hand. Her books had warned her Faerie was a perilous place and this sidhe left her terrified, but she couldn't deny a small thrill at seeing this strange and heartbreakingly beautiful world.

Ellian led her to a manor home, peculiarly mundane. It

nestled among a grove of trees on a low hill. A fence made of wrought brass extended off into the night on both sides. No iron in sight, not in Faerie. Lanterns lined a white gravel pathway, glowing a pale and steady blue in the night.

"You're safe now." Ellian released her hand. "Or as safe as you can be in Faerie. This is my home, and yours for the next year."

Cirelle stared at the house.

The faerie narrowed his eyes. "What?"

"It looks so... normal." She blurted the words before she could stop herself, her mental walls shattered by this evening's horrors.

The sidhe stepped through the open gates, the ghost of a smile dancing on his lips. "Sorry to be such a disappointment." His voice, halfway between liquid-smooth and gravel-rough, was unexpectedly droll.

He continued down the path, and Cirelle hastened forward. The gate closed and the latch fell into place with an ominous click. Luxurious prison this may be, but it may as well have been the padlock to a jail cell.

Wildflowers dotted the lawn. Some of them bloomed even this deep into the night, their faces tilted upward to the double moons. Trees grew scattered here and there, a sharp contrast to the carefully planned rows Cirelle was accustomed to. With all the rampant greenery, she waited for the back of her throat to itch and her eyes to water, but the feeling never came.

The front door's fittings were all wrought from shining silver and brass, some of them as intricately filigreed as those unusual boots that tinkled like bells with Ellian's every step. The doorknob sparked blue when he touched it, a flicker of magic.

Cirelle flinched. "What was that?"

"My wards. They keep out...undesirables." He threw open the door and entered with Cirelle on his heels.

The wooden doors creaked shut. Her boots echoed softly against a stone mosaic of whorls and undulating patterns in warm earthen hues. Vaulted ceilings arched high above, topped with a gigantic skylight. Two chandeliers framing the skylight cast a pale yellow glow, and a pair of gracefully curved stairways embraced the space. Three doorways led out of the hallway on this lower floor; a heavy set of double doors straight ahead, and two smaller ones on the left and right walls near the base of the steps.

Shadows clung to the edges of the foyer, far from the chandelier's reach.

It was so very human, but what had she expected of a fae lord? A treehouse? A castle carved of ice, perhaps?

A door at the top of the stairs opened. "*Saila dir*," a man said as he entered, his tone subservient. "*Brose*— Oh!" The man caught sight of Cirelle. "Sorry, my Lord," he said in Trade. The man smiled softly at Cirelle and gave a little bow. "I didn't realize you had a guest."

She couldn't place the man's accent, a clipping of consonants and a flatness of vowels that tugged at the edges of her memory. He was human, past middle age, with pale skin and ruddy cheeks. Silvery gray threaded through his honey-gold hair and crow's feet crinkled the corners of his pale eyes.

"Toben," Ellian greeted the servant. "This is your replacement. Her name is Cirelle."

The man sketched a brief bow after he descended the steps. "Welcome, my Lady."

Ellian didn't bother giving either human another glance as he took the stairway on the right. As he passed under the chandelier, his hair shone a rich midnight blue. Not black, then, and no color that could ever belong to any mortal.

"Toben," Ellian said as he ascended the stairs, "see she's washed and garbed before supper."

"Yes, sir," Toben bowed. "Might I ask where the lady will be staying?"

Ellian waved a dismissive hand. "Wherever you think best."

With those words, the jingling of his boots faded as he slipped into the wing at the top of the stairs, the door closing behind him with a soft click.

"This way, my Lady," Toben said, gesturing for her to follow him into the hall on the right. The corridor was drenched in shadows, an ominous darkness extending into the distance. It was like descending into the Void itself. Sconces flared to life as they passed then dimmed behind, so they walked in an ever-shifting island of golden illumination. Outside that circle, the dark of this place pressed on her, a hungry presence like a wolf stalking outside the edge of a campfire.

Cirelle shivered as they ventured further into the depths of this house. She cleared her throat. "*My Lady?*" The title felt odd, after being called "Your Highness" her entire life. Still, Toben didn't know that. "Aren't we both servants here?"

"Not yet," he said amicably. "Oh, I most certainly am, but you aren't. For precisely three days you are a guest." He shrugged. "So, I serve."

"I see. Is that one of those faerie rules?" One constant in her reading on fae; a series of intricate rules and customs bound them, including hospitality rituals.

Toben's grin widened as he turned and winked. "Got it in one," he smiled. "The fae are awful finicky about host obligations. For the first three days under your roof, newcomers are guests. After that, well, then you'll be a mere servant like me."

She nodded as they trailed down the long corridor. The man's easy demeanor felt unsettlingly out-of-place in this house of darkness, ruled by a cruel master who could take a human life in a blink.

Cirelle's stomach clenched at the thought of Lydia, of Aidan, of Briere, and she swallowed back another round of panic. Not now. Not yet.

Toben took her through several turns, along halls adorned with sculptures in alcoves, framed mirrors, and other bits of art. It seemed a shame to leave it in darkness most of the time.

When they passed the first mirror, Cirelle halted. "Oh, Stars," she swore. No wonder the faerie had looked doubtful when she declared her royal heritage. A stray leaf still clung to the top of her scalp and a smudge of blue paint adorned one cheek. Prickly burrs and fluffy seed pods clung to her clothing in a loose scatter. She didn't look like a princess. Cirelle more resembled a wayward peasant girl, lost and wandering the forest for days. She picked the leaf from her hair and continued following Toben.

The house was beautiful, but their footsteps echoed through empty halls. "How many people live here?"

"Just Lord Ellian, myself, and perhaps two dozen brownies that do the cleaning and cooking."

Toben stopped at a door like every other they'd passed. Cirelle was already lost. A well-lit parlor lay behind the door, with velvet armchairs and sofas around an open central area. The walls were a soft white, all the furniture palest blue or coated in silver.

Sconces lined the walls, glowing with a steady light like miniature suns. Not candlelight, but more faerie magic. A sharp contrast to the dim corridors outside, it was a haven in this dark, empty place.

Or a trap.

ELLIAN PACED IN CIRCLES, the luxurious bronze carpet softening his footsteps. Or it would, if the chime of his boots' filigree didn't drown the sound anyway.

A princess. Never had he claimed so lofty a servant before. It had been too tempting a plum to collect a pretty human royal.

He caught his reflection in the mirror and leaned forward on the desk. Alone, he didn't bother with glamour, and his eyes gleamed like dark emeralds. Worried. *Of course,* he laughed bitterly to himself. Only a few months remained and he decided to introduce this girl to the mix. What could possibly go wrong?

It was that damnable defiance, the spark in her eyes when she'd stared down her nose at him and scoffed. Just for the barest moment, before she remembered her courtesies, something fierce and determined had peeked from that regal facade.

Something he could use.

He sighed and finger-combed his hair, tilting his chin to admire his reflection and how the light caught the silver hoop at the tip of one ear. Tugging his shirt back into place, he left for his study. An hour remained before dinner. Enough time to review this new playing piece, and just how she might affect his plans.

Chapter Four

CIRELLE GLANCED AROUND THE AIRY PARLOR and trailed a hand over the flocked, sky-blue velvet on the back of one chair. What had she stepped into? Her new faerie master was obviously wealthy and could easily have afforded other servants. Why bring in humans? For sport, perhaps?

A trickle of fear slid down her spine. Mysteries upon mysteries, and the greatest was the sidhe himself.

Toben led her through the second doorway into a huge, open closet. An endless selection of gowns hung on posts. A set of shelves held an array of jewelry and elegant slippers, with a full-length mirror in a gilded frame beside it.

Cirelle had dresses aplenty at home, of course, but always in the latest Arravene fashion. Beribboned confections, corseted and full-skirted with panniers and petticoats to spare. She owned elaborate hairpieces and hats galore, but there remained a sameness to their opulence.

Here, the sheer variety overwhelmed her.

At any other time, Cirelle would have sighed dreamily and drowned herself in silk and satin. But all she could think about was the murderer—now her master—who owned them.

Lydia. She and Cirelle had grown up together, spending idle days playing with the other palace children. The quiet girl who'd always been Cirelle's voice of reason, the cautious one who kept the worst of Cirelle's antics at bay. Later, when they were older, she'd become the guard and chaperone who attended Cirelle when she went into the city.

Gone now, along with the cure that could have saved Aidan and Briere. A terrible blankness echoed in Cirelle's mind, a hollow spot in her chest. In this house with its vicious master and shadowed halls, these riches seemed too tempting, a lure on a hook.

"I don't know which of these would fit," Toben said, gesturing at the wardrobe, "but there's all sorts here. Just pick through and find whichever one you like after your bath is over. Speaking of which..." He made his way to the opposite door. It revealed a bathing chamber with a claw-footed tub and vanity.

A spout rested above the tub, with a dial on it like the wheel of a ship. "Turn that for water," Toben explained. "To the right for hot, to the left for cold."

Cirelle reached out to touch the brass dial with one finger. "Without bringing in water to be heated?"

Toben nodded with a grin. "Service in Faerie has a few perks, my Lady." He opened a nearby cabinet to show her an array of towels, soaps, and scented oils. "You should have everything you need here. That door opposite leads to a privy closet. If you'll be all right, I'll let you bathe and dress?"

Cirelle nodded slowly. During the walk through that enchanted forest, she'd steeled herself for any number of horrors at the hands of the sidhe. Not this comfort.

Without warning, a yawn threatened. Though Cirelle stifled it, Toben looked at her in sympathy.

"Sorry, my Lady. I know it's indeed very late into the night or very early in the morning, depending on which side you're looking from. Our lord wakes up when the sun sets and goes to bed when it rises. You're probably knackered, and I apologize, but the lord will want to dine with his new guest first, and then you can sleep early tonight."

Of course I'd get one of the nocturnal ones, Cirelle thought. Some fae preferred moonlight to the sun. It seemed fitting, with her host cast in the colors of midnight.

Toben interrupted her musings. "When you're dressed again, leave your old clothes on the rack over there," he gestured. "The brownies'll pick them up and get them cleaned up for you. They'll leave them on the shelf tomorrow, all nice and tidy-like." He stepped through the door and poked his head out. "I'll be in the room across the hall when you're ready." He left, closing the door behind him.

With Toben gone, the utter silence of the house fell upon Cirelle, stifling and thick. At home, sounds echoed at all hours. The chatter of servants going about their business, the ticking of clocks, a whinny echoing from the stables or a flurry of barking from the kennels. Birdsong outside the window.

Here, there was nothing. The quiet was a solid presence, a muffled weight in her ears. Not even a single cricket's song. In the absence of that constant small symphony of life, her mind invented its own sounds. Whispers in the corners, a scrape of claws on the stone floor.

Still, she needed to wash away the filth of the forest despite the oppressive silence. A pot of astringent liquid for removing cosmetics helped her scrub away the oil paint that remained on her cheek. Tears sprang to her eyes as she stared at the rich blue color, her last lingering link to Aidan in this empty place.

Her chest clenched, and she tossed the rag aside to draw a bath. The water cascading from the spout fractured the quiet.

Some of the scented oils in the cabinet were familiar aromas, some less so. She added a bit to the bath, one that smelled like bright sunshine and golden peaches to combat the unsettling darkness of this house.

As she sank into the hot, fragrant water, Cirelle's shoulders eased. The steam soothed her scratchy throat and cleared the last stuffiness from her nose. She breathed in deeply.

The panic hit her suddenly, a dash of icy water. All the fear and worry and dread had been slowly filling a glass bottle that now shattered in her mind, breaking into a thousand tiny shards.

What have I done?

One by one, the consequences of her choice piled up in her mind, weights added to an invisible scale. What of Aidan and Briere? Palace Arraven held the best healers in the kingdom, but were they enough? With Lydia and the horn gone… Cirelle sucked in a rasping breath. She'd abandoned them to die.

If Aidan didn't make it, Cirelle would return to Arraven a queen. Unease bubbled in her gut.

No. The healers would help. There was a slim survival rate, and they would pull through. They had to.

The hot burn of tears stung the back of her eyes. Rhine's charming, sensitive gaze swam in her vision, and she wanted nothing more than to throw herself into his embrace. But he was gone, just like the rest of her world.

Arraven went on without her while she endured twelve months here and hoped Faerie would not consume her. If her books told the truth, mortals who found their way into Faerie came back *changed*. Some were addled and half-dreaming. Others—the cold ones—were drained of humanity, their compassion gone and their minds turned to a preference for idle cruelty. *Fae-touched.*

That is, when they returned at all.

The worries harried her, grasped at her with greedy fingertips and dragged her down. It was no stranger to her, this bleakness, a hollow void of despair that sometimes drowned her in the deepest hours of the night.

Stupid. She'd been so stupid. The pit of self-loathing yawned so deep no human should ever survive it. She was a miserable failure, not even capable of ensuring her people's safety. A poor excuse for a princess.

Giving in to the darkness, Cirelle choked out sounds too raw to be sobs. She dug her fingernails into her palms. The sharp sting focused her thoughts and held the worst of the mental agony at bay.

Eventually, she cried herself hollow. Cirelle was left feeling gutted, like a melon rind after all the flesh had been scooped out. She took long, shuddering gulps of air and collected herself piece by piece. Uncurling her fists revealed reddish half-moons on her palm. As always, a wave of shame washed over her now that the spell had passed.

Another steady breath, and an old habit surfaced. She composed a small bit of melody in her head, the notes clearing away the last of her anguish. A forlorn phrase of music, it encompassed all her fears and her sorrows, fitting them neatly into notes and pushing them from her mind. Her composure returned, her tears running dry.

It was one of their family's most shameful secrets, this darkness that tangled inside, waiting for the opportunity to claim her. Cirelle's aunt suffered from the same bleak spells, alternating with bouts of restless, giddy energy and occasional violent bursts of temper.

Healers had been hired in secret when Cirelle's mood swings had grown severe a few years ago, but they could help her no more than her aunt. Leeches, religious rituals, disgusting draughts and creams and odd diets all did nothing.

Only the royal family knew the worst of it, and Cirelle's suitors had not been warned. It remained hidden from Rhine on his three visits so far, but would his face fall in disappointment when he discovered his bride was a broken thing? Would Beddig look upon her with simpering pity or derision for her fatal flaw?

Another sob caught in her throat, the despair lifting its head again, but this time Cirelle forced it down. She swallowed back her bitterness and stood. A pinkish hue stained the bathwater, the dye seeping from her hair. The color was pretty enough, but Cirelle couldn't shake the thought of diluted blood in the water.

Chapter Five

CIRELLE DRIED with the towels provided, grimacing when she stained the fluffy cream-colored fabric with red splotches. Despite the dye that had leeched out in the tub, her hair still held the color of dark wine. A comb banished any tangles. Though it felt strange to leave her hair loose rather than in one of Arraven's elaborate updos, she could never manage to style it on her own.

Such an array of dresses littered the closet, and there was no semblance of order to them. Nestled behind a crimson gown that would have fit in perfectly well last season in Arraven, she found a garment similar to one worn in her great grandmother's portrait, absurdly high collar and all. Behind that one lay a gauzy confection in no style she recognized. As assorted as the garments were in design, they varied as much in size.

Cirelle tried to ignore the telltale signs these dresses had once belonged to others. A name embroidered on the inside lining, a small stain, a worn hem. Some had faded with time, the fabric growing crisp and brittle.

She chose a flowing, gossamer gown in a Nycenine style that tied in a bow below her bust. The cut of the dress skimmed her ample figure and clung to her in all the right places. She twirled, admiring how the skirts billowed and flowed like running water. When the light caught the fabric, it glimmered in iridescent reds and oranges like a sunset.

The airy garment was a welcome change from the heavy skirts and tight stays of current Arravene fashion. At home, Cirelle would never have been allowed to wear something so foreign.

Despite—or perhaps because of—her lingering nervousness, Cirelle couldn't help twirling in a few fidgety steps of a reel. The fast-paced dance set the dress rippling and shimmering like fire curling around her. Yes, this gown was made for dancing.

On the wall of accessories, Cirelle found a pair of beaded red slippers that fit her comfortably. She almost bypassed the jewelry, but Ellian had said she should adorn herself. Hospitality was important to the fae. Would it be seen as an insult if she did not use what he had provided?

Just in case, she selected a few items. A ring dotted with garnet gems and a necklace that dripped rubies down her throat. As a final touch, she added a golden circlet worked in a pattern of roses and vines.

The general effect was regal enough, if strangely alien. She *felt* like a faerie in this delicate, flowing dress. The colors suited her golden complexion and red-stained hair, giving her gray eyes a bit of a blue cast.

Satisfied she'd adorned herself properly, she left the wardrobe. Stepping out into the hall plunged her back into the horrifying reality of this situation, outside the bubble she'd built in that parlor. Darkness swallowed her save a small pool of light.

Cirelle stood in the hallway for a long moment, gathering the frenetic chaos of stray notes in her mind into a semblance of a steady melody. When she knocked on the door across the hall, Toben answered with a smile, the crow's feet crinkling around his blue eyes. "Feel better?"

"Yes, thank you," she replied.

Toben opened the door wider and gestured her in. The bed-chamber was beautiful, of course. Rich tapestries left the space feeling smaller and darker than the parlor across the hall. The floor gleamed in polished wood, partially covered by a rug in charcoal and deep red hues. The rest of the room matched, including the plush armchair by the hearth and a heavy quilt on a large bed. Pillows heaped the mattress, half a dozen of them.

"These don't look like the chambers of a servant," she said.

"Perhaps not, but there are rooms aplenty here and Lord Ellian told me to give you whatever room I saw fit."

"Is yours this nice?"

"Not quite so lavish," he admitted, "but comfortable enough." He gestured back toward the door. "If I may, I'll show you to the dining chamber? The meal begins soon."

"Of course." Curious, she added, "You seem... comfortable here. How long have you been in Faerie?"

"Oh," he brushed the question aside with hand gesture. "Three years, or nearly so, anyway."

"Three years?" Her eyes widened.

"Aye."

What bargain had this man struck that he received thrice her sentence? "When does your service end?"

"Almost three months hence, by my count. Plenty enough time to get you used to things around here." Toben closed the door behind them and locked it. He handed Cirelle the key. "Take this. I'd keep this room locked even while you're in it if I were you."

A tremor shot through her. "Why?"

His frown drew out a crease between his brows. "It forces Ellian to knock. Also, there are guests sometimes, other fae. Not all of them are savory folk, if you don't mind my saying. Best to keep that door between you and them. Faeries have odd rules when it comes to mortals. Just the act of locking the door gives it a bit of protection. It's all about the intent, if you catch my drift."

Cirelle nodded. She wondered what 'unsavory folk' guested here sometimes. Her books on fae included more than a few nightmares. Tiny tremors prickled her skin, the scratching legs of invisible insects.

She still clutched the key he'd given her tightly in one hand. It was small, but she didn't know where to hide it in her gown without pockets. After a few moments' deliberation, she shrugged and tucked the key between her breasts.

Toben stared wide-eyed, then broke into a chuckle, turning aside. "Well, I reckon it'll be as safe there as anywhere," he noted with a nervous grin. Cirelle found herself smiling back until his expression faltered.

"What?" she asked.

"Nothing." He shook his head, but a darkness lingered in his watery blue eyes. He gestured for her to follow.

After they'd walked to the end of the hall, Toben asked, "So what do you do, in the human world?"

She grinned and curtsied. "Princess Cirelle telArraven, my lord."

"A princess," he muttered. "Well, I'll be."

"What, no formal bow?" She raised an eyebrow jokingly.

"Well, I'm not really a citizen of yours, my Lady. I'm Saedden, myself."

Ah. Saedda lay weeks from her kingdom, across a sea to the south and west. A cold and frozen land, Arraven traded with them often, swapping fine Saedda furs for her kingdom's rich grain. So that was the accent she couldn't quite place. "You speak the Trade tongue well," she complimented him.

"Aye. Well, as a dock clerk, it was a part of my job." His hand darted up to touch his earlobe, hidden beneath his thick hair. A nervous gesture? "Though I'll admit my Trade was a little rudimentary, before coming here." Again, Toben fell silent, choosing not to elaborate. A small frown of worry touched his lips. For a few moments, they walked in silence.

"My Lady," he blurted.

Something in his tone made Cirelle stop, clutching her hands together. "What?"

"If you pardon my saying, be... *careful* around Ellian." He ran one hand worriedly through his thinning, grey-streaked hair.

A sour tang filled her mouth. "What?"

Toben wrung his hands together, coughing nervously. "The last servant, she was a pretty thing like you, and..." He stumbled on the last words, shifting his weight from foot to foot. The old man's face flushed more crimson than a ripe red apple. He opened his mouth again, but only a small keening sound came out.

Fear trickled through Cirelle's body. "What happened?"

Toben's mouth worked as he began to turn purple. Half-formed words died on his lips. After a few moments he blew out a hard breath and shuddered. "Never you mind," he rasped out and turned.

Had Ellian blinked that girl out of existence like he had Lydia? Or was some unfortunate girl locked away somewhere in this hollow mansion? Panic made her angry, and Cirelle reached out to grasp Toben's shoulder and whirl him around. "No, I need to know."

Toben shook his head, his face still crimson. "It's nothing." But a forlorn weight in his words indicated otherwise.

A chiming bell cut the conversation short. Not the low clang of a heavy tower bell like back home, but a tinkling of silver. The sound came from everywhere and nowhere at once.

"That's the dinner bell," Toben said, cutting off any further questions. "I'll show you to the room where you will dine with Ellian. The lord will want privacy tonight."

A dinner alone with that sharp-edged, murderous sidhe. Cirelle clamped down on the swell of anxiety with steady breaths.

At a heavy wooden door, Toben stopped and said, "Our lord will be here shortly. I'll show you to breakfast tomorrow, but otherwise you're in Lord Ellian's hands for the next three days." He gave her another pensive smile. "Enjoy dinner, my Lady."

Unable to respond, all Cirelle could manage was a nod. And like that, he was gone.

Chapter Six

The dining room was small, intimate. An enchanted chandelier emitted a soft white glow, and each wall held paintings depicting the same landscape in varying seasons.

A small table sat in the center of the room, carved of the dark, polished wood that predominated here. Clever depictions of twisting vines and star-shaped flowers crawled up the table legs. The high-backed chairs were similarly adorned, upholstered in dark green velvet. Two places were set.

Cirelle shifted her weight restlessly from one foot to the other and ran a hand over the smooth woodwork of a chair. Which seat was hers? Should she sit, or wait for Ellian? If she offended, how would she be punished?

She was still deciding when Ellian swept into the room. Again, his presence was overwhelming, pressing against her skin with a tingling weight. He still wore those tinkling filigreed boots, and the pale gold of his silk shirt begged to be caressed. Next to the hue of the fabric, his charcoal skin looked like rich, dark suede.

Ellian paused halfway to the table. There was something of the predator in his posture, a stillness and watchfulness.

Dangerous.

Ellian watched Cirelle with a cool indifference. He met her gaze with a fire in his eyes, a silent question that made her glance away as heat surged to her cheeks. "Your Highness," he greeted her. "Welcome to my home."

With a nervous cough, she curtsied. "I'm pleased to be your guest, my lord."

A small smirk ghosted across his face. "No need to lie to me, Princess. I hope you are comfortable enough, nonetheless." Ellian gestured to the table, pulling out a chair.

Cirelle took the seat he offered, nerves still jangling. The faerie was the picture of propriety and courtly manners, but it rang false. A stage show, with Cirelle the entire audience. What horrors hid beneath that mask?

"You must have questions," he continued, slipping into the other chair and resting his chin in one hand. "While you are a guest for these three days, I will answer them. No need to fear dishonesty, as I'm sure you've heard we cannot lie."

"Though it's said you contort the truth until it might as well be a lie," she replied quietly. It was a challenge, her fear given teeth.

"Sometimes."

A soft knock rapped on the door and another faerie entered. He was small, his chin level with the tabletop. The creature's body seemed all out of proportion—a wrinkled face, long slim limbs, and large eyes above an equally big, knobby nose. His clothing was simple, in earthen hues with a gold cap. A brownie, one of the small fae that tended houses in exchange for saucers of milk and odd trinkets. In his arms lay a folded bundle of gray fabric with something small and silver glimmering atop it. The fae placed the items on the table, smiled briefly at Cirelle, and left as quickly as he'd entered.

Ellian gestured to the items, an invitation.

When Cirelle reached for the gleaming object, her fingertips never touched it. The items darted away from her grasp, and the shining bit of metal rolled and clattered to the floor.

In the surprised silence, the ring of silver on stone echoed in her ears. Ellian held the edge of the fabric in one fist, the rest dangling off the side of the table. She hadn't even seen him move.

"Your first lesson in Faerie," he said calmly. "Never, ever accept a gift from the fae. We do not give *gifts*. There is always something owed in return. Balance. Favors, debts, and cost. Always ask the price."

She knew that. How could she have made such a stupid mistake? Anger flared. "Is this how sidhe always treat their guests?"

He laughed, a bitter chuckle that vibrated deep in her bones. Ellian tossed the lump of cloth back onto the table, bent over to pick up the bit of fallen metal, then placed it back on top of the fabric. "Oh, this is much kinder than most fae treat mortals." He pointed at the items. "These, however, are not gifts. They are a condition of employment. The price is simple. They are on loan to you, to be returned at the end of your servitude here and to be used for my benefit during your service. They still belong to me, technically."

Nagging fear gnawed at Cirelle's core, begging her tongue to snap, but she bit back the urge. Her mother had despaired of ever making a passable ambassador of the temperamental princess, but a scant few of the lessons lingered.

Cirelle plastered a cold smile on her face and reached for the bit of metal.

A glittering black teardrop of opal dangled from a small silver hoop. An earring.

"That," Ellian said, "is to be worn by you at all times. Its enchantment will grant you the ability to understand and speak various languages. I speak several of your human tongues, but many of my associates and clients do not."

She hadn't even considered that. Her stomach clenched in apprehension at donning a piece of fae magic, but what other choice did she have? *In for a step, in for a hike.* She slipped the earring into the second hole in her right earlobe.

The bundle of fabric came next, a cloak of light wool in a middling gray hue, lined in rich black cotton that spilled over her hands with a pleasant weight.

"A cloak of camouflage. When your service begins, I ask that you keep it near you at all times. You will wear it to shadow me on summons to the human world. Bargains require a witness."

Toben had been at the mansion, though, not in the woods with her. Or did Lydia count as witness? Cirelle folded the cloak again, placing it on the seat of one of the empty chairs. "Tha—"

"Don't," he cut her off. The word was clipped, his eyes gleaming brightly. "Never thank a faerie. If you give us the opportunity, we will claim a debt."

Cirelle chewed her lip. Such different courtesies and rules here. Could she master them all before they ensnared her? "I understand."

"Now." He pulled an item from his pouch and set it before her. A small vial, filled with a pearlescent liquid. "Drink that."

As Cirelle stared at it, something invisible and slimy crawled in her gut. "What is it?"

"Water treated with unicorn's horn. Since you came to me with worries of a plague-ridden kingdom, I feel it necessary to share that cure with you. I've no wish to bring human illnesses into my home."

With a shaky hand, Cirelle picked up the vial. This precious bit of liquid could have healed Aidan or Briere. She closed her eyes, swallowed hard, and spoke. "What's the cost?"

"A lock of hair. Not much, less than the width of your pinky finger. A small price to pay for possibly saving your life."

Cirelle swallowed, hating the truth in his words. Still, giving this faerie a piece of herself left a cold feeling in her chest. "What will it be used for?"

"I'll trade it away to some witch or alchemist who needs a maiden's hair for a spell or potion."

She couldn't help it. Cirelle snorted softly at the word *maiden*.

Ellian arched one eyebrow and cast her an intrigued smile. "Very well, someone who needs a mortal's hair. It will be burned away into the potion, a mere ingredient."

"It won't be used to harm me?"

"No, on my oath."

One thing her stories had all agreed upon: faeries could not break oaths or promises. Cirelle hesitated, then nodded. The vial's cap came off easily. One swallow and the liquid was gone with a taste of floral tea.

Ellian produced a small pair of silver scissors from that mysterious bag. He stood but Cirelle recoiled and shook her head. "Let me do it," she said.

After a moment's pause, he placed the scissors in her palm. Cirelle snipped off a lock from the nape of her neck. When she handed it to Ellian, he tucked the hair into a bottle and everything went back into the pouch before he sat once more. "With that settled, we dine, and you may ask your questions."

As if they were listening—and perhaps they were—brownies knocked lightly before entering the room. One held the door open while the rest filed in carrying plates of food and two full glasses of wine. The brownie bearing Cirelle's plate had to stand on tiptoe to place it in front of her.

Tendrils of steam curled up from the bowl of stew. Poultry,

cooked in a rich brown gravy. A loaf of dark bread rested in the middle of the table next to a crock of creamy yellow butter. So human. Even the silverware was mundane.

She picked up her fork and poked delicately at the meal. She'd read all the old lore: *Never eat the food of Faerie.* It could bewitch a human, trapping them forever.

"You needn't fear the food," Ellian said, as if reading her mind. "It hasn't been enchanted. It's as plain and mortal as food gets, in Faerie. Besides," he added, picking up a wine glass and peering at the golden liquid inside, "your bargain with me removes the usual obligations. You've no need to worry about the food entrapping you. The same goes for the clothing you wear while you are here, your rooms, and use of anything within my property outside of my personal chambers. For the duration of your employment, you are a member of my household and entitled to your meals and lodging."

Well, that was spoken plainly enough. She speared a bit of the fowl on her fork and took a bite. The flavor burst on her tongue, salted and stewed in fragrant herbs.

He gestured to her untouched cup. "You should try the wine."

Cirelle lifted the glass. The pale liquid caught rays of light and tossed them about the room like fine crystal. Certainly not a human concoction. She took a cautious sip and an immediate flush of warmth swept through her body. A pleasantly sharp sensation lingered on her tongue, like the heat of spice.

Why did Ellian accept offerings of human brandy if he had this at home? She let the wine roll over her tongue before swallowing, savoring the sudden, giddy rush of light through her veins. She set her glass down. "It's delicious," she replied. "A fae vintage?"

"Made by dryads from the fruit of their own trees." Ellian watched her with a cat's patient, hungry stare. The faerie licked his lips without breaking her gaze. A sultry promise danced in those eyes.

Cirelle wasn't entirely sure whether her responding shudder was trepidation or something else. A rather enjoyable tingle settled into her limbs, the worries drifting away from her like debris caught in a river's current. For a moment, something dark flitted to the forefront of her mind, a stray note in an otherwise soothing sonata. Someone she should remember, something terrible. Before she could grasp it, the thought was gone.

She drank more deeply, rolling the flavor over her tongue. The wine tasted like glimmering spring sunlight. It sang to her, a melody she couldn't quite grasp, notes slipping through her fingers.

She met the faerie's eyes, searching them for answers. Had she imagined the heat she'd seen there, just for a moment? He did look so elegantly delicious sprawled in his chair, with that lean chest and stomach so brazenly exposed.

Her cheeks warmed, and she glanced down into the wine glass. *This is how Midwinter started.* Sparkling wine, indecent thoughts, and rash actions. She found herself sinking into the golden haze of the memory. And Ellian was far more beautiful, more tempting, than the boy who'd been her Midwinter merriment. Gadd, a simple soldier, earnest and sweet. A far cry from the fae who sat opposite her.

There it was again, that discordant note, quickly drowned by the lilting lullaby that coated her thoughts in sunbeams.

Cirelle was startled by a brownie at her elbow who took her empty plate and replaced it with a new one. The interruption was welcome. She should not be thinking such salacious things about a creature as alien and deadly as this faerie lord. Or *anyone* she had met scant hours ago, for that matter.

Not that it's stopped me before. She lifted her fork and took a bite of the dessert.

The dish was as lovely as the rest, a pastry with a flaky, golden crust. Deep red berries spilled from the sides, and a dollop of sweet whipped cream sat atop it. The tartness of ripe fruit and the sweetness of sugar filled her mouth. She took another gulp of wine to wash it down.

Ellian coughed politely, drawing her attention from the food. "A question, if I may? Do you know why I receive so few summons from Arraven?"

"My father passed laws banning contact with the fae and locked up every bit of lore in the castle before I was born. It's a crime even to share knowledge about you."

"So, you disobeyed your father, your king." His voice was a purr. "An outlaw princess."

The idea seemed suddenly ludicrous to Cirelle, and a small giggle bubbled up. "Yes." Another sour moment interrupted the siren's song, but she shoved it aside and took another sip of that lovely wine.

For a few moments, the faerie's eyes were unreadable, cool chips of slate. He leaned forward on both elbows again. "Do you disobey your king's rules often?"

Cirelle's hand lifted to tug on the end of her braid, a blasphemous garnet hue. She thought of other rebellions, so many lessons ditched to sneak out of the palace down to the city. There weren't many rules at home she hadn't broken, pushed, or at least skirted.

Briere. Gadd. Her two greatest secrets sprung to mind, the alcohol coating the memories with a nostalgic fondness. She'd yet to cross any lines with Rhine, but only because the opportunity had not presented itself in his few brief visits.

A wistful grin tugged at her lips. "Often enough."

He watched her closely for a moment. "I should ask you what memory makes you smile like that," he mused.

Cirelle drowned her flush by finishing off her glass. Without warning, a dizzy wave made the room seem to tilt. She gasped and closed her eyes.

Ellian frowned. "You're drunk."

"No, I'm not." Cirelle shook her head. The world spun around her, forcing her to close her eyes again. *Maybe I am.* Cold dread sluiced through her veins. She was alone with a dangerous creature, half-addled by faerie wine.

"That's... unfortunate." There was something cold in that voice now, a chill that brushed down her spine.

Cirelle's eyes snapped open to meet his silvery ones, icy as the surface of a frozen lake. He was watching her in a distant, analytical way, a small grimace lingering on the edge of his mouth as if she were an apple tree that had yielded a disappointing harvest.

Her tears had run dry an hour ago, and only bitter anger remained.

"*Unfortunate?*" she blurted. "Then why give me only faerie wine to drink?"

In one graceful motion, Ellian stood, delicately setting his own glass on the table. "I needed to test your tolerance for it," he said, voice cool and matter-of-fact. "Which is, apparently, practically nonexistent. Toben can drink thrice that much without losing his wits."

Cirelle's thoughts had narrowed to a single furious pinpoint. She leaned forward, hands flat on the table as she snarled. "You baited me. Did you seriously get me drunk on purpose to see how much it would take?"

"Yes." The response was blunt. "We will be dealing with other faeries, and they play many games. I need to know your limits, your weaknesses. Now I know one of them." His lips curled and he sighed. "Which seems to be a single glass's worth."

"I'm supposed to be a guest!" The words were thick in her mouth, her tongue tingling.

"Indeed. I did nothing to violate our laws, even those of guest rights." He extended a hand to help her up.

Cirelle slapped it away before he could touch her, shoving her chair back from the table to stand. The floor lurched beneath her unsteady feet. Ellian's hand caught her elbow, and she stared down at it in outrage before yanking her arm away. The momentum caused her to stumble into the table with an impact that was certain to bruise. "Don't touch me."

Something tightened around his eyes, his lips pulling into a straight line. The teasing mirth and cultured distance were both gone. "You can barely walk." The words felt like soft silk caressing her skin. "Nor, I suspect, could you find your room in this state." He lifted a hand, his fingertips hovering a few inches from her skin. "Let me help you."

His scent surrounded her. The comfort of a crackling fire, faint woodsmoke and resinous burning logs. Beneath that lay a subtler aroma of fresh-brewed spice tea and the sweetness of honey. It was a comforting smell, one that spoke of warmth and safety indoors while a savage winter raged outside.

His eyes met hers once more, and something deep and sorrowful lingered in their depths. And like sand seeping through her fingers, her anger slid away, a slippery thing drowned in the rise of those beautiful, calming notes. Worry was too hard to cling to, and she sank back into the delicate lullaby.

Ellian's eyes could hold a softness when he let them. His full lips were no longer curved into a taunting, arrogant smirk nor pulled into a cool grimace of disdain. While he waited for her response, his mouth parted slightly, expectantly.

Such an intriguing mouth.

A delicate shiver curled through her. Licking her lips and clearing her throat softly, Cirelle nodded. "Just help to my room."

Was it another faerie trick, whittling her away by inches? Ellian's gentle smile seemed genuine, though. His hand brushed her elbow, his arm sliding over and around hers as if he were escorting her onto a dance floor. Due to his height, she had to reach up a little to place her other hand on his bare forearm.

Cirelle willed the walls to stop moving, for her stomach to stop cartwheeling so alarmingly. It was a chaotic counterpoint to the giddy softness of the song in her veins, and she concentrated on keeping the floor steady beneath her feet.

As Ellian led her out of the room with slow, even footsteps, Cirelle found herself far too preoccupied with the small bit of contact, skin to skin. It was like a warm mug of tea against her fingers.

She wondered if he burned so hotly all over. It wouldn't be the first time she had done something scandalous, after all. Though a faerie was a whole new step, she had to admit the spice of risk added an irresistible allure.

There it was again, the sudden sharp note, a wrong key struck. Gone in an instant.

The lean muscles of Ellian's arm corded beneath her hand. "Your room is the third hallway on the left, then the second turn on the right," he told her as they turned down a darkened corridor. She had a brief moment to wonder how he knew which was hers, but he spoke again. "Last door on the right."

That voice. Like sand and suede. Cirelle closed her eyes and let it wash over her, through her, and imagined what it would feel like to hear him speak more intimate words in her ear.

She was emboldened again by the golden light that danced through her. A flush of warmth had settled in her belly. Her

head still swam, but it was a pleasant spinning now rather than
a sickening lurch. Tentatively, Cirelle traced a small circle on the
exposed skin of his forearm. His breath caught, and she grinned.
She felt powerful, a hunter stalking deadly prey. Some tiny voice
deep inside her screamed at what she was doing, warning of the
foolishness, the sheer *indecency* of it all.

A bigger part of her relished the utter thrill of it.

Indecency had never stopped her before, after all. Cirelle had
done so many things a princess shouldn't. She let go, immersed
herself in it like diving into a pool of clear, shimmering water.
She took in the peculiar fragrance that clung to Ellian, smoky
and warm and sweet. Her heart beat madly in her chest, fierce
and exultant.

"Princess," Ellian whispered softly, turning to meet her eyes
with those unsettling silver ones. He stopped walking.

"Yes?"

"How do you feel right now?" He tilted his head.

Giddy. Dizzy. Wanting. "Wonderful."

His grip on her arm tightened. He leaned in closer until she
could smell the wine on his breath, summer fruits laced with a
sour tang. The nearby sconce encircled them in a pool of light,
shadows swallowing all else.

Little shivers trembled through her core, and Cirelle tilted
her chin up.

But he didn't kiss her. His head canted sideways at the last
moment to whisper in her ear. "Summerwine. I suspect I could
do anything I wanted to you right now, and not only would you
let me, you'd beg me to."

Her throat went dry, and a fire sparked within her.

"Another lesson." He let her go, taking a step back. "Don't
ever be so careless around a faerie again."

A curse burst from Cirelle. She pulled her arm away from his and stumbled, steadying herself against a wall. He didn't offer his hand again. The melody that sang in the back of her mind was shattered, and she remembered what the song had been hiding.

Lydia. Aidan. Briere. How could I forget what he did to them? She swore again.

"Such language," Ellian said. "Not particularly regal."

"I'm too drunk to be regal," she snapped.

They walked the last distance to her room in silence, the lights kindling and dying to briefly illuminate the darkness. Cirelle followed. She had no choice, really. Panic suffocated her, horrified by what she'd almost done.

Ellian stopped before her doorway, lit by the golden glow of the sconce near her door. She placed a hand flat on the smooth, dark-stained wood.

"Good night, Princess." His boots jingled like a jailer's keys as he walked away.

When the corridor had gone silent, Cirelle took her key from its hiding place between her breasts and slipped into the dimness of her room.

ৎৎ

ELLIAN FELL INTO THE plush armchair in the Archive's antechamber, his arm still tingling where the princess had been tracing delicate circles with soft, teasing hands.

Humans were always cool to the touch, and her chill had settled into his skin in tiny pinpricks. Her reaction to the wine had been...unexpected. He was still staring at that spot on his arm when Toben entered.

"My Lord?" The servant asked, settling into the opposite chair.

"Well, she's not intent on murdering me, at least."

"That's reassuring, after the Paloma incident." The old man smiled and eased back further into the seat. "But did you have to bring her at all?"

Ellian ran a hand over his face wearily. "No. I couldn't help myself."

"My Lord...now is not the time to have a repeat of—"

"I know." Ellian bit the words off sharply. He sighed, his voice softening. "I know, Toben."

"How does this affect the plan?"

A shake of Ellian's head. "For now, we move forward. Don't tell her anything about the Key or the mission."

Toben's forehead creased with worry, but he nodded. "Yes, my Lord."

Chapter Seven

Cirelle woke to a pounding agony in her temples, her mouth dry and eyes crusted shut. Wan light trickled around the heavy velvet curtains of her lone window.

The full recollection of last night came flooding back. For a few painful breaths, Cirelle thought of Lydia, gone in a heartbeat. Sorrow clung to her, as did worry about Aidan and Briere's fates. Would the most skilled healers in the kingdom be enough? She said a small, fervent prayer.

And there was a more pressing concern. Last night, she'd acted as shamelessly as some moon-eyed barmaid before a wealthy patron. Playing such games with the cruel master of this manor was utter madness.

No wonder legends warned humans away from faerie wine.

She sat up and sank her head into both hands. Her stomach twisted and her temples throbbed in time with every heartbeat. With an effort, she kept last night's dinner down and slid out of bed. A glance out the window showed only Ellian's sprawling lands. Twilight painted the sky purple.

Last night's dress was a pile of gossamer fabric on the floor.

She threw the chemise on and quickly crossed the hall, carrying the shimmering overdress in her arms.

All was quiet in the hallway, the yawning darkness extending in both directions.

In her parlor, she closed the door and threw the latch. She needed to compose herself, slake her thirst, and try to ease the pain that threatened to turn her head inside out.

Cirelle couldn't shake the fear she had failed a test of some kind. Misery coated her like a black, sooty film she couldn't scrape away. In so many ways, she'd failed. Her brother. Her oldest friend. Her beloved. Their alliance with the coastal kingdoms. All her fault, and for nothing. Any hope of a cure disappeared with Lydia.

When she entered the oversized closet, the cloak Ellian had given her hung in front of all the other items. He'd told her she was to have it ready at all times, and she'd already left it behind in the dining hall. Another failure.

The cloak was warm to the touch and thrummed with silent energy. Enchantment. She couldn't resist trying it on, the fine cotton feather-soft against the skin of her throat.

She stepped over to the full-length mirror. Her face was clear above the cloak, but everything below her neck was nearly invisible, as though the room behind her were viewed through a foggy bit of glass. Throwing the hood up made her face disappear as well. Shaking her still-throbbing head, she removed the garment and hung it up again.

As she dressed, Cirelle's mind flitted back to the previous night. Her stomach tensed at the memory of brushing Ellian's arm with a fingertip, at how a fire had sparked inside when he shuddered at her touch. Could such a wild and beautiful creature truly want her? Or in true faerie fashion, had Ellian merely toyed with her just to make a point? Worse, how could she have forgotten what he'd done, to simper at him so wantonly?

She'd flirted before, of course, the toothless wordplay the upper class practiced at balls or at tea. A fluttering of eyelashes, all downcast gazes and gentle blushing. But there was always something more lingering just out of reach. Something fiercer, more honest. Briere gave her that once, but those days were long gone.

And what would it have done to Rhine, had last night gone differently? As soon as she returned to Arraven, either Rhine or Beddig would wed her. Surely, they would wait for her, for the fertile harvests Arraven provided and the political alliance that would end the escalating tension between the princes' kingdoms. Her parents could choose Beddig, but she'd prayed so often to Harena that the goddess must have heard her prayers for a match with Rhine.

Of course, she was expected to remain chaste until her marriage bed. One of the many rules she'd broken without regret. Both her lovers had left her with fond memories. Briere had been seasons of playful kisses and laughter, both teasing and generous by turns, a bright beam of sunlight in an otherwise dull life.

Gadd had been a one-time affair, with the spice of danger and eager, fumbling excitement. The bubbling wine served at Midwinter had certainly been a factor, along with the heartbreak of knowing Briere would soon bear her new husband their first child. The viscount had been beaming, telling everyone the news. Drink made the soldier Gadd bold enough to flirt with a princess. And so, her heart aching, Cirelle had seized what balm he had coyly offered, if only for a night.

She suspected Ellian would be an entirely different sort of lover, with his sidhe charm and that deadly aura of danger. Her face flushed hot.

He's a killer.

The thought doused the last fading buzz of the wine—at least, she hoped it was the wine making her feel this way.

She finished lacing the front of her dress and retreated to her parlor to curl up on the couch and sip cool, clear water. A magical pitcher on a side table remained full no matter how much she poured into the elegant crystal cup. There were items for making tea as well, with a similarly-enchanted teapot.

Today she chose familiar clothing from the closet, a comfortable linen day gown in deep green, a style common in Arraven. Silver beadwork twined about the edges of the skirt and the long sleeves in a pattern of leaping fish. A strip of pale white leather embellished with emeralds rested above the flare of full skirts.

As a reminder to both herself and her sidhe host, Cirelle had chosen another diadem today. This one was wrought into a fine braided pattern and dotted with golden topaz gems. She would not let anyone in this house forget her rank, not yet.

Cirelle pinched the bridge of her nose. Her headache was fading, but even a touch of cosmetics couldn't hide the weary shadows beneath her eyes.

When the knock came, Cirelle was ready. The agonizing ache had settled into a dull throb. "My Lady." Toben greeted her with a shaky, nervous smile when she opened the door. "How fare you, if you don't mind my asking?"

"I've been better, but I've also been worse," she said cautiously. Just the thought of food made her stomach heave. How much did Toben know of Ellian's little test?

"How many glasses' worth?" The servant's eyes crinkled with concern.

Well, that settles that. "One," she said, squaring her shoulders against the embarrassing admission. She pierced him with her most regal glare. "You knew?"

"I wasn't allowed to say anything about it." He rubbed the back of his neck with one hand and at least had the grace to look sheepish.

"One, huh?"

"Yes," she replied through clenched teeth. "I was told you can do three times as well."

A wide grin split his face. "More than. Three is where I start going fuzzy. It takes about five before I'm out. And I know that through painful personal experience." He coughed. "I'll leave you be. Ellian will expect you at breakfast, but sudden duties require my attention. Do you think you can find the way?"

She nodded. A lie. She wasn't going anywhere. If Ellian took offense, so be it.

After Toben left, Cirelle stared at her door. She wanted nothing more than to lie down and sleep for hours, but she made a pot of tea and sipped it carefully.

She was ravenously hungry, but when the breakfast bells rang, she remained in her parlor. Let Ellian eat in solitude, for all she cared.

Part of her wanted to venture out into this house, to see what secrets those dark halls held. A more rational part imagined all the enchanted dangers that could lurk in those rooms.

She didn't know how long she sat there, deciding, before the knock came.

With a frustrated huff, she went to open it.

Ellian swept past her, looking polished and fresh and not at all hungover. His trousers were a pale gray twin to those from the night before, topped with tall black boots that lacked the strange filigree. At least today's shirt covered his chest, more or less. The long coat he wore over it was midnight blue brushed silk, dotted with knots of silver thread and beads that twinkled like stars.

He'd left his hair loose, only the tips of his elegantly pointed ears peeking through the cobalt waves. Circling his throat was a simple band of silver. A scattering of mismatched rings still adorned the fingers tapping a staccato rhythm on the sideboard as he poured himself a cup of tea.

"Princess," he greeted. His smile turned cold. "You missed breakfast." A rebuke. "How are you feeling?"

She lifted her chin. "Like I lost a fight with a bear." She matched his grin with her own bared teeth. So much for courtly manners. She'd never been good at it anyway. Her temper had always gotten the better of her, especially when she was high-strung and anxious. It was like a monster living inside her, clawing its way out of her throat and spilling vitriol from her lips.

Would he blink her out of existence like Lydia, for such impertinence?

He laughed, a sudden, startling burst of sound, and sat opposite her. He nodded to her cup. "Tea does seem prudent after last night."

"After you poisoned me," Cirelle accused him.

"I did nothing. You chose to partake."

"You invited me to drink it."

"You could have refused."

Cirelle scowled. Her face burned with shame and anger.

Silence held for a few moments, until he broke it. "You're angry with me."

She merely stared at the sidhe, feeling the icy chill in her own gaze.

Ellian opened his mouth, hesitated, and closed it again before taking a sip of his own tea and crossing one leg over the other. He remained unmoved by her wrath, drumming the fingers of his free hand on his knee, making his rings clink together softly. "Last night," he began, "you think I gave you the faerie wine purely for sport." She did not reply, and he continued. "As

I told you, I need to know your tolerance. It may be of import later."

"You made a fool of me," she said, revealing the true source of her cold fury.

He shrugged. "Dryad summerwine generally has a rather interesting effect on mortals." Cold amusement danced in the depths of those silver eyes. "It reveals your most secret desires."

She nearly flung her teacup at him. "You told me it wasn't enchanted. I thought faeries couldn't lie."

"I said the *food* held no enchantment. I didn't mention the wine."

Cirelle's vision turned black and red. She was so livid that words completely failed her.

"Yet another lesson, Princess."

She simmered in silence, physically biting her tongue to keep the poison inside. Did other people—normal people—have to deal with this unsteady tempest inside, this seething rage always lurking under the surface, aching for a victim? Did they have to hold back a tide of vicious words at any irritation? Or was the savage beast within her just a part of Cirelle's curse, the one she shared with her aunt?

A soft tapping at the door interrupted before she could respond.

"Yes?" Ellian called, and the door cracked open.

Toben's head peeked through. "Terribly sorry to impose, my Lord." The man's gaze flickered over to Cirelle and his lips drew into a pinched, worried line. "There's, er, an *issue* that requires your attention."

Ellian's gaze darkened and he set down his tea. "I see." He glanced at Cirelle then back to Toben. "I'll meet you in the Archive shortly."

With a nod, the servant left.

"My apologies," Ellian said to Cirelle in a cool purr, but his hand gripped the edge of the table too hard as he stood. "You're welcome to explore your new home while I attend to this matter."

Cirelle swallowed, a taste like dust in her mouth. "What's going on?"

"You shouldn't concern yourself with it." He slipped through the door.

It didn't escape her notice that it wasn't an answer.

છ૭

When Toben closed the door behind Ellian in the Archive's antechamber, the servant didn't bother with pleasantries. "We have a problem."

Issen stood in the center of the room, a slender figure painted in sunshine shades and draped with golden robes. Buttery skin, daffodil hair that fell to his shoulders, and eyes of salmon orange that currently darkened with worry. He, too, didn't mince words. "Orwe hasn't reported in."

Ellian hissed a curse. "He didn't check in with you last night?"

A shake of Issen's head.

Ellian paced and weighed the possibilities, but came up with only one conclusion. Heavy remorse settled over him. How much did their enemies know now?

"Issen, return to court. Keep your eyes and ears open, and report anything of note back to me through the mirror." A slim chance, that. Though Issen was not unwelcome at the Unseelie Court, his friendship with Ellian was no secret. If Orwe's knowledge now lay in the hands of an adversary, they'd be too cautious to let anything slip around Issen.

The smaller sidhe's eyes fell, but he nodded. "Understood."

"Toben, try to call Dirilai and she what she knows."

The old man snorted. "As likely to bite my head off as tell me, but I will."

Issen asked, "What are you going to do?"

A sigh. "I'm going to entertain a princess and pretend things aren't falling apart."

Chapter Eight

CIRELLE FINISHED HER TEA in lonely silence, then mustered her courage and abandoned the room for the corridor outside. She couldn't just sit in her parlor forever. Fear fluttered as she looked into the hallway, a sea of black on either side of the golden sphere of light.

Squashing down apprehension, Cirelle crept through the halls. She was able to find her way out of the guest wing without too much trouble and headed into the first-floor opposite wing where the dining chamber lay.

Lights in each room flickered to life when she opened the doors, and she poked her head into one after the other. Among the various chambers, there rested a vast, empty ballroom with a pale stone floor. She scuffed one foot on the dusty marble and imagined dancing here in a clean and well-lit ballroom. What would it be like to witness a crowd of achingly beautiful faeries spinning in time underneath those chandeliers?

Mournfully, she left.

Another room seemed intended for gaming, with inlaid woodwork patterns on tables. She recognized a few of the boards, including the circular pattern of fox-and-hounds, something she'd played with Aidan when they could each snatch a spare moment.

Aidan. Cirelle's eyes stung as one fingertip traced the lines of the game board. Lifting her hand from the smooth wood, she turned to explore the rest of her new home with a heavy heart.

The house was lovely, of course, but it held an eerie beauty. Polished wood and rich, cream-colored stone dominated. Ghostly lights danced about the main chandelier in the front foyer, but the rest of the manor lay painted in shadow.

As Cirelle passed a panel of delicate silver filigree along the walls of one hallway, she brushed the whorls in the metal, cool to her touch. A serpent hid among the spirals with feathery wings outstretched in flight. A repeating motif. Now that she looked for it, signs of the winged serpent lay everywhere. The abstract lines of the mosaic in the foyer floor echoed the sweep of wings, the ridges of feathers. The banister of the stairwell was etched in a diamond pattern; not merely a geometric design, but implied scales that slid under her hand.

Heraldry, like the fox and ivy of Arraven. She was certain of it.

Cirelle suspected Ellian's chambers lay in the halls above the guest wing. The doorknob tingled with magic when she touched it, and she left that one alone.

The heavy double doors in the back of the foyer were locked, Ellian and Toben's voices murmuring within. She pressed her ear to the wood, but they spoke too quietly to make out words.

As she neared the west door at the top of the stairs, a bell rang. Unlike the tinkling bells that signaled meals, a deep resonance vibrated in the walls. Cirelle glanced around for the source of the noise, only to see Toben exiting the locked room. When he opened the front door, the murmur of conversation echoed up to her, and Toben stepped back to let the faerie in.

The woman was petite, her bare skin shimmering like gold dust. Her lower half resembled the hindquarters of a mountain sheep, covered in long, cream-colored fur that crinkled like the coat of a Durlish ewe. The hair framing her face was more of the same, a fluffy, wooly mass. Large, curling horns emerged from that chaos, glinting a deep gold, as if they'd been dipped in brass. The creature glanced at Cirelle and their gazes met. The faerie's eyes were citrine yellow, with the sideways pupil of a goat.

Toben continued speaking to the guest, sketching a bow and gesturing for the woman to follow. Her wide cloven hooves were as gilded as her horns and clacked on the tile.

Cirelle slipped away. She headed through the doors into the darkness of the second-floor west wing. There, she explored rooms of storage, some stacked with paintings half gone to rot, others filled with furniture in much the same condition. Parlors lay abandoned and coated with a thick layer of dust that tickled her nose, as if all these things had been set out for use and then forgotten.

Two rooms stood out, havens of illumination spilling into the inky black. Beacons in the night, like lighthouses on the coast.

The first was a library, lacking even a speck of dust. Along the walls, rows of books sat on crowded bookcases stacked to the ceiling. The center of the room was filled with scroll racks, surrounded by comfortable chairs and heavy mahogany desks. Despite its spaciousness, the room felt more like an overgrown study than the austere library back home.

The other well-lit room brought tears to her eyes. Instruments lined the walls, a dizzying assortment of flutes, harps, lutes, bells, and others she didn't even recognize. She wandered through it in a daze. A glossy fortepiano sat in the center, beckoning.

As Cirelle circled the instruments, Ellian appeared in the doorway. He did not speak, and she barely paid him notice. A full-size harp rested in a corner, its strings begging her to strum them. She lifted a hand but hesitated with a glance at the faerie.

Ellian nodded, his face unreadable.

She ran one finger lightly down the row of strings. The sound shimmered and her bones thrummed in tune. Giving in to her impulse, she positioned herself behind it and practiced a short bit of the plaintive melody she'd begun mentally composing last night.

The sound wove through the air, carrying a mournful quality she'd never been able to coax from her harp back home. She could play this for hours.

Reluctantly, Cirelle let her hands trail away as the last notes echoed and died. "It's beautiful," she admitted.

"Your duties will not take up all of your time," Ellian told her. "Aside from my chambers, everything in this manor is open to you. Play whenever you wish."

Cirelle opened her mouth, then shut it so quickly her teeth clicked together. *Never thank a faerie.*

Ellian's eyes sparkled with amusement as he gestured her to follow him into the hall.

Among the forgotten ballroom and the abandoned rooms of storage, the library and music rooms were pristine, the lights never snapping off. Islands of warmth in this cold place, ruled by a cold man. She had to know why. "Do you play any instruments?"

"No." His expression faltered for the briefest of moments, but she couldn't interpret what had risen to the surface before it was drowned again. "But I listen."

Without further explanation, he led the way upward. The third floor contained only a narrow staircase and a door that led onto the roof. As they stepped onto the open rooftop, it was obvious why the lower grounds grew wild. Who would care about those when such beauty grew in abundance up here?

The space overflowed with flowers and greenery. Scattered lampposts held faerie lights, illuminating such a vast array of plant life that Cirelle was left speechless. Rose bushes were covered in pale pink blossoms the size of her outspread hand. *Roses that bloom at midnight.* Climbing tendrils clung to trellises, heavy with bell-shaped flowers as vividly blue as a summer sky. The stone walls lining the roof were dotted with balconies that overlooked the grounds below, but the remainder of the walls were covered with vines.

A heady aroma lay thick in the air, the perfume of every flower she could imagine all at once. Cirelle waited for the familiar itch in her nose, the scratchiness at the back of her throat.

It never came.

Perhaps this faerie garden was the one place in which plants would not set her to sneezing. The thought made her smile.

The starlight here was brighter, too, twin moons hanging in the sky. They shone like polished ivory, one smaller than the other. It was a dash of cold water in her face, a bracing and undeniable reminder that this was not her world.

She was so far from home, a distance that could not even be measured in miles. Stars crowded thickly overhead, the constellations unfamiliar and alien. Cut off from her gods as well, it seemed; there was nowhere for them to dwell in these strange heavens. Did Aizhiu the Traveler still watch over his people when they wandered to other realms?

A stab of homesickness caught her by surprise. She couldn't stop her thoughts from constantly flitting toward the deep void in her chest left by Lydia, or the special knot in her gut for Aidan, or the crushing ache for Briere and her unborn child.

They'll be fine, she lied to herself. *The healer will see them through.*

She tried to slow her pounding pulse as she stared up into

that unfamiliar sky with its foreign stars, bereft of any gods to hear her prayers. Cirelle crossed her arms, feeling very small.

Ellian's voice beside her was a murmur, a cool puzzlement frosting the words. "What worries plague you so?"

Cirelle's head snapped sideways to look at him.

"Your thoughts are written too plainly on your face."

Cirelle gritted her teeth. She'd been schooled in how to conceal her expression, in the trickery and art of court. But it had never come naturally to her, her unstable temperament too strong. "You killed my guard. My friend. And you doomed my brother and—" Her voice cracked. "And Briere by destroying the cure."

The sidhe's eyes narrowed. "I fulfilled my part of the bargain. I gave the guard the horn."

The sharpness in his voice kindled a nervousness within her, like hearing a high violin string caressed slowly. Suddenly, it was all too overwhelming. The intensity of his presence, that magic aura beating against her skin like afternoon sunlight. Needing to measure every word carefully. Trying not to let her homesickness and grief swallow her whole.

Unable to bear another moment in his presence, Cirelle fled. He didn't follow.

The quiet beauty of the garden was at least a small balm. Outdoors, the heavy silence was finally broken by a soft chorus of insects. The scattered statuary was a perplexing mix of art, both familiar and alien. Some were depictions of beasts she didn't recognize, in detail too exquisite to be wrought by human hands. A few were twined with vines and creeping flowers, their growth carefully guided to become a part of the piece.

One of the sculptures forced Cirelle to halt in her tracks, a thick lump forming in her throat. It was a tall disk of shining black stone, embedded with tiny dots of glimmering silver.

Her sky. The home of her Arravene gods.

The specific constellations of the deities were marked by diamonds, with enameled lines connecting the shapes. She placed a hand against Irri's constellation. The Defiant, her favorite goddess among the pantheon. Tracing the lines lightly with one fingertip was a mantra, a prayer.

Cirelle murmured a fervent prayer for Lydia, for her soul. Would the soldier find her way to her spot in the heavens if she weren't burned on the traditional funeral pyre? Cirelle's stomach turned another flip. Her gods were here in this miniature sky. Did Ellian know what this stone meant, or was it merely a pretty piece of decorative rock to him?

She sucked in a steadying breath. *I can do this.* She wiped her eyes with the back of a hand and moved on.

Cirelle wandered aimlessly for a time. Her hand grazed the back of a rearing horse cast in bronze. *Aidan would have loved this.* Her brother would have spent hours out here with his charcoals and pastels, sketching the lines of these sculptures. Then again, aside from her portrait, she couldn't remember the last time he'd drawn anything at all.

A blur of motion caught her eye as a shimmering green insect buzzed by her to land on a nearby flower.

No, not an insect. The creature's body was a brilliant, iridescent emerald like a beetle's carapace but human in shape. It couldn't have been larger than her thumb, its eyes large and black. Translucent wings fluttered, a blur of golden-green. Without taking those uncanny eyes from Cirelle, it plucked a tiny bug from a leaf and shoved the whole thing in its mouth. It crunched down, swallowed, and gave Cirelle a toothy snarl of a grin before flitting away.

"Florafae," Ellian's voice said behind her. Cirelle cried out in surprise and whirled. How long had he been following her?

The sidhe leaned against a stone pillar, arms crossed before him. The half-smile was back, but Cirelle was beginning to recognize it for the mask it was. She had learned to hide her sorrow behind a smile when it was needed. What lay beneath Ellian's indifference? The heartless face of a predator?

He nodded in the direction the small creature had flown. "They're harmless. Relatively speaking, that is. Those teeth are tiny, but painful."

Cirelle stared at him, ignoring the light remark. "Why did you bring me here?"

His grin faltered and his face grew cold. "You wanted a bargain, and I made one. Don't ever give a faerie an inch, Princess, or we'll take everything."

Chapter Nine

"Come." Ellian said. It was not a request. Cirelle followed, but only because she knew how fickle the fae could be, and wondered just how far she'd already pushed him tonight.

He led her to one of the parlors she'd noticed before. Another cozy space, rich wood panels lined the walls, the floor a matching parquet. Various gaming tables dotted the room, all with matching chairs upholstered in the deepest blue silk.

Ellian indicated the tables while he watched her a bit too intently. "Choose a game."

Cirelle glanced down at the nearest table and its circular pattern. "This is another test. What if I say no?"

He shook his head and his voice sank to a glacial tone. "You *will* play."

With a shudder, Cirelle took a seat at the game board. Fox-and-hounds, her favorite. Another painful reminder of her brother. Cirelle closed her eyes. When she opened them, the faerie was watching her intently.

He helped her place the pieces in their starting positions, his nimble hands making short work of it. Cirelle pointed at the red piece. "I'm the fox," she said flatly, gesturing at the white pieces for him. "You can be the hunter. I'm always the fox."

He regarded her for a few moments, eyes dancing with humor and one eyebrow raised. "Are you?"

Her cheeks flushed at the purr of his voice, silk and sand. "Yes."

That made him laugh, a deep sound with a hint of a rasp that felt like a hand sliding across her belly. She pushed the shivery little warmth down, burying it deep, and set the last piece. "Your move."

While they played, Ellian changed. A white tension clung to his features, his shoulders growing stiff. All mirth faded. His motions were tight, the hint of a crease forming between his brows even as he cast her empty smiles.

"Who was the woman?" Cirelle asked. "The one with the horns?"

"A client. She finished her dealings and left."

A client. What Toben had said earlier...

"What happened today?" Cirelle blurted. "What did Toben mean when he mentioned an issue?"

"More business." His smile was banal, but his eyes flickered solid black and then bled through with emerald green, like ink spreading in water. Cirelle hissed in a breath. He blinked, and they melted back to gray.

"What was that?"

Ellian glanced down at the game board with a grimace.

"You promised to answer my questions," she reminded him quietly.

He was silent for so long Cirelle thought he wouldn't answer at all. "My eyes shift colors," Ellian finally said.

"They didn't before."

"Glamour," he said, settling back more firmly in his chair.

Cirelle let that sink in. Glamour. Faerie magic, and he spoke as if performing such magic was as easy as breathing. His jaw still clenched. She tilted her head and squinted, trying to see any flash of color beneath the silver. "You hide them with the gray."

"I hide many things."

Cirelle grimaced. She longed to peel off that supercilious mask, to crack him open and see what lay inside. Trapped here in this place, she needed all the information she could get about her capricious host. "Like what?"

"Secrets." The glamour dropped again. Ellian's eyes practically glowed cerulean now, like blue flames. His left hand flipped a spare game piece over and over, then twirled it in idle circles on the tabletop. He smiled, a sly, feline grin. "If you're digging for information, I'd trade one of my secrets for one of yours. Maybe your deepest regret, or the most sinful fantasy you've ever concocted in that pretty little head." The comment was only a shade above a whisper, the molasses-coated sand of his voice sending a small shiver up her spine.

Cirelle swallowed back the feeling, the game forgotten.

No. He's a murderer, she reminded herself. As before, the thought doused the flutter in her belly.

Whatever she would have said next was interrupted by the doorbell clanging. Not the single echoing ring of yesterday, but a repeated clamor as if someone yanked on the bell-pull over and over. Down the hall, a voice shouted Ellian's name, a teasing cry punctuated with a sharp laugh like broken glass.

Ellian's eyes widened, the color draining and leaving them dark as obsidian. "Stay here." He pushed his chair away from the table. Halfway across the room, he added, "Please." Then he was out the door and gone.

His footsteps echoed as he raced down the hall, and Cirelle could not shake the icy claws of fear that had sunk into her chest.

For a flash, terror had filled his face when his eyes turned pure black. Fear trickled along her spine, like the legs of an insect skittering over her skin. He'd said 'please.' Did faeries even say 'please'?

Ellian had left the door open in his rush to leave. Beyond it, she could hear him talking to Toben in worried tones while the bell continued to ring and that brittle voice kept taunting.

Cirelle steeled her resolve. *He is not my master yet.* She crept down the hall. The doors between the foyer and the corridor stood propped open this evening, and she could see both men clearly as she peered around the threshold. They stood staring at the front door, all while that relentless sound kept clanging and that voice shouted.

Ellian gestured at Toben and the servant stepped back, his face grim and his hands wringing one another. Squaring his shoulders, Ellian donned his affectation of casual confidence like a cloak. But his jaw clenched too tightly, his movements stiff. Was it her imagination, or did his hand tremble as he reached for the knob?

The ringing and the cries ceased when Ellian opened the door. The sudden silence was more deafening than the racket had been.

"Ellian," the voice on the doorstep said, a sound like boots crunching over shattered glass. It was the voice of a monster that lurks in darkness, of a wraith, a shadow. "We found this vermin slinking about where it wasn't welcome." The stranger laughed, an awful, rasping sound, the bray of a madman. "So, we took care of it. I think it might belong to you?"

"Get out." Ellian's voice was low, filled with cold fury and power.

"Only fulfilling our obligation and returning your property," the voice cackled again. A loud thump turned Cirelle's stomach, a heavy, wet sound. Then the clatter of footsteps crunched away down the gravel walk.

"Oh, Orwe," Toben croaked. It sounded like a name. His hands clasped tightly together before him and his shoulders sagged, a flower suddenly wilted. He bowed his head to whisper something under his breath that sounded like a prayer.

Cirelle's world had narrowed to a single pinpoint. She couldn't tear her eyes from the small, lifeless hand spilling limply through the front door. It lay perfectly still, its webbed fingers curled up like a dead spider's legs. The skin shone a pallid white with a faint blue tint.

The hallway grew stiflingly hot, all the air sucked out. Her heart beat a panicked staccato against the back of her ribs, and she was unable to get enough air despite sucking in lungfuls of it.

Ellian lifted the limp hand gently and tucked it back out of her view. When he leaned out to pick up whatever—whomever—was outside the door, Cirelle's world tilted, going blurry and dark around the edges.

She must have made a small sound. Toben's head snapped around, eyes widening. Ellian stood and turned toward her, his face expressionless. It may as well have been carved of stone. His eyes were flat gray, his voice cool. "Cirelle." The way he said her name, icy and terse, created a new lump of dread heavy in her stomach. "I asked you to stay in the game room."

She couldn't find her voice to reply, not when she saw what Ellian cradled in his arms.

The faerie was smaller than Cirelle and slender of build. A hairless creature with a broad, lipless mouth like a frog. It—no, *he*—was garbed in tatters of green fabric that resembled nothing so much as damp seaweed. His eyes were open, milky-white and sightless, his body unmoving. A mottled pattern covered his blue-white skin, and—*oh, Stars.*

As if a curtain had been drawn back, the truth crashed down on her. "Stars go black," she breathed, the curse slipping from her lips. Bruises covered him, ugly purple and yellow blotches scattered all over. Her eyes drifted to his feet. One of them ended in a bloody mess of bone and flesh. His skin was split in dozens of places, open welts and dark slashes that oozed a black liquid. Faerie blood.

He'd been beaten to death.

Cirelle's hand flew to her mouth. Ellian held the dead body of a faerie, cradling it as gently as a sleeping child. He seemed heedless of the black blood staining his pale, fine shirt.

Ellian closed his eyes. "Cirelle," he repeated, and her eyes darted to his face. That voice which had teased, scoffed, and purred so softly was now eerily flat. "Stay within the manor. We need to see to this." This time, Cirelle could do little but nod hollowly as both men slipped past her and down the hall.

Dead. The faerie was murdered and dropped off at the front door with little more than a mocking laugh. Cirelle felt strangely calm and distant, as if she stood outside her body. Her limbs grew heavy and numb.

She knew where they'd gone. Past the dining rooms and gaming parlors, past the door leading to the brownies' wing and the kitchens, there was an exit that opened onto the fenced grounds of Ellian's property.

Ellian had told her to stay within the manor, and she wasn't foolish enough to follow them out into the wildlands beyond the home. But she couldn't stand here and wait. Still dizzy, she dashed up to the third floor and out into the garden. She stood on a balcony and watched, clutching the railing tightly in a feeble attempt to still the tremor in her hands. Her skin burned so feverishly hot, and the damp breeze was welcome.

The wildness sprawling in front of the house stretched out

behind and to the sides, growing into waist-high grasses and copses of thickly-leaved trees. A band of shimmering silver twined through the gently rolling hills, a narrow river glittering in the moonlight.

Despite the serene surroundings, a chaotic jumble of thoughts warred in Cirelle's mind. Ellian had not been surprised to find a dead body left at his front door. Emotionless, cold as a glacier.

Toben and Ellian left the house, illuminated by the light of Faerie's strange moons. The lifeless form was still cradled in Ellian's arms. Who had he been, the faerie? Toben had said a name. *Orwe.* Cirelle closed her eyes, but that dead, milky gaze stared back from behind her eyelids.

She'd never seen a corpse before, never confronted gruesome death so closely. People had died in the palace, of course. Old age, a knife cut that festered, a fall from a horse. But Cirelle had never been present when someone passed. In Arraven, the bodies of the dead were wrapped head-to-toe in fabric that had been soaked in holy herbs and oils before they were committed to the funeral pyre. She'd never had to look into unseeing eyes and confront the unsettling, empty shell left behind.

And this was not just some accident, not the hopeless tragedy of illness, but *murder.* Someone had wanted the faerie to suffer before he died. Cruelty in its purest form. How scared had he been, how tormented with the agony of his wounds? Had he hoped someone would come and save him, or died in bleak despair?

Terror swept through Cirelle, like a sudden gust of winter wind. She blinked away the tears, wiping her eyes with the back of a shaking hand. *No, don't panic. Think.* She took a long, deep breath and tried to assemble the pieces of this mystery, but she didn't have any clues. Just a dead body and more questions.

The men's dark silhouettes emerged from a group of trees

in the distance and came to a stop at the riverbank. Both knelt for a time. Eventually, Ellian let his arms drop, slipping the still form of the faerie into the water. They stood, staring down at the pale body as the steady current swept it away. Then, in a sudden movement, milky-white arms rose up from the water and dragged the faerie's body beneath the surface.

Cirelle gripped the railing so tightly her knuckles hurt. Was this a faerie funeral or a quiet disposal of incriminating evidence?

As the two men made their way back, she almost left the balcony. But no, the moons were high overhead, the awning leaving her in shadow. And if Ellian saw her, so be it. She had questions for him.

Their voices carried to her on the crisp spring breeze. At first, they were a murmur with no discernible meaning. When the men drew close to the house, she could make out enough of their conversation to give her a few more tantalizing clues. They spoke in a language she did not know, but the earring Ellian lent her allowed her to make out the words.

"...you tell her?" Toben's voice asked, heavy with concern.

"I don't know yet. For now, only what I must." The deep rasp of Ellian's voice was empty, flat.

"What were you thinking, bringing her here so close to Thieves' Night?"

"I didn't have much say in the timing, Toben, and it was too good an opportunity to pass up."

Opportunity for what?

"Thieves' Night is a bad idea," Toben grumbled. "We still don't have a way in."

"But we know more than we did before," Ellian replied, the ice in his voice cracking and weariness seeping through. "We can't get in by water."

Toben's retort was an angry, anguished croak. "Orwe *died*

for that scrap of knowledge, and we still have no decent plan."
They were nearly to the side door now. Cirelle could have tossed
a stone and hit them, but neither noticed her.

"He willingly volunteered."

"So, we'll just throw someone else at it and let them die as
well?"

There was a pause before Ellian answered. "We only have
weeks left, and this will be our best chance. So yes, we will, if
there is a volunteer." He sighed. "Summon the others."

They entered the manor in silence.

Cirelle waited at the top of the stairs when they entered the
main foyer, arms crossed. The smear of dark, sticky blood by the
front door was already gone, the work of the dutiful brownies.

"What's Thieves' Night?" Cirelle bit off the words, sharp
and jagged.

Ellian exchanged a glance with Toben, who refused to meet
Cirelle's eyes. The servant cleared his throat. "I'll, er, be in the
Archive," he stammered before escaping through the doors in
the back of the entry hall.

Cirelle held her pose, staring down at Ellian with the question lingering in the air.

He closed his eyes and sighed, wiping his face with the
back of one hand. The silken fabric of his shirt was splotched
and smudged with the faerie's blood. Dark streaks marked his
hands, too. When he started up the stairs to meet her, the cold
mask was gone, replaced with deep green irises edged in darkest
black. His steps were leaden and weary.

"I'll tell you in the garden." Without looking back, Ellian
slipped past her and through the door to the rooftop. Cirelle
followed. He led her to the same balcony where she'd stood
minutes before, his eyes unfocused as he stared distantly over

the grounds. "At the corners of Faerie," he began hoarsely, "there are three great trees."

Unsure how this related to Thieves' Night, Cirelle stood beside him. She couldn't bear to look at him, not after she'd been so harshly confronted with his faerie callousness. Her gaze pierced the heavens instead. The sky here still seemed too crowded, a dozen stars scattering the void for each one in the heavens she knew.

"Those trees echo the same cycle as mortal ones," Ellian continued, his voice sounding hollow. "Their leaves flourishing, withering, and falling to bare their branches, though each blooms and dies at a different pace. They're known as the Lhyrria, in the sidhe tongue."

Anchors, Cirelle's earring provided the translation.

"They are the source of the magic at Faerie's heart. When all three are vibrant with life, leaves green and thick, the magic runs strongest. However, when all the Lhyrria are bare, only the smallest sliver of magic remains. No spells can be cast. Wards and magical shields fade to nothing. We cannot even hold a glamour until one of the trees begins to sprout again."

Ellian turned his own gaze up to the stars, and Cirelle wondered what he saw there. Did the sidhe have constellations of their own?

"We call it Thieves' Night. Sometimes it occurs during daylight hours, but the name remains the same. Weeks from now, the last leaf will fall from the last tree. All fae will be vulnerable for the span of several hours." His gaze fell, staring at the back of his hands. "With our enemies weak, it is also a time when grievances are settled. Treasures stolen, children kidnapped. Hence the name."

All magic would die. Including whatever mystical locks kept his doors shut to other fae. "Anyone will be able to enter your home," Cirelle whispered. "Even the faeries that killed your... friend." She wasn't sure that was the word. Ally, perhaps.

"They could, but you will be well-guarded. And if my home is breached, they will go for the Archive, not a mere servant."

Cirelle swallowed back the sharp pang of fear. She didn't even know what the Archive was, and she hated the thought of that murderous *thing* crawling about Ellian's home. *Her* home too, now.

"The sidhe laws still apply," he added, voice growing hard as granite and hollow as an empty grave. "If any trespassers are caught, they will be subject to faerie justice."

Cirelle had little doubt as to what that might mean. "Faerie justice." She turned the words into a blade. "Is that what happened to Orwe?"

Ellian winced, eyes flooding deep indigo twined with the green of emeralds. He looked away, jaw clenching. "Yes," he croaked, but offered no more.

Still, he had flinched at the name. Guilt? Sorrow? Was that what one of colors meant, the dark blue or the rich green? The tension in her shoulders eased, but she would never again forget that his morals were not the same as her own.

She thought back to what she'd overheard between Ellian and Toben. The words echoed in her mind. *We can't get in by water.*

Get in where?

"You're planning something on Thieves' Night." It wasn't a question and he didn't answer. Ellian's hand gripped the balcony rail tighter, his eyes narrowing as he avoided her gaze.

Who was her sidhe host? There were layers here Cirelle knew nothing about. Plots and ploys, in which she knew neither the rules nor the objective. "What are you, really?" she asked.

One corner of his mouth twisted in a bitter smile. "A sidhe."

"What are you planning for Thieves' Night?"

"I'm planning to protect my home."

It was not the answer she wanted. Focusing her most determined gaze on him, she enunciated the next question clearly. "Whose home are you planning to break into during Thieves' Night?"

That gaze was inscrutable, despite the flicker of colors swimming through it. Goldenrod, emerald, obsidian. He glanced away again. "An enemy's."

Another brick wall, but he'd at least confirmed he planned something.

"That's enough questions for now," the sidhe said crisply, turning to leave. "I must clean up. If you still want answers, I will meet you in the library." His tone left little room for argument and Ellian strode away, leaving Cirelle alone in the starlight with more questions than before.

Chapter Ten

THE LIBRARY STOOD OUT as a cozy haven in spite of its high ceiling. A few heavy wooden desks and plush armchairs rested on one side of the room, all atop an immense sandy-brown rug. The lighting shone bright enough to read by, but warm enough to feel intimate despite the shelves lining the walls. The scroll racks that stood in the center of the far end of the library were less imposing, only as tall as Cirelle could reach, but packed together with narrow aisles between.

Cirelle scanned the books, reading spines or tugging out unmarked ones and thumbing through them. There had to be clues in here, some scrap of information about what she'd leapt into.

She was disappointed to discover that her enchanted earring only interpreted verbal speech. Foreign script remained unintelligible, though she recognized some of the languages by their appearance. Nycen's flowing script, sharp Saedden runes, even the looping vertical strings of Kishi. Others were new to her, shapes she couldn't begin to decipher.

If there was a semblance of order to the books, Cirelle could not find it. She was fluent in two tongues, her native Arravene and the common Trade tongue that borrowed bits and pieces from a dozen languages. She knew a passable amount of Gilbran, along with a few words of Miskau. However, it was no surprise to find a lack of books in the Miskau tongue; her grandfather's people kept mainly to oral traditions.

Botany guides bumped shoulders with fictional tales of heroes and damsels, if the illustrations were any indication. Beside those lay atlases full of maps to places she didn't recognize. Then there were dense tomes without pictures, just rows of tightly-packed text. She managed to find a few books in Trade, but they were distressingly mundane; a treatise on the care of goats, an anthology of children's nursery stories, a popular epic poem.

It was as eclectic a collection as everything else in Ellian's home, the hoard of a barrow-bird collecting any bit or bauble that passed its way. Frustrated, she settled into a chair with one of the few books in Arravene, a collection of romantic poetry.

The words became increasingly difficult to read as she waited and her terror silently grew. Someone had been *murdered*. The panic threatened again, a cresting wave ready to crash over her. Could she fall prey to those creatures when Thieves' Night fell upon them? Her breathing shallowed and increased, a frantic flutter taking root in her breast. Her hands still trembled, and Cirelle gripped the edge of the book so hard her knuckles ached. She forced herself to set it down and was still massaging her fingers when Ellian entered.

If she'd still been holding the book, she would have dropped it.

He'd traded his ostentatious clothing for a plain robe of faded red and trousers with simple boots, no scandalous ensemble or jingling silver filigree. His jewelry was gone, every earring and ring absent, and his fingertips were inky black as if he'd dipped them in dye. The tips and nails swallowed light, the color of pitch fading to his slate gray skin at the knuckles.

Ellian's face was emptier than she'd ever seen it, a yawning abyss of nothingness. The silvery gray of his neutral eyes had gone dull, the color of dust. "You have questions." His voice was hollow as he took a seat at one of the small desks. Even his motions lacked in grace. It seemed a different person sitting before her, in plain clothing and blackened fingertips.

Something about the stain on his hands tugged at her memory. "What is that?" she asked softly, nodding at them.

She'd expected a flicker of something in his eyes, but they remained lifeless. He held up one hand and stared at the black stain. "A penance."

"For your friend." She hesitated. "Do you grieve? As humans do?"

"Sometimes."

Bile rose in her throat. How dare he treat Lydia's life like that of an insect, then mourn this faerie? She stared at those sooty fingertips, wanting to reach out and smash them with one of his heavy books until the bones crunched.

It hit her in a sudden flash. The dye on the fingertips, the plain crimson robe.

"That's not a faerie custom," she whispered. "It's a human one, from Kishir." She dredged up her old history lessons. Kishir, the continent across the eastern sea, a fallen empire. Red, the Kishi color of death and grief. Mourning garb. The stained fingertips were a funereal custom for their leaders, for a lord or a military officer whose choices led to the death of a subject or soldier. They wore the dye until it faded, to cleanse the blood from their hands in the eyes of their god.

Kishi's last emperor had been given the moniker of Black-hand for that very same custom. She struggled to recall the rest of the lessons. There'd been a rebellion over something or other. When the peasants' revolt was quelled, the emperor had borne those black-tipped hands until the day he died, a reminder of the untold amount of blood the war had shed.

Though he'd perished decades ago, the custom of dying one's hands remained, tied to the monotheistic religion that still dominated the continent.

"Stars," she swore. "You're Kishi."

The rich, dark wood that covered this home made sense now. It was Kishi halwood, or a mimicry of it. The intricate filigree throughout the home's decor and in his wardrobe, it all reflected Kishir's influence mixed with elements from other cultures like her own. His fascination with human things, with her world, it all fell neatly into place.

He nodded. "Yes."

"How?"

"As an infant, I was swapped with a human baby. A change-ling." Ellian's cold emptiness cracked, his eyes flickering darkest blue for a bare instant, his jaw clenching. He stared at an un-opened book on the desktop.

"What were they like, your human family?"

A sad ghost of a smile played at the corner of his lips, though his eyes remained distant and gray. "Kind. Brave. Reckless." He paused, swallowing something he was about to say. "Painfully mortal," he added instead. "They didn't know what I was. Neither did I, until they all died. And I didn't." Ellian stared with those cool, colorless eyes, his face back to his mask, and changed the subject. "You must be confused and frightened about what happened today, but there are things it's safer for you not to know."

"I'm trapped in this house. Soon, the *thing* that dropped off your friend's corpse could come for us, too."

Ellian flinched, then frowned. "You'll be well-guarded. I'll see to that." His fingers tapped a tentative rhythm on the desktop, and he canted his head to regard her with narrowed eyes.

"Like you saw to your friend's safety?" Vicious, but the words tumbled out before Cirelle could stop them. "How am I to survive living here, drenched in secrets?"

"If you want to endure Faerie, you'll need to sharpen certain skills. Tell me, Princess; are you a good liar?"

Was she? She'd fooled her parents and the guards often. "Good enough."

"Get better," Ellian responded, the velvety quality returning to his voice. Even his posture slowly returned to normal, his shoulders straightening.

Her eyes widened. "That's why you use humans. To lie for you."

"One of many reasons, yes." He regarded her for a few moments, and she watched those eyes brighten from ash gray to polished silver.

Lies. Deception. One of her specialties. Her hand lifted to pull a lock of hair between her fingers, staring at its bloody new hue.

Ellian watched her carefully. "I've been curious. The night we met, dye stained your temples. Your hair is freshly tinted. Why?"

"Because one of my suitors follows a religion that considers the color red a bad omen."

"Were you hoping he'd withdraw if he saw your red hair?"

A lump grew in her throat, unexpected tears stinging her eyes. "Yes."

"One of. There are more?"

Cirelle nodded. "One other."

"Do you love that one, then?"

She hesitated. What she'd had with Briere, she'd never hesitate to describe as love. But Rhine...they'd only met thrice. Charmed, yes. Smitten, perhaps. But in love?

Ellian measured her silence. "Every leader must weigh the

greater good against the singular desires," he said softly, his eyes gone dark and a sorrow lingering in the words.

She cast him an accusatory glare. "That's what happened to Orwe? The greater good?"

Ellian winced but nodded. "A queen must sometimes sacrifice one life to save many. Would marrying your unpleasant suitor be so much more difficult than the soldier living at a barren outpost, keeping a watchful eye on the border far from home? Or the mother who frets about her son's ship carrying important messages through rough waters?"

The words tightened around Cirelle. "Perhaps it isn't. But that doesn't mean I can't hate it, that I can't stop feeling I was meant to be more than a mere bargaining chip."

His thoughtful, cunning eyes met hers. "Maybe you are."

Chapter Eleven

CIRELLE SOUGHT REFUGE in the one place she knew would clear her head. Though the darkness clinging to the halls still left her uneasy, she found her way to the music room, an island of cheerful brightness in this silent, somber manor.

The harp still stood in the corner, heavy and elegant. No elaborately carved relief decorated it, just smooth curves and the natural grain of the wood. Cirelle sat on the matching stool behind it. She strummed a few strings and it came to life beneath her fingers.

First, she played a familiar melody, a romantic serenade about a cursed prince and the knight who redeemed him. As always, her thoughts calmed as the song wove around her. It was like taking a bundle of spilled sticks and gently setting each one into alignment with the other. Her worries did not disappear, but they no longer screamed in her head like carrion birds.

When the doorbell rang, Cirelle's pulse jumped as she recalled that sharp-edged voice calling Ellian's name. The chime only sounded once, and she breathed a soft sigh of relief.

She finished the ballad and began plucking out the tune

she'd started composing in her first hours here, experimenting with possible harmonies.

The second ring sent a shiver down her spine. Cirelle forced down her anxiety and continued playing.

At the third ring in a brief span of minutes, Cirelle's curiosity rose to a fever pitch. Abandoning her song, she left the music room. She peered into the foyer as Toben led a faerie through the doors in the back of the entryway. The creature looked like he was carved of rough grey stone and stood so tall he had to duck to fit through the doors.

The bell chimed yet again. Toben emerged and scuttled over to the front door. A cloud of small faeries fluttered in, each a miniature, sparkling replica of a human but with the bright feathered wings of tropical birds. These, too, were led into the mysterious room opposite the main entrance. The Archive, they'd called it. An archive of what, if his library lay upstairs?

Toben returned to the entryway and turned to her, his kind eyes dark with worry. "I fear you'll make our guests uneasy, my Lady, gawking at them like that."

Something snapped inside Cirelle, a tension kindled to sudden spark and flame. "Oh, my apologies," she spat, not bothering to hide the nervous venom in her voice. "Stars forbid anyone feel frightened around here."

Toben wrung his hands and opened his mouth, but she cut him off. "Don't."

She swept down the stairs past him and crossed the foyer into the guest wing where her room lay, slamming the hallway door behind her.

On the way to her room, a plan formed. Cirelle dashed down the corridor, the lights flickering off almost as soon as they lit her path. She took two wrong turns before she found her parlor.

There, Cirelle tugged the magical cloak off its peg and swept it over her shoulders before making her way back.

The closed door between the wing and the foyer presented a small problem. She crouched and peered through the keyhole. Little more than blurry silhouettes were visible through the small opening, but it was enough.

Toben greeted the latest newcomer and led them into the Archive. The moment both figures were out of view, Cirelle made her move. She darted through the doorway, closing it as quietly as she could, and scampered up the stairs. At the top of the steps, she pressed herself into the corner near the door to Ellian's private wing. From here, she had an excellent view of the front entry. Not two heartbeats later, Toben re-entered the foyer. Cirelle's heart raced as she stared at the back of his head, but he seemed to notice nothing amiss. He hovered by the door, waiting for the next guest.

Which of these faeries would risk themselves now, searching for a weakness in this mysterious enemy's defenses? What was so important it was worth such a sacrifice?

Back at home, one of Cirelle's few duties had been the mediation of minor personal grievances between her kingdom's gentry, alongside her mother. When lords held such grudges, it always boiled down to a few things: greed, revenge, or a lover caught between the nobles.

Which of the three would motivate her sidhe host? Mere hours spent in Ellian's presence left her with more questions than answers. No matter what mortal affectations and customs he adorned himself with, he did not bear a human's moral compass.

The next guest was human-sized but more bat than man. He bore large, leathery wings instead of arms, clawed hands at their uppermost tips while their longest ends brushed the floor behind. And he was only one member of an increasingly odd parade. A woman composed entirely of cloudy white crystal, a squat and gnarled faerie with skin like knotted tree bark, a sleek black cat the size of a wolfhound with hauntingly human blue eyes.

The doorknob to Ellian's private wing clicked softly. It was the only warning Cirelle received. The door swung open, hitting her squarely in the nose. Pain blossomed in her head, sparking like shooting stars. She yelped and clapped her hands over her face.

The door slammed shut. Ellian hissed, "*Avesh!*"

All Cirelle could do was try to breathe through the shattered-glass sensation in her nose. Her stomach turned and she counted out long, painful seconds. When the agony faded enough to think, fear and embarrassment smothered her.

Ellian was staring with wide, ember-orange eyes, nostrils flared. For a brief moment, he merely glared. Then a hand darted out, lightning-fast. She flinched away, but he only plucked at the back of the hood, tugging it off her head. "Princess." Despite the fury in his face, his voice was low and frigid.

She was caught. What punishment had she earned?

Still, Cirelle wouldn't meet her reprisal while cowering. she tilted her chin up, squaring her shoulders and meeting his gaze defiantly.

"That cloak was loaned to you *only* for use in my employ." He stepped closer, not touching but uncomfortably near. The polished stone of the wall was hard and cool against her back as his aroma surrounded her. A burning scent, smoke and embers overpowering the softer notes. "You've stolen something from a faerie, Princess, by using it in direct contradiction to the terms you agreed upon." This was a new Ellian. Something dark and glacially cold twisted its way up out of him. His eyes were red-rimmed, jaw tight, voice crackling like frozen branches.

Cirelle held her breath but did not break his gaze. Her heartbeat drowned out any other sound, and the pain of her injured nose washed over her in black, crashing waves.

Ellian still wore the red of Kishi mourning. A mad light shone in those eyes, a flickering orange ringed with the deep, brilliant blue of sapphires. Maybe faeries didn't have human morals, but this one felt anguish as keenly as any human. It was obvious in the crease of his brow, his clenched teeth, the coiled tension in his body.

It stole the wind from Cirelle's sails, her bravado withering in the face of his pain. She swallowed back the retort she'd been ready to hiss at him. Her arm lifted and her hand moved to touch his shoulder. Ellian flinched away.

"I'm sorry." Her voice rang strangely in her head, her nose already swelling. "I just wanted to see—"

"Don't," Ellian cut her off, voice brittle. "There will be repercussions."

Balance. The word echoed in Cirelle's mind, his explanation on that first night. Faerie rules. Insults met with reprisal, bargains held and kept, all in equal measure.

Ellian walked away, pausing with his foot still on the top stair. "Never use the tools I loan you to spy on me or mine again, Princess."

Chapter Twelve

A FEW MOMENTS AFTER the door closed downstairs, a slow trickle began deep within Cirelle's nostrils. She swore and darted down the steps, flying through the darkened hall to her room as she held her hand over her nose. The coppery tang of blood dripped over her lips before she'd reached her parlor.

Great, Cirelle thought darkly as she tended the wound before her mirror, tilting her head back and shoving wads of gauze up her nose. She prodded at the sides and tip lightly, wincing at the pain, though she was narcissistically pleased it didn't seem broken. She bore her father's prominent nose, regal and distinctive. It was a feature common in his family, he'd told her, and the unmistakable stamp of royalty among his father's clan. Or the closest thing that passed for royalty among the Miskau, at least. Arravene courtiers now painted their faces with cosmetics trying to create an illusion of the new telArraven features, but they were pale imitations.

Cirelle sighed. She rested her chin in one hand and waited for the bleeding to slow while her mind plucked at the puzzle of her faerie host. What was he? Thief? Spy? Conqueror? Or just a man with a grievance and a lot of people who owed him favors?

When the door hit her, Ellian had uttered a curse. *Avesh.* "Shit." Her earring had provided the meaning, and she rolled the harsh word around on her tongue. It sounded like Kishi. Not a faerie word.

Though she was fluent in two languages, Cirelle swore in Arravene. When her grandfather let a stray curse slip, he'd done so in his native tongue of Miskau. If Ellian still used Kishi expletives and clung to mortal mourning customs, perhaps there was yet something human mingled with his faerie nature.

The bleeding had slowed. Cirelle gently removed the blood-soaked cloth from her nostrils, discarding it in a waste bin with a grimace. Her nose was grotesquely swollen, the skin an angry pink. The tang of blood filled the back of her throat, and she spat red into the basin.

Cirelle did not know how long Ellian's clandestine meeting would last. Her head pounded too fiercely for reading or music to be an option, but a restlessness had settled under her skin. She wandered out of her parlor, uncertain where she intended to go. Her thoughts rattled around her brain like river stones tumbled in a current.

Orwe. A corpse left at Ellian's door like a gruesome gift. It was hard to escape those eyes, wide and unseeing. There was something gut-wrenchingly *wrong* about the way his head had lolled on those narrow shoulders. That laughing voice still echoed in her mind like the crunch of broken crystal. Now that she'd opened the door to the fear, it came swirling out, thorny vines that wrapped Cirelle and strangled. Her steps hastened, but there was nowhere to run, trapped in this shadow-coated, silent house.

She headed to the garden, to her gods.

The black stone disk stood tall and proud, the diamond stars of the pantheon's constellations winking in the moonlight. It rested in its own alcove, a curve of hedges framing the sides and back of the piece. Trembling, Cirelle pressed her hands flat on the cool stone and leaned her forehead into it. She wept, letting the terror and fear wash over her. Her head pounded and her nose ached, but it was nothing compared to the panic that threatened to consume her.

Even now, Ellian met with others downstairs to decide who would follow in Orwe's unfortunate footsteps. A committee of death.

When the tears finally eased, she wiped her nose on her sleeve, uncaring if she damaged the fine fabric. A sudden, intense lance of pain drove into her skull, causing her to snarl out a curse. Cirelle squeezed her eyes shut until the red waves subsided.

She traced the constellations, her fingertips following the paths worn into the stone by hundreds of other hands before her. How long had this stone stood in her world, and where? Had it been a prized piece in some rich lord's private sanctuary? Or was it once part of the lost mountaintop Temple of Basre, the one that had crumbled a century ago in a terrible earthquake?

"Divine Iska." The words rolled off her tongue easily. "I stand beneath you and ask your guidance." As she continued the prayer, the words built a wall in her mind, brick by brick, keeping the fear at bay.

The familiar rite kindled a new sorrow, though. A wave of homesickness struck Cirelle. She longed deeply for something small and simple from home; Cook's spiced mincemeat pies, the familiar curves of her favorite lap harp, the sweet scent of the sachet she kept beneath her pillow for peaceful slumber. The sight of her brother rolling his eyes at her latest outlandish behavior.

Aidan. Her chest grew tight. Cirelle said a prayer for her brother and Briere, then sketched the lines of Irri's constellation one more time, adding a wish for the inner strength to survive twelve more months surrounded by faerie cruelty.

"Please," she prayed. "Don't let this place change me."

Orwe's blank eyes stared back from her memory. No one ever deserved to die as he did. She didn't know what sort of person he had been, but such cruel and vicious suffering left a wound in her chest, a nameless horror and pity.

Staring at the glimmering gemstone constellations before her, Cirelle realized why her steps had truly led her here.

"Iska," she asked her gods, "there's a faerie. Orwe. I never knew him, but he died a terrible death. I'm sure his people have their own rites for the dead, and maybe his spirit doesn't belong among your stars. But if your reach extends this far, please help his soul find peace. Wherever that may be."

A deep breath, and a bit of the darkness subsided. Cirelle turned.

Ellian stood behind her, arms crossed. In the silver of the moonlight, she couldn't tell what color his dark eyes shone, intense and yet indecipherable.

She jerked back. The sudden movement sent another stab of pain through her skull. Cirelle stood with her hand over her heart. How much of that had he heard? Her cheeks flushed. "Were you spying on me?"

Ellian arched one dark brow. "Have you already forgotten how half your face became a bruise?"

Humiliation surged and her cheeks warmed. The hateful monster that lived in her mind rose up in response, twisting the embarrassment to fury. Cirelle bit back a sharp retort. Her fists clenched so tightly her nails dug into her palms, the sharpness of the sensation grounding her. It was soothing, the pain. It was solid, and real, and eased the pressure that built in her chest.

Cirelle tried to stalk past him, but Ellian moved to block her path. He stood in the center of the hedge rows so she would have to brush uncomfortably close to him if she wanted to slip past.

"About your injury." His face was still cool and unreadable. "I can heal it."

"Maybe you should leave it as punishment for spying. Balance and all that."

Ellian shook his head. "Your wound is not appropriate restitution for your deception."

"Not harsh enough, I suppose, given what I've seen of your people's idea of justice." The words were bitter. Her nose hurt. Her eyes were dry and scratchy. And a permanent flutter of anxiety had settled in her stomach, feeding the beast that growled and hissed in her mind.

"A mismatch." He shook his head again, those eyes dark. "Neither too strenuous a punishment nor lacking, but an ill fit."

"Well, perhaps I enjoy having you owe me one." She tried to squeeze past him, but Ellian stepped backward and blocked her path yet again. Never touching, but still an obstacle.

"As your host," he said firmly, a small furrow forming between his brows, "I brought you harm. Even by accident, that demands repayment."

"Too bad for you, then," Cirelle snapped, taking a quick step sideways and forward. He moved to block her once again, but she was gaining ground. She repeated the motion on the other side, a strange dance of diagonal steps as she advanced and he backed away.

"I can't let you meet the others with your face looking like that," he blurted.

"What?"

Ellian sighed softly, running a hand through his hair in a nervous gesture she hadn't seen from him before. "They asked to meet you. Against my wishes, I might add, but they've refused to help me further unless I introduce the new human living in my home. It is unacceptable to show them a woman who looks like she lost a fist fight." His lips thinned into a tight line, and he glanced away. "I do owe you healing for dealing you the wound anyway."

Cirelle blinked. The faerie guests were still here. She'd assumed Ellian's appearance meant the meeting was over, that they'd left.

But now they wanted to meet her.

Her headache grew slowly worse, spreading to her temples in a ceaseless barrage of black waves. In a quick, painful movement, she nodded. "Okay. You can do what you must, but only to heal my nose."

Ellian stepped forward. He drew a vial of purple liquid from his pouch and unstoppered it, then dipped an index finger into the potion. At first, Cirelle winced and shut her eyes when his hand came close, but she forced them back open. His touch was gentle when his unusually ice-cold fingertip brushed her nose. The chill soothed the pain instantly, Cirelle let out a small sigh of relief. As her nose cleared, the pungent smell of the potion filled her lungs. Like lemon and mint mingled with something dark and earthy.

Ellian narrowed his eyes and leaned closer to peer at his work. Cirelle flinched away again. He frowned. "Hold this." He pressed the vial and stopper into her hands. A moment later, his left hand cupped the back of her neck, sliding under her hair. His thumb rested against her cheek, and a fluttering heat blossomed in her belly.

She tried to pull away, but he held her in place. "What are you doing?"

His smile was a wry one. "You keep twitching. And you told me to do what I must to heal you." He dabbed more of the liquid around her nose.

Cirelle could have tried to slip away, but the tonic was working. She forced herself to relax and tilted her chin up, meeting his gaze squarely.

His eyes were so close, silver in the moonlight. He tilted his head to inspect what was left of her injury as his thumb stroked a soft line across her cheek. Shivers rippled outward from that touch.

Cirelle's breath caught. There was something new in his gaze that might have been concern. His right hand drew back from her nose slowly, and Cirelle realized her pain was gone.

Ellian didn't move away. His eyes were locked onto hers, haunted. His left hand still caressed her cheek. It would take so little for him to pull her close, to meet her mouth with his own. Cirelle licked her lips, an instinctive motion. Ellian's eyes darted down to catch the movement and the silver flickered into a new hue, a brilliant violet.

Within a heartbeat, the gray slammed down again. The strange tension that had built between them faltered and faded away. Cirelle slipped from his grasp and stepped back. How could she have forgotten what he did to Lydia, to Aidan, to Briere? Her forbidden books had contained stories of humans so bewitched by the fae that they forgot all common sense. *Could that happen to me?*

She shoved the vial back at Ellian. Without a word, he stoppered it and tucked it back into his pouch. "Come." His voice was hoarse, his movements stiff. "They're waiting."

Side by side, they traced their way back through the garden.

Cirelle grimaced. If there was one thing she should be avoiding, it was irritating her murderous host. "For what it's worth, I'm sorry... For spying."

Ellian shook his head. "What else should I expect from an outlaw princess?" When he glanced back again, his lip curled in a small, bitter smirk.

Cirelle returned a wan smile of her own.

Something nagged at her. In her research, she'd uncovered one reassuring detail about the fae. They could do nothing to a mortal without consent or giving affront first. Unless her books were filled with lies, Ellian shouldn't have been able to hurt her. "About my nose, about the injury... Doesn't that violate fae rules?"

"If it were intentional, it would," he replied while they descended the steps from the garden. "But I didn't know you were standing there. Accidents are another matter."

"But even if it's an accident, you still need to balance it?"

"Yes."

"That seems a finicky rule," she muttered.

Ellian shrugged as he held open the door onto the second floor. "With the fae, all the rules are particular and complicated. I'm beholden to them as much as the rest of my kind." He sounded weary, and Cirelle cast a glance at those blackened fingertips. His rings had returned now, and he twisted one around his thumb.

"Where did they come from, the rules?"

"Faeries have our own myths and legends, Princess, just as humans do, but none of us truly know who laid this curse on the entirety of Faerie."

At the doors to the Archive, Cirelle hesitated. She took a small step back and a long, steadying breath. His hand on the knob, Ellian's eyes glimmered sky-blue, and a teasing note lingered on his words. "You seemed so eager to observe my guests earlier. Why hesitate now?"

"Watching them is one thing. *Talking* to them is another." What if one of them tricked her into saying something stupid or agreeing to another bargain?

"For now, they merely want to see if you can be trusted."

"Do *you* even trust me?"

"So asks the woman who was caught spying not an hour ago." He cocked his head, his smirk pulling down into a small frown. "No, not yet. Someday, perhaps you'll earn it."

With that comment, he opened the door and Cirelle crossed the threshold.

Chapter Thirteen

The antechamber behind the doors seemed too small, over-crowded with fae.

Golden light bathed the space. A scattering of gray arm-chairs and a sofa lay around the west side of the room. A low, round table rested before them. Directly opposite stood another set of heavy doors. A large wooden desk sat to the right of the doorway, with a round mirror hanging on the wall beside it. Tapestries lined the walls, Ellian's feathered serpent woven into one of them.

The stone giant hunched beside the far doors while the other fae lounged on the furniture. Everywhere she looked, the winged creatures rested on the others' shoulders, armrests, or the table. The feline rested beside an armchair to Cirelle's left. Like an overgrown house cat, its long tail curled in front of its feet while it stared with brilliantly blue human eyes.

On the sofa, the bat-like man kept his wings tightly wrapped around his body to avoid nudging the small birch-skinned wom-an that perched on the back of the couch, her feet on the cushion. Beside her, the translucent glass woman sprawled elegantly, a clever sculpture made of milky quartz given life. The squat tree-stump faerie crouched on the floor next to her. In an armchair along the far wall sat a tall man covered in white fur with a snout that was more beast than human.

Strangest of all was the dark form in one corner, standing silently. When Cirelle stared directly at it, the faerie was little more than a faint shadow cast on the wall, a silhouette of a lanky, spiky shape that was only vaguely humanoid. She glanced away and the form grew more solid, darkening into an opaque murkiness of corners and angles, with four burning violet eyes.

Only a single sidhe numbered among these faeries, a petite man standing near the desk, all in hues of buttercup and cream.

Ellian said, "As requested, this is Cirelle telArraven, Princess of Arraven." The language he spoke was a new one, twisty and laden with consonants. A faerie version of Trade, perhaps.

One by one, he introduced the others, a litany of names she knew she wouldn't recall despite her training in courtly courtesies.

"Kith." The cat, his sleek black fur looking soft as velvet and his blue eyes luminous.

"Vilitte." The crystalline woman, clouded and translucent, draped in sheer golden silk. She tilted her head and watched Cirelle with eyes like polished silver orbs. Her long plait of silver hair glittered like strands of steel.

"Agdarr, Es, Leilarie, Carid, Ixikki," he introduced those around the sofa. "The sidhe is Issen. And the flock of winged fae are the Ulim."

He didn't name the dark shape in the corner.

Cirelle nodded to each as they were introduced, though a thin thread of panic unspooled in her chest. More than a dozen faeries crowded here, any one of them capable of winding her in a snare of their words, of cursing her. Her mouth went dry and she swallowed hard. Awkwardly, Cirelle resorted to familiar habits. She gave a small curtsy and said, "Pleased to make your acquaintances." The faerie tongue came to her easily, thanks to the enchanted earring.

"Liar." This came from Kith, the cat, the accusation thrown casually as he yawned wide and stretched, curling up on the floor. His voice dripped with arrogant disdain. "I can smell your panic, little human." His tone made it an insult, an epithet uttered with a bitter taste in his mouth.

In spite of the danger, Cirelle snapped. All her terror and unease boiled over into a sudden desperate fury. "Very well. I'm *not* pleased. I also won't stand here and bear your condescension. I have a name, and you will use it."

The cat stared with narrowed eyes, but the crystalline woman laughed, her voice airy. "Ooh, I like her."

"Vilitte," the little birch woman sighed, "don't goad Kith, please. You remember what happened last time."

"I paid for the damages," Vilitte replied, her silvery voice laden with honey and amusement.

Without even glancing at Vilitte, Kith gave a rumbling growl and a soft hiss. His eyes were glued to Cirelle's. She kept her chin lifted, her mouth set in a firm line.

Eventually, the cat blinked and settled his head on his forepaws with another lazy yawn, as if to say Cirelle was not worth the effort. Prickly as any feline.

The wolf-like man snorted. Carid, his sharp teeth gleaming white as his lip curled in disdain. "Ridiculous. A human princess? Not much help she'll be."

Cirelle's anger bubbled up again. "I daresay you're correct, and it seems there's little need for me to stay where I'm so *useless*." She whirled on a heel to leave.

Throughout the exchange, Ellian had stood quietly at her side, between Cirelle and the door. She circled around him, ignoring the confusing, weighted glance he gave her, and slammed the door when she left. Vilitte's bell-like laughter echoed behind her, even through the heavy wood.

Stupid, arrogant, condescending faeries. Cirelle huffed out a frustrated breath. She stormed off to the music room, a furious song roaring in her mind, full of sharp staccato notes and heavy, pounding drums. The drums she could not provide, and the harp was too delicate an instrument for her anger. Her eyes landed upon the glossy fortepiano in the center.

Cambiare. The word flitted through her mind, a musical term. A change. A switch of instruments.

So, she sat on the padded bench and pounded out the notes. She was not as proficient at this instrument as the harp, but it better suited her mood. With every dissonant note, she hoped the stupid faeries could hear the racket ringing through the walls.

Anger was good. It was comforting, powerful. A mask for the quaking terror that hid behind it.

Cirelle's fingers were sore by the time Ellian came to find her. He sauntered into the room, leaning against the wall beside the door and crossing his arms. Cirelle pointedly ignored him as she struck the keys in a sharp, vengeful melody. She punctuated the end of the song with several loud chords that echoed in the air. As the music faded, Cirelle closed the cover over the keys, letting her hands rest on the polished wood.

She stared at the back of her aching fingertips. "I suppose you're here to chastise me for being rude to your friends."

"Your display earned their respect, oddly enough. Kith is still put out, but that's typical. Offend the sidhe, however, and you could lose your head."

"So, I passed another test, I guess." Cirelle sighed, letting her hands fall to her sides as she stood. "Everything here is a test. It's exhausting." When she glanced up, she was startled to see his eyes a soft shade of pale copper.

"It is. It never ends. Do you have the strength to stand it?"

"I don't know." Her anger spent and her song finishe, Cirelle stifled a yawn. Her new sleep schedule, coupled with the never-ending waves of stress, fear, and worry, left her a pitcher drained dry. She wanted little more than to retreat to her room, curl up under the plush coverlet, and sleep for days.

"Tell me what's going on," Cirelle pleaded, her voice pitiful, weary, and weak. Somewhere deep inside, she was furious at herself for breaking apart like this, but the dam had collapsed and there was no stopping the flood. "Please." Her voice cracked on the word. *I don't want to die like Orwe did. I don't want to follow in the footsteps of the girl Toben warned me about.* It wasn't as if knowing would make her any safer, but it was better than this gnawing, nameless dread.

Ellian was silent a few moments, staring at the floor to avoid her gaze. "No." The word was little more than a whisper, flat and emotionless.

Despair's greedy teeth gnawed at Cirelle, and broken shards of glass filled her chest. "Sly, elusive faerie. I shouldn't be surprised. You're exactly what all the books said."

She stood and scrambled to leave but stumbled on her skirts. As she righted herself, Ellian sighed and reached out to give her a helping hand. He paused, waiting for her to lean into it, to accept his aid.

Instead, she growled and pulled away sharply. "No." Her mind flickered back to that uncertain moment in the garden, the softness in his eyes when his mouth had been so close to hers. Never again. "I'm going to bed. And I'll get there on my own."

At the door, she paused with one hand on the frame. "You try to placate me with a fancy garden and pretty instruments and a thousand books." Cirelle's gaze focused on the back of her hand against the dark wood trim. "But back at home I also had a garden, and instruments, and books I could actually read. You think such bribes are a substitute for honesty, but they're not."

Cirelle didn't give him the chance to reply.

Chapter Fourteen

THE NEXT DAY, Cirelle's parlor seemed too bright with its white walls and pale blue furniture. It was a false cheer, another veneer over the darkness lingering in this house, a thin coat of white paint over wood gone to rot. Her bedroom better fit her mood, all deep grays and burgundies, paintings hiding the pale stone of the walls. She bathed and dressed quickly, so she could return there and read the only book on her small shelf written in the Trade tongue. It was abysmally dull, a treatise on the merits of various sailing vessels. Still, it was all she had, and Cirelle was reluctant to go to the library when she might encounter Ellian or Toben in the halls.

She couldn't avoid them forever, of course. With that knowledge, Cirelle had girded herself for battle. She'd garbed herself in a dress the rich purple color of crushed grapes, a garment of angles and edges. The neckline of the bodice emphasized the curve of her breasts and swept upward into a high collar that cradled the back of her neck. A choker of silver and amethysts circled her throat. She eschewed the simple circlets this time, instead choosing the most ornate silver tiara she could find, all twining curves and delicate points, dotted with pale purple gems and blood-red garnets.

She looked like a cruel queen, especially with the dark kohl smudged on her eyelids. Her skin smelled of cinnamon and amber, a spicy aroma chosen specifically to drown out Ellian's scent.

The brownies had left a small platter of fruit in her parlor, so she stole an apple, made tea, and took both back to her bedroom. She drew the curtains closed against the last of the day's fading light. They were lavish things, hanging to the floor and made of heavy velvet in charcoal gray.

The precise shade of Ellian's skin.

Sudden anger wrapped around her at the thought of her host, making her jaw clench. *Faeries. Damn them all.* Cirelle sipped her tea and ate her apple, silently stoking the fear and the fury as she failed to read the book.

When the breakfast bells rang, Cirelle ignored them.

She didn't know how long she tried to read before the anger grew too deep, too hot. She thunked the book down on the side table. The darkness of her bedroom was comforting, but her legs itched to move, to do something else. Her fingers twitched, and she knew what she needed to do.

Cirelle kept one ear out for footsteps as she made her way up the stairs and into the wing that held the music room once more. Ellian would hear, but she needed to play. This restlessness in her fingers was a familiar sensation, and there was only one definite cure for it.

Choosing the harp again, Cirelle tried to soothe her agitation with the forlorn melody begun on her first night here. In her mind, she'd started calling it her Faerie Nocturne, a dedication to her endless nights here.

The notes thrummed through her, unlocking the sadness that lay beneath the anger. The panic scraped with sharp talons, but she pushed it aside, letting the sorrow spill free. The song untangled the threads within her, twisted into a knot of worry and fear and rage. She tried different counterpoints and harmonies, measure by measure. In a corner cabinet, she found a pen and ink along with parchment sheets already marked for music. Some held markings she didn't understand, but others bore familiar bars and notations.

After an hour or so, she grew weary of the piece and let the last notes trail off. She left her papers on the small table near the door, trusting they wouldn't be disturbed. Ellian had confessed he didn't play, and she was sure Toben wouldn't move them if he stopped by.

As she stacked the pages on the table, a familiar sound echoed outside the open doors, a soft chiming accompanied by the regular rhythm of footsteps. Ellian's silver boots. The noise trailed away down the hall.

Cirelle paused. The open door had been clearly in her line of sight, and he hadn't walked by. Cautiously, she stepped out into the corridor. The last light at the end of the hall flickered off as she watched. She pressed a hand to the wall beside the door. The pale, copper-threaded stone was still warm.

How long did Ellian lean against the wall to suffuse it with his body heat? And why?

No, I don't play, he'd said. *But I listen.* She recalled the music box that had been one of the offerings to summon Ellian, his soft smile when he'd listened to its lullaby.

Something twisted in Cirelle's chest. Not irritation, which she would have expected. She had no name for this feeling. It wasn't pity, nor was it sadness, but it was akin to both.

It was nearly lunchtime. She'd planned to skip it, as she had breakfast, but the music had leeched away most of her ire.

Cirelle straightened her shoulders and headed down the dim
hall as the bells rang.

℘

It seemed Ellian had dressed as spitefully as she did this evening. The faerie wore no jacket and a black shirt that once more
bared an indecent amount of skin. No jewelry circled his throat,
but his ink-stained fingers still wore his many rings. Some were
as simple as a thin silver band, others dotted with a variety of
gemstones. Cirelle was certain they were all enchanted. Weapons,
as surely as a dagger at his hip would have been.

When she entered, Ellian's hand paused halfway to his
mouth. His eyes betrayed him when they raked up and down
her, pupils widening as they flooded with violet.

A vindictive little smile curved Cirelle's mouth as she swept
past him and took her seat. Wordlessly, she began serving herself, cutting off a piece of bread and a thin slab of cheese. There
was cured, thinly-sliced meat as well, which she layered on top.
Taking a bite, she met his gaze. He'd cloaked it in gray again,
but there was a faint flush in those charcoal-colored cheeks.

Ellian cleared his throat softly, opened his mouth, and closed
it again. As if suddenly remembering it was there, he finished
the bit of food that still hung on his fork, frozen partway to his
lips. He stared down at his plate.

"Less glib today, I see." Cirelle poured herself a cup of rich
black tea, the aroma comforting as it steamed before her.

For a few moments, the soft clink of silverware on plates
was the only sound in the room. "You think I'm some sort of
monster," he finally said. "A beast from your bedtime stories."

"I think you're a killer, and a faerie," she replied, sipping her tea. It was the perfect temperature, warming her from the inside out. "Whatever that means. You have your own morals, and they aren't human ones."

His lips thinned and his brows drew together, but Ellian didn't respond.

How many other humans had died at his hands? *The last girl, she was a pretty thing like you.* Her pulse pounding, she asked, "What happened with your previous human servants?"

Ellian's met her eyes squarely, a wan echo of a smile touching his lips. "I've been alive a very long time, and I've had a great number of servants. You'll need to be more specific unless you wish my answer to take days."

She hesitated. "The last one, before me."

He broke the stare, his eyes focused downward on the hand that toyed with his fork, those black-tinted fingertips like soot against the shiny silver. "Toben tried to warn you, didn't he?" Another pause, a soft sigh. "Kyrinna was a mistake."

"What happened to her?" Cirelle's mind conjured a dozen horrible fates for the poor girl.

Ellian was silent for a long moment, one black-stained fingernail picking at a scratch on the tabletop. The doorbell interrupted his reply, and Cirelle flinched. Fear scratched at her, but Ellian seemed unfazed.

He stood. "It seems tonight's appointment is early."

Cirelle quickly chewed and swallowed the last bite of her food, washing it down with a final sip of tea before pushing her chair out from the table. She refused to let the matter rest. "What happened to Kyrinna?"

He grimaced. "She trusted the wrong faerie."

Cirelle's heart leapt into her throat. Before she could ask how, Ellian slipped into the corridor. She was left to follow him as she simmered with dread. Toben was already at the door when they arrived in the hall, standing beside a sidhe woman.

Her skin was the color of mint cream, a pale, frothy green. A shock of turquoise hair brushed her shoulders in wild curls. There was something uncanny about her face, her cheekbones too sharp, Void-black eyes too far apart. She stood slim as a willow, garbed simply in loose trousers and a white tunic. Her feet were bare.

She spoke softly to Toben in words that Cirelle was too far away to hear.

"Ah, here they are," Toben said in the sidhe tongue as she approached. He bowed to Ellian. "I'll be back to my duties, then?"

Ellian dismissed the servant with a nod. "Princess Cirelle telArraven," he said with a courtier's grace. "I present Tallia, a fellow sidhe."

The woman looked her up and down with unfriendly eyes. She, too, was taller than Cirelle, but only by the width of a few fingers. She smelled like green growing things, of moss and pine needles and freshly-cut hedges. It made the back of Cirelle's throat itch instinctively.

Tallia's thin lips were set into a brittle smile as she nodded. The expression didn't reach those dark eyes, and her teeth were slightly pointed. Her voice was rich molasses, at odds with her delicate frame. "So, Ellian, you found a replacement for Toben. Pity. Let's hope she's at least more clever than the last two."

Ellian's smile faltered, but he did not reply.

Giving her voice the weight of her regal upbringing, Cirelle stared the woman straight in the face when she responded, her voice laced with sarcasm. "Perhaps in keeping with the custom you have just shown, I should convey to the next guest my hopes that they are more pleasant than the previous one." The words emerged from her lips in the sidhe language. It was a strange sort of speech, lilting and airy.

Ellian stared at Cirelle with a sudden, keen interest.

The woman ignored Cirelle. "A princess, Ellian? What are you thinking? It will take ages to break her."

Cirelle bristled at the comment, even as she shivered at the woman's words. The woman spoke as if she were a willful filly. What did it mean to the fae, to 'break' a human?

Tallia snorted and turned to face the inside of the front door, running her hands around the frame. A faint glimmer of light trailed behind bony fingertips, clinging to the polished wood before fading away. She worked around the entire door then held out a hand to Cirelle. "Your hand," she demanded.

Cirelle took a step back.

"She's tuning the wards on the doors," Ellian said, "so the house recognizes you."

Cirelle looked back and forth between them while Tallia's lips thinned in impatience. "But I'm already *in* the house," Cirelle pointed out.

"And I'd like for you to remain here without the wards rattling their alarms in the back of my head," Ellian replied.

"Wait, this whole time—"

"The house's alarms have been going off because you're here, but I'm the only one who can hear them."

Even in his sleep? How does that work? Or do the sidhe even sleep at all?

Reluctantly, Cirelle placed her hand in Tallia's. The other sidhe tightened her grasp. Her touch was as warm as Ellian's but hard as steel. A tingling sensation spread upward from Cirelle's hand until it suffused her entire body, like she was full of bubbles.

Without warning, Tallia drew a small blade from a pocket. "Now the blood."

"What?" Cirelle yanked her hand out of reach.

"It's just a tiny bit. Don't act like a child."

Ellian nodded. "A drop of blood is part of the enchantment. She'll take no more than is needed."

Tallia snorted again, giving him a mocking little bow. "On my honor as a sidhe."

"Only as much as you need for this spell," Cirelle confirmed. "Your oath."

Tallia stared at Cirelle as if the family pet had demanded a seat at the dinner table. The sidhe woman glanced back to Ellian. "I could just leave now and let you fend for yourself."

"You could. I'm sure I could find someone else to refresh the wards. Someone who might truly appreciate the grimoire."

Tallia's brows lowered into a deadly scowl, those black eyes shooting daggers. "Fine," she said to Cirelle. "You have my word."

Cirelle waited a moment more, then held out her hand. Tallia was not gentle. The point of the tiny blade pierced her palm. Cirelle bit her lip and glared at the woman despite the sudden tears that sprang to her eyes.

A bead of blood welled up. Tallia dragged a glimmering fingertip through it and smeared the drop onto the door frame. *How much blood has soaked into that dark wood?* Cirelle wondered.

Tallia yanked on Cirelle's hand, dragging her over to the doorway of the guest wing of the home. They repeated the process for each of the wings, as well as all of the doors leading outside. The spell was even set along the ivy-covered walls that edged the rooftop garden.

The heavy doors to the mysterious Archive were last, the ones at the back of the antechamber. The sidhe pressed Cirelle's palm to the solid weight of the wood as she traced a sigil in a tingling line of fire along the back of Cirelle's hand. Her fingertips glowing gold, Tallia drew a matching symbol onto the door.

Cirelle yelped at the sensation of cold, of leeching pressure. It was as if the door inhaled an icy breath against her skin. She yanked her hand back, but Tallia didn't seem to care. Instead, she stepped away, wiping her own hand on her trousers like she'd touched something foul.

"The wards are restored, and your *princess* has been added to them," she confirmed.

"I know." Ellian's voice was cool. He stared at Cirelle's hand for three long seconds, then turned toward the door opposite the entry. "Cirelle, please return to the foyer while we settle our business."

Cirelle bristled at the command, but her hand hurt and she was all too eager to leave Tallia's presence. She massaged her palm gently as she stepped through the doorway. She barely caught the woman's last words as the door creaked shut. "Did you tire of the easy ones for a while, Ellian?"

Tallia left shortly thereafter, clutching a heavy book to her chest and Ellian trailing behind her. She cast one last snooty look in Cirelle's direction before uttering her parting shot. "Enjoy it while you can, Ellian. When Adaleth gets his way, you'll have to tally your own books and warm your own bed." The implied insult made Cirelle grit her teeth and clench her fists. A pain lanced through her injured hand.

Ellian's reply was a warning. "Get out of my house." Without another word, Tallia stalked out the door. Ellian threw the latch with a disgusted sigh.

"I take it you don't like her much."

"No." Ellian gestured at her wound. "Let's get that hand treated."

"It's fine." She tucked the hand behind her.

"She was rougher than she needed to be. You shouldn't have provoked her like that."

"Well, she shouldn't have acted like an ass."

"You don't insult a sidhe and expect to come out of it un-scathed, Princess." He led the way to the nearest room and gestured to a small table with two velvet-upholstered chairs.

"It's okay. Really." Cirelle didn't know why she was so hes-itant. Perhaps it was the lingering sensation of Tallia's magic, a tingling in her fingertips and a twitchy energy that made her unwilling to top it off with yet more enchantment.

Or perhaps she remembered too clearly what had nearly happened the last time she let him treat a wound.

Ellian sat, gesturing again at the opposite chair, a pinched look on his face. "You're my guest, and I allowed you to take injury under my roof. Again."

He wasn't going to let this go. With a sigh, she sat and placed her hand on the table with its palm up. "Fine. But only what you absolutely must do to fulfill the minimum demands of hospitality."

"One would almost think you don't trust me, Princess." His lip quirked as he took her hand, cradling it in his palm. He tucked his hair back while he bent to inspect her injury. A series of small silver studs ran along the edge of the ear, glittering in the soft white light.

Cirelle forced herself to look back down at her hand. The bleeding had slowed, but it still hurt. The skin was already start-ing to discolor around the edges where Tallia had pinched it. A shadow flickered in Ellian's eyes, his smile fading. A sigh escaped him as he set her hand back down on the table.

With quick, sure motions, he once again retrieved the purple potion from his pouch, along with a small square of white cloth. He uncorked the potion and tipped it over to soak the fabric. Its aroma filled her nostrils, mint and citrus and damp earth.

As Ellian slid his hand under her own, Cirelle tried to ignore the warmth of his skin. His touch was so light that she shivered. Ellian's eyes flickered up to hers before concentrating again on his work. A wickedness settled in his smile as he added casually, "I knew a faerie once that could heal wounds with his tongue."

Cirelle's heartbeat stuttered, taken by a sudden mental image of Ellian lifting her hand to his lips, placing a gentle kiss on her palm and a warm, slow stroke of his tongue.

No. She would not be swayed by his faerie trickery.

Still, those long-fingered hands were smooth, his grasp gentler than Rhine's commanding touch, softer than her soldier boy's callused hands, and stronger than Briere's small, deft fingers.

Briere. The thought evoked a sharp pang within Cirelle. Did she suffer even still? The vibrant young woman had been Cirelle's first true act of rebellion. That contagious smile had so charmed her, and she ached at the memory of those copper-colored curls that felt like cool silk twined around Cirelle's fingers and skin that tasted of Briere's honeysuckle perfume.

Cirelle had been fifteen that first time. Young, foolish, and impulsive, breaking every rule to go where her heart led. Their brief liaisons had continued during Briere's visits to the palace, a flash of light and heat and joy. Cirelle's cage seemed less lonely with her beloved curled up against her side. The memories still stung with a bittersweet burn, an old injury half-healed, a tiny needle forever embedded in her chest.

"I'm very curious," Ellian asked, his voice a purr. "What—or who—makes you smile so sadly?" He brushed the potion onto her hand, and Cirelle shivered from the chill of it.

The secret unspooled within her, a skein of yarn tumbling, unraveling. The words spilled out unbidden. "A courtier. A secret. A wild, brash girl with a ready laugh and beautiful brown eyes." *A rich voice like liquid amber that could halt the breath in my lungs when it whispered my name in my ear. Gentle, playful hands and a teasing smile that haunted my dreams.*

It had been Briere who showed Cirelle the many ways to defy her status. She'd helped Cirelle climb out a window and shimmy down a tree for the first time. They'd spent that day in Palace City disguised and exploring the city streets while free of bodyguards and reverent stares.

"What happened?" His question was soft, quiet.

"She got married. And now she lies dying because of you." Cirelle yanked her hand away. The wound already looked better, the skin closed and the bruise gone. Only a shiny pink dot of mostly-healed skin puckered her palm.

Ellian fell silent, lips thinning. He collected his things, then stood and left her in silence.

Chapter Fifteen

CIRELLE'S FEET TOOK HER to the library, where a new stack of books rested on the table nearest the door. One heavy tome lay open in the center. A paperweight rested on the pages, a circular bit of heavy glass ringed with silver.

The words that lay outside the circle were some complicated language, all loops and swirls. However, the writing viewed through the glass was in Arravene. When Cirelle touched it, the thing tingled with magic. She traced the glass over the words, her pulse racing.

Hand position is key when learning the ittar. A finger placed in the wrong position will result in flat notes, and bad habits will be impossible to break if they are learned too early.

Cirelle turned the page to find a detailed illustration of a complicated flute. She slid the paperweight over the spines of the other books in the stack. Every single one was a book on music. Diatribes on the benefits of one instrument over another, collections of sheet music, the history of various genres.

At home, I have books I can actually read. Her words last night.

Every time Cirelle thought she had a handle on her strange host, he surprised her. The puzzling sidhe shifted personalities as often as his eyes changed hue. *Which one is the true Ellian, deep down?* Uneasiness settled in her stomach as she flipped through pages. Whatever his motivation, Ellian had opened a door for her.

With the hours remaining, Cirelle curled in a plush armchair and lost herself in a volume of music history in Faerie, full of events that happened a thousand years ago or more, illustrated with beautiful wood prints.

The jingling sound of Ellian's boots startled Cirelle from a particularly fascinating passage. She leapt up as he entered, dropping the book and the glass behind her.

His gaze flickered down to the objects. "Your time as guest has ended." He gestured to a small table. "Sit."

Cirelle, still flustered at being caught using his gift, took the chair while he sat opposite.

"Now that you are no longer my guest, there is the matter of repercussion for your theft."

"For using the cloak?"

"More than that. You mocked my hospitality by declining not one but two meals. You wear your impertinence like a badge of honor, a challenge. And yes, you stole something that did not belong to you, then used it to spy on me."

She bared her teeth. "What are you going to do?"

The faerie pulled a small jar from his pouch and set it on the table. It was an elaborate thing, beautifully molded in sparkling facets. He pried off the lid and withdrew another item from his enchanted bag. It glittered beneath the warm fae light, an amber stone in a silver setting.

Briere's ring.

Ellian dropped it into the jar with a clink and pushed it toward Cirelle.

She blinked. "What is this?"

"A memory jar." Ellian rested an elbow on the table, chin cradled in his hand. His eyes remained gray, cold. "You wounded me, and I take equal injury in return." He pointed at the ring, distorted through the shapes of the glass. "You claimed that ring was from your first love."

Cirelle gritted her teeth. "It was."

"I want the memory of your first kiss."

"What?"

"A theft for a theft, princess. You have disobeyed and now shall pay. Close your eyes and summon the memory to mind. Then breathe into the jar and seal it. The memory will be lost to you, mine to claim and keep."

Her breath tangled in her lungs. "No." That sun-drenched afternoon was hers and hers alone. "I won't."

"One way or another, you will." Such darkness in his eyes, a faint flicker of orange flame peeking through the gray.

Cirelle swallowed. If she said no, what would he do? Imprison her? Starve her? Drug her as he had that first night?

She was still tempted to call his bluff, until she thought of Lydia, gone without a single scrap of remorse from this cruel faerie. With shaking hands, Cirelle reached for the vial. *A memory, nothing more*, she tried to console herself. Only one in a string of happy, golden days she'd spent with her countess.

It had started so innocently. Before Cirelle had found her teeth and begun bending the rules, she'd met Briere at some inane tea party and the girl's wicked grin had charmed Cirelle instantly. They'd become inseparable while Briere's parents visited court.

One day, they'd slipped their leashes for an afternoon walk on the hills outside the palace, taking a picnic beside the creek and hiking their skirts up above their ankles to skip along the stepping stones like children. A game of dares ended in raucous laughter, a careless slip, and a tumble into the knee-high water for Cirelle. Briere teased and offered a hand up the slippery bank, but some fey impulse made Cirelle pull her into the chilly creek instead.

Briere's indignant shock gave way to her bold, contagious laugh a moment later. She'd looked so beautiful in the autumn sunlight, damp copper hair clinging to her skin in wet curls, water dripping from her nose and chin as she grinned, golden-brown eyes dancing with merriment.

Cirelle kissed her, suddenly and without thought, her chilled, wet hands cradling either side of Briere's face. That first kiss was fumbling, a wild and impulsive thing, Cirelle's heart pounding harder than she thought possible. When they'd parted a few moments later, giddy and breathless, Briere had smiled at her. "I knew it."

Ellian's voice interrupted Cirelle's thoughts. "Now."

Her chest tight, she lifted the jar, filled it with a single puff of breath, and sealed it. Briere's ring rattled inside as she set it on the table.

Her first kiss, gone. When she tried to recall the first time her lips touched Briere's, her mind became a misty fog. She searched through the haze, but it was like trying to remember a dream. Dozens of other stolen kisses—and more—she remembered with absolute clarity but not the first.

The sound that erupted from her throat was a sharp thing, a jagged shard of metal. The faerie's hands tugged the jar from her iron grip, the patterns in the glass pressed into the flesh of her palms. He stood and tugged his sleeves into order as the jar went back into the pouch.

"Balance," he reminded her. "Your debts have been paid, Princess. It would do you well not to incur more."

Her lip curled, but before she could retort, he cut her off. "I'll take you to Toben to start your training."

ᘓᘔ

IT WAS THE FIRST TIME Cirelle had been alone with Toben since their first meeting, and the Archive was the smallest of the mysteries she wanted to ask him about. Questions clustered her mind. *What is Ellian planning? Who are those faeries? Who was Orwe, and what's so important it was worth his life? What happened to Kyrinna?* But the words wouldn't come. Toben wouldn't answer them any more than his master had.

The old man explained the intricacies of Ellian's business dealings. The sidhe made bargains with humans and fae alike, trading treasures for treasures. It would be her duty to meet with his faerie clients, take their requests, and pass out the items after Ellian had approved the exchange. She would also shadow him when he was summoned to the human world, to witness his deals under the concealment of that magical cloak.

"And this," Toben said, "is the Archive." He opened the heavy doors at the back of the antechamber. "No one—and I mean no one—except Ellian and his personal servants can get in here."

Cirelle followed him through the doorway. A tingling sensation brushed her, icy goose-pimples erupting. It was like stepping outside on a chilly autumn day, fine mist settling on her skin. Except it was perfectly dry, and the prickling little more than a phantom.

All her discomfort was forgotten as she stared into the Archive.

The room was immense, taking up two full stories and

stretching back far into the north end of the house. It was filled with tightly-packed shelves, the aisles barely large enough for one person to walk through. They extended to the ceiling throughout the enormous space, with rolling ladders along each end. Trinkets galore rested atop the shelves, some glowing or humming softly. Books, jewels, tiny sculptures, an apple made of gold.

Toben led her along the wall to a smaller room. Here, rows of wooden cabinets sat in neat lines, each engraved with number codes on the drawer. In one corner, a small set of shelves held the items she'd given Ellian as offerings; the music box, the carved statuette, even the empty brandy glass.

And the jar with Briere's ring.

"When Ellian puts new things in his pouch, they show up there," Toben explained. He then opened the top drawer of the nearest cabinet and showed her what lay inside. Sheaf upon sheaf of papers. "Apart from keeping the Archive neat and tidy, we document every item that comes in and sort 'em into the shelves outside. We'll start with the jar." He gave her a sympathetic glance. "Sorry." Cirelle closed her eyes, clenching her fists.

Toben lifted a sheet of parchment off the shelf. He opened the ink, dipped in the pen, and showed her the process of paperwork and filing.

It was an abysmally long and dull evening of scribe's work. Toben's former career as a dock clerk left him far more suited for this sort of task than Cirelle. Grief for Lydia and worry for her other loved ones shadowed every thought. Her mind darted back and forth. What was happening back home? What dark conspiracy brewed within these walls, and what did Ellian want so desperately despite this treasure trove?

They were filing away the last of her items when the dinner chime rang, and Cirelle winced. She wasn't ready to face their

host again, not yet. Not while her memory sat in a jar on one of his shelves like some useless knick-knack.

"You'll be at dinner tonight, won't you?" she asked Toben.

He gave a small grunt of agreement as he made his way down the ladder to stand beside her. "Though I've a feeling it won't be a pleasant meal," he replied, his eyes sparkling with a wry humor.

Cirelle stared down at the floor. "He's a killer."

"He's a faerie." The old man shrugged.

Cirelle clenched her fists as she followed Toben down the narrow aisle out of the Archive. "How do you just accept it?"

"They can't help what they are. It's like living with a cat. You learn how to deal with it, after a time. Besides, they can't do anything to a mortal without permission."

"I know." She stared down at her feet as she walked. "So what did Kyrinna agree to?"

Toben sighed.

Kyrinna was a mistake.

"I can't speak to you about her," he admitted.

"At least tell me if she made it back home safely?"

Guilty silence was his only reply.

Chapter Sixteen

ELLIAN STOOD before his coterie, twisting one of his rings idly about a thumb.

"We still don't have a good candidate, and time grows short," Kith growled.

"I know," Ellian replied. The cat was right. Thieves' Night drew closer, the Key almost in their grasp save one gaping hole in the plan.

"Well, it's a pity I can't play the role," Vilitte purred, flipping her silver braid over one crystalline shoulder. "I'd excel at it."

Ellian had no doubt of that. "You've already agreed to your part," he reminded her.

"And I'll perform it perfectly."

Leilarie swung her feet as she perched on the back of the couch. The tiny salcha appeared almost childlike, slim and wide-eyed, with skin like pale paper. Only her sharp teeth and a capricious glint in her eyes gave away her true nature. "It can't be me, either."

Ellian cast his eyes over the rest of the crew. The Scath was absent, as he was from most of the meetings. The Shadowed

General had his singular task, and there was no need for him to assist with their other plans.

The stone giant hunched in the far corner, his forlorn voice like gravel crunching underfoot. "I won't even fit through the doors."

Ellian's heart twisted a little for the gentle creature. "I understand, Ixikki."

Carid's wolf-like muzzle twisted into a snarl as Ellian's gaze snagged on him. "Don't even think about it, pretty boy."

Agdarr the spriggan huddled on the floor at the corner of the sofa, toying with one of his wooden puzzle boxes again. The squat creature glanced up for the briefest of moments, his gnarled face a picture of indifference. "I only do locks. Told you that before."

Ellian nodded, though he wouldn't have asked Agdarr anyway. The spriggan was ill-suited to the task of debauchery and fomenting drama.

Issen was too well-known at court already.

When his eyes lingered on Kith, the cat's lips curled up to bare his teeth. A warning. *I could ask anyway,* Ellian thought. No oath bound him. But if he uttered a word of Kith's secret, the cat would disappear into the wind, gone and taking their plans with him. Possibly to their enemies. Ellian's lips pressed together, holding the words inside.

But there was one last chance to find the player they needed. "The full-moons revel," he said, leaning back against the desk. "I'll find someone there."

Vilitte scoffed. "We can't give away our plans to someone new, not now. Not when this is our one chance at the Key."

Ellian shook his head. "I'd just invite them to the festival as a guest. They need not know more to accomplish their task, if unwittingly."

Kith hissed. "I don't like this."

Ellian swept his gaze over his crew and sighed. "Neither do I."

❧

THE COTERIE'S CHATTER ECHOED up the stairs and down the hall as they crossed the foyer. Cirelle caught only stray words, but it was never anything consequential, no clues to their scheme. Just the mindless everyday prattle of colleagues. Asking after relatives, comments on the weather, idle conversation.

She sighed and went back to playing the sonata she'd been practicing. Soon enough it would be supper, where Ellian would once more deflect any questions with faerie wordplay and steer the conversation toward other topics.

Over the past weeks, an uneasy and unspoken truce had grown between Cirelle and the men as she settled into her duties. She reluctantly accompanied Ellian on a handful of summons from the human world, taking over for Toben. The faerie collected an odd assortment of trinkets, from a hand-knitted scarf to an elaborate jeweled belt to a small vial of a woman's tears. And he traded such simple things to fauns and nixies and spriggans for wonders aplenty. A pear that replenished itself from the core within moments of being eaten. A necklace that glowed with inner fire. Stones that turned to fluttering songbirds then back into simple rocks again.

Her new life became routine. Even her sorrow and worries turned into background noise. Toben and Ellian still held their secrets close, their allies coming and going at all hours. She lost herself in music, her work duties, and endless hours of sleep. She

grieved for Lydia, prayed often for Aidan and Briere, and let the bleak despair claim her.

The bribes worried her, though.

After Cirelle confessed her love of spice to Toben, the next night they'd dined on peppery pork soup with a burn so hot it made her lips tingle. From time to time, a brownie would bring a tray of her favorite tea during a long day in the Archive. Once, she found a book of Arravene songs sitting on the stool of her harp.

And yet Ellian never spoke a word of those small kindnesses. At meals, the three shared tales and casual conversation. After supper, they would pass the time with games of chance or skill, erupting into laughter when one of them bested the other.

Ellian's laugh was a rare, smoky sound, twisting about the room when it bubbled to the surface. Sometimes, when Toben told a particularly outrageous story, Ellian's smile took on a new quality, wide and unfeigned. And so, on those infrequent occasions when she forgot herself, lulled by the camaraderie, Cirelle's eyes would linger on him perhaps a moment too long.

Cirelle tried not to stare while Ellian traced the whorls of the wood grain on the tabletop and cast his hooded gaze her way. He continued to parade about in those flagrantly scandalous garments and jewels like a Nycenine courtesan. Something uncomfortably familiar began to settle in her chest while he was near, a lingering heat that crackled and scorched.

Lust, simple and undeniable. It was merely wanting, a craving both simple and savage, equal to her loathing. The more she tried not to imagine how his skin tasted or what those fingers would feel like exploring her body, the worse her fantasies became. She watched him reheat his tea with one of his magical rings and wondered what other tricks he could do with an artifact that warmed whatever it touched.

She despised herself for desiring such a cruel, capricious monster. He'd killed without thought, had stolen her memories of Briere and held them on a shelf.

She hated him, and she wanted him, and it was driving her mad.

There were moments when it seemed his thoughts echoed hers. A flicker in his eyes, the cant of a smile. She'd never be so foolish, despite how her stomach wrenched itself into knots in his presence. But when her eyes met lavender ones, she remembered how warm his hands were, how close his lips had once been to her own. How gently his fingers had caressed her skin.

And there were the touches, testing herself like holding her hand close to a flame. She initiated them, of course; he couldn't. With faerie laws binding him, Ellian couldn't so much as brush her skin without her permission or without her touching him first. So she faked little mistakes. Reaching for the salt at the same time, touching fingertips. Ellian would not flinch away, and for an instant his eyes met hers and his fingers stroked the back of her hand.

Danger clung to Ellian like a well-fitted jacket, a dark halo lingering around his edges. Secrets lingered around him like an exotic perfume. Cirelle wanted to touch it, to wrap that aura around her fingertips.

She was no stranger to risk between the sheets, after all. Briere had been nearly two years of possible scandal. And a few months ago, that one night of wild, perfect recklessness with Gadd had shown her a man could be as pleasurable as a woman. Two secrets, each carrying a decadent thrill.

A small, constant pang of guilt in her gut reminded her of Rhine, of his sweet promises to her, but his memory had already begun to fade. Her human life seemed like a dream, and Faerie her waking hours. Everything here was so sharp, so vivid.

It was not all sparks and flame. Sometimes, Ellian would come to listen when she played her harp, leaning against the wall with eyes closed and a distant smile on his lips. Other times, she'd stumble upon him scribbling in a journal, sprawled on a bench in the garden. When she drew near, he would slam the book shut, heedless of any ruined ink. Cirelle burned to know what he wrote in those pages. His secret plans? A private diary? Did he fantasize about her as maddeningly as she did him?

A part of her wondered if she kissed him hard enough, could she draw his secrets from his mouth and shove them into jars to peruse later? If she took him to her bed, would he tell her of his mysterious plans while he drew constellations on her stomach with those long fingers?

And all the while, a parade of fae continued to slink into the manor for hidden conversations.

She slept fitfully. Some nights, her dreams were things of fire and ice, of bodies entwined in the dark. But in her nightmares, Orwe's lifeless eyes haunted her. If Ellian's faerie companions were so expendable, what of a human? A clueless mortal girl, stuck in this home of intrigues?

She feared that come Thieves' Night, she would find out.

Chapter Seventeen

CIRELLE TRIED EAVESDROPPING at doors and poring through papers in the desk of the Archive's antechamber but found nothing. She even hunted for Ellian's journal, but to no avail. Toben was as tight-lipped as his master despite Cirelle's best attempts at sorrowful tears and heartfelt pleas.

When her snooping yielded little fruit, Cirelle devised another strategy. Toben said it himself—Ellian was like a cat. So, she would treat him like those half-wild strays around the palace. Ellian may not be interested in saucers of cream or table scraps, but there was one lure that Cirelle knew would work.

She retreated to the music room. The lucky discovery of a book of Kishi folk songs had spurred this idea. The magic glass translated them into Arravene notations, and Cirelle had laboriously copied them over onto music sheets.

Sheets that now rested on the stand before her.

Her hands hovered over the strings, and she began to play.

It didn't take long. At the end of the first song, the soft jingle of those absurd boots came to a stop beside the door. She finished, but all remained silent in the hall.

"You can come in, you know," she called. "I won't bite."

Ellian stepped into the doorway. "That razorblade tongue of yours is sharper than any bite," he noted with a wry grin.

Cirelle began the next piece. "No insults tonight, I promise." Some sudden impulse made her add with a smile, "Besides, my tongue has other uses."

He laughed. His real one, the resonant sound that plucked at something warm and giddy inside her. Ellian stepped into the room and sat in a chair opposite her. His long legs sprawled before him and he nodded to the harp. "These are Kishi songs."

"I know."

"So, this show is for my benefit?" he asked, propping his elbow on an armrest and leaning his head on one hand.

"Perhaps."

He lifted an eyebrow. "Do you intend to seduce me with your music, like the Mad Violinist of Sheppet? And then I'll spill all my secrets to you?"

Cirelle felt her cheeks grow hot, and she bit back a curse.

"It's not the subtlest tactic, Princess."

Her hands stilled on the strings. She opened her mouth, hesitated, and closed it with a click.

His grin widened. "Yes, you did promise to withhold your insults for the evening, and it's a very bad idea to break an oath to a faerie." His free hand tapped out an idle rhythm on the armrest.

Cirelle clenched her jaw so hard sparks flickered behind her eyes.

"Do feel free to play on." Ellian said, his eyes gleaming like brilliant aquamarines. "Maybe I will be charmed enough to let slip some juicy little tidbit."

She considered refusing. "*Maybe,*" he'd said. One of the half-way words faeries hid behind. He wouldn't hold up to it.

Yet she couldn't let even this slim opportunity pass. She strummed the strings once more and mustered her voice. "I just want to know what happened to Kyrinna. Why is that such a grievous question?"

Ellian's eyes flickered a pallid green, then deepest midnight blue. "Because I don't talk about that. To anyone."

"What if it happens to me?" The words were quiet, her fears given shape.

He hesitated.

A jolt of dread made her stumble on a note.

"I can't control your actions, Princess," he admitted.

"And *I* can't control *anything*, it seems." Cirelle blinked back sudden tears. She'd bitten down to the core of her anxiety, her anger. Helplessness. She'd thought unveiling Ellian's mysteries might give her power back, but here she was, walled off again.

Her fingers trembled, but Cirelle shuffled the pages on her music stand and started another piece while her thoughts swirled in a mad dance.

As always, the melody calmed her and her breathing steadied. Ellian closed his eyes, his fingers tapping out the beat on his thigh. The tension that so often tightened his shoulders slipped away. A faint smile played at the edge of his lips.

When the last notes died, Cirelle let the silence hold until his eyes opened. Silver and sapphire, and strangely vulnerable.

"You've given me your music," he said. "And I owe a boon in return. An answer, to any one question other than Kyrinna or my Thieves' Night plans."

"Give me a secret about yourself. Something you've never told anyone."

Ellian watched her for a few moments, his eyes dark and conflicted. Then he licked his lips. "I've dreamed about you." A low purr.

The air in the room thickened and grew hotter. Had his dreams been like hers? Visions of tangled limbs and the taste of sweat on skin? Her voice came out hoarse. "What kind of dreams?"

Ellian held her gaze for a few seconds too long. "You only asked for one secret."

Cirelle's eyes narrowed, and his wicked grin grew wider.

In a single languid motion, Ellian stretched and stood. "Well. Toben is working for the rest of the night. If you would like the chance to glean more of my deepest mysteries, I've an impulse to take advantage of your sweetened tongue for an evening."

She swallowed, her throat gone dry. "What do you suggest?"

"Drinks. Conversation."

A flutter blossomed in her belly, as those eyes pierced her, sharp and intimate like a finger sliding down her spine.

She nodded.

Chapter Eighteen

HE LED HER TO a cozy parlor room. In lieu of a fire, the hearth held a steady yellow globe of light. Framed paintings of flower arrangements hung on the walls, while a matching rug covered most of the floor.

Cirelle sank onto a rust-colored sofa as Ellian rang the bell to summon a brownie for refreshments. She leaned back into the soft upholstery, tracing one hand over the flocked pattern in the velvet. The fabric bristled against her palm as she brushed it the wrong way and smoothed it out again.

Ellian sprawled on the other side of the sofa, one ankle resting on the other knee, arm draped casually along the back of the cushions. His eyes wandered over her, and she wondered what color they would gleam if he dropped the glamour.

She cleared her throat. "What did you want to talk about?"

He grinned. "Whatever you wish. I wanted to see what you're like when you're not slicing me to ribbons with your tongue." He arched one sweeping brow. "Although I see the scowls remain."

Cirelle deliberately composed her expression before a brownie entered and set a tray on the table before the sofa. Berries and slices of tangy white cheese were arranged upon it. Ellian was served a wine glass, while a pot of tea rested beside a cup and saucer for Cirelle.

She poured a cup of tea and plucked up a bit of cheese. "So how much goodwill have I garnered with my songs?"

"I doubt I'm as enraptured as the Mad Violinist's victims, but I'm inclined to be generous tonight."

"Why?"

He shrugged. "Call it a mood."

She snorted and asked a question she'd pondered since arriving here. "So how did you end up with all this? The house, the Archive, a full library?"

Ellian closed his eyes and took a long, thoughtful sip of wine. "When my human family died, they left me adrift in a world of mortals, having just discovered my faerie nature. I had only one sliver of knowledge to go on. A scrap of forest several miles from my village was known to be dangerous, for it housed a host of fae beasts. It was said no mortal who entered ever came out alive.

"I ventured into the forest and met creatures both wondrous and dreadful. One in particular took a keen interest in me. He was an ancient faerie, the only one of his kind. Urisk. Hideous by human standards but wise, quiet, and lonely." A wistful smile curved Ellian's lips. "He taught me the ways of faerie glamour, of the laws that bind our kind. I'd never known it was faerie rules that always tied me to truth and kept me to my word when others would have broken their promises."

"And what happened to this Urisk?"

"He was old and tired of his existence. Faeries can live forever, but we can be killed, as you've seen. Urisk gave all he owned to me in exchange for the escape of death."

The tea turned bitter on her tongue. "You killed him." Like he'd killed Lydia.

Ellian stared into his glass with eyes like dark sapphires. "He begged me to."

She swallowed. "How many people have you killed?"

"In a cruel world, sometimes cruelty is the only way to survive."

Not an answer at all. Cirelle drank her rapidly-cooling tea to drown the icy cold wriggling in her belly.

A deep and weary sorrow lingered in Ellian's face. The pain of decades. How could he be so sad for these others, yet feel nothing for the life he'd stolen from her? "Do you regret them?" The words tumbled from her lips before she could hold them back. She didn't expect an answer.

He closed his eyes. "Some."

"So even faeries make mistakes."

He barked a broken laugh and tossed back the last of his wine. "Too many." The gaze he turned upon her was pensive, full of sorrow.

That stare felt far too personal. Cirelle rasped out the words, "Am I a mistake?" That old self-loathing flickered to life, the small whispers of doubt in her mind. "Just a pest peppering you with endless questions. A useless, pathetic excuse for a princess."

Again, his eyes turned her inside out, razor-sharp. "I don't regret our bargain. And Cirelle?"

Hearing her name made her shiver. Ellian almost always called her 'Princess', and he'd never uttered her name so softly. Her mouth went dry. "Yes?"

"I don't ever want to hear you call yourself pathetic again." Dead serious now, no hint of mockery.

The silence that wrapped around them was a living thing, choking and thick. Her pulse was an arrhythmic beat, and she couldn't remember how to breathe.

Cirelle cleared her throat and set down her tea. The cup

clattered loudly against the saucer. "I think I like you better when you're mocking me."

"Oh, I can do that, too." He smiled softly, and the pressure in the room lightened.

He ate a deeply purple berry and his gaze flickered lavender. "Should I tell you the sordid details of those dreams I mentioned earlier? Perhaps I should ask you what thoughts linger in your head when you look at me like something to eat? Have you, too, had dreams of your own?"

Cirelle flushed. "I don't know what you're talking about."

"I think you do." Summer blue bled into that gaze, threading through the violet.

"You just want to mock me without being insulted in return."

"It *is* a nice change of pace." But the violet remained.

Did he truly mean all the wicked and delicious things his eyes promised, or did he merely toy with her, as fae were wont to do with humans?

I've dreamed about you.

A test, then. As she took a berry and slipped it between her lips, Cirelle played idly with the dangling jewels of her necklace. One finger trailed slowly down from the gems until it reached the edge of the fabric. She twisted and untwisted the ribbon there, the bow at the apex of the lacings that held the front of her gown closed. She tugged on it gently, loosening the bow. A tease, nothing more.

When Ellian glanced back up, she smiled. His eyes widened a fraction, nostrils flaring. The hint of blue fled, and the purple grew brilliant as amethysts in sunlight. Those soft lips parted in surprise. His breath hitched.

Cirelle's grin sharpened, a huntress scenting her prey. This hadn't truly been her plan. She'd meant to soothe him with music, to begin to earn his trust. But maybe the role of seductress better suited her. "Now that you have me here, sworn to speak gently, what do you want of me?"

The apple of his throat bobbed as he swallowed. "More than you would give."

"My soul? My firstborn? My eternal servitude?" she asked. "Those are all faerie things."

He shook his head. "No."

"Then what?"

Again, a darkness filled those eyes, the hue of rich violet petals. He licked his lips.

A tremor slithered through her, a heat blooming in her belly. She poured another cup of tea and leaned back against the arm of the sofa, taking a delicate sip. Cirelle felt as if she hurtled headlong down a steep cliff, unable to stop herself. A new tension hung in the air between them, thrumming like a string pulled taut, and she tugged on it recklessly as the conversation turned back to playful taunts.

Something inside Cirelle sharpened as they teased each other, like a blade held to a whetstone. Ellian's posture was a carefully crafted pose meant to emphasize his beauty, and those eyes flickered with unspoken promises. As vengeance, Cirelle made it a point to eat slowly, licking the berry juice from her fingers with languid strokes of her tongue. A tight bundle of tension coiled in her stomach, waiting to snap.

"Princess," Ellian set his wine glass aside and leaned toward her, "be sure you don't start something you're not prepared to finish."

Cirelle's heart lurched in her chest. Did she truly want to take this a step further? Something inside her leapt at the thought. *Yes.* Would it really be such an awful thing to give in to that urge, just for tonight? To fulfill those idle daydreams?

Ellian leaned back onto his corner of the sofa, one long leg stretched out before him, the other foot flat on the floor with his knee bent. It was a lovely picture. Cirelle suddenly found herself fascinated with his mouth, stretched into a sly grin as he regarded her with darkened eyes.

Oh, yes. This careless, elegant sprawl was artfully planned. A display, a carefully arranged temptation. He was ripe fruit clinging to a vine. She merely had to pluck it from the branch to claim it as her own. So ridiculously easy.

The room spun about her, and Cirelle squeezed her eyes shut.

"Cirelle?" Concern lowered Ellian's voice. The sound of her name whispered by those lips was like a hand sliding up her thigh.

She had to end this.

"A headache," she lied, and kept her eyes closed. "I think I braided my hair back a bit tightly."

"Here." That velvet voice was closer now. Cirelle's eyes fluttered open to find him leaning toward her, one hand extended. Those long, dusky gray fingers hovered an inch away from the bow that tied her braid. "May I?"

She nodded, an instinctive response.

Ellian tugged on the loose end of the ribbon. She was surrounded by his scent again, faint woodsmoke and fresh-brewed tea with a dollop of rich golden honey. His fingers threaded through the end of her braid and tugged it loose, working upward as he unplaited her hair. Ellian's hands were so gentle as he worked it free and ran his hand through the waves left from the braid.

She shivered and Ellian smiled. Cirelle wondered what he would do next. More, she didn't know if she would stop him.

This close, she could see every striation of color in his violet eyes. Cirelle was frozen in place. His face was mere inches from hers now, and an uncertain quivering trembled in her stomach.

His breath warmed her skin. Cirelle began to close the gap between them. A hair's width from their lips touching, the remaining rational scrap of her mind screamed at her. She flinched away.

"No."

She'd expected to see a flash of irritation in his eyes as she stood up, a flicker of orange. Instead, they gleamed violet and aquamarine. A satisfied smile curled his lips as she fled.

ᚼᚾ

"I still don't like it," Issen said.

Ellian picked at a stray nick in the woodgrain of his desktop. He couldn't deny that his stomach turned in knots at the thought of Thieves' Night, but he had little choice. "Do you have a better plan?"

Silence held.

"Exactly."

Issen's gaze fell to the map on the desktop between them. He ran a hand through his daffodil hair, such a vibrant, cheery contrast to his steady demeanor. "I'm the only member of the group who's seen what you once were. I don't think it's a good idea for you to return to that, even briefly."

"Are you afraid I won't come back?"

"Should I be?"

Ellian hesitated. The memories of his time at court were sharp-edged things, dangerous and seductive. Wanton pleasures both cruel and exhilarating remained fresh in his mind, an intoxicating mix. It would be so easy to let go, to fall prey to the

pull of power and the thrill of sidhe games. Those machinations had once been his entire world.

Not anymore.

His reply was certain. "No."

With a doubtful stare, Issen sighed. He dropped the subject and pointed at the map. "Whether your plan succeeds or not, we still need to keep searching for the Lock." He pointed to a dark cluster of trees inked on the brittle parchment. "I've traced down clues that point to The Lisovyk's Wood."

Ellian hissed in a breath.

"My thoughts exactly," Issen muttered.

"It will have to wait until after Thieves' Night."

"By my calculations, the forest will open two months after. I don't know yet what we'll need."

Another mission to sort out and only scant months to do it. Too many threads to weave together, binding Ellian in their tangles. "Not much time to plan."

"That's what I'm here for, aren't I?" Issen's kind, canny eyes took on a sly gleam.

"True. Can you take point on organizing that mission?"

"Of course. Who should I include?"

Ellian mentally flipped through his list of allies. "Not Shai. Stealth is not her forte. Still, we need muscle, just in case." Unease settled into his chest as he added, "Kith. And me. No more than three. In and out."

Issen nodded. "I'll make the preparations. Is that all for today?"

"One more thing." His hands drummed out a nervous pattern on the tabletop. "The princess. She'll be here at the manor during Thieves' Night. I want you and Shai to guard her."

"Shai isn't going to like that."

Ellian's lips thinned. "She'll have to accept it. We all have our parts to play, even if we find them distasteful." Again, his chest tightened. Could he go through with Thieves' Night? Such a terrible sensation, to fear and crave something all at once.

Perhaps Issen had a point about sliding back into his former life.

With a shake of his head, Ellian dismissed Issen. "Keep me apprised of the situation with the Lisovyk. I'll see you at court." The Unseelie Court. A glittering haven of depravity, masked beneath a veneer of civility and razor-sharp words. A thrill rippled through him, and he shivered.

Issen's stare was piercing. For a moment, Ellian expected another warning. Instead, Issen merely gave a quick nod. "Farewell."

Chapter Nineteen

"How many times are we going to play this game?" Cirelle muttered as she flipped over her card.

Ellian grinned. He watched the princess's mouth curl into a grimace, her brow furrowing. A bit of his fae nature peeked through, to find such humor in her foul mood. "Until you take three hands in a row." He scooped up the tiles, his winnings for the hand.

Cirelle groaned. "You could just let me win. Then you could go scribble in your journal, and I can work out that new song." She lifted an eyebrow. "I might even let you listen, if I can quit this godsforsaken game."

Tempting, but this was more than a mere lark, and he could not allow himself to be dissuaded by music today. "Not yet, Princess."

"What's the point of this? Trying to humiliate me?"

Ellian had plucked her from the library over an hour ago with the promise of three full days' respite from Archive duties if she indulged him. *Though sweeping endless rows and sorting old paperwork likely seems a pleasant alternative at the moment.*

Cirelle had suggested a rematch of fox-and-hounds, but Ellian insisted on his favorite faerie game instead. Raven's Gambit, a game of trickery, of lies. A test.

It was deceptively simple. Each player chose a small hand from their personal deck before an hourglass ran out, a series of five cards, and lay them face down. The first cards were revealed, and the players could rearrange their other four cards at that time. The process repeated, card against card, until the hand was over. Tiles were wagered between reveals and awarded to the winner of each hand.

And cheating was encouraged, as long as you weren't caught.

Ellian was particularly adept at the sleight-of-hand needed. He'd been doing it right under Cirelle's nose the entire time. If he could manage to move his cards while she wasn't looking, or even swap one from the deck, it was perfectly acceptable. However, if he was caught doing it, he lost the hand entirely and forfeited any extra tiles.

He practically thrummed with a nervous energy, watching the princess's every move. She managed to slip a few cards around while Ellian pondered his own hand, but he made sure he called her out on it twice.

After a number of losses, Cirelle finally claimed her first victory with a smug grin.

Good, Princess. She thought the stakes here were merely game tiles, but Ellian smiled, feeling a surge of hope at her deception and determination.

Time to move on to the next test.

As they each chose their cards, Ellian lapsed into heavy silence. This part required little enough acting. He caught the princess's gaze with his own, staring at that expressive mouth and imagining what it would feel like to taste those lips. A tingle shivered down his spine and settled in his stomach.

Then he dropped his glamour, knowing full well how his

gaze would burn violently purple. After that night in the parlor, she'd haunted his dreams even more feverishly than before. A slow, wicked grin curved his mouth.

A flush of pink blossomed in Cirelle's cheeks, and he watched her chest rise and fall more rapidly. She hesitated for too long and the hourglass ran out before she could set all her cards. Cirelle lost the hand.

Ellian grinned and lifted a brow. It took her another hand of fiery glances before she caught on and ignored him, taking another round. After that, he moved on to the next trial. "Foolish move," he remarked when she flipped over a card. "I thought you were better than that."

"But I already knew you were a smug ass," she retorted.

He grimaced and continued to taunt her until she realized his new ploy and fell silent. Still, he caught her hands shaking with rage, her jaw clenched. For once, she managed to hold her poisonous tongue.

Still Ellian continued to win.

He almost let his relief and pride show when Cirelle began cheating ever more boldly. She stacked her tiles together and placed fewer of them in the center pile than she claimed she did. She peeked at the deck when she shuffled it. The princess even chattered away at him, reciting numbers and letters while he tried to concentrate on selecting his hand. Ellian made sure to comment on a few of her tricks but suspected even he didn't catch them all.

Once he was satisfied with the results of his tests, Ellian let her take three rounds in a row, and the princess threw her remaining cards down with a relieved sigh. "Finally."

When they tallied the tiles, Ellian still won the game by a long shot. He gathered up the cards and gave her an approving nod. "Not bad. Quite the cheat, Princess."

Cirelle cast him a remarkably innocent smile. "What?"

"You didn't put six tiles in that stack, princess. It was short by two."

She huffed out a breath and slumped in her chair. "So why did you let it slide?"

Ellian tried to ignore the growing warmth inside his chest. "Because no one has ever used that strategy on me before. You earned that round with cleverness and boldness." The grin faded as he placed the cards in a wooden box with a carved raven atop it. "But you still need to get a handle on that temper." He could feel his smile growing thin and strained as he warred with himself. If the revel came up empty, would the coterie agree to his mad backup plan?

Can I do this? He met the princess's stare. "You may have need of a cooler head soon."

Her proud expression faltered. "What's that supposed to mean?"

He kept his mask tight as he replied. "If you can manage that vicious tongue of yours, maybe you'll find out."

✧

THE DOORBELL RANG, but by the time Cirelle crossed into the foyer, Toben already stood at the door.

"I need to talk to Ellian," Kith said from the doorstep, half-growl, half-purr.

Toben ushered him in quickly. The cat glanced up at Cirelle. His eyes were chips of cold blue topaz and his lip curled up in a silent snarl. His footsteps made a small, sticky sound, leaving dark paw prints on Ellian's floor.

With a single apologetic glance at Cirelle, Toben followed Kith into the antechamber.

Heart thudding in her chest, Cirelle couldn't take her eyes from the trail of dark prints. *They're probably just mud,* she told herself. But they glistened wetly.

Her pulse roared in her ears, drowning out all other sound as Cirelle made her way quickly down the stairs and knelt beside one of the prints. Black as pitch, glossy as the moon on a midnight sea. Some dark impulse made Cirelle dip two cautious fingers in the liquid and hold it up to her nose.

That scent was unmistakable. Metallic and earthy, with the tang of salt and a hint of rot.

Blood.

Her fingers stung and tingled, as if they crawled with tiny spiders. Panic overtook her, and she bent to wipe them on the floor, but hesitated. She chided herself. Why the reluctance to mar that mosaic, when it already bore the blood of some unfortunate faerie?

Kith had not been limping or moving gingerly. It was not his.

The door at the top of the stairs opened. Cirelle scrambled to stand, hiding her bloodied hand behind her like a child caught playing in the dirt. Ellian stared silently for a few moments and made his way down the steps with slow strides. His eyes held hers the whole way, two shiny silver coins.

Still, neither one spoke. What would she say? Did she dare ask him why Kith arrived here with blood-soaked paws?

He wouldn't answer, even if she did.

Ellian skirted around the paw prints, gave her one last unreadable glance, and slipped into the antechamber.

Her fingers still burning, Cirelle dashed down the hall to her parlor to wash off the sticky black ichor that clung to her fingertips.

Chapter Twenty

CIRELLE BRUSHED HER DUSTY palms on her trousers and stood, knees protesting. Toben had assured her she'd become used to the physical labor soon enough, but crouching to clean the lower shelves still made her thighs screech afterward.

"Well that's it for today," she called to Toben, who nodded as he finished up his shelf opposite. She stretched and left for the library to fetch her latest book and the reading glass.

She wasn't prepared to find Ellian sitting at a desk with a small book open before him and his head in his hands. And she definitely didn't expect to see tracks of tears when he startled and glanced up at her. His eyes were a flood of deepest cobalt blue, the hue of misery.

He seemed a different creature in this single, frozen moment. Something terribly human and vulnerable. Her chest gave an unsteady lurch as silence wrapped around them. Ellian's eyes flickered back to gray as he donned that emotionless mask, but he could not take back what she'd seen. Nor could he erase the tears that stained his cheeks.

Though she wanted to flee, Cirelle's feet refused to obey. Her stomach turned an uncomfortable flip.

Ellian cleared his throat softly but did not speak.

Cirelle found her tongue. "I didn't even know you could do that."

His pensive stare was unsettling. "A long time ago, I wept often enough." His eyes flicked down to the open pages before him. "Less and less, now."

She dared take another step into the room. "Why?"

He snapped the book shut as she drew closer. A little of his usual coolness crept into his tone. "Because that's what happens to sidhe. We rot from the inside. Our human traits fade away over the centuries. The shell left behind is the stuff of your worst faerie stories. Hollow and cruel and insufferably bored."

"That's why they toy with us, with mortals?"

He nodded and brushed his cheeks with a sweep of a hand. "They fill that void with whatever they can. Hedonism, parties, and meaningless games. Useless violence."

"What about you?"

He barked a humorless laugh. "I'd rather be empty, if I must." A moment later, he closed his eyes and shook his head. "An impossible wish. When the void becomes so strong it strangles, anything that makes us feel alive will do. Power, pain, debauchery."

Cirelle reached the desk. She glanced down at the book, but the cover was only unadorned leather, incredibly old and cracked. It had been dyed a peculiar shade of rich purple but was otherwise unmarked.

His words had struck an uncomfortable chord within her. She knew the hollow ache that tore one to pieces, what it was like to drown in a black abyss of sorrow. Briere had been so good at sensing the onset of Cirelle's dark moods and filling that empty space with her golden light.

After Briere was gone, the numbness set in. Cirelle replaced her beloved with the thrill of defying the rules. She dulled the pain with drink, raced her horse across fields at full gallop just to feel the cold wind buffeting her face, relished the heady rush that followed the sting of painfully-spiced food. And the absolute reckless taboo of her wild night with Gadd. He, too, had made her feel so gloriously alive, if ever so briefly.

Yes, she understood what Ellian meant.

"If it takes centuries, how old are you?"

Another pause. "Not yet a hundred, I think, in human years." He picked idly at a worn spot on one corner of the desk. "One stops counting eventually."

Less than a century. That seemed awfully young for a sidhe, considering her books had mentioned fae a thousand years old or more.

A glimmer of insight flitted through her mind. "You keep mortals nearby to retain what makes you human."

"Empathy, passion, humor." The words were almost a whisper. "Yes." He shook his head again. "Not that it works in the long run. A temporary patch, nothing more." He stood, clutching his book to his chest.

Cirelle had no reply. Awkward silence fell and she made her way back to her small stack of books, a collection of various tomes written in Gilbran.

Ellian nodded toward the books. "You're not using the glass on those."

"No." She thumbed through one and bitterness crept into her voice. "I've been studying Gilbran for three years, since my parents narrowed down my suitors to the two coastal princes." Though each kingdom had their own government, they spoke the same language. "Best not get rusty, considering I'll be married away to Gilbras or Asheir as soon as I get back."

His eyes locked onto the book she held. "Do you dread it? Returning?"

Cirelle closed her eyes and took a deep breath. "Yes."

"Why?"

She opened her eyes and traced the edges of a Gilbran book. "Let me explain with a story. Of a man, a prince. He loved his people and his kingdom, but he left them both. A famine threatened, and a trade treaty with the bountiful lands to the south would save the people he loved so dearly. So, he married their queen and became their king. He abandoned his gods, his culture, and his language to adopt theirs. He was lost to his people and to everything his life had been before."

"Your father," Ellian guessed.

"Grandfather. He was Miskau, but I only know his culture through history lessons taught by tutors, can only recall the tidbits of his language he let slip before he died. He was a foreigner, come to Arraven to be king, and he was told the best way to soothe dissenters' ruffled feathers was to become Arravene, fully and completely."

She shook her head, tracing the edge of a Gilbran book with a fingertip. "Whether I go to Gilbras with Rhine or to Asheir with Beddig, I'll be asked to convert to Ordrae. Rhine isn't truly devout, but many of his people are. I'll publicly forsake my gods and go through a cleansing ritual to be sanctified as one of Ordrae's children. I'll speak Trade and Gilbran for the rest of my life. They don't speak Arravene on the coast."

"But your beloved prince would make the trip worth it." A bitter, almost sarcastic tone laced Ellian's words.

Cirelle was silent for a moment. *Is Rhine really my beloved?* She could still recall Briere's laugh, the exact color of her hair, her scent. Rhine, however, was a rapidly fading memory, a charming man she'd met a few times. A pretty face, a few stolen kisses, and little more.

Her eyes flicked up to meet Ellian's. "No. I adore my home

more than I could ever love any foreign prince. I miss Arravene dances and our famed music hall in Palace City. Our baked apple tarts and slow-roasted chicken drowning in butter and wine and herbs. Arravene summers, with the smell of dry grass and heat in blistering golden sunlight. To stay there with my brother, my friends..."

"Your friends. I know of your brother, of Lydia, your lost beloved. But I was beginning to wonder if you had any others."

Cirelle fought back the anger bubbling up within her. It was true. Oh, she was on polite, friendly terms with a number of the gentry, but little more than that. She shook her head.

"So few friends. It sounds...lonely."

Cirelle hissed out a short laugh. "I was rarely alone. Always someone wanting to curry favor with the royal family, invited to countless gaming sessions, horseback rides near the palace, afternoon teas."

"I said *lonely*, not *alone*."

"Aren't they the same thing?"

"No, they aren't. Not at all."

Chapter Twenty-One

CIRELLE HEARD HIM COMING.

The silvery jangle of Ellian's boots was a discordant note in her song, out of rhythm with the idle melody she picked out on the small instrument, a thing of metallic plates struck with a small hammer. Ellian's footsteps stopped and he leaned against the doorway of the music room.

Cirelle let the last note echo. "Yes?"

"In two days, there is a faerie revel. I will be attending." He hesitated. "You will be coming with me."

Cirelle nearly dropped the miniature hammers. She set them aside as she cleared her throat. "Outside the house?" What did a fae party look like? A host of faeries like Ellian's strange coterie, lost in celebration?

He nodded. "Yes."

"Is Toben going?"

"Toben will stay here to handle business."

"Why do you need me?" The silence that fell was absolute. Cirelle could hear her own breaths until he answered.

"I need to gauge how some possible allies feel about humans."

She snorted. "Why? The rest of your crew didn't seem terribly fond of me."

"They didn't eat you or charm you. That's generosity, for fae."

"So, you want to see who tries to eat me?"

"More or less." His lips turned downward. "I'll be keeping an eye on you. And as a mortal, you know they cannot harm you without permission."

"Can you swear to that?" Cirelle was surprised by the sudden flutter of excitement in her belly at the thought of a faerie revel.

"Yes."

Cirelle nodded. "Then I'll go." This was a chance to learn something of Faerie, and she was weary of living surrounded by unknown secrets.

"The day after tomorrow, dress in your best. You need to be visible, noticeable. Select the most brilliant garment you can find in your wardrobe and don't skimp on the jewelry."

She grinned. "I think I can do that."

$$\text{\emph{CO}}$$

THE DAY OF THE PARTY ARRIVED and Cirelle had more than exceeded Ellian's request. Her gown was brilliant blue silk, the color of Ellian's eyes when he smiled, embroidered all over with sparkling beads of golden topaz worked into the shape of tiny flowers. It was an Arravene gown and she'd had to call one of the brownies to help her into it. The skirts were full and layered over fluffy petticoats and panniers, with long sleeves and shimmering golden ruffles all over. A series of bows adorned the front of the bodice. A necklace draped her neck, encrusted with so many blue topaz gems that she glittered like the ocean. The tiara matched, a golden confection of delicate blossoms with sea-blue gems at their center.

Cirelle had even taken the time to soften her work-roughened hands with lotion and trimmed her now-unruly fingernails. Working in dust and paperwork every day had taken its toll on them. Her cosmetics were delicate and feminine, all in glittering brassy shades and rosy browns that accented the natural golden hue of her skin.

Ellian had dressed in his finest too, in one of those ridiculous, indecent shirts. It was a shade of pale copper that made his skin seem almost blue. The fabric shimmered when he moved like the feathers of some exotic pheasant. The silly filigreed boots were present as well, chiming a little melody when he moved. His jewelry was nearly as ostentatious as Cirelle's. Though Ellian had said there would be no fighting, he still wore the many rings, along with his silver stud earrings and a wide torc about his throat. His hair was swept partially back from his face so one could appreciate the full glory of all that silver.

He arched one eyebrow at Cirelle while he stood in that artfully casual pose, a supercilious grin on his face.

She rolled her eyes at his posturing. "Let's go."

Ellian held out his hand and Cirelle took it. The world misted away. It was dizzying, alarming to blink and realize you were in an entirely new place. Though she'd been whisked away like this before to attend and witness Ellian's summons in her camouflage cloak, the sensation always left her giddy.

When the sensation settled, they found themselves in a stone cavern as lavishly appointed as any castle. Cirelle stared, wide-eyed. It was obviously a cave, there was no doubt of that. The walls were slick grey rock, with stalactites hanging from the ceiling and stalagmites craning up toward them. The floor was polished to a smooth shine. Strings of faerie lights in a myriad of colors dangled from the rock formations. Arching high over their heads, a gap in the stone ceiling revealed the real stars. The moons were both full, bathing the scene in additional silvery light. Garlands of flowers hung everywhere, their fragrance overpowering.

And the faeries. Never had Cirelle seen such a variety of folk in one place. Tiny to enormous, they mingled and danced and ate. This festival was not the formal affair of an Arravene court party. No, the music was full of wild, pulsing drums and the cavern rang with the sound of laughter. Food was piled high on tables in untamed disarray, a chaotic spread. Fried dumplings lay heaped into tiny mountains, whole steaming potatoes sliced open to ooze with melted butter and herbs, an entire roasted pig—or something like a pig, anyway. There were fruits and vegetables galore and even a plate of something that looked suspiciously like cooked insects, with prickly legs and crispy carapaces.

The faeries here were like Ellian's little rebellion, but multiplied tenfold. An ethereal maiden made of moonlight and shadow, all pale skin and cobweb hair, whirled past with a wild grin on black-stained lips. Grotesque goblins gathered beneath one of the tables, laughing raucously and shoving each other with startling violence. A large hunchbacked creature with greenish skin and a massive, fanged underbite danced with a slim dryad, tossing her into the air and catching her with ease.

"Try not to stare," Ellian murmured beside her.

"What, jealous I'm not staring at you?"

His lip quirked. "Mingle," he told her, pointing at the tables. "Don't eat anything here, though. The rules are very different at this party. See who approaches you, who speaks with civility, who tries to trick, who casts insults."

"What will you do?"

"I, too, will be making the rounds."

A faerie flitted a bit too close while twirling batons that flared with green flames. The heat pulsed from the spinning orbs of fire, and Cirelle flinched back with a gasp.

Ellian's reaction was harsher. He fell back a full step and spat a Kishi curse. His dark eyes followed the fire even as the faerie left them behind.

"Are you alright?" Cirelle asked.

Ellian blinked, took a deep breath, and shook his head. "I was startled." With a single, indecipherable backward glance, he plunged into the crowd.

This party was so much *more* than Cirelle could ever have predicted. Louder, more chaotic, wild and utterly inhuman. The music was a frenzy of untamed notes, heavy and frantic and pulsing. The musicians stood on a far dais, a group of indefinable faeries with a scattering of instruments that sang in notes nearly discordant. A cascade of drums accompanied a violent cacophony of strings. It lit something in Cirelle's blood as she watched the faeries dancing. It was a free-for-all, no set steps to this revel. Everyone moved as they wanted, letting the music take them.

Suddenly, with a surprising intensity, Cirelle couldn't resist any longer. She *needed* to join them.

She stepped onto the dance floor. The world became only her twisting, turning feet, hair tangling in her face. A myriad of faeries swirled around her, always near but never touching. Time slipped from her, lost in the rhythm of that strange beat and the whirling dance.

Finally, out of breath and her cheeks sore from laughing, Cirelle glanced around the crowd and locked gazes with Ellian on the opposite side of the cavern. His eyes were a dark glower, his mouth set in a line of disapproval.

Right, Cirelle thought sourly. *Mingling it is, then.*

Chapter Twenty-Two

THE PRINCESS'S SMILE was a new thing, and Ellian didn't like the uneasy feeling it stirred inside him. Cirelle spun merrily on the dance floor, her caution and prickliness melting away.

She'd grinned occasionally at the manor, barbed smiles that accompanied a tongue-lashing and even the occasional laugh during their evening gaming. This one, however, was unguarded. Joy, pure and simple and uncontaminated.

Ellian grimaced and turned away from the dance floor. *Stay on task.*

He wove his way through the crowd, all cool smiles and witticisms. A sidhe to the core, at least for tonight.

It wasn't long before someone's attention snagged on him. As the faerie approached, Ellian gave him a quick glance up and down. The fae's eyes were at a level with Ellian's, but the wide antlers that branched above his head made him taller. A lean face, feral, eyes larger than human ones. Gold and crimson coated his eyelids, his lips curled into an insouciant smile. He, too, gave Ellian a once-over, slower and more intense.

The man exuded fiery elegance, with glittering hair like strands of pure bronze. His long jacket of rich red shimmered a brilliant orange when the faerie lights struck it just so. He cocked his head, that smirk never fading. "Sidhe."

"Ellian," he introduced himself with a nod.

"Devir."

It took only a few heartbeats to take this man's measure, to decide what role to play here. At least Ellian had learned some useful skills playing the games of the sidhe court. Sultry and submissive, that's what this faerie craved. His energy was confident, dominant. And the look in those flickering-flame eyes was hungry.

Ellian shifted his posture, his shoulders tipped forward, his eyes cast at the man's mouth and throat rather than meeting the gaze that glimmered gold and orange and pale blue.

"So, Ellian," Devir purred, "what brings you here?"

"It's a full-moons revel. All are welcome, are they not?"

Devir grinned, leaning in closer. He lifted one gold-nailed hand and stroked the edge of Ellian's jaw. Bold, as the older faeries so often were. "Very welcome."

Out of the corner of his eye, Ellian caught a flash of brilliant cerulean. Cirelle, dancing past with her head thrown back in a laugh. Ellian couldn't help his expression faltering, his true emotion spilling out if only for the briefest of breaths.

Devir's eyes flicked to Cirelle and back to Ellian. "You want her, don't you? I've heard about you," the faerie confessed, his hand slipping to cup the side of Ellian's neck, just below his ear. "The sidhe who wants to be human. Who cavorts with mortals."

Ellian swallowed. He couldn't have thought of a better segue.

"Does it bother you?" he whispered as he shifted his body closer to the other faerie. "That I deal with humans?"

"Why should it?" Devir leaned in, his lips brushing the edge of Ellian's cheek, inviting him to turn and make it a kiss.

Demanding wordlessly. "Humans are just another species. You and I aren't the same species, either."

He's a possibility. Ellian's mind was casual, calculating, even as he accepted the faerie's invitation and shifted his head to meet Devir's mouth. "Yes," he murmured before the man's tongue urged his lips open.

It was only a breathless kiss or two before Devir teasingly drew away. As he left, he slipped a coin into Ellian's jacket pocket, a silvery faerie thing. Ellian knew all too well what it was. A calling card. An invitation. He could use the coin with his enchanted mirror to contact this man later.

Ellian's hand dipped into his pocket, fingers caressing the warm, smooth metal. He leaned back against a stalagmite and pondered. Devir was not hostile toward humans. He could possibly be wooed if it was necessary to tell him the full plan. The faerie was confident, and certainly lovely enough to offer the necessary distraction.

And yet Ellian's eyes drifted back to the dance floor, to the whirling blue-and-gold princess in the center of all that chaos. *Maybe...*

He frowned at himself. *It's a stupid idea, and you know it.*

Cirelle glanced up and met his grim eyes. Her own expression fell, the merriment fleeing in the face of embarrassment and irritation. She scowled and stormed off to continue her mission.

Chapter Twenty-Three

CIRELLE MADE HER WAY around the edges of the cavern, meeting a strange parade of creatures. A faerie that was half-serpent, a gossamer-winged woman that would have fit in the palm of Cirelle's hand, a leering goblin man with a hat that dripped red streaks down the side of his head.

They were, by turns, friendly or predatory or dismissive. Cirelle noted them all.

She also noticed Ellian. He seemed to always watch her, but forever on the opposite side of the room. He danced with a nixie now, a woman with dappled blue skin and a sheer white gown that clung to her lithe frame wetly. She was fluid in motion, a waterfall come to life. Ellian shone with wildness and strength and grace as he spun the girl about, her head thrown back in a laugh.

A bitter, poisonous emotion blossomed inside Cirelle, white-hot and sudden as a flash flood. For one brief moment, she wanted to storm the dance floor and rip that woman from his arms. She tore her eyes from the floor and returned her attention to the faerie beside her. The woman still prattled on about this party's improvement over the last revel.

As the night wore on, faeries approached her or disdained her. Cirelle composed little ditties in her head to remember their potential allies, simple rhymes set to nursery songs. The predators, she ignored.

Still Ellian continued to dance. With a faun, a sylph, and a woman covered in nothing but tiny glittering emeralds. He'd chosen a slender man with skin like carved onyx now, gleaming and sharply beautiful. Ellian's hand curled around the faerie's hip as his burning gaze bored holes in Cirelle, a blue and violet so brilliant she could see it even from a dozen paces away. Ellian's head dipped forward as he whispered something in the man's ear, nuzzling the faerie's throat. But his eyes never left Cirelle's.

Her face flushed and she turned aside to meet the eyes of a peculiar, birdlike faerie standing beside her. He plucked something from a heaped plate on the nearby table. Small, black, and glistening wetly, Cirelle didn't want to guess what it might be. Throwing the bite of food in the air, the faerie caught it in his massive beak and tossed it down his throat like a buzzard. His face was a fan of tiny red feathers around gleaming yellow eyes, his beak dark and glossy. He wore human garb, a vest and trousers over a scarlet shirt with billowing sleeves. No wings. Instead, his fingers were like winter-bare twigs tipped with spiky nails. He stabbed another squishy morsel with one of those claws and snapped it off with his beak.

"Such a pretty little thrall," he croaked, tilting his head like a crow who'd found something shiny. "Whose tasty pet are you?"

This creature may have the beak of a scavenger vulture, but he stood with the unmistakable posture of a predator. He leaned forward, piercing Cirelle with those yellow eyes.

"I'm not a pet," Cirelle snapped, though her pulse ramped up a notch. The faerie stood easily a head and a half taller than she, that beak large enough to crush her skull if she gave him reason to.

He laughed, the sound of a raven's caw. "Oh, I beg to differ. Humans only exist in Faerie as playthings or as food." Those yellow eyes pierced hers. "So, which are you?"

She never got the chance to reply.

A sidhe woman appeared beside them, blinking into existence between one breath and the next. Cirelle had never watched a faerie flit between locations before, but it was the matter of half a heartbeat. One moment the space beside them was empty, and the next it was filled with this unfamiliar faerie.

She was perhaps Cirelle's height and curvy, if not quite Cirelle's size. She bore skin the color of the whitest clouds and hair like spun silver thread. A narrow nose rested over dark, pouty lips and a pointed chin. Cirelle couldn't stop staring into the woman's eyes. Yellow as citrines, there was nothing human in them. The cold eyes of a hawk, glinting with a spark that could have been a touch of madness.

Her gaze locked on Cirelle's. "Mortal." Her voice was a clear bell, dripping with disdain. The birdlike faerie gave a small hiss and scurried away.

Cirelle didn't miss the sharp crystal crown atop the woman's head. A white gown heavy with draped strings of champagne-colored beads clung to her form, a garment that would have been considered scandalously short in Arraven. Barely brushing her thighs, it was almost a tunic. Better to bare the knives strapped to her tall boots. The hilts sticking out of their sheaths were black leather and well-worn. The sidhe's slim fingers brushed the pommels of the small daggers, long nails clinking against the metal.

A clamor arose nearby and Cirelle looked over the woman's shoulder to see the dance disrupted, a single figure parting the

ocean of revelers as he barreled toward them. Ellian, and the
expression on his face was unmasked fear. That, more than anything, made Cirelle's own panic rise to the surface.

"What is a human doing here?" the woman said to Cirelle,
oblivious to Ellian's approach. Her golden eyes narrowed, and one
hand tightened about a knife's hilt. But she didn't draw it, not yet.

Ellian forced himself between Cirelle and the stranger. The
woman did not move. Then Ellian did something Cirelle would
never have thought she'd witness. He knelt before the woman,
his head bowed. "Your Majesty." The greeting was said through
gritted teeth, his shoulders tense.

Majesty. The word rattled back and forth in Cirelle's head.
A word for a queen, in the human world. Did fae bear the same
customs?

The woman slid her blade from its sheath. She used its
gleaming tip to tilt Ellian's chin upward and meet his gaze.
"Ellian," the woman purred, poison in her tone. Her lip curled
in a small snarl. "I should have known she was yours."

A queen.

With a knife at Ellian's throat.

"Let him go," Cirelle blurted.

The woman blinked. She withdrew the knife and darted
forward to press in close on Cirelle. The tip of that silvery-white
blade reflected the faerie lights an inch from Cirelle's eye, and
her heart ceased to beat for a moment.

As always, the beast in her mind twisted the fear to anger.
She lashed out. "You can't do anything to me. I've given you no
permissions." The light in the queen's eyes turned to blazing-hot
rage. Cirelle smiled, a savage grin.

Ellian still knelt, though he'd shifted to watch them, jaw
clenched and his eyes a new shade of burning crimson. A small
line of dark blood trickled down his throat.

"Ellian, stand," the Queen said, without taking her eyes from Cirelle's, that knife's tip still deadly-close.

He did, hands clenched into fists at his sides. Before Cirelle could so much as blink, the queen whirled and buried the short knife up to the hilt in Ellian's shoulder.

"No!" Cirelle's shout rang through the chamber. Only then did she notice the silence and the sharp faerie stares all turned upon them.

Ellian cried out and stumbled into the table as the woman withdrew the blade. Dishes clattered to the floor. A splatter of sauce landed on Cirelle's face and stained her fine dress. A knife flew past, narrowly missing the edge of her cheek. Ellian's free hand flew to his injured shoulder, his left arm hanging limply and covered in bits of food where it had landed amongst a platter.

The queen smiled, her knife now slicked with black blood. She watched Cirelle with those cold, mad eyes. "I suppose I can't hurt *you*, no. But your master is another story."

A dark stain slowly spread on Ellian's coppery shirt. There was only one way out. His eyes met hers, deepest green and black mingled. Cirelle lunged toward Ellian, past the Queen and her bloody knife. Ellian's good hand darted out, grasped hers, and they were gone.

Chapter Twenty-Four

ELLIAN FLED TO HIS ROOMS the moment they returned from that revel. He'd since evaded all of Cirelle's questions about that icy queen with the golden eyes, but surely a sidhe queen would be mentioned somewhere in his library.

"How does he ever find anything?" Cirelle snapped, slamming another useless book onto the floor. She spoke only to herself, of course. Ellian and Toben lay reasonably abed at this hour, long after dawn.

Weariness tugged at her, but not as strongly as the restless, twitchy energy that had prodded her to leave her bed and come here. Another of her accursed moods had consumed her, one of the frenetic ones that felt like imaginary ants crawling over her skin. She sought answers here in the library while everyone else slumbered.

Now, hands flying rapidly to thumb through endless pages, Cirelle traced the reading glass over the spines and stacked books aside in rows. Her temper built as she unearthed one worthless tome after another. Cookbooks, diagrams for building carriages, a book full of paintings of cats. There was no semblance of order in this entire library. Somewhere in here, there had to be clues to *something*.

Cirelle kicked a book across the room as tears stung her eyes. She wanted to destroy something, to lash out, to give her anger life. She threw books to the floor, biting back a scream of frustration. Instead, a choking sob slipped from her and she collapsed onto the floor as that familiar blackness swallowed her again.

She cried herself empty, curled in a ball with her arms wrapped around her knees. Useless. It was all useless. Trapped here in a mansion full of secrets and half-truths, surrounded by a storm of creatures that were nowhere near human.

So, she wept and dug her fingernails painfully into her wrist until the agony passed.

The despair vanished as abruptly as it always did, leaving her feeling foolish and ashamed of her outburst. She picked up the book she'd kicked and tucked it back on the shelf, along with the others.

When footsteps echoed outside the door, Cirelle swore and began tidying ever faster.

"Dare I ask?" Ellian's voice from the doorway was gentle. Too soft, too sympathetic.

"No." She knew her face was still blotchy and swollen, her eyes still shining with the last remaining tears. She slid another book back on the shelf. "I thought you were asleep."

"I was, until the house's alarms woke me up, warning me someone was tearing my library to pieces." Still, no anger filled the words, only a deep pity.

Cirelle hated pity.

Still, she *had* just been hurling his books about. She bit her lip. "Sorry."

He shrugged and began helping her put the books back. "I

suppose I'll need to take something for it, though. You broke the spine on this one."

Remorse washed over her. "Like what?"

A shake of his head. "I don't know. Maybe an honest answer?" He turned to look at her with eyes of pensive sapphire blue. "What are you looking for?"

She hesitated. "Clues. Something, anything. That queen. Thieves' Night. Kyrinna."

He flinched at Kyrinna's name and guilt fell over his face. Stars, what had happened to the girl, and why did it wound Ellian so deeply?

Ellian shelved another book, still favoring his injured arm.

Cirelle motioned toward his shoulder. "Why haven't you healed that with your magic potion yet?"

"That elixir is meant for smaller wounds. It closed the skin and started the process, but a stab wound will take time to heal."

A flash of memory, that cold queen piercing his flesh with a cruel satisfaction. The black blood that seeped through Ellian's shirt, the loathing in his eyes. And yet he'd answered none of her questions about the woman so far. She sighed. "I'm so tired of living surrounded by secrets. Why can't you tell me anything?"

He opened his mouth, hesitated, then closed it again. A moment later, he asked, "Have you wondered *why* Orwe died as he did?"

"Because faeries are cruel."

Ellian shook his head. "I have enemies. They wanted what he knew."

The truth took a moment to sink in. *Torture.* Cirelle sucked in a breath.

He continued, "And if those enemies manage to discover or capture one of my other allies, they'll confess that you are only a clueless human, a mere servant who knows nothing of my plans."

Cirelle felt dizzy.

Ellian cleared his throat. "So, that's your answer."

"Stars," she breathed. "Enemies. Like the queen?"

"That... is a very long story."

"I have time. Why does she hate you?"

"I honestly don't know," he admitted as he continued to tidy the scattered books. "She's despised me from the moment we met, and I've given her little cause to change that opinion."

Cirelle bit her lip and settled a book on a shelf. "So, you weren't...together?"

He barked a laugh. "Certainly not."

"Good," Cirelle said with a soft smile. "She's terrifying."

"She has to be. She took the throne by force and holds it with more of the same."

"Why?"

"She and her son Adaleth killed her consort, Adaleth's father. The reason why varies by the telling. The king and queen exiled them for it. Centuries later, mere decades ago, they returned with a small army of stray sidhe and took the kingdom through treachery and bloodshed."

Cirelle pursed her lips. "You said you were under a hundred years old."

"I did."

He didn't elaborate further, but Cirelle prodded. "Were you there?"

Ellian shook his head. "Some sidhe fled and swapped their children with human ones rather than see them raised in such a regime. I believe I was one of those."

"Where are your sidhe parents now?"

"I suspect they are dead." He spoke so tonelessly, but a crease in his brow conflicted with his carefully-gray eyes. "There were...

executions, after Ayre took the throne. Anyone who didn't bend a knee was killed."

"No one knows about the children switched as changelings?"

"I didn't say that. But no one will speak of it, regardless of what they know. It's a messy history, one we don't prod at too deeply." Another shake of his head and he met her eyes. "Something *I* don't poke at. My birth parents aren't the ones who raised me."

"You aren't just a little bit curious?"

The corner of Ellian's lip curled upward in a small smile. "Awfully persistent, aren't you?"

"Not that it pays off."

"Not yet." There was a strange emphasis on those words, but when Cirelle opened her mouth to ask, Ellian arched one eyebrow and pushed the last book into place. "But please, spare the books? It's not their fault."

"No." Cirelle's mouth drew into a grim line. "It's yours."

Chapter Twenty-Five

Thieves' Night draws ever closer. The more I try not to think on it, the stronger my dread grows.

And my anticipation.

A cry broke Ellian's concentration, sudden and harsh. His pen skittered across the page, leaving a jagged streak of ink. He closed the journal, setting both it and the pen aside. A quick glance around the garden showed only the usual trees and flowering shrubs.

The noise echoed once more, and this time he recognized it for what it was. A sob. Not the pretty, delicate kind, but a visceral, raw agony.

Cirelle.

*I should leave her be. But h*is traitorous feet led him closer instead, cutting through the winding garden paths. He found her seated on the ground, her back to the large black prayer stone, arms wrapped around her knees. Alarm jolted through him. "Princess? Are you hurt?" He stepped closer, but she glared up at him with red-rimmed eyes full of shame and fury.

"Go away." Her lips curled into a snarl.

It would have been wiser to follow her orders, to retreat. But as happened more and more often these days, his common sense fled around this woman. He took another cautious step forward.

"I said go away!" She bit off the words, picking up a nearby stone and hurling it at him. It was a small rock, almost a pebble, and he batted it away with a hand. After a moment's pause, he turned.

"Wait."

Ellian hesitated. "Which is it, Princess? Go, or stay?"

"Would you do whichever I asked?"

He nodded.

"Why?"

A very good question. "I've no wish to cause you pain."

She barked a laugh at that one. "You've caused me nothing but pain since I got here."

The words stung more than the stone she'd thrown at him. Still, a tiny fleck of anger bloomed. "Have I? I've housed you in comfort and given you only the most menial tasks to pay your debt." His voice dipped into a growl. "Yet you hurl insults at every turn. You snarl at me like a feral cat when the worst I've done is withhold secrets that are rightfully mine to keep."

Cirelle's reply was shrill, sudden, sharp. "You *murdered* my friend!"

"I didn't kill her!" Ellian clamped his mouth shut. *Why did I tell her that?* This girl already trod too close to the line Kyrinna had walked. He closed his eyes for the span of a sigh. Too late now. The words rang in the air. "She still lived when we left your world."

The shock on the princess's face was piercing. She gasped in a labored breath. "What?"

"I transported her to the nearby city. With the unicorn's horn."

A dozen emotions washed over her face. Surprise, relief, joy.

Fury. She stood, her stare hot enough to melt steel. "You let me think she was dead."

A nod.

The princess took a step closer, hands balled into fists. "Why would you do that?"

Carefully, he let his mask fall back into place. "I'm a faerie."

"That's not an answer."

"It's the only one you'll get." He turned away. This had spiraled too far out of control.

She lunged forward and grabbed his wrist, yanking him toward her. Ellian caught his balance and twisted his arm from her grasp with a startled glare.

"Tell me," the princess demanded.

His lip curled.

The fury in her eyes faded, doused by an aching sorrow. Tears still flowed, but she made no move to wipe them away. "Make an exception, just for tonight." She stepped closer. "Why did you spare her? Why did you lead me to believe she was dead? Was it merely a faerie game, toying with me like a cat with a half-dead beetle?"

I should say yes. "No."

"Then why?" She whispered.

He couldn't bear the sight of those shimmering trails on her face. And she had just touched him, giving him the opportunity to lift a hand and brush the tears from one cheek with his thumb.

The princess stared up at him with those wide, tear-stained eyes. For one brief, weak moment, he was tempted to tell her everything. Foolish. But he could spare a single truth. "You shouldn't become comfortable around faeries."

"So you made me think you were a murderer instead?"

"I am."

"But not Lydia. And not without serious cause."

He shook his head, his hand still cupping her cheek. Her features twisted in agony and she withdrew sharply, another violent cry clawing its way from her throat.

Ellian pulled his hand away and let it hang at his side. "I'll go."

The princess shook her head. "Wait, no... I just get like this sometimes." She spoke around another sudden sob that broke from her. "It's my curse."

"Curse?"

"These moods. They swallow me whole, then just disappear."

"Is that what happened to my library when you decided to start throwing books?"

Her lips turned into a grimace. "Yes." She wrapped her arms around herself again. A pause. Indecision flickered in her eyes. Then, almost a whisper, "Stay, please? I don't want to be alone."

He held out a hand with a sad smile. "All right. But perhaps it would help if you were more comfortable?"

She hesitated, then placed her fingers on his palm. Within a moment, he'd worldwalked them into her parlor. They arranged themselves on the pale blue sofa, Cirelle's hand withdrawing as she tucked her feet beneath her and stared at the floor. Ellian sat beside her, keeping a careful space between them. His tongue remained still as he picked at a button on the upholstery and discarded a dozen things to say. Her sobs rose and fell like ocean tides, coming rough and jagged, then subsiding until they rose up again shortly afterward.

When Cirelle's hand brushed his arm, he startled. A moment later, she buried her face in his shoulder, clutching his jacket with an iron grasp as her tears stained the fine gray suede.

Her touch gave him the permission he needed to stroke her hair as she curled against him and wept. The princess's words spilled as freely as her tears, a litany of all her sorrows. Homesickness, restlessness, feeling trapped. Loneliness.

Ellian let her speak, her hair spilling through his fingers like cool water. No longer the color of wine, it had faded to an auburn hue, the roots a middling brown.

After the flood of despair slowed to a trickle of sniffles, the princess lifted her head. "Th—" She stopped herself, pressing her lips together.

Hesitantly, slowly, as if he were afraid to spook a skittish cat, Ellian lifted his other hand to hover beside the princess's cheek. A request. This time, she gave a shuddering sigh and leaned into it.

"I hate being worthless," she said.

"You're anything but worthless, Princess." A smile curled his lips. "And I can't lie."

Her breath caught, their gazes still locked together. Ellian realized he'd let his glamour slip. He wondered what she saw in the color of his eyes, but didn't replace the illusion.

He spoke. "Faerie can be terrible." *I can be terrible.* "I'm doing my best to keep those things away from you."

"I know," she admitted with an exhausted sigh. His hand withdrew from her cheek to curl in his lap. She didn't pull away, though. Cirelle still watched him with those new eyes, unguarded and swirling with a dozen emotions.

He sucked in a soft gasp of breath, accompanied by a shudder in his bones. A slow and steady heat built in his belly. The tears still glistened on Cirelle's cheeks, but something dark and needy sparked in her stare. A tiny flame twined itself around the slurry of guilt and gentleness in Ellian's chest. He couldn't tear his eyes away from hers, so stormy and hungry and earnest.

Everything happened in a single motion. Her hand slid from his shoulder to the nape of his neck, and she shifted up onto her knees to lean closer. His mind registered what was happening just as their lips met.

An involuntary sound slipped from his throat. She pinned his head in place with her hands as her mouth claimed his, demanding and certain. In another smooth movement, she swung a knee over him to straddle his lap, her body draped deliciously against him. That small spark inside Ellian burst into flame. His heartbeat sped into a sprint, his lips surrendering and parting for her persuasive tongue.

Yes. He groaned, his hands sliding down to her sides as she moved against him in ways that forced all common sense from his brain. The princess kissed him deeply, seizing control as her hips pressed into his. She tasted like salt.

Like tears.

Rational thought returned. Ellian lifted his hands to grasp her wrists and pull away. "What—"

"Don't talk. Please." Her words were breathless, hurried. "I just need to...not be alone, or useless, or empty. To feel something." Her eyes were turbulent, a deep well of sorrow swimming in their depths.

Ellian gently forced her arms away from his face. His lips still tingled with her tear-drenched kisses.

She saw the rejection in his eyes before he could utter it, and rage turned her features into something harsh. "Stupid faerie." The princess scrambled off him with fury and self-loathing in her eyes.

He didn't let go of one wrist, tugging on it until she turned to look back at him with a snarl. The words scraped like knives leaving his throat. "You don't want me. You want a warm body. I won't be your drug of choice, Princess."

Hypocrite, his inner voice said.

"Your loss," she hissed, yanking her hand free and stumbling out of the room.

Ellian groaned and ran a hand through his hair, staring up at the ceiling for answers it could not give.

Chapter Twenty-Six

ELLIAN TURNED THE COIN over and over in his palm as its magical warmth seeped into his skin. He paced in front of the calling mirror in the Archive's antechamber, deliberating.

Who should he wrap in his intrigues? Time was running out, and Devir remained the clearest option. The fiery fae didn't even need to know about the Key or the mission. All he had to do was attend a few parties, look pretty, and share a few scandalous public kisses.

And yet…

The coin clacked as Ellian set it on the desk. He stared at every curl in its embossed design, unique to its owner and duergar-made as all such coins were. If the pattern held any clues, Ellian couldn't find them.

Devir was the perfect candidate, so why did Ellian's hand balk at tucking that coin into the notched frame of the mirror and calling him?

You know why.

Ellian brushed aside the voice in his head, squashing it down deep.

It refused to be buried. The princess's face appeared in his mind's eye. *She is mortal. She can lie,* his traitorous thoughts tempted him.

He had to admit, it was more than mere practicality that whispered to him. Cirelle had avoided him since the incident in her parlor, leaving Toben to go on summons. But he'd eavesdropped on her music, fierce and achingly beautiful. Moreover, the memory of those few lurid moments would not leave him. Cirelle's weight straddling his legs, her lips pressed demandingly to his. Cool, mortal hands pinning his head in place so she could claim him.

He shivered. Could she really do this? Cirelle had passed most of his tests well enough, after all. Deceit, seduction, theft. Her temper was a worry, but could she dampen it if the mission were important enough?

Ellian sank his head into his hands, wiping his face in weary resignation. With a sigh, he slipped the coin into a desk drawer and prepared to summon the coterie.

ᘓ

ELLIAN'S CREW ARRIVED ONCE more, even the strange shadow creature visible only at the corners of her vision, all broken-glass shapes wreathed in darkness. When the last of them entered, Ellian and Toben shut the antechamber door.

Cirelle padded down the steps and pressed her ear to the door, but only heard muffled snatches of conversation.

"Next week..."

"Our last chance..."

Then her name. Distinctly, in Ellian's voice, raised above the din. "I think it should be Cirelle."

There was an uproar at that.

An argument ensued, too many voices chattering at once.

"Quiet!" Ellian's voice rang through, command in his tone. Silence fell. "This is our only shot at the Key. We have to try."

Chaos erupted once more, a dozen voices talking over one another in unison.

An idea sparked. Judging by the shouting, the debate showed no signs of ending soon. A giddy rush clamoring inside her, Cirelle dashed up the stairs to the library. She clutched the reading glass in her hand and approached Ellian's wing. The doorknob buzzed against her hand, like holding her palm against an angry hive of bees. With a deep breath, she turned the knob and pulled the door open.

No alarms sounded, and no one burst from the antechamber doors below. Still, Ellian would know. She had little time to spare.

Cirelle slipped into the forbidden corridor, as dark as all the others.

This wing seemed smaller than the rest, though she wasn't sure how that was possible. It consisted of a single long hallway with a handful of rooms on either side. She peeked into each as she passed. The first bore shelves cramped with an assortment of items. No magical treasures here, each trinket as mundane as the last. A handwoven basket. A necklace of carved wooden beads. A child's plush toy cat with a singed ear. Most of the items were well-worn and faded, though not a fleck of dust marred them.

The next room gave her pause. Contrary to the hues of Ellian's wardrobe, his bedroom was decorated in warm autumn shades; russet, gold, and crimson. The coverlet was a silk so fine it looked like polished bronze, and the bed it rested upon was enormous, a four-post monstrosity in dark polished wood.

Here, once again, the winged serpent held sway. The posts of the bed were carved in scales, gilded to highlight the pattern.

Wooden wings arched over his headboard, and the coils of a snake danced in the rug in the center of the floor. There was a single door opposite the entry, cracked partway open to reveal a sliver of what appeared to be a bathing chamber beyond.

Cirelle closed the door once more and made her way to the third room. This one was more promising. A study of sorts, cozy and comfortable. Bookshelves lined two walls, and a soft burgundy chair rested before a small, solid desk of halwood.

Two books lay upon it. Hand shaking, Cirelle opened the first, bound in deep purple leather. The paper crackled with age, the ink faded. It was filled with vertical columns of linked whorls and loops. Kishi.

Tracing over the text with the glass, Cirelle grew more puzzled than ever.

I can't believe tomorrow is my nameday! Perhaps Rikai will be the one to steal a kiss. Oh, I hope so.

It was a short note. The next page bore a different handwriting.

You can do better than Rikai, and you know it. Aim for the stars. What about Shidal?

Cirelle flicked through the book. On and on it went, a series of communication passed back and forth between two writers. Inconsequential things, the worries of adolescents. Minor humiliations blown out of proportion, friendships torn apart by romantic entanglements. What was this doing hidden in the study of a faerie? She flipped through more of it, looking for any mention of her host, but there was nothing. Just two teens and the small dramas of their everyday lives.

With a growing sense of urgency, Cirelle set it aside to flip through the other book. This one turned out to be a portfolio of letters. Much newer, by the look of them.

My love…, the first letter began in Trade, and something

slithered in Cirelle's stomach. This was no longer a mere search for clues to her predicament. This was personal.

Still, she read on.

… I hope this reaches you. I know you heard my summons, even if you did not answer. What must I do to feel your touch again? Name it and it's yours. I'll be in the same spot next full moon, and the one after, and each one ever after that.

Signed,

Your Dearest Kyrinna

The letters piled together, each bearing the same sentiment with varying levels of desperation and longing. Every note started the same. *My love.* The lover's name was never mentioned, but a knot in Cirelle's gut tightened as she skimmed one after the other. At least a year's worth of letters, each begging for a suitor's attention.

Kyrinna was a mistake.

A dull roar filled Cirelle's ears. Some of papers had been crumpled and smoothed back out. The ink in a few places had been splashed and blurred, smudged into illegibility. The tears of the writer, or damage done later? Cirelle stacked them back together with shaky hands and closed the portfolio, rearranging both pieces as she'd found them.

Footsteps rang outside, steady and purposeful. Cirelle's heart skipped. The silvery chime of Ellian's odd boots was far too pleasant a sound to accompany the dread that filled her.

Doors creaked open and then closed again. She glanced around, but there was nowhere to hide. She'd never fit under the small desk.

The doorknob clicked.

Cirelle stood straighter, grasping the reading glass tightly in one fist.

The steady light of the sconces cast Ellian's face in sharp lines as he stood in the doorway. A flicker of orange flame lit his eyes, doused by a wave of black when he glanced from her to the desk and back again.

"The antechamber, now." The words were wearier than they were angry, but they brooked no argument as he turned and led the way.

Cirelle followed. The faeries were gone, the Archive's antechamber empty. Even Toben was nowhere to be seen.

"Sit, please." Ellian pointed to a chair.

Cirelle lifted her chin and made no move toward the seat.

His jaw clenched, but Ellian fell into one of the chairs with a wave of his hand. "Suit yourself."

Now that he was sitting, it made her look foolish. Cirelle took the other chair. Realizing she still clutched the reading glass, she set it on the low table between them and waited for him to speak. Excuses were useless.

"I warned you not to use my own tools to spy on me ever again."

She bit her lip but couldn't stop the words from tumbling out. "I'd have no reason to spy if you would just tell me what's going on."

He stared at the reading glass.

Irritation prodded at her. "So, what punishment have I earned this time?"

"A choice." Ellian finally glanced up. "A bargain. Four nights hence, there is a sidhe festival. I'm allowed to bring a guest. You will accompany me."

Cirelle's heartbeat pounded against her ribs. "Why not Toben?"

Instead, his voice held wry amusement. "This task requires far too much deception for Toben. I need a liar and a spy. Someone unafraid to get their hands dirty. Skills you've demonstrated admirably."

Realization struck her like a blow. "That's what Raven's Gambit was about. The wine. All those tests."

He nodded.

"Was that why you teased me so often?"

"Oh, no," he grinned. "That was just for me." His smile faded, his eyes flickering dark. "So, Princess, do you think you can corral your temper around the sidhe?"

She glowered, her hands gripping the armrests of her chair.

"I..." Ellian cleared his throat, his next words quiet. "If you do this, I will be forced to include you in my plans for Thieves' Night."

Cirelle's breath caught. The great mystery solved. Her gaze slid upward, meeting eyes of purest green, emeralds in sunlight. "What if I say no?"

"Then I choose another punishment for your spying and trespassing. You will remain ignorant of my plans, and another takes this task."

Cirelle cleared her throat nervously. "Does that mean you trust me now?"

"Of course not. But my options are limited. I risk everything on you, Princess. You will either be my savior or my ruin."

Cirelle watched him closely, the tightness around his mouth, the bob of his throat as he swallowed. He wore black finery tonight and picked at the edge of a sleeve.

A mission. *A liar and a spy.* It must be killing him, to need her help. His eyes returned to hers. Cirelle nodded sharply, a grim smile dancing on her lips. "I'm in."

Chapter Twenty-Seven

WHEN ELLIAN INFORMED HER of his plans, Cirelle's temper erupted.

"The prince?" She paced the antechamber. "You want me to lie right to the face of your queen and your prince?"

Ellian ignored her. "You'll be glamoured to play the part of my faerie guest during the festival. The masquerade is only the beginning."

"There's more?"

He barked a bitter laugh. "Of course. The sidhe can't resist a good party. Two full days of revelry precede it. Parties, performances, dances, banquets. For the time leading up to the final Hunt, all I need you to do is provide a distraction. Help keep all eyes on the two of us so my other spies can fulfill their tasks without being caught." He shifted his weight. "But as my festival guest, you'll need to accompany me during the Hunt itself."

A Hunt. She'd never participated in one at home, but hunters didn't always come back unscathed. "Is it dangerous?"

"Yes." He didn't mince words. "All I need you to do is follow me. I'll protect you, on my word."

"Your oath. That you'll keep me safe."

Ellian met her gaze squarely, deadly serious. "I swear it."

"What is this Hunt?"

"A contest." Ellian pushed away from the desk and circled it to flip open a book laying on the desk. "It occurs once every hundred and fifty years. The royal court is obligated to host a Great Hunt in memory of an ancient sidhe king, and to grant a boon to the winner."

"Any boon?"

Ellian shook his head. "No. This time, the reward is a place in the prince's Inner Court, his small circle of advisors and companions."

"And you want it."

His lip quirked as he glanced up from the book. "I need it, but I do not particularly want it."

"It seems a slim chance, if it's a contest," she pointed out.

"I have a backup scheme, but this would save my allies from bearing the brunt of the plan on Thieves' Night."

"Which is?" She lifted an eyebrow.

"Still a secret." He smiled at that, eyes glimmering sky blue.

A flicker of anger, deep in her chest. She tilted her head and narrowed her eyes. "What is the Key?"

"Stone and sea and sky, Princess," he swore. "Where did you hear that?"

She stared.

"You were eavesdropping."

"You wanted a sneak."

Ellian sighed, gripping the edge of the desk. "It's a powerful artifact. A weapon the prince intends to use. I want to keep it from him."

"Why is it so important?"

Ellian spoke as if the words hurt to spill from his lips. "If he finds its matching piece, Adaleth will close the gates between our worlds. There will be no more travel between them, and anyone on the wrong side of the doors will be trapped there forever."

Silence held. Locked in Faerie with no way home. Never to see her family again, or Briere. No more of those beloved, lazy Arravene summers. She swallowed back the lump that formed in her throat.

Cirelle stared down at the floor and uncrossed her arms. "So, I'm supposed to be a distraction. That's it?"

"That's it."

"How?"

"The Unseelie Court is insular. Though you'll be glamoured to appear fae, you'll still be an outsider. You merely need to be noticeably present at all times."

Cirelle snorted a laugh. "That I can do."

ᘓᔓ

ON THE DAY OF THE MASQUERADE, Cirelle found an unusual golden gown hanging at the front of her wardrobe.

Thin metal triangles the size of her thumbnail covered the backless halter dress, dangling free and clinking together like bells with every movement. It clung indecently to her and bore a slit to her thigh. A feathered mantle covered her shoulders and neck, shimmering deep bronze and cobalt blue.

The mask was a perfect match, delicately etched with a pattern of scales. Two wide fans of blue feathers swept back from its sides. The dress was a cool weight against her skin, its silken lining soft in spite of its sharp-edged exterior. She twirled, listening to the metal jingle.

She was still contemplating the overall effect in the mirror when Toben knocked at her door. "A feathered serpent," he murmured, staring at the mask.

Ellian's heraldry, the creature that inspired the decor of his home.

Cirelle grimaced. "Isn't it a bit... obvious?"

The old man's eyes crinkled. "I think that's the idea."

She fidgeted with her bracelets, two heavy pieces in gold that hinged and clamped over her wrists. Turning before the mirror, she admired how the scales rippled and shone in the light. It was beautiful, even if that slash in the fabric up to her thigh was brazen. When she danced, the gown would bare both her legs for all to see.

Cirelle couldn't deny it thrilled her more than it left her scandalized. A poor example of a princess, indeed.

Ellian waited for her in the Archive's antechamber. His garb was a perfect match for hers, a jacket of midnight blue trimmed in a pale gold. A shimmery bronze shirt peeked from under the coat, a flare of lace covering his wrists. A simple brooch glimmered on one lapel, the golden serpent with blue enameled wings outspread.

His eyes flickered a myriad of colors, each flowing into the other so quickly she couldn't discern them. Like a door closing, the color drained, fading to that inscrutable gray. Still, a faint smile clung to the corners of his lips.

"Here," Ellian said, slipping a new ring off his finger and holding it out to her. Reluctantly, Cirelle held out a hand, letting the small band of metal fall into her palm. It still held his warmth, and she closed her fingers around it.

"What's this for?"

"After I cast your glamour, the ring will hold it in place."

She nodded toward one of his hands. "You're missing a few of *your* usual rings. Why?"

"Anything that can be used as a weapon won't be allowed into the palace. Your translation earring is an exception, as is glamour. If they forbade that, no one would attend. Sidhe are many things, but 'incredibly vain' is somewhere toward the top of that list."

Cirelle gave him a long, pointed look, her gaze sliding up and down to take in all his finery. "You don't say."

After a brief, startled laugh, Ellian shook his head. He made a vague gesture in her direction. "There. Now the ring."

Cirelle had to try the ring on two fingers, but when it settled on her middle finger, a small shiver ran up her arm.

"So, what do I look like?" Cirelle was surprised at her own nervousness. It was only temporary, but the idea that she wouldn't be *herself* was a disconcerting one.

Ellian gestured toward the mirror beside the desk.

Cirelle stared at her reflection. Her skin had lost its golden luster, now a faded gray-brown with dappled markings like sunlight filtered through tree branches. Her hair was a tangle of russet, half-wild and windblown. Her nose was slimmer, longer, her lips fuller. In fact, her whole face had taken on an angular quality, making her now-green eyes gleam even larger. Incredible.

"A sylvan." Ellian finally answered her unspoken question.

"Not a sidhe?"

"No. Our numbers are too small. The sidhe are all known to one another. It's common knowledge that I consort with other species, so a sylvan will not be unbelievable." His reflection in the mirror grinned back, eyes sparkling sky-blue. "Even better, sylvans can eat only uncooked plants and can only drink water. They're oathbound. It's the perfect excuse to keep you well away from the wine."

Cirelle snorted. "What are sylvans, anyway?"

Ellian leaned in closer, his presence a weight at her back.

His breath brushed her cheek. "They're temptresses who lure mortals deep into the forest."

A sudden heat shivered through Cirelle, and she swallowed.

"Another thing." Ellian stepped toward the desk and picked up an object. Cirelle recognized the dancing figurine that had been her offering to Ellian when she summoned him. He shoved it toward her so quickly Cirelle was forced to take it or let the small sculpture fall to the floor. While both their hands brushed it, Ellian murmured something quietly and Cirelle's fingertips warmed where they touched the stone.

She pushed it back reflexively, letting out a yelp. "What was that?"

His eyes glimmered as he set it aside. "You'll see." Cirelle glared, crossing her arms and giving him her stoniest stare. The scowl that had backed down soldiers did nothing, and only made his grin widen. "Also, sylvans are not known for their cleverness."

"What?" Abruptly, it all clicked into place. The dangerously high slit in the skirt of her dress. *Sylvans are temptresses.* Cirelle's fists clenched. "Stars go black," she swore. "You want me to play the part of some dim-witted arm candy?"

"Precisely." His lips curled into a positively wicked smile.

"You insufferable ass," she snarled.

"It's all in the bluff, Princess. If my guest is a fluff-brained sylvan, no one will suspect you of deceit."

It *was* a sound strategy, even if it made her skin crawl. "Fine."

Ellian's eyes darkened. "And... there is one final thing I need from you, if this plan is to succeed."

Cirelle crossed her arms. "What now?"

"I need permission to touch you."

Her heartbeat ran laps in her chest. "What?"

The white tension around his eyes was back. "If we're to

play these roles, I need to be able to grasp your hand, to touch your shoulder."

Cirelle swallowed and chose her words carefully. "I give you permission to touch only skin that is not covered by clothing, or to touch me over said clothing. No sliding hands under my dress." With a grimace, she added, "Be a gentleman."

His smile was faint. "No one is truly a gentleman at the Unseelie Court. But I will agree to the rest of your terms."

Unease skittered down her spine with spider's legs as the air shuddered to acknowledge their bargain. She crammed down her fear and held out a hand. "Then let's get this over with."

$$\text{\small \textbf{ᏉᏋ}}$$

THEY LEFT FROM THE FRONT WALKWAY. When the mist cleared from their worldwalk, a promenade of tiny shimmering pebbles lay beneath their feet, like a scattering of pure white pearls. Floating globes of cool light lined the pathway on either side.

At the end of the path stood the royal palace of the sidhe.

It was larger than her home in Arraven, constructed entirely of gleaming white stone that sparkled in the starlight. Spires curled up toward the sky in strangely organic shapes, the doorways and windows sculpted into unusual arches. It all resembled nothing so much as frosting swirled artfully on a holiday cake.

And yet, there was something cold about it. The pale marble, the blue-white lights, the guards in their silver uniforms beside the door. Though the air was heavy with the warmth of early summer, goosebumps prickled her skin.

To their right, ocean waves crashed. The palace stood on a cliff overlooking the vast sea, shining black in the moonlight.

We can't go by water. The information Orwe had died for. Cirelle shuddered.

Gravel crunched behind them and a pair of sidhe brushed past, their skin and hair in bright rainbow hues. The closest woman cast a disparaging sidelong glance at Cirelle and murmured something to her companion. They burst into a fit of small giggles as they continued down the path.

Cirelle's jaw clenched, and Ellian's fingers tightened around hers. She pulled away sharply. "When you said it was known that you fraternized with other species... that's not a good thing, is it?"

Ellian's gaze skittered away from her. "Not in the eyes of our illustrious prince or his mother. Or anyone they've deigned to accept into their Unseelie Court, their chosen, the elite." A bitter smile crossed his face. "I'm not one of them, if you hadn't guessed."

"So, I'm a second-class citizen, less than dirt."

His grin widened. "As am I. Let's track some muddy footprints all over their pristine floor." Those eyes sparked palest blue.

Despite her anxiety, Cirelle found herself returning that grin, wild and impetuous and untamed.

Ellian offered his arm. Cirelle took it, and they walked into the palace side-by-side.

Chapter Twenty-Eight

They entered through the large doors and were ushered down a broad hallway. The entire palace was crafted of that shimmering white stone, inside and out.

The ballroom was no exception, blinding in its paleness. The floor, the walls, the ceilings arching high above, all shone like polished alabaster. An icy blue glow left the air misty and dreamlike. Chandeliers dripping with crystals glimmered in the eerie, thick light.

Music echoed without any apparent source, a strange song made entirely of bells. Soft chiming ones, deep resonant ones, and a staccato metallic cascade of notes in the background. It was like a song woven from moonbeams. For a few moments, Cirelle was entranced by the music alone, wondering if she could replicate the melody on her harp later.

Until she noticed the host of sidhe scattered throughout the room. The mingling of fragrances was so strong it was like walking into a perfumery, a collective smell that made Cirelle's eyes water.

Faeries whirled together on the dance floor or clustered in small groups, all masked for the ball. Eyes peered through gilding and feathers, some reflecting light like a cat's, some of unnatural hues like brilliant gemstones. Mouths grinned beneath half-masks, lips in red or black or purple showing teeth that were only sometimes an imitation of human ones.

Though the room was filled with sidhe in their assortment of skin tones and hair colors, all were garbed in colorless shades. The glittering white of diamonds, the soft gray of ash, the deepest black of onyx. Their masks matched, not a drop of color to be found there, either.

Cirelle glanced at Ellian's strikingly cobalt jacket, then at her own shimmering, golden dress. "Apparently you missed the message about the dress code," she remarked wryly.

"Oh, the message was recieved. I simply don't care." The grin he cast in her direction was irreverent and reckless. Another new facet of her faerie host. All night, Ellian had been more fey than usual, a wildness clinging to him.

Something clicked into place. Cirelle reached up to touch her red-dyed hair, only to meet the glamoured, unruly tangle she now bore. But her real hair lay hidden beneath, a fading, unlucky scarlet.

Was Ellian's choice to disregard the garb of the ball anything other than a similar rebellion? Perhaps he was fickle and full of sly secrets. For tonight, though, Ellian was her partner in this game. For one brief second, she felt a moment of kinship, a key sliding into a lock.

Heads turned when they entered, more than a few displaying mild disgust. Several cast curious glances at them instead, eyebrows raised and heads cocked like inquisitive birds. Cirelle met the eyes of one enigmatic sidhe, a mousy-faced woman with an ebony cascade of hair that half-masked her lavender face. She stood against a wall, arms crossed, wearing a dress that looked like tattered cobwebs. Her eyebrows rose when she glanced up and down at Cirelle, and something piercing in her gaze made Cirelle uneasy. Those eyes were chips of obsidian, cold and calculating.

Worse, Tallia was here. Her mask was feathered all over, a pure white swan, making her dark eyes all the blacker. The woman glided up to Ellian. With a wicked laugh, her eyes darted to Cirelle and she grimaced as if she'd smelled sour milk. She clicked her tongue. "I didn't think you could be a worse disgrace, but it seems I was wrong. Are you so eager to pick up where you left off?"

Cirelle bit her tongue with an effort. She cast her eyes demurely at the floor, simmering with fury. What did Tallia mean, pick up where he left off?

"It matters little what you think, Tallia," Ellian said, his voice icy cold.

"But it *does* matter what our dear queen and her prince think, doesn't it?" Tallia crooned. "Sooner or later, you'll push them too far. Perhaps it will be tonight. It would certainly enliven the evening." With that parting shot, she swept away in a flurry of flowing white skirts.

Cirelle huffed out a breath through her nostrils and Ellian glanced sidelong at her. "Come, let us refresh ourselves." He led the way to a banquet table where a garnet-skinned sidhe stood. Picking up a wine glass, he leaned back against the table and took a sip. "Hello, Shai."

"Ellian!" The woman's returning smile was wide and contagious. She gave Cirelle a brief once-over.

Cirelle remained silent. Her eyes roved over the array of food on the table. With all the preparations for this ball, she hadn't eaten yet this evening. Ellian had told her the food would be safe, as an invited guest. One pitcher seemed to be full of water, and she filled an empty glass with it. She gave it a sniff, confirming it was safe before taking a sip. Remembering Ellian's warning about a sylvan's diet, Cirelle plucked a few orange berries from the table and popped them in her mouth. They were pleasantly sour, like green grapes.

Shai grinned at Ellian. Her short brush of crisp white hair peeked out around her mask of dark metal, plain and simply styled. More of the same metal graced her throat and wrists. It was dark like iron but obviously couldn't be, not if it touched her skin. She wore a knee-length dress in a pale gray, layers of girlish ruffles draping her frame like an upside-down rose blossom, though decorative leather pauldrons rested on her shoulders.

Shai shook her head. "Oh, the prince is going to spit nails when he sees the two of you."

Ellian took a small sip of his wine, a sly smirk curling his lips. "Iron ones, I hope."

Shai snorted. "Shit, Ellian. You're going to get yourself killed."

"I say nothing that isn't common knowledge."

"Yeah... but the outfit? And bringing a sylvan into the castle?"

"I'm allowed one guest," he pointed out coolly, plucking a small pastry from the table and taking a bite.

Shai grunted and shrugged. She didn't look like a courtier. The woman had the build of a fighter, all muscles and mass. But her face was heart-shaped, her lips curled into a perpetual smile, and her short halo of snowy hair looked soft as downy feathers. Her eyes were a startling shade of golden orange as they stared into Cirelle's.

"You have a name?" Shai cocked her head at Cirelle.

"Ibrafel. Ibra." Cirelle deliberately kept her voice small and airy. Here, she was not a princess, just a stupid piece of arm candy in a shimmering golden dress and a serpent's mask.

"Good to meet ya." Shai grinned and tossed back the rest of

her drink. "Well, I'm off to find a front-row seat for when the sparks start flying."

After the woman walked away, Cirelle whispered to Ellian, "Is it really going to be that bad?"

He hesitated. "Maybe."

Cirelle suppressed a shiver. "Are we actually in danger?"

"Not today," he shook his head. "Guest rights keep them from doing us harm. Adaleth will almost certainly have something to say about your presence, though. The queen will make an appearance, but not much more than that. She's grooming Adaleth for the throne, and he will take the lead."

Cirelle took another sip of her water. More faerie laws, rules and bureaucracy knotted into a tangle. Interrupting her thoughts, Ellian set his glass aside. It vanished as soon as it touched the table. The music stopped and shifted into a delicate melody, gentle and flowing like a river of sound. "Well, our goal is to be seen. Let's dance." He held out a hand.

Cirelle stared at that dusty gray hand for three long seconds. Her heart stopped, then lurched back to life.

"I—" she stammered, forgetting her role in the small surge of panic that jolted through her. "I don't know the steps."

Ellian's eyes twinkled with mischief, his glamour dropping as they sparkled cerulean for the briefest of seconds. "Yes, you do."

She glanced out at the dancers, a host of sidhe swirling and dipping, spinning gracefully in an elaborate pattern. She *did* know this dance. Not as if she'd read it in a book, either. Rather, her feet knew the steps as if she'd learned and practiced it for years.

The realization struck her. A tingle of warmth and magic had stung her fingertips as Ellian pressed the tiny dancing statuette into her hand. "The figurine," she breathed. "That's what it does."

"Yes."

Cirelle shook her head, hesitant to accept the gift of knowledge. "What is the price?"

His lips curled into an insufferably smug grin. "Dance with me."

She bit her lip, holding in the angry retort she wanted to spit at him. That old, familiar fury boiled inside her. *Damned faerie tricks.* But she had a role to play. So instead she plastered an insipid grin on her face and placed her water glass on the table, where it disappeared. With a deliberate effort, Cirelle glanced down shyly and took Ellian's hand.

As always, it was warm in her own. Did she imagine the faint trembling in those fingers? His eyes were clouded gray once again, his face back to the indecipherable expression and slight superior grin that was his mask. Her dress tinkled softly as the scales brushed one another. Heart thudding against her ribs, Cirelle followed Ellian as he wove his way through the crowd and claimed a space for them amidst the other dancers.

Sharp gazes followed them. Cirelle felt like a mouse among vipers. Her heart stuttered as Ellian guided her into the steps of this dance. A disdainful snort behind Cirelle made her first step a stumble. Without missing a beat, Ellian slipped an arm around her waist to catch her, twirling her into another step.

"Ignore them," he said, pulling her in close again, his breath soft against her ear. "Just focus on the music." His warm hand slid down her bared spine. A flush crept into her cheeks and a small tremor rippled along her skin.

The eyes behind Ellian's cobalt-feathered mask flickered a brilliant emerald. His smile faltered in an expression she recognized. *Worry.*

Ellian's fingers tightened on her own as she led him into the next move. She had agreed to play this part, and she would do so. To all eyes, she should seem merely a bit of mindless fluff enamored of her sidhe escort.

So, she danced. The cascading melody made her steps light as they slid through the weaving patterns. It was like riding a current of water, completely unlike the stately gallanads and baliterres she knew.

Cirelle's heartbeat pulsed in time to the rhythm as her feet led her where they wanted to go. The music flowed through her and she forgot the stares. Ellian played his part well enough, a small smile painted on his lips as they whirled on the dance floor.

Then, the song faded, trailing into silence. It was replaced by a low, steady thrum like a heartbeat, dark and haunting. It tugged on something in Cirelle's chest, a sensation she couldn't name. A heavy stone settled in her stomach as the other pairs drew close, swaying to the deep, sultry rhythm.

Ellian's hand shifted in hers, his fingers interlacing with her own. Cirelle was certain he could feel the racing pulse in her fingertips. Her cheeks were aflame. The steps that accompanied this beat would have left Arravene courtiers gasping in shock.

She couldn't withdraw now, not without breaking the role she'd agreed to play. So Cirelle let Ellian pull her into his arms as her feet slipped into the slow steps. A writhing and serpentine set of movements left their legs twining around each other then untangling, their bodies pressing together in ways that would have been obscene in her court.

A teasing smirk lingered on Ellian's lips, a glimmer of pale blue in his eyes. So arrogant, so sure that he knew what lay in her heart. But she also knew what lay in his.

I've dreamed about you.

Cirelle was not prey. She was a hunter, too, and she could make him ache for her.

She gave herself over to the sultry melody with abandon,

let her hands wander as their bodies touched in places that kindled a fire in her belly. She was rewarded with a shudder, his eyes widening and that smile vanishing. His lips parted, pupils dilating. But those eyes remained frustratingly gray, the color of river stones.

It wasn't enough. Cirelle was determined to *win* this game. She turned in his embrace, guiding his hands to her waist as her hips swayed to the steady beat of those pulsing drums. Her memory flashed back to that moment she'd dared not mention ever again, that brief lapse in judgment when she'd kissed him.

When she'd asked for more than that.

He'd turned her down then, but tonight Ellian's eyes told another story.

His hands slid across her stomach, making the scales of her dress chime against one another. Every move of her body made its own music, like tiny golden bells. His hands on her hips, Cirelle faced him once more, pressing her palms flat against his chest. The silk of his jacket was cool beneath her fingertips. Her smile widened, making silent promises with her eyes. Her hands slid down his chest and slipped under the lower edge of the jacket, only the thin fabric of his shirt separating their skin where her fingertips rested above the waistline of his trousers.

When his glamour slipped and those eyes burned violet, Cirelle laughed, a vicious sound she'd never made before.

In answer, his hands tightened against her lower back, where the dress lay open to bare her skin. Ten spots of pressure, of warmth. Her own breathing stopped as she imagined the grip of those hands elsewhere.

Ellian grinned, and the game was on.

It was both wonderful and awful at the same time. His feather-light fingertips trailed lines of teasing warmth down her bared spine. She wrapped herself around him, writhing in his arms until he made a small, involuntary sound that sparked a shivery need in her body.

By the time the song ended, Cirelle's veins burned with fire and she was coated in Ellian's smoke and honey scent. His eyes blazed a brilliant purple, pupils dilated and his glamour in tatters.

Then the melody died away, slipping into another song of whirling steps and light feet. The sudden shift in music woke her from this game gone much too far. All too suddenly, Cirelle was brutally aware of the crowd that witnessed their display.

She sucked in a long breath, stepping out of his arms. Ellian let her go.

"Water," she blurted, her cheeks burning as she realized how many faeries now gaped, aghast at the sylvan whore Ellian had brought to their party.

Those stares followed her all the way to the refreshment table, where she gripped the pitcher with a shaking hand and poured a glass, downing it in one long swallow. Cirelle wanted to dump the whole thing over her head to cool the flames deep inside.

⟡

PRINCE ADALETH'S GLEAMING BLACK BOOTS clicked on the colorless stone floor of the gathering chamber as he paced before the row of mortal thralls. They stood silent, their bodies swathed in gowns of ephemeral fabric as white as Adaleth's shimmering hair. A dozen pairs of eyes stared blankly forward, empty and insipid.

Adaleth's lip curled in subtle disgust. Humans. Certainly not his preference, but one must keep one's court happy, after all.

Another ball, another festival. The Grand Hunt this time,

but a few months hence there would be another celebration just as dull. And more after that, an endless chain of parties until the end of time.

Adjusting his collar, the prince waved at the thralls. "These will do," he told the wrangler.

The man blinked his dark, beady eyes. A sidhe, but not their most shining specimen. Hence why he stood here herding entranced humans, rather than entering the ballroom right now. "All of them?"

Adaleth gave a nod, followed by a bored little shrug. "Why not?" After all, there was no shortage of mortals eager to bargain with a faerie. Greedy for wealth, for power, or merely desperate to survive, they came flocking to the sidhe like brainless moths to flame. Meivre could easily collect more of them to keep his people entertained.

The wrangler bowed his agreement and ushered the thralls into line behind the prince. Music already drifted down the corridor from the ballroom. The same songs, the same dances. Even the promise of the darker pleasures that would end tonight's revel could not assuage his ennui.

Still, it was the duty of their future king to make his presence known before his court. To smile, to satisfy their indulgences, and most importantly, to remind them of his authority. Within the century, his mother would abdicate, and it would be left to him to hold the Unseelie Court in his icy fist. But first, the party.

As he turned away from the thralls, the queen swept into the room, her golden eyes aflame with anger. "He's here," she hissed, her hands curled into furious claws.

Adaleth blinked. "Who?"

"*Him.*"

Her meaning sank in. Adaleth's stomach flopped over, though he couldn't have said if it was dread or anticipation.

It didn't particularly matter which, however. It was something visceral and real, a rare sensation that rippled down through his bones.

So Ellian has returned.

The virulent trickle of loathing that crept into Adaleth's heart was both dizzying and welcome. Now the evening would be a true challenge. He hadn't even realized how thoroughly he'd missed Ellian's participation in the cat-and-mouse games of his court. A slow, cruel grin curved his mouth.

His mother's eyes narrowed. "Don't do anything rash."

Adaleth cast a pointed glance down at the queen's hands, now clenched into fists. "Me? I'm not the one that stabbed him at a full-moons party, mother."

She backhanded him. Though it rattled his skull, Adaleth responded with a bitter, crystalline laugh.

"I'm not just your mother, but your queen," she reminded him, not for the first time. "I'd have another sidhe's head for that."

"But not your dear son's." Adaleth rubbed his cheek and settled his diadem more firmly on his head.

At her burning glare, Adaleth backed down. He may often toe the line, but even he knew when to stop pushing. Still, his heartbeat pounded just a little harder as he took his mother's arm and walked down the hall.

Ellian. His most treasured rival. A shiver skittered over his skin, and he smiled once more.

Chapter Twenty-Nine

HALFWAY THROUGH her second glass of water, Cirelle realized she'd lost Ellian among the crowd. She scanned the room for any sign of him while the dancers whirled past, but the otherworldly, foggy quality of the ballroom made her head spin. Figures danced past her in an array of clothing: gowns, suits, and ensembles that were neither or both.

As she scanned the crowd for Ellian, her gaze landed on Shai. She danced with the golden-haired sidhe Cirelle had seen in Ellian's antechamber before. Issen. His eyes met Cirelle's, glanced around, and widened. He said something to Shai. She nodded, then left him to approach Cirelle.

"You lost, sylvan?" Then, in a whisper,, she added, "Play along, or one of these jerks will come find you instead. Care for a dance?" Shai's eyes were far too kind for her brash energy, a pulsing power that pressed against Cirelle's skin. She smelled dangerous, like old leather, sawdust, and soured red wine.

What to do? Ellian had treated the woman as an ally, and he was all too noticeably absent. If Cirelle declined, who would find her next? A thread of worry uncurled in her stomach, and she nodded. "Yes."

Shai led her out to the floor. She was half a head taller than Cirelle and built entirely of muscle. Her ruffled dress bared corded athlete's arms.

The introductory steps of this dance were careful, sedate, until the song exploded into a whirling dervish of music. It was a merry one, all rapid spins and quick footwork. Despite the metal scales of her gown, Cirelle's skirt flared out around her legs as she twirled, the slit up her left thigh baring more skin than she'd ever be allowed to show at home. It was thrilling, exquisitely reckless.

Shai was not as graceful a partner as Ellian had been, her motions full of power more than elegance. She grinned as she led Cirelle about the floor, heedless of the stares.

"So, why ask me to dance?" Cirelle confronted Shai breathlessly between steps. She kept her tone bubbly, air-headed. "They're all watching. Don't you care?"

With a grin, Shai spun her out so quickly that a brief wave of dizziness washed over Cirelle. "Nope."

Cirelle laughed. "Where is Ellian, anyway?"

Shai pointed with a grimace. "Over there."

Ellian stood within a cluster of other sidhe, barely visible through the misty haze. They ringed him like wolves, harrying him with mindless chatter. His mouth was frozen in a lackluster smile, that tightness around his eyes giving away his irritation. Cirelle knew the look of that group, the backbiting and two-faced smiles of the gentry. Apparently, it was no different in Faerie.

Cirelle caught Ellian's gaze for one frozen moment. His eyes widened, flickering to Shai and back. A glimmer of relief washed over his features before Cirelle twirled away.

Then the dance ended, the music faded to silence, and the crowd hushed as a set of large doors on the far side of the ballroom opened. They were elevated on a low dais with wide steps leading down to the dance floor.

A pair of figures emerged. The queen stood tall and elegant. Her crown of jagged crystal nestled atop silver hair, her dark lips stained with a crimson so deep it was nearly black. Even from this distance, Cirelle could see a cold gleam in her amber eyes.

At the queen's elbow stood a sidhe with skin of palest blue like a frozen winter sky. His white hair held the soft sheen of a pearl, but his features were sharp as jagged ice. Lambent green eyes were stark in his face, a firefly's glow. His garb was the opposite of his mother's, an inky onyx jacket embroidered and beaded with glossy black stones. His head bore a silver band with a single row of obsidian stones running along its length.

Both unmasked. Through the strange haze in the air, they looked otherworldly, like ghosts emerging from mist.

Behind them stood perhaps a dozen figures, wearing sheer garments of ghostly white. Humans... They remained perfectly still, their eyes hollow and empty.

As one, every sidhe in the room knelt, even Shai. Cirelle followed suit, casting her gaze downward. A part of her rankled at the motion, somewhere deep beneath the fear. Cirelle had never knelt to anyone in her life, not even her parents. In Arraven, a princess curtsied to a king but did not kneel. But here, she faced the queen and the prince of the sidhe. In this guise, she was nothing but a mere commoner. A sylvan.

Her pulse raced. She and Ellian were glaringly conspicuous, in his brilliant blue jacket and her glittering golden gown. She stared resolutely at the pale floor.

"Rise," the queen said, her voice still cheerfully sweet.

Shai stood and offered a hand to Cirelle. Cirelle took it gratefully, hauling herself to her feet.

Dread churning within her, she dared a glance up, only to

meet the prince's unsettling green eyes. He stared as if he could turn her inside out with a glance and spill all her secrets on the floor.

Shai grunted lightly beside her, and Cirelle realized she'd gripped the woman's hand too tightly. Immediately, she let go, murmuring a quick "sorry" as quietly as she could. Shai returned the apology with a small smile.

The sidhe stood silent while the royals regarded the crowd. The prince's gaze hesitated on someone toward the back of the room—Ellian. It was impossible not to notice that Cirelle was costumed as the beast of Ellian's heraldry. It marked her as his, completely and without question.

Her cheeks burned.

After a few heart-stopping moments of silence, the Queen waved a hand and the music started again. She remained on the dais, but her son descended the steps to mingle.

"I'd find Ellian if I were you," Shai muttered. "And fast." The prince cut a path through the crowd, headed unerringly for Cirelle.

She fled as quickly as she could without running. The crowd before her tightened, sidhe drawing closer to bar her path, while those behind stepped aside to let the prince through.

He caught up with her in matter of moments, staring with those cold, empty eyes.

"Whose pet has disgraced my party?" He gave her a grin that would have been appropriate on a cat before it pounced on a helpless mouse. His voice was absent of any kindness or gentleness, a vast abyss of empty space.

He reeked of magic, if it could be called a scent. Sang with it, if it were a sound. It hung heavy in the air and danced along Cirelle's skin, raising goosebumps on her bare arms. She'd been awed the first time she met Ellian, but this faerie stirred a primal part of her brain, a deep urge to run. He did not fill her with wonder like a brilliant sunset.

No, Prince Adaleth was a carefully contained hurricane, a cyclone, an earthquake.

Like all sidhe, he had his own aroma as well. The frigid air of winter, mingling the fragrance of damp leaves with the crisp scent of half-melted snow.

That angry beast inside Cirelle wanted to snap back at the prince, to stand her ground and lash out at his sheer arrogance. But with the weight of his presence pressing down on her, she couldn't. Neither was that the role chosen for her.

She curtsied and said in a trembling voice that was only half playacting, "I came here with Ellian, Your Highness." There would be no use in lying. The whole point was to be seen.

The time to play her part had come, the test of her skill. *A liar and a spy.* "You are so lovely." She tried to appear awestruck, watching the prince from beneath her lashes. "If you'll forgive me saying so, Your Highness."

The prince didn't seem quelled by such flattery, and she hadn't expected him to be. He did dismiss her compliment with a scowl. He gestured for her to follow as he swept past. "Come."

He didn't glance back.

Ellian awaited their approach, the crowd that had harried him only moments before now conspicuously absent. Though the music still played, no one danced. Instead, they watched the coming confrontation with rapt eyes, some clutching wine glasses or plates of food as if this were the evening's entertainment. And perhaps it was.

"It seems I've found a stray," Adaleth said in that hollow voice, staring up at Ellian. Despite the difference in height, it was all too obvious who held the power here.

Ellian's eyes sparked with defiance, though their silver glamour was firmly in place. Yet he bowed his head. "Your Highness."

"It is unfortunate enough we were forced to let you enter the palace again. But this is the last time you will defile it by treating a creature like this as a guest." The prince made a move to shove Cirelle forward and a surge of panic spiked. His hand would stop, unable to touch her, and their game would be up. If the prince felt so strongly about a sylvan, how would it anger him to know a glamoured human had guested in his palace?

So Cirelle stumbled backward a step, deliberately meeting Adaleth's hand. She'd expected his touch to be icy cold, but his handprint burned into her skin. With a sudden motion, he shoved her forward. Her arms flailed and Ellian pulled her into his embrace and his smoky scent.

"Lovely party," Ellian told the prince, voice dripping with cold venom. It was a tone she'd heard only once before, when Orwe had been dropped at his door. "But I think my guest should retire for the evening." He traced soothing circles against Cirelle's back with one hand, chin resting atop her head.

"The party is just beginning." Adaleth's voice was polite with a dark amusement. Cirelle dared a glance over her shoulder. The prince's bared teeth were anything but a smile. "You're both welcome to stay and participate in the festivities." His gaze flickered toward the glassy-eyed humans who were each being escorted down the dais by a sidhe. Vapid smiles adorned their faces as they swayed to the beat in the arms of the fae. One man's sidhe partner dug sharpened nails into his back hard enough to draw blood. He didn't so much as flinch.

Cirelle shuddered and looked back down at the polished stone floor.

Ellian didn't look away from the prince. "I'll return shortly, Your Highness." Poison in those words, a deep hatred seething beneath the surface. Ellian turned Cirelle in his arms, giving Adaleth a small bow before herding her out of the hall.

This time, the other sidhe parted for them, but not without a myriad of unusual expressions. Cirelle had composed herself enough to put on her bland mask again, eyes downcast and body trembling.

At the exit to the ballroom, an attendant stood outside the door. His gray tunic bore a crest, a single drooping snowdrop emerging from a crown. White stag's antlers crowned his head and short silvery fur coated him all over. "This way, sir."

Cirelle tried to still her jangling nerves as they followed the faerie deeper into the palace. She could not shake the sight of that human man's blood welling up against his skin like gleaming garnets.

Ellian remained silent, though his jaw clenched tightly while they walked. He refused to meet her eyes until they were shown to their room and the attendant left.

"I have to go back," Ellian told her without emotion. "Stay here, please."

Cirelle swallowed a heavy stone in her throat. "What's going to happen to those people?"

Ellian's gaze slid away from her. "That depends on the whims of my queen and her son."

Fear plucked at her. "We have to help them."

"We can't."

"How... how did they get like that?"

His eyes grew dark. "They made the wrong bargain." He swallowed and shook his head again. "Wait here. I'll be back as soon as I can."

The door slid shut, and Cirelle was left alone.

Chapter Thirty

ELLIAN WISHED HE COULD forget what he'd once suffered at the hands of Adaleth's court.

Tonight, he walked back into that ballroom to endure it all over again. Though it chafed to leave the princess alone in this empty place, it was far better than allowing her to witness what was about to happen.

At the door to the ballroom, he hesitated, a slithering sensation in his gut begging him to flee. The antlered servant tugged the doors open and it was too late to turn back. Ellian straightened his shoulders, swallowed his good sense, and walked through the door.

The foggy quality of the room had grown thicker, distorting the light refracted from the chandeliers like a fever dream. Sometimes, the sidhe preferred dark corners for their debauchery, but tonight only the misty haze concealed their depravity. He ignored the sounds coming from the human thralls. He could do nothing for them. He'd tried once and the consequences for both the humans and Ellian himself had been grievous enough he dared not make another attempt.

"Ellian," the prince said coolly, gliding up beside him. "So eager to return to our court. What price are you willing to pay to stay this time?"

Ellian let his glamour slip. He knew what color his eyes would reveal. Crimson hatred. "Enough games. We both know the cost. Throw me to your courtiers, your wolves." His voice dipped into a growl. "You'd better enjoy the spectacle while you can. When I win the Hunt, you'll need my leave to so much as touch me ever again."

The prince grinned, a slow and predatory smile. "We'll see about that."

ℰℱ

CIRELLE WAITED.

And waited.

She paced the length of the chamber. It was a spacious room, with a bathing tub behind a screen and an attached privy closet. A tall wardrobe sat in one corner, holding an assortment of fine clothing in colorless shades. Everything in this place lacked even a splash of vibrancy. The room's decor was a sea of gray and white.

Cirelle poked around in the drawers of a vanity table, discovering nothing save the usual amenities and a small pile of jewelry. She flopped down into one of the two chairs in a small sitting area. Her eyes lingered on the single bed while her stomach turned somersaults at the thought of sharing it. Hopeless to sit still, she got up and swapped her heavy serpent's dress for a sleeping gown from the wardrobe. Even it was made of fine silk.

Her pacing resumed.

After half an eternity, Ellian slipped through the door. His pupils were wide, his skin flushed a deeper gray. Cirelle cast him a wary look. "The buttons on your jacket are uneven."

A sudden flare of fuchsia in his eyes, then a pale green. He stared down at the floor as he unbuttoned the jacket.

"Ellian." Cirelle was startled at the horror in her own voice. "What did you do?"

His distant mask returned. "What I must." He draped the coat on a nearby chair, slipping the serpent brooch from the lapel and turning it over in his hands. His eyes were locked on the small bit of gold. "Please, let's just sleep."

That rare word again, *please*. The second time he'd said it tonight.

"Tell me," she demanded. "Did you hurt those people?"

"No." He shook his head. "I did not touch them, but that's all I want to say about them." A tremor lingered in his voice. He set the pin on the nightstand and began sifting through the items in the wardrobe.

She wanted to press him, to claw his secrets out of him, but he wouldn't answer. He could not tell a lie; he'd done no harm to those poor souls. That would have to be enough.

All other thoughts fled as Cirelle stared at the bed and its embroidered satin coverlet. Ellian's gaze drifted toward the mattress, then met hers. Heart hammering, Cirelle slid between the sheets.

He plucked a set of loose drawstring trousers from a drawer and set them aside. When he unlaced his shirt and pulled it up over his head, Cirelle rolled over to face the other way. She ignored the tense knot in her belly. And she most certainly didn't notice the slithering sound of fabric as it fell to the floor.

His footsteps barely made any noise as he crossed to the corners of the room to extinguish the cold blue sconces. He circled to the light on her side of the bed. Shirtless, the inhumanly gray hue of his bare back seemed even more surreal. The cold light made his hair gleam vividly blue, the color of the deepest ocean. The glint of the gold hoops at the tips of his ears were like stars reflected in that dark sea.

Ellian extended a hand to douse the light and she watched the muscles shift under his skin. He brushed a fingertip along the bottom of the sconce, and the light snapped off like a candle suddenly snuffed. Ellian turned and watched her in the dimness, his face and bare chest illuminated by the single remaining sconce. The trousers were tied low on his hips, beneath the planes of his stomach.

There was something thrillingly indecent about this, she had to admit. The forbidden so often flavored her relationships; first the delicious possible scandal of Briere, then the outright thrill of her wild, one-night tryst with that soldier boy. Now even more dangerously, here she lay tempted by a sidhe. The hint of danger was like the bit of hot, peppery spice in Cook Jana's cinnamon buns.

Ellian continued to meet her gaze, his lips falling into a lopsided smirk. "I can't help but ask what is going through your head, with your eyes so far away."

"Nothing," she muttered, burrowing deeper into the blankets.

He circled the bed to darken the light on his side of the room and she rolled over again to face him. The mattress jostled as he slid under the blankets and her stomach churned at the scents that wafted from him. A myriad of strange aromas. The smell of other sidhe. He moved closer.

"Cirelle?" His voice was a scant whisper.

Her heartbeat quickened. "Yes?"

"That dance earlier," he began. "Was that just for show, or for your own pleasure?"

A silence fell, neither of them moving. Her eyes closed

again. She was keenly aware of his proximity, a gap she could bridge so easily.

She wondered what he tasted like.

The dance tonight had left a tightness in her belly that still lingered underneath her frustration and fear. "Both," she admitted, her voice faint.

His laugh brushed something deep inside her, something tempting. "I know." The coverlet rustled as he pulled away.

Cirelle rolled over, yanking the blanket with her. She wondered if the sudden pang she felt was relief or regret.

Without warning, the exhaustion of the day smothered Cirelle, pressing heavy on her chest and drowning out everything else. Her fear, her fury... all shoved aside as sleep weighed down her eyelids. In that state of half-dreaming, she thought she heard him reply.

"For what it's worth," he whispered in that voice like velvet, "I liked it, too."

Chapter Thirty-One

THE NEXT MORNING, Cirelle awoke to sunlight filtering through the sheer curtains of the sole window in their room, over the headboard of their bed. Weariness dragged at her. She'd grown so accustomed to awakening in the night hours. Morning looked strange to her now, details too crisp and too vividly golden.

Ellian had stolen all the blankets in the middle of the night, and Cirelle shivered in the morning chill. Summer had begun to settle in, but the cold stone walls of this palace leeched all the warmth from her bones.

She tugged on one corner of the blankets, but Ellian sleepily pulled them back. Cirelle huffed out a sigh and pondered her faerie companion while he slept.

All her life, Cirelle had been trapped inside the cage of royalty, beating her wings against the bars to be free. It seemed Ellian was on the other side of those bars, a pariah of cultured sidhe society. Yet he reveled in his position. Their costumes had been recklessly blue and gold among a sea of gray ghosts. And he'd made an equally contentious choice of companion, the equivalent of Cirelle bringing a cockroach to a tea party.

Then he'd pushed her aside and left her to wait in this cold room while he engaged in more schemes. Unease flitted through her. His expression had been so haunted when he walked back through those doors.

None of last night's tension lingered in Ellian's sleeping face now. In the wan morning light, he looked... normal. Vulnerable, perhaps, with that smiling mouth slack with sleep and heavy brows neither arched in mockery nor furrowed in frustration. His hair had tangled overnight, spilling across the pillow in unruly midnight waves.

"If you're going to stare," Ellian mumbled without opening his eyes, "you could at least compliment me."

Cirelle jerked away. A flush of embarrassment washed over her.

As she slipped out of the bed, the shimmering white stone of the floor chilled her feet. A pair of slippers and a sleeveless gown of pale gray chiffon with a silver belt lay in the wardrobe. It was a gauzy garment, floating through the air when she moved. Like her dress last night, there was a slit up to her thigh on one side. A current faerie fashion, apparently.

She cast a quick, furtive glance at Ellian. His back remained to her, so she dressed quickly. The gown was loose, but she belted the chain around it anyway.

Cirelle grimaced when she caught her reflection in the long mirror beside the wardrobe. It was still shocking to see her skin a pale, mottled gray-brown rather than its usual gold. Her hair was a mass of tangles, even to the touch when she tried to rake her fingers through it. How deeply did that glamour run, to fool all her senses? For a frightening moment, Cirelle wondered if he'd truly shifted her form. If underneath all this, she was still even *her* anymore. She touched one fingertip to the pointed ends of her ears, and they felt solid.

"Are you quite finished?" Ellian asked from the bed, still facing away.

She rolled her eyes, though he could not see it. "Yes."

Ellian sat up and stretched, pulling the muscles of his stomach taut. The rosy light of dawn gave it the illusion of a faded brown rather than colorless gray. He tilted his head and smiled, his eyes a pale lavender-blue hue.

She swallowed hard and turned away. The thought of confronting that violet in his eyes left her with a conflicting swirl of emotions she didn't want to ponder. Instead, she picked up her discarded sleepwear and hung it in the wardrobe.

She already missed Ellian's home, the polished wood and plush rugs, even the darkness. Experimentally, she walked to the sconce by the door and ran her fingertip beneath it as Ellian had the night before. It hummed beneath her hand, flaring to light. Well, one mystery solved. She'd never quite figured it out back at Ellian's manor and had been too proud to ask.

Behind her, the sheets rustled. The thump of fabric hitting the floor made her heart beat faster. Cirelle resolutely stared toward the door.

A minute later, he spoke, the smile obvious in his voice. "I'm clothed. Though you didn't seem averse to admiring the show last night."

Cirelle whirled on him and rolled her eyes.

Ellian's ensemble was as monochromatic as her own. It made the blue of his hair brighter, the gleam of a sapphire in the sunlight. The jacket was purest white silk, flocked with velvet in a floral pattern. The deep black trousers were a sharp contrast. He picked up his brooch from last night, the golden heraldry of his feathered serpent with its brilliant blue wings, and pinned it to his breast. It stood out against the snowy velvet, gleaming and impossible to ignore.

"How are the clothes the right size?" she asked.

"They are every size. Guest clothing adapts to the wearer."

"But my dress is loose," she grumbled.

"That's the style of the Unseelie, all flowing and drapes. At least with gowns, anyway." He cocked his head while he ran fingers through his hair to loosen the tangles, eyes glimmering blue as the Nycenine ocean. "Why? Are you saddened no one gets to admire those tempting curves?"

Cirelle grimaced. "You ruin everything." She knew she should play along, adopt her role more fully, but couldn't seem to bite back the words.

Ellian laughed again, tugging at his sleeves so the lace trim brushed the back of his hand. "You can wear trousers if you like. There's no rule that says you must wear a dress."

"Would you wear a gown?"

"I could. No one would bat an eye. But I rather like jackets."

"And I like dresses," she said. "Just not these flimsy ones." Cirelle slipped on the equally insubstantial faerie slippers with a frown. "So, what's the schedule today?"

Ellian smoothed his jacket with a grin. "First, there is a performance to attend. I think you're going to like this one."

"What is it?"

"Oh, but that would ruin the surprise." He held out an arm, and Cirelle took it with a sigh.

The palace was beautiful in its icy way. Every wall was carved to depict scenes from faerie history or myth. Some of them seemed to match tales she'd read in her books. Eldemn's conquest of the selkies. The marriage of the Autumn King to his annual bride. Cirelle had little time to admire the art, though. They converged with other sidhe along the way, a small herd of fae headed in the same direction.

The faeries gave them a wide berth, as if she crawled with

vermin. So, she 'accidentally' stumbled a few times, lurching toward a nearby sidhe before Ellian caught her. The horrified looks on their faces were worth it.

Then, without warning, Ellian spun her toward a wall and his lips were on her neck, beneath her ear. She almost shoved him away but stopped herself at the last moment. *All a part of the act.*

"I'm sorry," he murmured, so quietly none of the other sidhe would hear. "But Agdarr is down that hallway opposite, where he isn't supposed to be." Agdarr. One of Ellian's allies, the spriggan.

The other sidhe stared at her, their mouths agape, not a single glance spared for that side hall. Cirelle, though, could clearly see a small figure hunched in front of a doorway, hands fiddling with small tools wedged into the lock on a door.

She wrapped her arms around Ellian. If he needed a show, she would make one. Her skin felt tingly and flushed all over. Ellian nipped her throat lightly, and her hands gripped his jacket so hard her knuckles ached. His lips pressed gently over the spot he'd just bitten. When his tongue caressed her skin, Cirelle gasped out loud, a line of lightning jolting from that spot down through her core.

Agdarr, finished with his work, glanced up and met her gaze, then hurriedly put away his tools and scurried back into the main corridor. Now just a servant in the palace's silver livery. Practically invisible.

She turned Ellian's head aside, ostensibly to nibble on his earlobe. She whispered, "He's done."

Still, Ellian's hands slid from her waist slowly and his eyes burned a fierce purple. She'd asked him once if he could glamour his eyes to show a different color, to mislead. "No," he'd replied. "It's common knowledge what my eyes show. I can conceal it entirely, but to portray otherwise is apparently considered a lie by whatever curse constrains us."

So, she knew the violet in his gaze was utterly real as they continued down the hall, seemingly oblivious to the rest of the sidhe. Again, her stomach flopped, a war between desire and uncertainty.

Along the way, they passed by the open doors to a music salon. Cirelle cast a longing glance at the silver harp sitting in one corner, but they were ushered into the room next door instead. Here, comfortable chairs were set in a broad circle. Seats clustered in groups of three or four, with enough space between them to allow a person to slip through. Ellian guided Cirelle into theirs.

Small tables lay beside some of the chairs, filled with dainty trays of pastries and pots of tea. Cirelle looked at the food with a sinking stomach. She was allowed to eat nothing here, not in this guise.

Ellian took her hand in both of his and she leaned her head on his shoulder. Their performance wasn't done yet; she must continue to draw the stares and ire of the sidhe so Ellian's spies could accomplish their tasks. Spies like the Ulim. Cirelle tried hard not to let her gaze flicker toward the tiny, feathery wings she'd seen fluttering as one of the creatures wriggled under a tapestry.

After their display in the hallway, the other sidhe already stared and whispered. Some of them were equally as amorous, but they weren't sylvans. Lowly, less than sidhe.

With a soft giggle, Cirelle rested her free hand lightly on Ellian's forearm. His lip twitched, the beginnings of a small smile squashed down quickly.

Whatever he'd been about to say next, it was interrupted by Queen Ayre and Prince Adaleth's entrance. Adaleth was a winter scene in white and gray and faded pale blue, save those eerie peridot eyes. Ayre was resplendent beside him in a gown dripping with white beads like droplets of ice. Her crimson lips were stark in her face and her golden wolf's eyes gazed out on the crowd with cool indifference.

Everyone bowed their heads for a few moments.

The queen and her son sat in chairs along the innermost ring of the circle. More intriguing were the handful of sidhe in the seats nearest them. Ellian had briefed Cirelle on the Inner Court before the mission started, five sidhe who acted as confidants and advisors to the prince and the queen.

The two twin men were Rhael and Sholle, with brawny frames and skin almost a human shade of pale, shimmering gold. Thatches of unruly hair bore the yellow-green hue of Nycenine grapes. The one seated next to the prince glowered at the floor, while the other smiled warmly and boldly at the queen. Cirelle didn't know which was which.

Beside them sat a tall and curvaceous woman with berry-colored hair and skin like the whitest lily petals. She glanced around with a casual interest. Ysven. Her hand rested possessively on the arm of one of the twins.

Next was Meivre, a petite female sidhe with wide eyes and a charming face like a doll. She was the pale pink of cherry blossoms, her hair an amethyst cascade. Yawning with boredom, she admired her plum-lacquered fingernails with an appraising eye.

Lastly was someone Cirelle recognized all too well. Tallia, her froth of aqua curls bobbing as she laughed at something one of the twins had said.

Cirelle next caught the gaze of a black-haired sidhe woman with dusty-lavender skin and tattered clothing, the one who'd stared at her with such canny scrutiny at the ball. She was not a part of the Inner Court, sitting on the opposite side of the circle, her expression grim. Her sharp black eyes pierced Cirelle's and narrowed in suspicion. Something about her put Cirelle in mind of a rat, with her long nose and those dark eyes in such a narrow face.

Shai sauntered up and took a seat in the chair beside Cirelle, holding a plate full of pastries. "Morning," she greeted them with a grin. Issen stood behind her, his expression serene.

While they waited for the show to start, the other sidhe chatted and mingled amongst themselves, but now pointedly ignored Cirelle, Ellian, Issen, and Shai. The warrior seemed oblivious, engaging them both in idle chitchat. Shai ate with relish, speaking before she'd finished chewing. Her hands gestured wildly while she regaled Cirelle with stories of her journeys to the mortal realm, and her smiles were both genuine and frequent.

Cirelle couldn't help but return the sidhe's grin while biting her tongue to avoid commenting on the human world. Once, Shai mentioned Arraven, and it was a struggle not to reveal the chord of homesickness it struck.

"Shai," Issen sighed once, wiping his fingers delicately on a napkin. "Please don't speak with your mouth full."

She glowered at him. "At least I enjoy my food. You act like it's a burden."

"I enjoy it." Issen took a small bite, chewed, and swallowed with a smile. "Mmm."

Shai rolled her eyes and returned to chatting with Cirelle, pointedly ignoring Issen's reprimand.

All the while, Cirelle did not forget to brush her hands through Ellian's hair, to let him lean in and whisper something in her ear. *A show, nothing more*, she reminded herself as a shiver wound its way through her insides.

After a brief time, a dozen faeries entered, none of them sidhe and each carrying an instrument. They wasted no time beginning to play, dancing in serpentine paths around the chairs.

The instruments wove the air itself into dreamlike patterns of sound, the music changing as they moved around the room.

True to their roles, Ellian had taken her hand before the show started, his thumb brushing across the back of her knuckles. Cirelle breathed out a sigh as one of the musicians spun before her, playing a strange, echoing flute.

Cirelle's chest tightened and she blinked back tears. She couldn't even thank him for this. Instead, she lifted their entwined hands to her lips, placing a kiss on the back of Ellian's hand. A faint pressure, gone as soon as it started.

His hand tightened. A flutter of warmth twisted her stomach, the frantic brush of a moth's wings.

Chapter Thirty-Two

AFTER THE RECITAL, Ellian led the princess to the selection of competitors for the Hunt. Twenty-three sidhe had thrown their names into the ring, but only five could participate. The Queen would also join, due to ancient custom. Ellian's stomach dropped at that thought, knowing full well what her focus would be.

They filed into the throne room, a space larger than the ballroom but equally colorless and cold. Too many memories tainted the whole of this palace. Just standing here left Ellian nauseated. He cast a glance at Cirelle, a pang of guilt lancing through him at bringing her here. *Necessary*, he reminded himself.

The prince took his throne on a high dais, Queen Ayre seating herself in the larger throne beside him. On either side stood the Inner Court, with expressions ranging from curious to distinctly bored.

Five of them, soon to be six.

Out of place at the base of the dais, a small salcha stood, a fae with skin like birch bark and a wild white tangle of hair. No stranger either. This one bore a familiar round face. Leilarie. Like Agdarr, she blended in perfectly with the assortment of fae that served the court. To the Unseelie sidhe, one salcha looked much like another.

Those who had submitted their names for contention stepped forward, forming a line before Leilarie. She held a tray of tokens, neat rows of dark wooden discs, and peered up at them with eyes like spring leaves.

The salcha's gaze slid past Ellian and Cirelle, but the edge of her lips quirked ever so slightly as she did.

The princess's hand twitched in his own, but she remained silent. Not a peep from her, no suspicion on her face. A liar and a spy, indeed. So far, she'd played her cards perfectly.

As each competitor came forward, they selected a token. Ellian's fingers danced over the tray until Leilarie blinked. He plucked one up and flipped it over to reveal a star painted in gleaming silver. Adaleth hissed. Ellian tossed the prince a smile and a bow that bordered on irreverent. "I'll see you at the Hunt, Your Highness." He bowed also to the queen. "And you, Your Majesty."

A hint of a snarl played on the prince's lips. "At the Hunt, then."

Four other sidhe pulled tokens with stars, Ellian's fellow competitors. Three of them he knew only in passing. Dirilai came last, all pale purple skin and inky black hair. She still insisted on dressing in tattered gowns, thumbing her nose at the rest of the court. His heart gave an uncertain twist at accepting her alliance, but when he'd taken her oath his allies had been few. Her onyx eyes met his, cold and bitter as always before her gaze slipped away.

Ellian tossed his coin back onto the tray and placed a hand lightly on Cirelle's shoulder, bared in her filmy Unseelie gown. Her skin was chilled, and she trembled under his touch. Was it just the warmth of his fingertips, or something else?

He didn't like this uneasy sensation that settled in his gut whenever the princess was near. They'd still never spoken of that moment in her parlor, the offer she'd made to him. No, what she'd *demanded* of him. Still, that lust was safe, simple. The invisible tug between them was far more dangerous.

Kyrinna's letters lay scorched into his mind. *My dearest love,* she'd written, over and over. Never knowing, never wanting to believe Ellian had not felt the same. Not wounded, nor trapped in an enchanted crystal, nor her soul drained dry. None of the typical awful fates that could happen to a mortal in his realm. Lovesick. A painfully mundane injury to take home from Faerie.

His grip tightened around Cirelle's hand, but she didn't turn to look at him.

At the meal, they once again dutifully performed for their rapt audience, a dance of caresses and breath on skin and wandering hands. Only a show, a spectacle, he reminded himself. Except the cool touch of her hand on his thigh was all too solid, and only a scant few of his soft hisses were solely affectations.

Whatever her motivations, a streak of faerie-like cruelty possessed the princess. Was this truly a dance, or had it become a battle? Brazen with her hands and lips and tongue, Cirelle took the lead in this performance, made bold sorties in this skirmish. If it was indeed warfare, he was rapidly losing. When his fingers trailed down her throat and stroked the top of her breast along the edge of her low neckline, it was not just a feint. He pressed right up to the edge of his oath. No sliding hands under my dress, she'd demanded. The fire in her eyes told another story now. If he pushed farther, would she relinquish her command and let his hands wander the rest of her?

Was she still even playing a game? Was he?

And all the while, Adaleth's eyes burned fiercely, his lip curled in a snarl of disgust. A small thrill of victory rippled through Ellian. Another piece of kindling on the flames of his desire, that vindictive satisfaction. Ellian stared down the prince as Cirelle's breath warmed his throat, drinking in the revulsion on Adaleth's features.

By the time they escaped the dining hall to seek their own room, Ellian was wound tight. Too tight. Reason fled as he closed the door. "You little vixen," Ellian hissed, then kissed her.

She tasted sweet, like the berries she'd just eaten so tauntingly, sliding them slowly into her mouth with a sultry little spark in her eyes. With a wordless murmur, she melted into him, her lips yielding to the sweep of his tongue. His heartbeat fluttered, something warmer and softer tangling with his desire.

No.

Abruptly, Ellian stopped and slipped from her arms.

Cirelle's eyes snapped open. "What was that?"

I don't know. "Payback," he growled. "For being such an exceptional tease."

"Isn't that what you wanted?"

Yes. No.

She stepped closer.

Ellian blurted the first vicious thing that sprang to mind. "Don't you have a prince waiting for you back home?"

She looked as if he'd struck her, eyes wide and wounded, sucking in a deep breath.

The sweet taste of strawberries coated his mouth, his tongue, and he hated how much he loved it. "I have to go. There's another event I must attend. Alone."

He wondered how much of Cirelle's play had been false and how much truth. When he left, would she give in to her own desires? Perhaps once she were alone, her hand would dip between parted legs as her mind soaked in thoughts of him. Or now that he'd reminded her of the man's presence, would she instead ache for her lost prince as she pleasured herself?

Ellian shook his head. It didn't matter. He knew where to quench his own lust. Earlier, he'd dreaded tonight's revel. Not anymore.

As the princess still struggled to find words, he stepped out and let the door click shut behind him.

Chapter Thirty-Three

Alone, Cirelle grew restless. Her thoughts drifted. To the kiss, tense and tantalizing and wonderful. To her actions at their meal. She'd been vicious, ruthless, steering this game in a safer direction. Those moths in her belly were terrifying things, but desire? That she could control.

And she had, until he ruined it with that kiss.

She paced, her belly tight with frustrated lust. Maybe she couldn't attend whatever party they held, but she couldn't stay inside these four walls either. She could try to find that music room again, the one with the harp that had called to her. Or perhaps this palace had a garden, a courtyard, *something* to disttract her.

As she made her way through the castle, her hands caressed the cold, hard stone of the wall's sculptures. A scene of seabirds in flight over delicate whorls of ocean waves. A creature half horse and half serpent. A garden of fantastic flowers surrounding a sleeping unicorn.

The corridors twisted and turned, an endless sea of white. She passed other sidhe for a time, but they grew less frequent as she made her way along. Soon, she was well and truly lost in an ominously quiet and empty hallway. A heavy silence hung in the air, thick and stifling.

A door opened beside her.

Adaleth, prince of the sidhe, stepped into the hall and stared at her with eyes like luminescent fungus.

"I—" Cirelle started to say, but the words died in her throat. *He's royalty, and you're just a lowly commoner here*, some tiny, sensible part of her brain shouted. As much as it chafed her to do so, she knelt. "Your Highness," she said meekly.

"Stand," he commanded and Cirelle did, heart in her throat.

His face was impassive, a frozen mask, those sickly green eyes vicious. The prince took a step toward her as she backed into the wall, a sharply-pointed leaf of a sculpted tree poking her neck. He lifted a hand, and time seemed to slow.

He's going to try to touch me. For what, she didn't know. To hit her? To drag her back to her room?

Whatever Adaleth's purpose, his hand would stop before it touched her, hitting that invisible wall, and the ruse she had constructed would all fall apart.

Only one thing to do, one gamble to make.

Cirelle forced her eyes to soften, gave him a sultry little smile, and lifted her hands to press against his chest. The prince stepped back, shock and anger falling over his features.

"I saw you watching me earlier," she said quickly. "I know what you want. What I do for Ellian... you can do to me what he does, if you like."

The prince reached out to clutch her wrist, and she hoped the phrase had been enough.

Stars, let this work.

The prince grasped her wrists tightly with both of his hands and Cirelle almost let out a sigh of relief despite the pain. She'd given him the same permissions Ellian had while she was here, to touch her anywhere her clothing did not cover. Her mortal nature remained hidden.

In a movement so fast it wrenched her shoulder, the prince slammed her arms into the wall, leaning in close. That stone leaf dug painfully into the nape of her neck, but she forced herself to smile.

"Here?" she teased, voice breathy even as her stomach turned.

At the same time, panic screamed in her brain. She'd tossed the dice, relying on his disdain for her. What would she do if her ploy failed, if his hands wandered? Cirelle's skin crawled and nausea threatened.

The prince's green eyes pierced her as his lips formed into a snarl. "Don't even imply such a thing, filth."

Cirelle nearly wept. With a vast effort, she was able to maintain her role and squint at the prince in slight puzzlement. "But you have many non-sidhe in the palace."

Adaleth's face pressed close to her, but it was far from intimate. No, this was the threatening stance of a predator glaring down upon prey. "I employ them, but I do not fuck them," he spat the obscenity with such venom that Cirelle flinched.

He stepped back, yanking Cirelle's arm and tossing her down to the floor. Her hands and knees smacked hard against the stone. The prince ignored her yelp of pain and bit off his words. "To take a plow horse or a hunting hound into your bed is obscene." He stepped over her like she was a fallen log in his path. "What are you doing in the royal wing, so far from your master?"

Cirelle kept her head down, her unruly, glamoured curls masking her face. "I got lost, Your Highness." She didn't need to fake the tremor in her voice.

Adaleth pointed, his eyes full of hate. "Guest rooms are that way. Do not come further into our wing, or there will be consequences." His eyes narrowed. "I should clap you in chains for being so bold as to touch me. If you weren't under the protection of guest rights…" He cocked his head, a small smile on those lips. "Would Ellian find your back as appealing with stripes, I wonder?"

Cirelle shivered and remained silent, hands on the floor and legs curled beside her.

"Unfortunately, as much as I would adore the expression on Ellian's face while he watched your punishment, my obligation as host prevents me from doing those things. Unless you commit further offense after receiving this warning, of course." That voice. How could one speak with such an utter lack of emotion, with the sound of a bitter wind?

She risked a glance up. That hair might have looked like a fluffy snowdrift, but Adaleth was not soft at all. His face was narrower than Ellian's and his lips thinner, with high cheekbones and a jawline sharp as steel. Everything about him was jagged.

He laughed, a brittle sound, tossing his head so the silver diadem caught the pale blue light. Then, with a click of his cloud-gray boots, he strode down the hall. "Go back the way you came, sylvan," he called over his shoulder. "If I catch you in this corridor again, you'll find my threats aren't idle ones."

Cirelle waited until his footsteps faded before pushing herself up off the floor, arms and legs still trembling. She'd come so close to ruining everything, and she'd given that terrifying beast permission to touch her.

The knowledge felt like a beetle skittering over her skin.

Chapter Thirty-Four

CIRELLE MADE HER WAY back toward their guest room on trembling legs.

Ellian had told her that sidhe lost their humanity over centuries. However old the prince was, there wasn't a scrap of it left within him. Those eyes held no warmth, no humor, no compassion.

She shuddered just as she passed the open door to that music salon. Empty. She paused. A harp stood in the corner, shining silver and oh so tempting. Cirelle took a cautious step into the room. She was a guest here, right? This room lay open in the common halls of the castle. Slowly, inexorably, she made her way over to the instrument. As if compelled, she took a seat and strummed a few strings. It was lovely, but the sound was not quite as rich as Ellian's beautiful harp. This one was more crystalline, glittering but hollow.

She practiced a bit of her Faerie Nocturne. Slow and haunting at first, then fretful and full of a nervous anxiety. And underneath it all, a low and sultry counterpoint.

Movement caught Cirelle's eye and her hands abruptly stilled as she glanced up. A sidhe stood in the doorway, leaning against the frame. Meivre, one of the inner court. She looked like a painting, with delicate features and full lips, that waterfall of hair like lavender petals. She was shorter than Cirelle, slimmer, in a gown of sheer black lace that allowed a scandalous amount of her carnation-pink skin to show through.

"Don't stop on my account," she purred with a soft smile. Her voice was lower than Cirelle would have expected with her tiny frame. She entered the room and took a seat nearby, crossing her legs so the slit in her skirt revealed their full, shapely length.

Cirelle cleared her throat. She was alone with one of the prince's most trusted confidants. "I apologize if I'm not supposed to be here. It was empty, and..." She let the sentence trail off.

Meivre shook her head, waving a hand. Her nails, coated in a glossy lacquer the color of rich red grapes, caught the light. "The music salon is open to guests, and that is a rather enthralling melody. Please play on."

"If you insist," Cirelle said, afraid to offend. She recalled the prince's wrath and wondered if such cruelty lingered beneath this woman's elegance. Her fingertips shook a little and she missed a note with a wince, but the sidhe didn't seem to care. "I thought the sidhe attended a party tonight. I'm flattered that you choose to listen to me instead."

Meivre smiled, eyes gleaming in the richest shade of magenta, the color of raspberries. "Many do, but I find today's party... ill-suited to my tastes." She grimaced, the faintest downturn of her sensuous lips. Every move she made seemed practiced, flawless and lovely.

Cirelle let the notes trail away, admitting, "I'm still writing this one. That's as far as it goes."

"Do you know any others? The harp seems an odd choice for a sylvan."

Cirelle's heart skipped a beat. She hadn't thought of that.

Not many harps in the woods, were there? Instead of trying to come up with a lie, she just shrugged. "Do you know much of sylvans, my lady?"

Meivre's mouth curled into a smile, and something dark flickered in her eyes. "Some." She tilted her head coquettishly. "I have... *known* a sylvan or two in my time." A small, silvery laugh.

There was no mistaking her meaning. Apparently not all of Adaleth's court shared his disdain for a lowly non-sidhe faerie.

"We could while away the hours, you and I, while other sidhe fritter away time at that party." She peered at Cirelle through thick, violet lashes.

Cirelle swallowed. Was this faerie trying to seduce her? This beautiful, luxurious creature?

A moment later, reality crashed down. *She just wants to hurt Ellian by taking one of his toys.*

With another light cough, Cirelle shook her head, gazing demurely down at the floor. "Oh, I couldn't dream of stealing any more of your time. You've already honored me with your presence. I should go back to the room to await Ellian's return."

The woman cocked her head again, a soft sigh of disappointment slipping from her. She smoothed her lace skirts as she stood. "His creature entirely, it seems. A pity. Well, I suppose you must, then."

When Meivre left the music room, Cirelle also exited but turned the other direction. Sadly, that left her lost once more. Just as panic began to settle in, an unfamiliar sidhe woman turned a corner and smiled. A rare sign of friendliness.

"You," the faerie said as she approached. "Ellian's guest, right?" She had cute dimples that graced her cheeks when she grinned. "Lost? I'll show you to him."

"Um, he told me I wasn't welcome at this event."

"Nonsense." The woman giggled. "You're his guest. Come."

She gestured for Cirelle to follow and turned to go. After a few steps, she looked over her shoulder to find Cirelle still frozen in place. "Well, what are you waiting for?"

Speechless, Cirelle followed.

The woman laughed as she led the way to a set of doors. "Ah, here we are." She shoved them open and gestured Cirelle inside.

The room was dimly lit, and a smoky haze hung in the air. The pungent smells of dozens of sidhe mingled into one choking scent. There was no music, just a chorus of conversation and mumbles and moans that could have been either pain or pleasure.

As her eyes focused, it became apparent this was not a ballroom. No dancing here. Cushions and settees and chaise lounges scattered the large room, and sidhe had claimed them in writhing pairs or trios or more. Curtains hung here and there, though they framed the tableaus like sordid stage plays more than they offered any real privacy.

It was debauchery.

Over the scents of all those faeries, the acrid smells of strong alcohol and herbs burned her nose. The smoke had an aroma too, sweet and cloying.

Cirelle took a step back, shaking her head. A mingling of horror and desire swirled in her gut. She wanted nothing more than to run away, but the faerie woman stood behind her, blocking the door. "Come now." This time, a sinister shadow lingered in her smile. "Don't you want to find your master?" The faerie reached for her wrist and Cirelle was forced to grasp the woman's hand first.

The sidhe's grin had grown catlike, her teeth sharper.

Cirelle tried not to look at the scattering of fae throughout the room. Still, she caught glimpses. One sidhe's pale hair spread on a crimson pillow. A woman ran sharp nails down his bare chest, her tongue caressing the bloody furrows left behind. On another sofa, a trio tangled together, a riot of jewel-toned skin.

It felt like a bad dream. Cirelle was beginning to grow light-headed as the scratchy smoke filled her lungs.

Her anxiety and panic only grew as they wove their way through this party. *Run run run run,* her brain screamed, but she couldn't seem to obey. A dark curiosity lurched in her breast. She didn't want to know where Ellian was in this mess, but a part of her needed to find out, nonetheless.

And then she did.

In a shadowed corner of the room, that familiar face was thrown back with eyes closed. One of the twins pressed his mouth to Ellian's throat, hands pinning Ellian's wrists to a wall painted black as night.

Ysven stood beside them, nipping at Ellian's ear with lips the color of overripe grapes. One hand disappeared into Ellian's half-unlaced trousers. His jacket lay unbuttoned, the front of his shirt slashed open.

Nearby, the prince perched in a plush chair and watched, his elbows on his knees and fingers steepled beneath his chin. His yellowish eyes glowed fiercely, and a small, cruel smile curved his mouth.

Cirelle's stomach heaved, and something sharp tried to burrow its way out from her chest.

The woman leading Cirelle dropped her hand. "Oh, here he is," she said loudly enough to draw stares.

Cirelle couldn't tear her eyes from Ellian. He, too, had startled at the cry, opening his eyes and catching her gaze. The brilliant violet of that stare quickly flooded with black, swirled with a pale color she couldn't make out in this light. His mouth opened as if he would say something, but he couldn't seem to form words.

The other two sidhe stopped and turned to watch Cirelle with greedy eyes. The man did not relinquish his grasp on Ellian's wrists, and Ysven barely moved.

"Oh, look," the twin purred. "It's your pet."

"A new player." This voice came from behind Cirelle, a liquid sound like honey.

"No." Ellian's reply was hoarse. He coughed and spoke again. "She's mine."

"Tsk," another faerie said. "Too selfish to share? That's not really in the spirit of the party, Ellian."

The stares had grown hungry, like sharks circling. Cirelle met Ellian's eyes in terror. His expression was glassy. *Stars, he's drunk.* Ellian could not protect her from these creatures. Only her humanity saved her, but if they found that out, what then? Those humans at the ball sprang to mind, hollowed-out husks. That was what happened to mortals in the Unseelie Court.

Cirelle turned to run, but the faeries ringed her too tightly. No escape. They loomed closer with wanting eyes, hands outstretched. She barely had time to close her eyes before they surged toward her, hissing a terrified whisper under her breath. "I give you permission to touch me." They reached for her, grabbing hands and mouths and nails. Claws scraped ragged lines across one shoulder, and she yelped in pain. Another sidhe laughed and held Cirelle's head firmly in place as his tongue claimed her mouth for his own. He tasted like the bittersweet burn of faerie liquor.

Then Ellian was beside her, growling at the sidhe who'd lain a hand upon her. Almost violently, he yanked her into his arms and retreated. The other sidhe didn't follow, though the prince's eyes did.

Cirlelle pressed into Ellian, though her hands grasped his

shoulders tightly enough to bruise. "Why?" she whispered. "How could you do this?"

"I wanted to wash away the taste of you." Ellian's eyes grew dark and unreadable as he leaned closer. He caught her mouth with his, nipping at her lower lip. "But it lingers on my tongue no matter what I try."

They were trapped in this horrific nightmare room, surrounded by sidhe that ringed them like starving wolves. Wolves with tangled hair and lustful eyes, their clothes in disarray. Sweat gleamed on skin, on faces flushed with heat. Delicate tongues licked swollen lips. Their mingled scents were overpowering and Cirelle's mouth was covered in the taste of Ellian's honey and salt.

And alcohol. The faerie spirits coated his skin, his lips, his tongue. Even that small taste sent a shivery warmth trickling through her. Stars, he'd been drinking some strong liquor tonight.

Breathing in another gasp of smoky air, dizziness slammed into Cirelle.

Ellian's hands moved to her hips, greedy, pulling her into him.

Beneath the horror, the panic, something inside her sparked. A heat flared in her stomach and between her thighs. Giving in to the sudden impulse as her head spun, she sighed against his throat, scraping his collarbone lightly with her teeth.

Adaleth spoke. "Ellian." The word was sharp. Not shouted, but enough to cut through the murmurs of the crowd.

Cirelle turned to meet the prince's gaze. It burned with barely-contained fury.

"Get that thing out of here. I don't want to look at her."

Ellian's nod was sharp. He yanked on her arm, guiding her through a sea of leering faces and back to their room.

"What was that?" Cirelle's voice shook as she shut the door behind her.

"That," Ellian said, discarding his torn jacket and shirt in a basket in the corner, "was the Unseelie Court."

"And that's normal?"

His steps were still sluggish, his pupils dark and dilated. He took a few strides toward her, and Cirelle retreated until she was pressed back against the door.

Ellian leaned in close and the scent nearly overwhelmed her. His own smoky aroma mingled with the smells of baking bread and a bitter flower. A hint of a snarl caught the edge of his lips. He pressed both hands to the door on either side of her head.

"This is what it means to be sidhe, to be a part of this court. That is what I will become. Do you still want me?" His voice was cruel, his eyes a flat and cold gray. But something in the slant of his eyebrows and a tension around his jaw gave him away.

Conflicted. Bleeding inside.

His breath washed over her, wine and whatever other spirits he'd been drinking. The taste of him still danced on her tongue and her mouth tingled with the memory of his teeth scraping her lip in desperate hunger. Somewhere beneath, she threatened to fall apart, her panic and anger seething. But this craving drowned out all else.

Cirelle met his eyes without fear. "Yes." She lifted both hands to cup his face and pull it to hers.

The kiss was gentle. He sighed into her mouth, and his hands left the door to tangle in her hair.

Cirelle spoke against his lips, "Let them steal your humanity away." She pulled back enough to meet his silver gaze, caressing his cheek with a thumb. "And when they do, I'll bring you back."

He made a small, choked sound as he leaned in to nuzzle her neck. "You won't be here forever. Someday, I won't come back. I'll be fully sidhe, made of ice and emptiness."

"You're stronger than that."

His tongue swept across her skin and Cirelle threw her head back to let him. *Yes.* The tight knot in her belly began to loosen. His hands slid downward to rest at her waist. "Who are you to say? After today, I think you're as likely to turn sidhe as I am. There's something dark inside you, Princess, and I'm afraid I'm setting it free."

Something flickered in her stomach. Cirelle had enjoyed toying with him today, that much was true. It had been a thrill to tease him without mercy. To feel this dangerous creature shiver at her touch.

Fae-touched. Was this a first step toward becoming one of the cold ones? Her fingertips stroked through his hair, a cool weight. "Perhaps. And maybe we'll save each other."

His lips followed the edge of her dress's neckline. "Maybe we will."

Sparks jolted through Cirelle. She made a noise inappropriate for a princess and tugged him up for another kiss, this one greedy and breathless.

Ellian's lips stopped moving. A small, pleading sound escaped her, but he shook his head. "I can't do this."

"What? Why?"

He wiped a weary hand across his eyes. "Because I'm still drunk."

Frustration simmered inside her chest, that snarling beast raising its hackles. "Fine." She shoved him away, too hard. "At least wash off their scents before we go to supper."

Chapter Thirty-Five

Dinner was another show, though an uneasy one for Cirelle. Ellian's refusal stood between them, a wall he'd built. For supper, he'd donned more finery, his serpent brooch again pinned to his breast. He looked tidy once more, and very nearly sober.

At the table, the rest of the sidhe watched her with sharp, curious gazes. Wondering. She was the evening's entertainment, whether she willed it or not. She squashed down her painful slurry of anger and hurt and desire, met their gemstone eyes fearlessly, and focused only on Ellian.

His movements were stiff and hesitant. He brushed her skin with trembling, feather-light touches. When his eyes met hers, he kept them carefully cloaked, a faint furrow between his brows.

It almost undid her, forced to meet his gaze and confront the roil of feelings that tried to drown her. She was so weary of arguing with herself, of pushing back at those violent emotions until they quelled themselves. Temporarily, though. Always only a fleeting respite. Later, they would ignite and consume her.

After an eternity, the meal finally ended. They returned to their room with weary steps. The door closed behind them, and

Ellian wasted little time beginning to shuck off his clothing for bed. No mention of what had happened earlier.

He faced only the armoire as he disrobed, allowing Cirelle to quickly slip out of her dress and into the nightdress folded neatly on her side of the bed.

A kindness, or a rebuff?

Cirelle snuffed out the light on her side of the room and slipped beneath the sheets with a sigh of comfort. The flimsy Unseelie clothing she wore was little protection against the chill of the palace and these heavy blankets seemed an immense luxury after hours of bearing the cold.

When Ellian switched off his light and slipped into the bed, he turned away from her without so much as a word.

The window's heavy outer drapes remained open and starlight seeped through the thin inner curtain. In the crispness of the soft white light, he was colorless, that deep blue hair faded to an inky black. Before she realized what she was doing, Cirelle's hand stretched out to comb through the silky strands where they draped across his pillow.

He tensed, the bed shifting.

If asked, Cirelle couldn't have said why she'd done it, save some sudden inexplicable impulse. She found herself leaning into the compulsion, threading her fingers through that hair, stroking the waves into even lines on the pillow.

Ellian remained perfectly still. The quiet held for several long seconds. When he did speak, his voice was toneless and faint. "I'm very tired."

It stung like a rebuke. An instant later, anger bloomed. Not with Ellian, but with herself. She slipped her hand free of his hair and rolled over, drawing the blankets tighter.

Cirelle awoke the next morning to an empty bed. Early sunlight filtered through the window above her head.

Today was the Hunt, and a new set of clothing hung in the

wardrobe. Practical trousers rested next to a cotton shirt with a light vest, and boots made for trekking through woodland terrain, all dyed a deep black that swallowed the light.

I look like a villain in a story book, she thought as she observed the effect in the mirror.

A restlessness overwhelmed her, a familiar twitchy energy. It was a need to move, to ease her pent-up anger by doing something, anything. So, she left, closing the door behind her and uncertain where she intended to go.

Too late. She came face-to-face with Ellian as he neared the door. He, too, was garbed all in black for the Hunt. A matching pair, though his golden serpent gleamed at his collar.

Cirelle's heart stopped, her cheeks aflame and mouth suddenly dry. For the briefest instant, Ellian's eyes flared a faded yellow, then palest green and back to silver again.

Last night haunted her. The kisses that had left her feeling sick and hungry, the way her stomach had turned when she entered that party.

Before either of them could speak, the summons came, the rumble of the earth beneath their feet. The Hunt was to begin.

Chapter Thirty-Six

THE MORNING AIR PROMISED a sweltering early-summer day, a sticky dampness already clinging to Cirelle's skin. It was welcome after the icy chill of the palace.

The Hunt's participants knelt before the prince near the stables, with a small crowd gathered to watch. Cirelle downcast her gaze, her palms flat against the dewy grass. She hadn't even known there were stables, hidden behind the palace as they were. They, too, were built of that same white stone.

Even stranger were the beasts housed within, if the sounds coming from the building were any indication. Those growls and roars and screeches belonged to no horse.

Five enormous wolves stood behind the prince in a row, their fur bristling. They were easily the size of plow horses. Cirelle met the eyes of one and its lip curled to bare yellow teeth.

The prince held up a heavy silver collar. "Your quarry wears one of these." He practically gleamed in the rising sun, his white hair nearly translucent. The queen, as ever, stood behind him. Her gaze was flat as she scanned the crowd with her amber hawk's eyes. She, too, wore practical clothing in ghostly gray. Knives were scattered about her person and her silver hair was pinned into a tight crown about her head.

"Your trial is simple," Adaleth continued. "Track the faerie that wears the twin to this collar, find them, and bring me a hunter's trophy from the body."

No. Cirelle fought back nausea. Ellian had never told her the prey was a faerie. She turned to ask him the question with her eyes, but Ellian refused to look at her, jaw clenched.

Adaleth continued, though Cirelle barely heard him through the ringing in her ears. "The prey cannot move more than three miles from the palace. If Queen Ayre finds the quarry first, you all lose. When a participant brings me the trophy, I will sound the hunt's horn to signify the end of the trial. At that time, all competition is to cease, and you will return without delay."

The prince's words turned to nonsense in her brain. She couldn't focus.

A faerie. Ellian was going to hunt and kill a faerie. Not a stag, not a fox.

Adaleth handed the collar to an attendant, who scurried away to store it wherever such things were kept. The members of the Inner Court stepped forward, each holding two blindfolds. The hunters would be led into the woods, each team left at a separate location with a tracking amulet.

Still reeling, Cirelle barely felt the blindfold as one of the twins tied it about her eyes. She was guided up onto the back of one of the wolves, behind Ellian. A musky scent that could only be described as animal surrounded her. The fur was coarse and thick beneath her hands. There was nothing resembling a saddle. For lack of anything else to hold onto, she was forced to slide her arms around Ellian's waist and hoped his hands held tightly to the ruff of the wolf's neck.

Then they were off. The wolf had a long, loping stride unlike any horse, and the wind buffeted her ears. After a time, the wolf stopped and gave a low whuff. Cirelle was all too grateful to remove the blindfold as they both slid off the wolf's back. The beast immediately set off again at a run and was hidden by the trees before she could take two breaths.

They stood among heavy forest, the canopy clustered so thick it left the light dim and green. It smelled overwhelmingly of soil and moss and leaf. One would almost mistake it for a deep forest in her own world, save the prickling sensation on her skin and the glimmering quality to the air. The sounds were different too, unfamiliar bird calls and the hum of strange insects.

Ellian's hand nervously touched the hilt of the sword strapped to his hip, the slim blade of a dueling nobleman. His hair was pulled back from his face in a single plait, and an empty knapsack was slung over one shoulder. "Let's go," he said.

Cirelle shoved him with all the force she could muster, forcing him back a step. "You're going to *kill* a faerie?" Fury made her tremble.

Ellian regained his balance and shook his head. "No one dies today by my hand. I swear it."

"Then what?"

His smile was a ghostly thing. "I'll show you." He set off toward the east.

Cirelle blinked. "What about the amulet?" She pointed at the necklace around his throat, the stone levitating and urging them north.

"It lies. They all do. The amulets point to a very unfortunate hare."

It took a moment for that to sneak in. More trickery. Ellian had thoroughly stacked the deck on this game. "So, now what?"

He grinned. "Now, you follow me."

She wasn't sure how Ellian knew where to go. Occasionally

he'd catch glimpses of the sky, but he also watched for landmarks. A twisted set of trees woven together as they'd grown. A small creek lined with glittering blue stones. A set of rocks arranged in a circle. Finally, they emerged from the tree line onto a ledge overlooking the ocean. A mile in the distance, the palace rose above the treetops.

"Ah, here we are." He led her along the cliff's edge, his steps casual like a deadly drop didn't hang a few paces away. Looking out over all that vast ocean left Cirelle dizzy, and she focused on her feet. Ellian found what he was looking for. A small path carved directly into the cliff that led downward along the outside of the alabaster stone.

Cirelle took one look at the ledge, barely three feet across, and shook her head. "Are you crazy?"

His lips drew into a thin line and his brows lowered. "Very well. Wait here." He stepped onto the ledge and disappeared from sight.

"Ellian!" She took one reluctant step closer. He was already descending with careful, steady steps. I'm going to regret this.

Cirelle set her feet onto the path and clung to the cliff's face with a white-knuckled grip. The stone was mostly smooth, offering little purchase, but she still scrabbled at it with trembling fingers.

Ellian had halted. When she was close enough to touch, he gave her another reckless grin. There was a rebellious spark in his eyes, gleaming silver.

The descent took far too long, one slow step before the other as the waves crashed below. Eventually, they approached a small cave cut into the cliff's edge. Cirelle stumbled into the hollow gratefully, her legs twitchy and trembling.

"Took you long enough." Vilitte sat cross-legged in the cave, tapping her crystalline fingers against the stone floor. Her quartz-like appearance nearly blended into the stone, in the slanting half-light of morning. She yawned widely, covering the gesture with a hand. Circling her neck was a silver band, a collar like the one Adaleth had shown them.

"Vilitte?" Cirelle blurted. "You're the prey?"

The faerie stood, tossing her long silvery braid behind her. "Humiliating," she snorted in disdain. She lifted the end of the braid away from her head, nodding at Ellian. "I can't believe I let him talk me into letting myself get caught by a sidhe."

"The things we do for the right price…" Ellian drew the sword at his hip.

"And I earned every bit of my pay," Vilitte sighed as she pulled the braid tight and Ellian slid the sword gently beneath it. The blade sliced easily through the metallic strands with a shrieking sound. Still clutching the end of the braid, Vilitte shook out her now-short hair. It was a lopsided cut, haphazard.

Ellian sheathed his sword and stuffed the plait into the knapsack. "Agdarr should be along soon to take care of the collar. There's not a lock that spriggan can't pick, magical or not. But stay hidden until then. The Hunt's not over until we return with the trophy."

Cirelle watched all this with wide eyes. Laughter bubbled up and slipped from her lips. "A trophy. He never said you had to kill her, did he?" She looked back and forth between the two. "This whole thing was rigged."

"How else was I supposed to win?" Ellian grinned. "But others will not be so generous with that loophole, so we'd best return quickly."

Vilitte sat down again, running her hands through her shortened hair with a grimace. "Farewell, Ellian. Princess."

The trip back up the incline was worse. By halfway, Cirelle's legs screamed in pain, her breathing labored. Even Ellian seemed winded, his cheeks flushed. They spoke little. At the top of the cliff, Cirelle collapsed onto the solid ground, her calves clenching.

Ellian held out a hand to help her up. "We can't rest. Not yet." He glowed with the thrill of victory, his smile broad and sincere.

Cirelle groaned, but he was right. They had to deliver Vilitte's trophy before someone else found her. She took his offer of aid and stood on legs that burned and shook. Her knees threatened to collapse, and Ellian caught her. His usual scent mingled with sweat and rock dust. One arm slid around her waist. Her trembling knees were suddenly forgotten.

He blinked, his gaze flickering a rosy color as it wandered down to her lips. His triumphant grin faltered. Indecision flickered in his expression.

"Am I interrupting?" A clear, silvery voice asked.

Cirelle jerked away and whirled to see the queen standing at the edge of the tree line. A long and wickedly-sharp dagger gleamed in one hand. She took a few sauntering steps closer.

A weight settled around Cirelle's shoulder. The knapsack. Ellian's voice whispered in her ear. "Run."

She turned to meet his black eyes.

"Go," he whispered with a nod toward the castle spires. "Get that back to the stables." Ellian unsheathed his sword as the queen approached.

Cirelle took an uneasy step back. Dread settled in as she analyzed Ellian's posture. She'd watched Lydia drill before, and Ellian did not have the balanced stance of a fighter. She hissed, "Do you even know how to use that thing?"

Ellian's jaw clenched. "Out!" He held up his sword in a manner that couldn't possibly have been effective.

The queen's dagger slashed out, lightning-quick, and sliced the arm of Ellian's sleeve open. He grunted in pain. "Run!" he shouted without taking his eyes off the queen.

"I'll get to the sylvan next, Ellian. Don't worry." Ayre purred the words as another slash flicked across his cheek. "Like we did with your little nacken, swimming where he shouldn't have been."

The blade lashed out again, piercing Ellian's shoulder. He cried out and stumbled backward.

When the queen grew bored of the game, Ellian would lose.

She didn't even turn. *She doesn't know I have the trophy, Cirelle realized.*

Ellian's eyes caught on hers one more time, a plea painted in their depths. There was only one way out. To end the Hunt, summoning all players back to the starting point.

Cirelle whirled and fled as fast as her aching, burning legs would carry her. Each step felt like glass shredding her calves, her thighs.

A cry of pain rang out behind her, followed by the queen's laughter.

Tears stung her eyes as she hurtled into the trees, toward the looming palace in the distance. She stumbled through underbrush. Branches reached for her with grasping claws, tangling in her hair, scraping at her hands. Still she ran.

It seemed like both hours and mere seconds before she reached the castle. The forest opened up onto the palace grounds. A small crowd still milled about the yard. Cirelle barreled through them, barely dodging a handful of courtiers. The prince sat at a gaming table brought out for him. Meivre sat opposite, nudging pieces across a lacquered board with a slender, pale pink hand.

Cirelle stumbled and fell at their feet, gasping for breath.

"The Hunt is over," she panted. *Hurry hurry hurry.*

"What?" This from one of the nearby twins, teasing a faerie hound with a bone.

Cirelle yanked Vilitte's braid from the sack and hurled it to the ground as she knelt before him. "Your trophy, courtesy of Ellian. We've fulfilled the terms."

Meivre leaned forward to stare at the unraveling cascade of metallic hair and laughed. It was a clear sound, ringing in the silence following Cirelle's pronouncement. "It seems she has, my prince." The faerie woman arched a violet brow.

Adaleth stood, his hands shaking with cold fury.

The other twin nodded before taking a swig from a flask he held. "She's right."

Anger painted the prince's face in ugliness, but he lifted the horn to his lips and blew a loud peal of sound, deafening. The end of the Hunt. All players were to immediately return to the palace. Including the queen.

Cirelle's legs gave out beneath her, and she fell to the soft, cool grass, rolling onto her back. Had she been in time? Would the queen truly kill Ellian? She stared up at the sun and willed her body to stop trembling. The drowning sorrow reached for her with ragged claws, but she pushed it away with all her might.

No faeries came to help her up. After a minute, Cirelle rolled over and lifted herself onto all fours, then stood. Everything still ached, but the worst pain was the tightness in her chest.

The other competitors returned, milling about as they waited. Then the queen stalked out of the forest, a cool glower on that beautiful face. A distance behind her walked Ellian, weary and heavy-footed. Seeing him alive, Cirelle blinked back tears. Her fingernails bit into her palms as she hurtled toward him. A dozen cuts marred his clothing. One slice dripped a smear of blood down his cheek. His eyes met hers and melted into a deep goldenrod hue as he caught her up in his arms.

She buried her face in his neck. A show, yes, but not entirely. Right now, she was too relieved to care. Ellian withdrew from her, twining his hand with hers as he walked slowly toward the prince. They knelt.

The queen took up a spot beside her son, her daggers sheathed and her expression unreadable.

"Your Highness," Ellian greeted the prince, indicating the braid that still lay on the ground, untouched.

"Ellian." The prince's voice was cool and clear. "You have fulfilled the terms of the Hunt. I name you champion. Tonight, we celebrate your victory. The ceremony is tomorrow."

Without another word, the prince whirled and left, taking his Inner Court with him.

Chapter Thirty-Seven

EVERYTHING HURT, but Ellian had felt worse. The moment he shut the door, he unbuckled the belt and tossed it into a chair, sword and all. The jacket came next, then the shirt as he fell into the other chair.

A bit disappointingly, the princess seemed unfazed by his bared skin. She wrung out a washcloth in the water basin and handed it to him before she shoved the sword off the chair's cushion and sat.

A host of cuts stung, ranging from shallow to painfully deep. The wounds seeped a green so dark it was nearly black. Some of them still bled freely, despite his efforts to staunch them.

"What are we going to do about those?" Cirelle's brow creased with worry.

A knock at the door interrupted his reply, and Cirelle hauled herself to her feet to answer it. Shai barreled into the room, holding a bottle half-full of that familiar purple liquid. His supply was getting dangerously low. He'd need to strike another bargain for more before Thieves' Night.

"Amazing!" Shai crowed as she handed Ellian the bottle. "Oh, the prince is seeing red."

Ellian winced at Shai's loud enthusiasm.

Cirelle nodded to the potion. "I'll get that, Shai." She gave the sidhe a warm smile. "But let me get Ellian patched up and then we can talk later?"

Shai waggled her eyebrows at Cirelle. "Ah, gotcha. Well, don't wear him out before the party." She left with a wave and shut the door behind her.

Cirelle handed Ellian the bottle and slid back into her chair.

He gave a tired smile. "You told her you were going to tend my wounds."

"It got her to leave, didn't it?"

He laughed as he began dabbing the potion onto his cuts. It was probably for the best, anyway. He wasn't sure how he'd respond to the princess's hands washing his wounds, her fingers spreading the potion on his skin.

Cirelle shifted in her chair and winced.

"Here." Ellian held out the potion. "Take a sip. It'll soothe the muscle aches."

After she'd done so, Cirelle handed it back and nodded toward his cuts. "So...do you actually want help with those?" A conflicted uncertainty hung on the words.

"So eager to get your hands on me?" The words spilled out, flippant, with a smirk. But they were only half a jest.

The princess didn't answer, her eyes locked on his. She licked her lips.

His gaze slid down to her mouth and back to her eyes, the healing potion still clutched loosely in one hand but forgotten.

Cirelle cleared her throat. "You're still bleeding."

The moment was broken. Ellian tried to hide his frustration as he soaked a cloth with potion and began working on the rest of his wounds. Cirelle sighed and made her way to the wardrobe to lift out a gown in the shimmering black color of a raven's feathers.

While Ellian tended his injuries, she slipped behind the screen and drew a bath. He didn't blame her. They both stank of the forest, of sweat and dirt and the tiny leaves in their hair.

Ellian remained silent while he catalogued every ripple of sound from her side of the screen and imagined her smooth golden skin bared as she scrubbed away the dirt of their morning's adventure.

Except it wouldn't be her skin. It would be the mottled gray-brown of Ibrafel's. Even were she to slide aside that screen, it wouldn't be the princess before him, but a creature of his own creation. Not what he truly wanted at all. And yet he still couldn't completely quell the tingling ache in his belly.

The water sloshed as she left the tub, then emerged with a towel wrapped around her glamoured hair and the gown draped over her form.

His ministrations done, Ellian stretched and stood, selecting his ensemble and stepping behind the screen for his own bath. He chose garb to match hers, all sleek lines in black velvet and leather.

As he washed off the day's dirt, Cirelle broke the silence from the other side of the screen. "Why do they all hate you so much?"

He hesitated. How much to tell? "I've left their court before."

"And now you're trying to get back in."

Ellian sighed. The water splashed softly. "Yes."

Cirelle let the conversation lapse. Eventually, he stepped around the screen, clothed and clean, squeezing the last of the water out of his hair and braiding it back once more.

"Will this..." Cirelle's voice cracked, and she cleared her throat. "Will this be like that other party?"

A shudder ran from his head to his toes at the memory. His head pleasantly spinning with the effects of the wintersweet, his blood simmering with it. Drowning in the sheer, simple pleasure of Rhael's lips and Ysven's deft hands. And the utter horror that had crashed over him at the stricken look on the princess's face.

"No," he said. "It won't."

૯৲১

Uneasy, Cirelle entered the room alongside Ellian. It was larger than the scene of last night's revelry, though no less dim or smoke-fogged. There was no food, but drinks aplenty were available. The hedonism of the last revel was either absent or had not yet begun. Sidhe mingled and chatted, waiting.

On the far end of the room, two chairs sat on a raised platform.

All eyes were on her as she and Ellian crossed the room to take those seats. His grip on her hand was tight, and it trembled as he stroked his thumb across her knuckles. Cirelle took a deep breath and almost choked on the thick scents of the sidhe. And under that, the sickly-sweet smell of the smoke, filling her lungs with a dry burn.

A small wave of giddiness rippled through her, a sudden sway of the earth. *Stars, the smoke.* Cirelle could avoid the wine, but she could not decline to breathe.

While the sidhe came to greet them one by one, each dipping their head to acknowledge Ellian's win, Cirelle grew ever more lightheaded. The smoke smelled like resin and pungent herbs, and left her throat parched. Her tongue was coated in sweetness and dust. By the time the Inner Court came to offer congratulations, a prickling sensation had settled into her fingers and toes.

Each nodded to Cirelle and Ellian. The twins first, broad-shouldered with their short, unruly hair of yellow-tinged green. Even in the dimness of the room, they shimmered with a dusting of metallic gold. Cirelle watched them with narrowed eyes, wondering which of them had tasted Ellian's skin.

Then came Ysven, pale as a dove's feathers with her lips and hair like drops of blood. Her smile was the closest to genuine, though it still lacked an indefinable something. Her gown was cut to emphasize her considerable curves. She, too, had held Ellian against the wall. Was her scent the one that had lingered on his throat afterward?

Next was Meivre, the petite woman with the enigmatic smile and hair like a cascade of amethysts. The one who'd tried to tempt Cirelle in the music room. Stars, was it only yesterday? She cast Cirelle a small grin and moved on.

Tallia came last, and her small bow was stiff.

To them all, Ellian did not bow or yield. He accepted their congratulations as if they were his due, without humility. He'd released Cirelle's hand when the well-wishers began filing through and she felt isolated, shut out. Ellian was one of them again tonight. Inhuman. Cold. The cant of his head was arrogant, his smile cool and indulgent.

Adaleth and the queen were last of all. The prince didn't dip his head even in the slightest. His luminescent peridot eyes met Ellian's, dismissing Cirelle entirely.

"Tomorrow, then." The flicker of a knowing smile twitched at the corner of his lips. It left Cirelle with a sour taste in her mouth.

Her eyes darted back to Ellian, to find his gaze glinting a rich and brilliant scarlet. The tension was back in his jaw, around his eyes. He nodded silently.

The queen was more eloquent, if just as imperious. She, too, did not lower her head. "Congratulations on your win, Ellian." Her voice was that pleasant soprano, but the words were emotionless. She swept after her son in a swirl of diamond-encrusted skirts.

Once the sidhe had all greeted Ellian, the party began in earnest. They mingled and chatted and danced without music. The few sconces burned Cirelle's eyes while her head spun.

A familiar itch had settled beneath her skin. "Let's dance." She held out her hand to Ellian.

"Not tonight."

"All I'm asking is a dance."

Still, he shook his head even as his carefully-colorless eyes roiled.

Irritated sparks flickered in her vision. "Fine. I'll find another partner, then." She stood and stepped out into the floor. Ellian protested behind her, but she ignored him.

A surge of unease fluttered as she descended into the crowd of sidhe. Their leering faces from the day before still haunted her. Her shoulder still stung where it had been scratched with sharp nails. Perhaps she should have used some of the potion on that, too.

"Looking for a partner?" A soft tenor voice asked beside her. She turned to find an unfamiliar sidhe holding out a hand. They were a sea of inky black, eyes and hair and skin, though a single streak of vibrant blue framed one side of their face. Even their teeth were like chips of obsidian. A tailored suit of dark velvet trimmed in shining silk clung to their slender frame, the jacket's hem brushing their knees.

But the most striking feature were those eyes. Solid black without a hint of white. A shark's eyes, or a crow's. A small smile decorated their lips. Enigmatic as any sidhe. Cirelle nodded before placing her hand in the faerie's. Through the haze of the smoke, it felt like they danced in a strange dream.

"And who are you?"

"You may call me Ren," the sidhe replied.

"Why dance with me, Ren?" *Why, when the others seem to hate me so?*

"Because you are the victors of the Grand Hunt. Who wouldn't want to partner you?"

Cirelle resisted the urge to retort, *Ellian, for one.* "I'd think you'd prefer dancing with Ellian. He's the one who will have a place in the Inner Court now."

Ren's smile faltered. "Ah, but will he live to take it?"

Dread settled over her. "What do you mean?"

Ren cast a long, meaningful glance toward the door, where Tallia slipped out of the party. Without another word, Ren slipped free to flit away into the crowd.

Cirelle looked back at the dais where Ellian sat. Even through the fog, she met his silver eyes. She mouthed the word "privy" and hurried out of the room.

In the hall, Cirelle sucked in a great gasp of clear air. Tallia was already most of the way down the corridor. There was nowhere to hide in the vast expanse of white stone, but Cirelle's slippers made little noise and Tallia seemed unconcerned about followers. Eventually, the sidhe stepped through an open door. The scents and sounds drifting down the hall gave it away; the kitchen.

Cirelle ducked into a nearby open room. A gaming parlor, empty for the evening. She waited. What if Ren was toying with her? But it seemed all too obvious now. The royals despised Ellian. Of course they would take whatever measures they could to keep Ellian out of the Inner Court. By any means.

Cirelle swallowed back bile as Tallia's purposeful steps strode past her hiding spot. When she was certain the hallway was empty, Cirelle quickly made her way to the kitchen. A blast of heat hit her, a wave of dizzy nausea following. Stars, what did the sidhe enjoy about that smoke?

The kitchen was a comfortingly familiar oasis in this warren of icy stone. An assortment of fae bustled about, doing the mundane tasks of food preparation and cooking. One little salcha stood on a stool to knead bread, while a girl with floppy rabbit's ears stirred a pot of soup. The chaos hesitated when she walked in. Cirelle didn't mince words. "What did that sidhe just do?"

The faeries glanced back and forth among themselves, communicating silently. After a long, heavy pause, one of them stepped forward. A brownie, much like the ones in Ellian's manor. "There," she pointed to the corner of a large table. A crystalline vial sat upon the corner, out of place among flour-covered earthenware and wooden utensils. A virulently orange liquid shimmered within.

Cirelle's heart stopped. "Is that... poison?"

The brownie wrung her hands together. "Aye."

"It's meant for Ellian, isn't it?"

With tear-filled eyes, the faerie nodded. "I'm sorry. I know he's a friend to our kind, but we're oathbound to serve the queen and the prince."

"Well I'm not." With two determined strides, Cirelle reached the table and snatched it up, hurling it into a nearby waste bin. The crystal shattered and a pungent odor wafted up. For one panicked moment, Cirelle belatedly feared the fumes were as deadly as the liquid itself, but the fae seemed unconcerned.

They pointedly avoided her gaze and returned to their tasks. Cirelle cast one more glance around the room, then made her way back to the party.

Chapter Thirty-Eight

As Cirelle walked back from the kitchens, a faint tremor took hold of her. That poison must have been intended for breakfast tomorrow, before the ceremony that would cement Ellian's place in the Inner Court. And they would try to kill him again. She wouldn't be lucky enough to foil another plot. Ellian must be warned.

Her head began swimming again after only a few breaths back at the party. Her thoughts became ephemeral, elusive things. Sconces had dimmed and the debauchery had begun. Cirelle caught glimpses of entwined limbs in one darkened corner, and some of the dancing pairs had become more intimate. Tongues flickered across necks, hands teased and wandered.

Cirelle's belly tightened, and she looked toward the dais through the haze. Ellian met her stare with his carefully emotionless mask. He sat in an idle sprawl, one leg stretched before him with the other tucked underneath. His chin rested on one hand as if he were unutterably bored by the proceedings.

A show, all false. Did the sidhe see that as clearly as she did?

The pose reminded her too much of Adaleth the night before, when the prince had been casually ensconced in a chair and watching two of his Inner Court toy with Ellian. Again, that image flashed in her mind, Ellian's lips swollen from kisses, his eyes gleaming violet. A phantom sensation gripped her, the sharp echo of his teeth at her earlobe, her throat.

Another dizzy surge rippled through her as she strode across the room, but she was caught by partners first. She'd given them permission to touch her last night, after all. She was whirled and passed from one sidhe to another, dancing without music.

Shadows wavered at the edges of her vision. Her skin felt too tight, too hot, and it tingled with pinpricks. The lightheadedness built and crested. They laughed at her, but she didn't care. Sidhe raked hands through her hair and slid warm fingertips up her arms, down her spine. A cruel and slow-burning ache began low in her stomach. The world spun and shifted beneath her feet.

The thwarted lust and helpless frustration of the past two days hardened into violence. She tasted sweat on sidhe throats, salty and floral-sweet. Her own fingernails scraped down faerie backs, digging in until the sidhe hissed and writhed for her. When one was bold enough to kiss her, she bit down on his lip until she tasted blood and he moaned for more.

A persimmon-skinned sidhe spun her away, and Cirelle found herself caught in familiar arms.

"Ellian." That stony and inscrutable expression rested on his face, but she knew it for the lie it was. She smiled. "Dance with me."

Indecision flickered in his eyes. She leaned into his embrace and licked her lips, startled to taste lingering faerie blood on them.

Ellian bent closer but did not kiss her. His lips nearly brushed her ear as he whispered. "You claim you'd preserve my humanity, but you're more sidhe right now than I am."

"Maybe." Her fingertips dug into his hips, frustrated by the layers of fabric between her hands and his skin. "And maybe we're both caught between." She moved to caress the skin of his throat with her tongue.

He sucked in a surprised breath before shoving her away.

Cirelle was shocked and furious at the violence of his rejection. "Fine," she said, grasping the arm of the nearest sidhe to spin away into the dance again.

Ellian's hand caught her other wrist in a tight grip. "You win. A dance. But not here."

❧

THEY ONCE AGAIN FOUND themselves in the ballroom. The tables of food were gone, and a scattering of white faerie lights lit the large chamber.

Other sidhe had made their way here, free of the smoke and depravity of the other party. Cirelle was painfully aware of Ellian's nearness, of his warmth and his scent. How his hand felt entwined with hers, and how badly she wanted those clever fingers to wander elsewhere.

A haunting melody played, again with no source. It would be accompanied by an airy dance full of rises and dips like a ship upon an ocean. Ellian tightened his fingers about hers and led her out to the floor.

He smiled, a soft expression that only prodded the violent, burning need inside her. Ellian had no idea what she'd just done. She should tell him, but here in this peaceful place, it seemed wrong. Later, in their room, she'd explain the crystal vial shattering, spilling out the vivid orange liquid that had been meant to end his life.

It was both soothing and a subtle agony to rest her head against Ellian's shoulder. Her fears and the smoke left her fragile, like a hollowed-out eggshell. Cirelle took a long breath of cool, clean air and let it out in a shudder. The shell cracked, a barrier crumbling.

Ellian must have felt it, too. His arms tightened about her for an instant, a small sigh tickling the back of her neck. Cirelle inhaled his charred-wood scent and built a small world around the two of them. In the dimness, it was easy to imagine they danced alone.

They didn't speak. Words weren't needed. Cirelle did not tease, did not try to play him like her harp. This was something gentler, sweeter. Their previous games had left a string pulled tight between them, the thread ready to snap. Now an invisible ribbon wrapped around them instead, binding them together.

Perhaps she should have fled, as she did every time before. But tonight she was tired of running, tired of fighting the thing that had been blossoming inside her.

Gauzy skirts fluttered about Cirelle's ankles as her mind emptied. She spun through the dances with ease; rapid reels that left her flushed and laughing, elegant ones that were all dips and spins, light-footed ones that spun her into the air. She barely noticed the other sidhe. These dances were not for them, not tonight.

After a time, the dizziness from the smoke cleared, leaving behind a trembling ache and a fuzzy numbness. This all felt like a play, where she'd become both spectator and actor.

The others slowly filtered out of the room in twos and threes, but she and Ellian danced until the last notes finally died. Silence held for several long moments. Ellian's eyes glinted a deep, rosy pink. He still held her, hands on her waist. The press of his fingers burned through the thin fabric of her faerie dress. His pupils grew wide. The conflicted expression on his face melted into surrender. His head tilted.

A violent fluttering jolted to life in her stomach. Cirelle rose on tiptoe to meet his mouth with her own. His grasp tightened on her hips as the kiss deepened, a gentle kindling of embers rather than their previous spark and bonfire. She savored his honey-and-salt sweetness as Ellian's tongue coaxed her lips open. She sighed into him, her body languid and heavy.

Did he taste the kisses of other sidhe in her mouth?

When the kiss ended, Ellian pulled away to meet her gaze. A dozen shades of violet danced around his pupils, and it sent a tremor down to her toes. The purple was ringed with purest emerald, bleeding into the center like oil paints mixed in solvent. For the shortest second, Cirelle remembered her brother, painting at his easel, but the thought was fleeting.

Ellian blinked, and the green was gone.

No words were spoken as he led her from the ballroom, through chilled halls now empty. It was as if she walked through a dream, a world a step aside from reality. Everything had shifted. Her steps were oddly light on the stone floor, Ellian's hand warm and trembling in hers.

As the door closed behind them, he pulled Cirelle into his arms and she went without protest. The palace's horrors had broken something within her. She'd been hollowed out, turned inside-out and emptied.

His kisses were gentle, tender things, like butterflies brushing her skin. They touched the edge of her mouth, her cheek, her throat. Her hands held him tight, clutching back of his coat. They shook, though she couldn't have said with what emotion.

Neither of them bothered to kindle the sconces to life, only a single one left burning by the door. It cast Ellian's face in deep contrast, bringing out the angles of his features. Not a human face, too perfect and too sharp for that. Letting go of his coat with one hand, Cirelle reached upward to touch those edges, tracing the line of his jaw before cupping one cheek. His eyes fluttered closed, and he covered her hand with his own.

He was so inhumanly beautiful it hurt, made her chest burn even as the moths in her belly threatened to break free. She'd forgotten how to breathe, her lungs working in fits and starts.

Cirelle didn't know how they got to the bed. Time skipped and jumped, lost in those violet eyes and the taste of his skin.

This was foolish and dangerous, and she found she didn't care.

At some point between the door and the bed, his jacket had been discarded. Only the tailored shirt kept her fingertips from his chest. He sat on the bed now, Cirelle standing between his knees as he looked up into her eyes.

With shaking fingers, she unfastened the shirt, one slow button at a time. Why did it make her knees tremble now when he'd bared more skin before?

The shirt joined the jacket on the floor and Cirelle stepped closer, leaning down to place a kiss on his shoulder. A shudder ran through him. His head turned, and their lips met once again. A gentle push urged him to lie down.

And then Cirelle was kneeling over him on the mattress, her faerie skirts puddled about her. Her breaths now came quick and shallow as her hands traced along the side of his face, tangled in his hair, drew lines down his chest. She carefully avoided the half-healed wounds from the Hunt.

Suddenly, jarringly, Ellian's violet gaze turned dark, and he closed his eyes, uttering the first word either one of them had said in over an hour. "No."

Cirelle sat up, confusion jolting her out of her dreamlike

reverie. "What?" Emotions shot through her so fast she could barely identify them. Hurt, humiliation, anger. "Why?"

One of his hands caressed the side of her face, and his eyes bled into deep sapphire blue.

He never got the chance to answer.

The door crashed open. Cirelle scrambled off the bed as faeries poured into the room. Sidhe guards swarmed her. One kicked her in the back of the knees and Cirelle collapsed with a cry, her shins colliding painfully against the stone floor.

How? She had a single terrified moment to wonder. How can they hurt me?

Ellian knelt in a similar position on the other side, but he wasn't looking at her. His crimson gaze was focused on the two sidhe standing in the doorway. The Prince and the Queen.

"Ibrafel the sylvan," Adaleth said, his voice glacially cold. "You have stolen something from me, and now you will pay the price."

Chapter Thirty-Nine

THEY WERE HAULED ROUGHLY to the center of the room. The guard once again forced her to her knees, and Ellian followed suit a moment later.

"Sylvan," Adaleth began, head held high. His mother stood beside him, golden eyes glittering as the prince continued. "You have destroyed what was mine. Do you deny it?"

The poison. Cirelle stared. She couldn't lie, not when she was caught. She swallowed a cold lump. "No."

Ellian writhed in the grasp of the soldier, his anguished eyes staring hard into hers. "What did you do?"

"I saved you." She glared at the prince. "And I'd do it again."

"Did you think I lacked loyal servants in the kitchen?" Adaleth asked. "That no one would inform me of the vial you shattered?"

Cirelle kept her silence. There was nothing to say.

"What?" Ellian's voice rasped, a soft whisper. He shook his head as realization flickered across his face. "You destroyed the poison meant for me tomorrow, didn't you?"

A heavy stone settled in Cirelle's stomach. "You knew?"

His eyes said it all; Ellian had already known of Adaleth's

_se. He had planned this whole thing down to the _y last detail.

Her act had been for nothing, and now the prince stared with empty firefly eyes. "I demand recompense for your theft, sylvan." He held up a hand and spoke to one of the guards. "Bring a cleaver from the kitchens."

The sidhe left. Terror washed over Cirelle, and blackness swallowed her vision.

"Place her hand upon that table," the prince commanded. He gestured to one of the small side tables in the sitting area.

"No!" Ellian struggled, but Cirelle stared down at the floor. An icy, numb panic consumed her. A low buzz rang in her ears while the guard yanked her across the room.

"A punishment equal to the crime," the prince said flatly. "The hand that threw the vial will be taken as payment."

"No," Ellian croaked again, though this time it was a plea.

A sidhe returned with the cleaver and placed it in the free hand of the guard who held her. His iron grasp pressed her right hand roughly to the surface. She tried clawing at him, but another sidhe held her opposite arm firmly behind her. She whimpered and writhed, but they only tightened their grips.

The guard raised the cleaver, and Cirelle's stomach lurched.

"Wait," Adaleth said, a simple spoken word. The guard froze. A wave of relief crashed over Cirelle until she realized her stupidity. This was not a pardon; they merely toyed with their prey.

"Ellian." The prince stared at Ellian, who strained against his own captor. A terrible despair had gripped his features, his eyes solid black pools. It wrenched something inside her, to see him undone for her sake. Adaleth continued, "A bargain. If you concede your prize and leave my court, I will not remove her hand."

Ellian hesitated. His eyes shifted to deepest blue, the color of anguish.

He's going to let them do it. Cirelle closed her eyes while angry, bitter tears scorched them from inside. She'd always known his mission was more important than anything. Even her. But it still carved out a hollow, ragged space within her.

The guard's grip was tight enough to bruise as he lifted the cleaver in his other hand.

"Done." Ellian rasped out the word.

Cirelle sagged on the floor, weeping tears of relief.

"Good." The prince's lips curved into a cruel smile. "She did, however, steal from me. I will not take her entire hand, but a finger will do." He gestured idly toward the guard. "Continue."

The sidhe who held her once more raised the cleaver high. Cirelle screamed. Ellian's shout rang in her ears.

"No." This from the queen, an icy tone of command.

Again, the guard stopped. Again, Cirelle held her breath.

The expression on Queen Ayre's face was positively feral. She drew a short, heavy knife from one tall boot. With slow strides, she crossed the room. "I'll do it." Her eyes held no mercy, no humanity.

She clutched Cirelle's wrist at once, her nails digging deep.

Cirelle had given none of these faeries permission to harm her, but she had given offense. It seemed whatever curse bound the fae deemed her crime worthy of such brutality.

The guard let go and stepped away. Time seemed to slow. The silence stretched out.

Cirelle should have tried to be brave, but she couldn't. Her will broke. Her shrieks and sobs shattered the quiet, while Adaleth watched with a disinterested smile. Ellian shouted in Kishi, obscenities she'd never have expected from his lips.

The queen grinned. The knife burned as it sliced through skin and flesh. So fast. The sting of the blade, then the wrenching jolt and audible crunch as the joint popped free. Skillful as a butcher separating a chicken thigh.

Cirelle screamed. The pain was all-consuming, burning and sharp. Her stomach heaved and glittering stars filled her vision. She felt suddenly too hot, the air growing thick and stifling.

And then darkness claimed her.

Chapter Forty

ELLIAN PACED in the Archive's antechamber, his thoughts circling like carrion birds. His gaze drifted to the unconscious princess lying on the sofa, at her bandaged hand. Toben had dressed the wound, since she'd only given Ellian permission to touch her during their palace stay.

Adaleth's cruel green gaze burned in Ellian's memory. Of course, the prince had relished the spectacle of Cirelle's misery. He was probably glad she'd broken that vial.

What terrible coincidence led her to stumble across the poison? Ellian had plotted everything out so carefully, only to have it all tumble down because of Cirelle's thoughtless actions. Noble actions, perhaps, but ones that nonetheless obliterated his plans. And yet, a part of him ached with something other than anger. The foolish woman risked her own hide to save his, even if she hadn't realized it at the time.

But now that this gambit had failed, he would risk yet more lives on Thieves' Night. Who might fall this time? Gruff Carid? Cheerful Leilarie? Sly Vilitte? Which new death could weigh on his conscience a fortnight hence?

Cirelle stirred, groaning softly. Ellian reluctantly took a seat in the chair near the sofa. The shimmering black Unseelie dress still draped her. He'd have to send it back soon or risk being accused of theft on top of the chaos he'd already caused.

The princess sat up and hissed sharply when she put weight on her injured hand. Her eyes latched onto the bandage, and Ellian watched a host of emotions unravel in her eyes.

In the end, angry tears won the day. She blinked them away and pierced him with a cutting stare. "What happened?"

He kept his indifferent mask in place. "Your punishment was complete. We left."

She clutched her wounded hand to her chest and a soft sob burst from her before she clamped her lips shut.

A moment of weakness, a tiny pinprick of guilt. "I—"

She snarled at him. "Don't try to apologize to me, faerie."

His own fury flared to life. Yes, she'd been hurt, but she also risked *lives* with her decision. "Why couldn't you have left the poison and warned me?"

"I was trying to save your stupid, worthless life," she hissed with lightning snapping in her stormy eyes. "Next time I hope you drink it and I'll be rid of you once and for all."

He bared his teeth. "You let your unstable temper get the best of you, and it cost us everything."

"Unstable?" Her voice rose to a shriek, and she launched herself to her feet.

Ellian stood to stare her down. "Do you know how many lives were risked—were lost—to give me that one shot at the Inner Court?" He took a step closer, forcing her to back up. "Now because of your decision, more of my allies will put their lives on the line."

"I didn't—"

"You didn't think. If I bring home another body to bury on Thieves' Night, that blood will be on your hands."

She blinked, and tears leapt to her eyes.

But Ellian would not take back the words. His hands curled into fists.

He watched her gray gaze harden, her jaw clench. The princess spat, "This isn't my fault. If you'd told me your plan, none of this would have happened." She held up her hand. "If you didn't hold your precious, damned secrets so close, I'd still have this finger!"

Ellian's jaw clenched.

She didn't back down. "You swore to keep me from harm. You gave your oath."

Every muscle in his body tensed, but Ellian was forced to nod. Grudgingly, he added, "And I owe you payment for breaking it."

A sharp, shaky breath. "I want to go home." Her voice cracked. Small, shattered. It tore at something inside him, found a crack in his fury and pried it open.

"I can't. You pledged a year in Faerie, that cannot be broken."

Anger flooded her eyes. "Faerie was a mistake," she spat. "And maybe the gates *should* be closed."

"You don't mean that—"

"Yes, I do. We'd be better off without monsters like you!"

He flinched. "If the Key is used, you would be stuck here. Could you endure being trapped forever with a creature you hate so fiercely?"

Cirelle's only response was a dark glare.

The trickle of warmth she'd kindled inside him at the palace turned cold, mere empty ashes left behind. He let the doors slam when he left.

ꞔꞓ

Cirelle had little time to adapt to the loss of her finger. The potion did what it could, and she learned to bear the pain. As payment for her sacrifice and for breaking his oath to protect her, Ellian bestowed upon her the ring that held glamour in place. With it, she at least bore the illusion of a finger once more. But the false finger held no sensation of its own, a mere phantom.

While a melancholy gripped Cirelle, Toben and Ellian scurried about in a rash of last-minute meetings.

And then it came: Toben's final night in Faerie. By his request, they celebrated with the gaming that had ceased after the incident. No talk of Thieves' Night was allowed, and Cirelle promised Toben she would remain polite.

A promise she skirted as much as possible.

"Care to make it interesting, faerie?" There was a sharp, bitter bite in Cirelle's voice as she glanced at Ellian across the table, a vicious smile curling her lips. She peeked under the cup at her dice and covered them again.

The knuckle of her missing finger itched and burned. She hadn't forgiven him for her injury or for the words flung at her in anger. But Ellian seemed determined to pretend none of it had ever happened. He met her poison with a cool smile. "You seem terribly eager to make another bargain, princess." He didn't even glance at his own dice trapped under the wooden cup before him.

"Not a bargain," Cirelle corrected Ellian. "A wager."

Toben pushed his own cup into the center of the table, dice and all. "If it's more than game tokens, it's too much for me," he shrugged. "I'm out this hand."

Neither of them responded. "I wonder," Ellian asked Cirelle, "what would you ask as my forfeit?"

"Dessert." Small, petty. But she dared not push him too far. So, she would take her vengeance in tiny pieces. She'd seen how he favored his sweets. "Loser forfeits their dessert at dinner tomorrow to the winner."

Ellian's lip quirked upward. "Perhaps you don't realize this, but the brownies could easily make extras if you ask."

"It's not about getting an extra," Cirelle said. "It's about you *not* getting one." A tiny bit of vindictiveness.

Across the table, her faerie host glanced under his cup and met her gaze again. His eyes were flat gray, his mouth frozen in a teasing half-smile. But there was a faint tension around those eyes. A sign Cirelle now recognized. She bared her teeth in a savage grin and asked, "Is it a wager, then?"

"Yes."

"Then show me."

Ellian revealed his hand in a casual motion. Three stars.

Cirelle lifted her own cup to reveal two moons and a star. "Your dessert is mine, faerie."

They played four more hands, each with varying wagers. The stakes increased as Cirelle angled to take more and more from the faerie. She lost access to the music room for a day but won the choice to select their dinners for a week. And she would make sure they were all of Ellian's most hated dishes.

Toben took the third round, coerced into joining the bargaining while Cirelle withdrew. He won a bottle of fine Durlish whiskey from Ellian's Archive, much to his delight.

Cirelle should have withdrawn on the fourth hand, and she knew it. Ellian stared her down, a faint cat's smile on his lips. His face was relaxed, without that tell. Still, Cirelle held a great roll, better than most. And he'd offered a juicy plum, the choice of any instrument in his music room, including the exquisite harp she played most often.

"And in return?" she asked.

"Every fortnight, you visit the ballroom with me, starting one week after Thieves' Night. Just the two of us." His grin turned sly, silver eyes piercing. "And we dance for one hour."

Cirelle swallowed back the sudden lump in her throat. Deep inside, those moths fluttered their wings. But her roll was excellent. And she'd never heard anything like that harp. She nodded.

"After you, princess," Ellian gestured.

Cirelle revealed three moons.

Ellian casually lifted his own cup. Two moons and a diamond. He'd won.

The moths turned to sparrows in Cirelle's belly. Ellian watched her with a burning gaze, his lips a cruel smirk. Cirelle's mouth dried out and her hands grew cold.

Toben broke the tension awkwardly. "One more round?"

Focusing on her dice, Cirelle tried not to think about that ghostly ballroom. The memory of those dances at the Unseelie palace wouldn't leave her, and a flush suffused her skin as she rolled her next hand with trembling fingers.

No. Ellian's secrets had left her with a permanent, painful injury. She still couldn't properly play her harp, and her chest hurt just to enter the music room anymore. His fault. She wouldn't let herself be swayed by the memory of a few stolen kisses.

The fifth round, Cirelle rolled the best combination in the game. It was hard not to reveal her delight, but she'd been practicing her facial expressions since they'd begun their gaming weeks ago. Her performance at the Unseelie palace only sharpened those skills.

"A final wager," Ellian suggested. "If you feel you can handle it, Princess."

"I can." Her hand was unbeatable, and Ellian's tell was written plainly on his face, the taut skin around those eyes.

This was the time to risk it all.

"The memory jar and Briere's ring." The answer came to

Cirelle without hesitation. Though she'd lost her first kiss, she could still recall every detail of the moment she received that ring. Her nameday, mere weeks before Briere was to be married. A bittersweet sorrow had painted the festivities. The memories still burned; Briere slipping the ring onto Cirelle's finger, the tender, tear-stained kiss that followed.

The blank space on her finger was an itch, an ache. That ring was Cirelle's last reminder of her only love, and she wanted it back.

Ellian leaned forward, elbows on the table. "I'll wager the jar and the ring you used to summon me. But if you lose, you add six months to your time in Faerie."

Cirelle blinked. Her hands tingled to peek under her cup again, to reassure herself she had a winning roll. But she held herself in check. A dull roar started in her ears. Six more months. Was it worth getting back her ring and her memory?

She tilted her head, eying her opponent across the parlor table. Ellian's gaze gleamed silver, his face an unreadable stone mask. But there it was, an indefinable tension.

His tell.

"You're bluffing," she said, taking all her willpower to keep her voice calm.

"Only one way to find out, Princess."

Cirelle *knew* she held the winning hand. There was not a single combination that was higher. She swallowed, then nodded. "Yes."

Ellian's smile widened, a shark's pointed grin, and he tipped over his cup.

Cirelle's heart stopped. Three diamonds.

"Now yours." The faerie stared expectantly, knowingly.

Her hands shaking, Cirelle lifted her cup, revealing another trio of diamonds.

Ellian plucked one of his dice from the table and dropped it into his cup. "It seems we roll a tiebreaker." For such were the rules of this game. A single die, rolled by each player at the same time.

Cirelle picked up her own die, holding it in her palm and placing the cup over it. She didn't trust her voice not to quaver, so she merely nodded as a faint buzzing sound rang in her ears.

Ellian casually jostled the die in the cup and flipped it on the table. Cirelle followed suit, her hands shaking so hard the die rattled loudly.

Together, they lifted their cups, and the world grew dim. She'd rolled a lowly circle, and Ellian's die bore a star. His smile turned wicked, his eyes like blue topaz gems. "I win."

Chapter Forty-One

ALL THE AIR LEFT Cirelle's lungs, and she sucked it back in a ragged gasp. "No."

"The wager was struck, fair and square. An extra six months here," he repeated.

Cirelle couldn't tear her eyes from that painted star. Everyone's voices sounded muffled and far away.

"You cheated."

"I didn't cheat. I didn't even start the wagering," he pointed out. He gathered up his dice with those graceful fingers and dropped them back into his wooden cup.

Cirelle's hand clenched into a fist on the table. Her anger filled the room, thickening the air.

"Please." Toben's gentle voice cut through the rising tension. "This isn't how I wanted to spend my last night here."

A sheepish silence hung in the parlor. His plea cut the cord of Cirelle's rising anger and she slumped, head in her hands. She still couldn't force her mouth to form words. She'd been so certain she'd win back Briere's ring. Ellian had a tell, for Stars' sake!

The realization settled on her like a smothering blanket.

Ellian knew she'd figured out his tell and had duped her

completely. She wanted to scream at him, to rail at Ellian for goading her into another half a year of service, but Toben was right. An argument wasn't the way to send him off.

She wouldn't forget this, though, and she'd get her revenge. Somehow.

"Ellian," Toben said softly into the silence. "I'll take my winnings now if you please."

Ellian tore his gaze from Cirelle to pull a heavy bottle from the pouch at his hip. He set it before Toben with a flourish.

"Glasses?" The old man asked next.

The faerie lifted an eyebrow but produced three small crystal glasses.

Toben poured a jot of whiskey into each and pushed them toward the two. Cirelle stared at hers, the dark amber liquid sparkling in the cut crystal. Human spirits, free of faerie enchantment. She grasped it with an unsteady hand. Perhaps the alcohol would drown the birds whose wings beat against the inside of her ribs.

Toben lifted his glass, but it seemed even he couldn't think of a toast. He shook his head and gulped it down.

The whiskey burned and scraped its way down Cirelle's throat, fire in a bottle. She coughed, her eyes watering. For a single worrying moment, her dinner threatened to come back up. Then the dizzy jolt of the alcohol hit her, a pleasant tingling wave that crashed through her body. It softened the sharpest edges of her anxiety and anger.

Toben sighed, pouring himself another glass. "Perhaps a different game this time."

"Yes," Ellian purred, "and I have just the one. Now we wager with truths." His eyes pierced Cirelle, bright as polished steel blades. He picked up one of the tokens from their previous game, placing it in the center of the table and clearing the rest.

"It's an old Kishi drinking game. Whomever has the token is the Emperor and can ask any one of their subjects a question. The subject then answers honestly and becomes the next Emperor or refuses to reply and drinks. If they don't answer, the Emperor asks a different subject a question until someone accepts or until we're all under the table." His cerulean eyes complemented his smirk. "A player can withdraw at any time, but only if they leave. No listening in on secrets unless you're willing to divulge your own."

Cirelle cocked her head. A chance to glean answers from the sidhe, now that she better knew what questions to ask. "Only if you promise not to sidestep the question. None of this tricky faerie nonsense. Answer the spirit of the question as well."

Ellian gave her a nod. The gesture of a rival in a duel acknowledging a point. "Accepted, on one more condition. No questions about Thieves' Night, whatsoever."

"Agreed."

Ellian nudged the token toward Toben, who'd been watching the exchange with silent interest. "As the guest of honor, Toben shall be our first Emperor."

"That's all well and good, my lord." Toben pulled his whiskey bottle closer. "But pardon my saying, and I like both of you well enough, but I'd prefer to keep most of my winnings."

Conceding with a nod, Ellian produced another bottle.

Cirelle shook her head. "Oh, no, I'm not playing this game with faerie spirits."

"Relax, Princess. It's human brandy, no enchantment or faerie meddling. Plain mortal alcohol, on my oath." He pulled her glass closer and poured a measure into her cup, then his own.

Cautiously, Cirelle sipped. Arravene pear brandy, the same liquor she'd given Ellian as one of her summoning gifts.

"Here." Ellian tapped the side of Cirelle's glass lightly with the back of a knuckle, one of his rings clinking merrily against the crystal as he did.

The glass chilled beneath Cirelle's fingers. Ellian lifted an eyebrow, and she narrowed her eyes. "Show-off."

With a chuckle, Ellian gestured to Toben. "Shall we begin?"

As Cirelle would have predicted, Toben started the game innocently enough, asking Cirelle her favorite food dish from home. "Cook Jana's spiced stew," she answered easily.

There were a hundred things Cirelle wanted to ask Ellian, but she started small. Or at least she thought it was a harmless question. "Why are some rooms in this manor filled with dust, while others like the library and music room are well-cared-for?"

Ellian's eyes darkened. A sad little smile brushed the corner of his lips. "My youngest sisters played their flutes to the point of irritation. My brother wanted to be a scholar before fate chose another path. Though truth be told, we had few enough books at our home. My elder sister tended the small garden, filling it with flowers and beautiful things as well as the vegetables for our dinner table."

Cirelle swallowed. Memorials. He'd saved these things to honor his family. She pushed the token toward him in silence.

For a time, the questions returned to simple ones. A favorite color, or a fond childhood memory. They sipped their alcohol as they played, even when the game didn't decree it necessary. It was fine brandy, smooth on Cirelle's tongue, cooled by the chill glass.

Cirelle asked Ellian once, "What do all of those rings do?"

Tapping each in turn, he listed them off. "Heat, cold, a sleep spell, teleportation of others without touching them, protection against poisoning, sight to see through some glamours, a light source, a temporary magical shield if I summon it, and," he tapped the last one on his right pinky finger, "a lie detector."

Cirelle blinked at him, a sour taste in her mouth. Ellian smiled, a feline grin.

"All this time, you could tell if I lied?"

He nodded.

Cirelle wracked her brain, trying to remember what lies she'd told him, but the brandy left her thoughts sluggish and she came up blank.

"Now, Princess," Ellian leaned forward on the table, tilting his head to watch her as he claimed his token. "What secret would you most like to keep buried?"

Her heart stuttered, and Cirelle's cheeks burned. *The curse of my moody fits. That I gave the prince permission to touch me. What we almost did at the palace.* With a glare, she downed her glass. At least the dizzy rush from the brandy gave her an excuse for the flush in her skin.

Ellian laughed, that arrogant chuckle that felt like a caress. Cirelle barely noticed when he moved on, asking Toben a question that was much less shameful and intrusive. The inquiries grew more ridiculous or sordid as they all proceeded into roaring drunkenness. Cirelle's anger loosened, a pleasant fuzziness taking its place.

In one round, Cirelle admitted that she'd gotten her belly button pierced at a town festival with Briere, in kitchen-maid disguises. It was another rebellion, a fashion adopted from Nycen. The piercing had festered, and she was forced to remove it, as well as sneak supplies from the healer's hut to tend it.

Toben told a tale of a fiery argument with his wife that left him in the Saedden snow in nothing but his smallclothes. He'd been forced to knock on doors seeking shelter until a neighbor's family let him in, much to the tittering amusement of their children.

With a yawn, Toben pushed his chair back, and even he was

a bit wobbly on his feet. "I'm out. Got some of this bottle left and I want to savor it later." He cast a quick, worried glance at Cirelle. "If you're wise, my Lady, you'll retire too."

With those last words, Toben walked out of the room.

Ellian watched Cirelle with hooded eyes. "So, Princess. Are you going to be 'wise' and follow Toben's advice, or will you be reckless and stay?"

She narrowed her eyes. "What do you think?"

His eyes shone azure, shot through with veins of goldenrod yellow. "I think it's too tempting to probe me for information with no one else around. You'll stay."

Just to be contrary, Cirelle wanted to leave. To prove him wrong. But he wasn't. This was her chance to find out everything she wanted to know. The brandy left her limbs tingling, her head swimming, and her good sense far behind.

When she didn't move, Ellian arched a brow. "Well, it seems I'm still the Emperor." He twirled his token on the table. His eyes met hers, a deep and pained blue. "Do you truly hate me now?"

The world fell out beneath her, Cirelle's stomach turning in knots. Anger still gripped her, yes. But true hatred? She gritted her teeth. "No."

Wordlessly, he slid the token to her.

Cirelle swallowed hard, stroking the edge of the token with her thumb. So many questions. She was surprised at the one that tumbled from her lips. "Why did you say no, at the palace? That night..." She let the words trail away, the memory burning within her. The agonized look on his face as he caressed her cheek and rejected her at the same time.

"Because when that happens between us, I don't want to be looking into the glamoured gaze of Ibrafel the sylvan. I want to see your face, your own gray eyes. And certainly not when you've been breathing faerie smoke." His gaze held hers, violet mingled with rose pink, a garden of color. No smiles, no taunting.

Cirelle's stomach flopped over as she was unable to muster a single word in reply. Her hands wrapped around her glass, and she tossed back the brandy without prompt. The warm flush of heat steadied her and numbed the flurry of inexplicable panic. She poured another glass.

Picking up the coin again, Ellian rested his chin in one hand. Melancholy settled over his face.

"I'm sorry." His eyes drifted downward. "For what I said to you that night we returned from the palace. And I'm even sorrier that you were hurt." Achingly sapphire, his eyes, like bottomless pools of agony.

Cirelle's heart turned a somersault. "That wasn't a question."

A sad smile tugged on his lips. "No, it wasn't. So, if you don't hate me... will you accept my apology?"

A pause. She scanned his face for deceit. The anger she'd been holding onto so tightly cracked and splintered. "Yes."

With clumsy motions, she reached out and took the token from his hand. His fingertips were so warm when she brushed them. Her head felt fuzzy, full of unspun wool, and she struggled to form another question. A single, unbidden thought emerged from the murk.

"Did you love her at all?" She didn't have to specify whom.

"Kyrinna? No." His fingers coaxed the coin from her grasp. "Do you worry you might follow in her footsteps?" There was something hesitant and guarded in that gaze.

Cirelle stared into those fretful blue eyes, guilt swimming in their depths. Memories flitted through her mind. The almost-kisses, the hollow hopelessness on his face when he confided his fears of losing his humanity, the softness with which he'd held her hand.

That one shining, glorious moment at the Unseelie ball, when she'd looked at him and saw something of herself reflected back at her: a rebel, a troublemaker. Or that shade of rosy pink that had painted his gaze and made her so very uneasy.

Her eyes darted to his rings, to the one with the lapis stone he'd called a lie detector. She swallowed, her throat going dry. "Yes." She shook her head even as she said it. She couldn't. She would not be *tamed*, turned into some moon-eyed maiden.

He slid the token over without another word, his motions lacking his usual grace. Cirelle's heart threatened to burst through her chest, it pounded so fiercely. The words burned her tongue, but she said them anyway, knowing the question was foolish. No matter his answer, she wouldn't like it.

Still, the question spilled from her lips. "Have you ever fallen in love with one of your human servants?"

He didn't look at her, but down at his glass. Utter silence held. Cirelle couldn't even hear her own breathing, nothing but the faint ring in her ears. "Yes."

"And you still let them go."

It wasn't a question. Ellian didn't have to answer, but he did. "The bargain was made. When their time was up, they returned to the mortal realm."

As Cirelle would, though he'd managed to add another six months onto her sentence tonight. "Yet you courted them, seduced them."

It wasn't a question, and he didn't have to answer, but he did. "Yes."

"Like you did with Kyrinna. Like you tried to do with me."

Silence.

"I'm done," she muttered, pushing her chair back from the table and standing. The room swayed, and she steadied herself on the table.

She expected Ellian to offer assistance, to try to walk her back to her room. In silence, he pushed the token back and forth across the table as she walked away.

The next evening, they bid Toben farewell after breakfast with aching, pounding heads. Even Ellian moved gingerly.

Cirelle pulled the old man into an embrace. "Thank you," she said. "For being kind."

He blushed. "It was nothing."

And like that, Ellian whisked him away and returned alone.

Chapter Forty-Two

IN THE DAYS BEFORE THIEVES' NIGHT, visitors arrived. Cirelle opened the front door to a familiar face as Ellian entered the foyer behind her.

"Shai," he greeted her, then nodded to the sidhe beside her. "Issen."

Shai tossed a forlorn glance at Cirelle. "Babysitting duty, Ellian? Really?"

The utter lack of recognition was jarring, but Shai and Issen had only known Cirelle in her sylvan guise, dapple-skinned with a sharp and narrow face. Right now, Shai looked upon Cirelle as if she'd tasted bitter, over-steeped tea.

Issen stood off to the side, watching the proceedings with those attentive, salmon-colored eyes. His short robe and trousers were pale ivory trimmed in cloth-of-gold. Cirelle was still fascinated with his hair, how it was composed of strands in a dozen shades from palest butter to deepest goldenrod, all combining to give the effect of a vibrant spring blossom.

Cirelle broke away from Issen's stare and looked back to Shai. The woman once again wore a strange mix of feminine lace and practical armor. A chest piece in a pattern of layered autumn leaves artfully complemented her blood-red skin. Beneath it, a fluttering gown of deep green fell to her knees over tall leather boots. A sword hung from a wide belt at her hips.

"Yes, really." Ellian remained unfazed by Shai's display of attitude. "You swore to help this mission in whatever way I thought best, and this is it. You will both guard the princess."

"Do I have to?" Shai whined. "I'm gonna miss out on the mission."

Ellian replied, "As a member of my household, however temporary, Cirelle is under my protection. This is final."

"Fiiiine." The faerie drew the word out in a groan.

Cirelle snapped. Misery gnawed at her daily, and she was all too eager to sink her fangs into someone else, to spread the poison. "I don't want a bodyguard who's acting like a spoiled child. For all I care, you can go back wherever you came from." She whirled off toward the Archive where they could not follow. "I have a job to do. Enjoy your time here," she snarled with biting sarcasm as she yanked the door open.

Once in the Archive, Cirelle gave in to her anger, kicking the heavy wood of the doors as the beast in her mind spat and growled, a sudden rage that could not be contained. Vivid pain erupted in her toe through the soft boots. She growled in frustration, almost a scream.

Cirelle stomped over to the shelves she'd been dusting before the newcomers arrived. She knelt to wipe clear another patch of the dark wood. The knuckle of her missing finger jolted with a spike of pain as she clutched the rag too tightly.

When Ellian entered, Cirelle didn't bother turning around. Instead, she just muttered, "Why are all faeries so unbearably arrogant?"

"I don't know. Why are human princesses so hot-tempered?"

With a frustrated huff, Cirelle kept at her task. Her eye

snagged on the memory jar that held Briere's ring, mocking her recklessness and stupidity. She should have known better than to try matching wits with the fae. She'd failed and lost a finger for it. And she'd added half a year to her sentence, as well as being stuck with those dances every fortnight.

Cirelle continued wiping down the shelf. The heavy silence between them stretched thin.

Ellian exhaled. "Shai is non-negotiable. On Thieves' Night, she will watch over you even if you despise it. You'd best become accustomed to the idea." His hand on the knob, he paused. "Shai and Issen have the run of the house. They know the rooms here and can select their own, but courtesy demands we show them to their chambers. They wait in the foyer still. You will escort them."

Cirelle scowled as she set her rag aside and stood. "Fine."

In the main entryway, he nodded to the two sidhe. "If you need anything, let one of us or a brownie know, and we will help you. Welcome."

Issen sketched a quick bow. Even Shai gave Ellian a respectful nod before regarding Cirelle with a cautious gaze. Cirelle only glared back. She made a curt gesture for the faeries to follow. Shai didn't even bother, leading the way herself while Cirelle and Issen trailed behind.

As it turned out, Shai's favored chambers were around the corner from Cirelle's. She clomped ahead and slammed the door. In contrast, an uncomfortable silence fell over Issen and Cirelle while she followed him to his chambers to ensure he had everything he needed.

"Don't mind her," he said, indicating Shai's door as they passed. "She's young and still full of fire, but she'll soften up to you soon enough." He cocked his head, eyes sly. His gaze flicked down to the hand that should be missing a finger, now glamoured even against this faerie's scrutiny. "Ellian's guest at the Hunt. It was you, wasn't it? The sylvan."

Cirelle's cheeks flushed. "What?" she feigned confusion. "I don't know what you're talking about."

"I think you do."

"You're not making sense."

Ellian had told her these two were on their side, but Cirelle still didn't trust them. Especially Issen. There was something all too clever in the slender faerie's demeanor.

He shrugged. "I make perfect sense." At the room, he opened the door and gave a quick glance around. "This is sufficient." He gave her another of those close-lipped smiles. "I look forward to speaking with you again, Cirelle. Or should I call you Ibrafel?"

Before she could manage a response, Issen shook his head and shut the door.

Chapter Forty-Three

WHILE THIEVES' NIGHT LOOMED ever closer, Cirelle mingled with their faerie guests. By suppertime the first day, Shai had warmed to Cirelle, her temper vented. Instead, she rattled off questions about life in Arraven. Also a changeling, Shai had been raised in a kingdom across the sea.

"Resangra," Shai told her. "Arraven hasn't discovered it yet."

The idea of an undiscovered country in her own world fascinated Cirelle, and their first night gaming was spent asking Shai about her homeland while Issen roundly beat them both at Nightswheel. Ellian was nowhere to be found, sequestered in a last-minute flurry of Thieves' Night plans.

Often, Shai would retreat to the garden or ballroom for weapons practice, while Cirelle and Issen would seek solace in song. Issen was excellent at musical improvisation, coming up with meandering melodies while Cirelle strummed background chords. She tried to ignore the pain in her knuckle, and Issen didn't comment on any missed notes.

They spoke of many things as they played, Cirelle often probing him for more information on Faerie and the sidhe. He told her of the Lhyrria, of faerie traditions and customs, and even some of their holidays. The small details that her books had skimmed or skipped entirely.

When she asked about his sidhe magic, Issen turned it into a lesson. Cirelle gritted her teeth at being lectured over things she already knew, but let him continue for the small nuggets of new knowledge he would scatter among the known facts.

"We all have varying gifts, the daoine sidhe," Issen told her as he oiled the odd stringed instrument he favored. "Some have only one or two, others have as many as four."

Seizing the chance to pry, Cirelle asked, "How many does Ellian have?"

"You haven't puzzled it out yet?"

"Just the eyes, if that even counts."

Issen focused on his work for a time, and Cirelle gave up on waiting for him to answer. The calm, stoic sidhe could fall silent at the drop of a hat and not speak for minutes at a time.

"Yes, the eyes. And a gift for glamour, strong enough to fool even powerful sidhe into thinking you were a sylvan."

Cirelle remained silent.

Issen sighed softly, but gave her a knowing smile, those blush-tinted eyes kind and canny. "Most sidhe can only glamour themselves, but Ellian can cast an illusion over others or inanimate objects."

"Except he can't keep a lock on those eyes."

"You think so?" Issen's smirk was small, sly. "If they shift around you, it's because he allows you to see it."

A pang twisted her chest.

Issen continued. "Have you never wondered how he always knows which items to pull from his pouch, and where they are in his Archive?"

Cirelle blinked.

"Yes, I know how the Archive works," Issen told her. "That's not the matter at hand. Ellian's third gift is memory. A cuimh-nesidhe."

"A what?"

"Some abilities crop up often enough they have specific names. The beansidhe who can predict death, cait sidhe the shapeshifter, and leanansidhe the seducer of mortals."

"Ha," Cirelle snorted and added, "Ellian's not the last?"

"No, child." Issen shook his head slowly. "If you ever had the misfortune of being at a leanansidhe's mercy, you would know. It is not nearly as pleasant as Ellian's affections."

Cirelle flushed. "So, what is the one Ellian has again?"

"Cuimhnesidhe. It means memory. He can recollect anything he's ever heard or seen, with perfect recall."

"Anything?"

Issen nodded.

Meaning he could still remember in excruciating clarity every regret and sorrow in his long life. Wouldn't that drive one mad, after decades?

But also... "That's how he knows everything in the Archive, and where to get it. That's why we have to update the list every time something new comes in, and the reason he insists on reviewing the notes when we do."

Issen nodded.

"Why are you telling me this?"

"I don't like knowledge kept from anyone."

"So, does that mean you'll tell me what abilities you and Shai have?"

Issen was silent for a while, rubbing the oil into the dark wood with small, circular motions. "Shai has an immunity to iron's poison."

"Wait, so that's actually a steel blade she uses?"

"Yes, and she doesn't shy from flaunting that gift before the other sidhe."

"Her mask—" Cirelle caught herself a moment too late, and Issen's sidelong glance was positively mischievous.

"How would you have seen her mask, if you know nothing of the ball that mysterious sylvan attended?"

Cirelle shuffled her stack of sheet music as her cheeks reddened. "Fine. It was me."

"I know."

"Why make me admit it, then?"

Issen shrugged. "Because I like knowing when I'm right." He put away the rag and began restringing his instrument.

Cirelle barked a laugh. "Well, that makes two of us." She marked the time and key signatures on her new sheet of music paper and toyed with a melody. "So, what are your talents?"

"I control elements. Light, water, and earth. Meager gifts, but effective if one knows how to use them."

"Meager?" Cirelle raised an eyebrow as she strummed the harp's strings. "If those are meager, what is a measly human?"

"Humans are passion, and wildness, and freedom." He tightened the screw on a string. "There's a reason so many of our kind are drawn to yours. And why so many others despise you. The prince loathes mortals because you are not bound as we are, chained by immutable rules and burdens." He finished tuning the last string and ran the bow along the instrument to test it. "You can tell blatant, utter untruths. You can break an oath. The prince covets such freedom. Therefore, he hates."

Issen tried out a few notes, and Cirelle matched them with a cascade of her own. "It seems like an awful waste of energy, hating that deeply."

"Yes," Issen agreed somberly. "Yes, it does."

❦

THE DAY OF THIEVES' NIGHT, the household awoke mid-morning. Their allies arrived one-by-one as the day wore on. Vilitte entered with a smile, her smoky quartz appearance even more unsettling in the sunbeams spilling through the foyer's skylight. Her new, shorter hair had been trimmed evenly.

Cirelle also heard the stone giant Ixikki speak for the first time, a surprisingly gentle voice like the low rumble of distant, crumbling mountains. Es seemed to maintain a perpetual expression of worry on his bat's face and spoke little. Leilarie took a special joy in supervising from a perch on Ixikki's shoulder.

Ixikki fortified the outer exits by hauling large boulders from Ellian's lands to block off the side doors. The garden was off-limits as well, the doors to the stairwell now barricaded from the inside with more blocks of stone.

The brownies locked themselves in their wing and refused to come out, leaving piles of food in the dining hall and retreating before mid-afternoon.

While everyone else performed their own tasks, Vilitte joined Cirelle in locking every door. The entire time, she peppered Cirelle with a series of questions in her calm, sardonic manner. How did Cirelle enjoy Faerie so far? Did she find the work tiresome? Who was the other human staying here?

There was a sly, patronizing note to the questions that made Cirelle's hackles rise. She kept her answers short. Her growing irritation only seemed to amuse Vilitte, the smile on the faerie's face growing wider with each inquiry.

Issen cast a wary, sidelong glance at Vilitte's conversation. He and Shai walked ahead of Cirelle, ducking into every outward-facing room of the manor to block the windows and spread iron shavings on all the windowsills. Issen gave the bits of dull gray metal a wide berth, but Shai brushed her fingers through them without batting an eye.

Vilitte's gaze followed the two sidhe, her lips curled in that cat's grin. "So, where were we? Ah, yes. How does a peasant's clothing suit you? Comfortable, or dreadfully drab?" Cirelle ground her teeth at Vilitte's interrogation as she continued locking doors with the skeleton key Ellian had entrusted to her.

All too soon, it was nearly time for Ellian and his crew to leave.

Kith and the wolf-like Carid both showed up at the last possible instant, apparently declining the opportunity to participate in preparations. The tiny flock of Ulim were absent. They were spies, not thieves.

A noticeable tension thrummed in the air, everyone's nerves on edge. The group would worldwalk closer to the palace before the magic faded. After the mission, they'd meet a short distance from the palace in a pre-designated area. They would retreat to the manor when magic returned.

That is, if everything went according to plan.

Cirelle fidgeted. The group convened on the pathway outside the manor. The sun was setting, and Cirelle could not steady the frantic, nervous energy that filled her.

In the hazy lavender twilight, movement flickered at the end of the pathway. A figure stood inside the gate, a vague black silhouette with burning violet eyes. It was the shadow creature, the one Cirelle could only see in her peripheral vision. A host of skittering forms followed in its wake, giant spider-like shapes that turned Cirelle's stomach. The eerie faerie approached the group, whispering Ellian's name. The sound was more like rustling leaves and snapping twigs than human speech.

Ellian bowed to the shadow.

"Scath," Ellian greeted the creature.

The creature didn't bother with a greeting. "As agreed, I've brought the ilthys." The Scath gestured at the shadowy shapes behind it, all spiky legs and angles. They grew more solid, more real as the sun sank. A faint chittering sound echoed, like a thousand clacking insect jaws.

"Cirelle," Ellian called without turning back. Did anyone else note the tension in his voice?

She approached, throat too dry to speak.

"Tonight, the ilthys will guard the manor, commanded by the Scath. Take the others back to your parlor and lock the door. The ilthys will be confined to the corridors." His gaze slid to the setting sun, then the Scath. "Don't come out until the sun rises." The words were strained, not a proper goodbye at all.

The clicking sound was getting louder, the spider-shapes growing ever more solid as the sun touched the horizon. They were twice as tall as a person, their legs as thick as Cirelle's thighs.

"Go," Ellian urged her, eyes flickering black and rose and emerald green in turn.

It wasn't the farewell she wanted, though Cirelle couldn't have said what she expected. An apology? A tear-stained good-bye? A last stolen kiss before he went into danger? They all seemed equally ridiculous.

She met his stare for several tense moments. Her missing finger still hurt, and a spiteful part of her hoped he'd come back empty-handed. As she brushed the back of her knuckle with her thumb, she remembered the prince's icy expression and the fervent, greedy look in Queen Ayre's eyes as she held the knife.

Ellian left to face them, to take the Key from beneath their noses. Even with the aid of his coterie, would it be enough to avoid getting caught? Or would he too pay the price of the Queen's wrath?

Cirelle's anger flickered and died, replaced with an anxious unease. Her tongue tangled on her farewell. *Come back safe. Please don't die. Don't do this.* They all flitted through her mind, but in the end, she blurted, "Good luck."

Swallowing back the sudden lump in her throat, Cirelle turned and fled from the ilthys with the others on their heels.

Chapter Forty-Four

THE UNSEELIE PALACE'S CORRIDORS were eerily quiet as Ellian ghosted through them, silent as a shadow. It was a skill he rarely used, one learned long ago in another life. His hand traced the lines of the sculpted marble relief on the walls as he walked. Gray fingertips brushed the horns of a giant stone ram locked in eternal battle with a mighty stag.

Odd, that these halls would still seem so familiar despite the many years and his best efforts to forget them. But he could never banish those nightmares, not with his gift of flawless memory. He took another turn, his feet leading the way. The entirety of this castle was etched into his mind, burned there forever along with the phantoms of what he'd experienced here.

Ellian had hoped to earn that spot in the Inner Court so he would already be inside the palace when Thieves' Night began, but that mission had failed.

Perhaps it would have been wiser to select someone else for the festival.

It had been a necessary bit of subterfuge. And except for that one grievous error, Cirelle had excelled at playing her part. A bit *too* well, if Ellian were honest with himself. That woman was indeed a vixen in a princess's skin. It seemed her family's heraldry had been chosen well, and her role in fox-and-hounds. *I'm always the fox.*

He'd let the princess think their brazen show was for the entire Unseelie Court, but it had been more than that. Ploys within ploys. Sidhe games. How he loathed them, but one didn't survive in Faerie without playing them.

It wasn't far to the royal wing now. Dread turned his stomach and made his hands shake.

I can do this. He had to. It was his responsibility to rectify what he'd unwittingly set in motion.

He passed through empty halls. On Thieves' Night, there should be a heavy guard presence over the castle, but Ixikki had performed his task perfectly. When the chaos hit, Ellian and most of the crew had been lurking outside the palace in a grove of fruit trees, waiting for the signal. That sign, as planned, was the stone giant storming right up to the front doors, swatting aside the guards like rag dolls, and punching a hole through the thick marble. Kith and Carid joined him, launching into the fray on the front line.

Ayre and Adaleth had secured their palace against sidhe intruders and espionage, but not against a brutal assault by a near-invincible living statue. It caused the intended disorder, pulling guards from many of their posts to fight the more immediate problem. As Ellian had expected, the small, hidden back entrance outside the palace was now unguarded.

It had been Ellian's last resort for entering the castle. The stone cylinder looked like a well, but it hid a tunnel full of traps and small, slithering creatures far more dangerous than their size suggested.

Ellian led his crew in through this passage. Es's wings would have caught on spiked walls, and he was left at the rendezvous point. The others crept along the small tunnel intended as an emergency escape route for the royal family. The traps were set to trigger only if one traveled up the tunnel the wrong way. Poisoned darts, tripwires rigged to deadly blades, and floors that collapsed to reveal pits lined with razor-sharp spikes.

On any night other than tonight, the magical wards were much deadlier.

With his immaculate memory, Ellian guided them through the traps. He let his crew think it had been merely the clever gathering of intelligence that gave him this information. They didn't know his secret, and he wanted to keep it that way.

Vilitte got them past the tiny, venomous beasts that occupied the passage, her crystalline skin impervious to their fanged bite. By the time they'd reached the hidden door, Vilitte was spattered in the creatures' blood and sickly yellow poison. Ellian lost his dagger in the process, not that he'd ever been much good with it anyway. His elbows and knees were scraped raw on jagged stone, his clothing dusty and torn.

Not ideal, but it could have gone worse.

It was a simple plan, but risky. Leilarie had been inside the palace in her servant's role. When Ixikki stormed the gates and drew the guards, she opened a secret door in a lower tower, cleverly hidden among the sculpted relief along the walls.

Once inside the castle, Ellian nodded to Vilitte, at the head of his crew. "Seek the treasury. I'll check other likely places, ones that are less guarded."

"I don't like this," Leilarie chimed in. "One of us should go with you."

Ellian shook his head firmly. "I know the sidhe's secrets, and I can talk my way out of it if I'm caught where I shouldn't be. You can't. Stick together, take out the treasury guards, and check it. I'll meet you back at the rendezvous."

Grudgingly, they nodded and went their own way. Ellian let out a slow breath. It was possible Adaleth had the sense to store the Key in the treasury, but it was doubtful.

And so he went alone to breach the serpent's lair.

Chapter Forty-Five

"WOULD YOU *PLEASE* STOP PACING?" Shai grumbled at Cirelle.

The three of them were ensconced in Cirelle's parlor, fitfully waiting out the evening. Cirelle nervously nibbled on an olive without tasting it. The brownies had left a small repast there before they'd barricaded themselves into their own wing. Cirelle wasn't hungry, not with her stomach doing backflips, but she ate out of the need to fidget. To do *something*.

The room was dimly lit, adding to her unease. There were no candles in Ellian's manor, only those mystical faerie lights. When Cirelle asked if they could use some candles for Thieves' Night, he'd responded by suggesting a strange, luminescent faerie plant they'd harvested from the garden. Cuttings now lay scattered about the room, leaving everything bathed in an eerie green half-light.

Strange, that these plants could still glow, but the sconces could not. *Thieves' Night dulls our active abilities, but not our innate ones, he'd told her.* Another faerie rule that seemed terribly fickle.

Cirelle paced in the wan light, trying to take the edge off her nervous energy. Issen's eyes lingered on her missing finger, the glamour gone, but he held enough courtesy not to mention it. It couldn't have been a surprise. Surely it was the height of gossip that Ellian's sylvan slut had lost her finger for daring to cross the prince.

Shai was armored, that strange combination of leather pieces over a frilly, girlish dress, with weapons hanging at her sides. Issen bore two knives strapped to his calves. He wore one of his short robes and trousers, his feet in soft boots.

Only Cirelle was unarmed, useless. The tiny voice in her head crept in, whispering that she was just a weakness to be protected. She told it to be quiet and continued to pace.

Shai tried to engage them both in distractions, in parlor games they'd hoarded from the game room. She started casual conversations since both Shai and Issen spoke Trade well enough. A stroke of luck, since the magical earrings were disabled for the evening.

Or perhaps not luck at all. Ellian had a carefully-laid plan for everything, after all.

Cirelle couldn't think straight enough to play a game, not even fox-and-hounds. The panic bubbled inside her. Stubborn pride was all that held her together, a refusal to let them see her fall apart. She clenched her hands, once again grounded by the sensation of fingernails biting deeply into flesh.

Hours passed.

Still the terror crested and built. She was on the brink of snapping when the front door slammed open, loud enough to echo through the silent manor. In the next moment, Ellian's voice cried her name. It was faint and far away, but the shout was one of unmistakable agony.

"Ellian." Cirelle rushed to the door before she could stop herself. But at the latch, she stopped. The ilthys.

"It's a trick," Issen said.

The next cry was strangled and wordless. It shredded at

something inside her. How loud must he call to hear him all the way down these corridors and through the wooden door? No. Issen was right. He had to be. If it truly were Ellian, he would come to this room.

Unless he was hurt so badly that he couldn't make it.

It's a lie, she told herself as the voice continued screaming. Still, she pressed her forehead to the door and concentrated on her unsteady breaths. In, out, in, out. Her fingertips trembled where they lay against the wood.

The clicking sound of an ilthys passed by in the hallway outside, then silence.

The door crashed open, the heavy halwood splintering.

Cirelle scrambled back, but not far enough. A sharp, chitinous leg stabbed through the opening and hooked around her waist. The nightmarish visage of an ilthys stared at her with its empty spider's eyes. *Stars, it has a face,* Cirelle thought in horror. Sharp, dark teeth crowded in its too-wide mouth. She scrambled under the beast's leg only to be encircled by another.

The sidhe burst into motion, but they were too late. The ilthys yanked Cirelle through the shattered doorway and darted down the hall. She screamed, writhing and scratching at the forelegs, but they held her tightly. The limbs were misshapen, as if they possessed too many joints, and they were as hard and glossy as steel.

This can't be happening. The ilthys were faeries, and she'd never given them permission to touch her.

A single compulsion crowded her head, a need to fight, to survive. Her heart beat hard, each pulse agonizing. She kicked at the thing's face in the dark, but it only hissed. It shifted her around , skittering down the hall. A sharp pain erupted in her abdomen and back, two curving rows of needle-like pinpricks. A warm dampness that soaked her shirt.

Teeth and saliva. Any moment now, it would bite down.

But it didn't. The beast held her in place as it dashed through the hall, turning a corner so sharply Cirelle's neck jerked painfully. Those hard forelimbs still clutched her knees and shoulders. She shrieked and clawed and tried to wriggle away, but it held tight. Every move of her torso caused those teeth to scrape and pierce.

The shouts and cries of her protectors echoed behind her, but they were not as fast as the creature that carried her. The ilthys burst through the open doors and skidded to a stop in the foyer.

Ellian was nowhere to be seen. A trick after all.

Two figures stood bathed in moonlight, clothed in black. A woman with long dark hair pinned tightly about her head held a pair of slim, curved daggers. The man was massive, with a nose that had been broken at least twice and a sour expression.

More ilthys lingered in the space, clinging to stairwells and walls, clicking softly.

Cirelle scratched at the face of the beast that held her, but she could not reach its insect's eyes and the rest was as impenetrable as the limbs that gripped her.

"Hold her tighter," the woman said, pointing at the ilthys with one of those bright, silvery knives.

Those jaws closed a little harder, the teeth piercing Cirelle more deeply. Not yet a grievous injury, but more than enough to leave her immobilized and gasping.

"Ellian's princess." The voice was a mocking coo, speaking heavily-accented Trade. "I'd stop wriggling if I were you." She took a step closer, and the hulking man followed silently. "I'd prefer to do this without killing anyone, but I will not hesitate if you give me a reason. One word from me and that creature will bite you in half. I can just as easily loot your corpse."

At that moment, Cirelle's defenders burst into the foyer.

"Stop or she dies!" The stranger's shout rang through the empty space.

The ilthys shifted, and a new burst of agony jolted through Cirelle. She cried out, and the sidhe went still. The male intruder circled around the woman with thumping steps, stopping between the ilthys and Cirelle's protectors. He lifted his axe at the ready.

Cirelle's mind had gone blank, a constant hoarse scream rattling through her. Still, she managed to choke out a response. "What do you want?"

"The key to the Archive. I know Ellian gave it to you."

"I don't have it," Cirelle lied.

The intruder shook her head and clucked her tongue. "Bite a little deeper." Those teeth ground into Cirelle's flesh again, and she screamed.

"One more lie like that, and it's over." The thief's head tilted. "The key."

Cirelle swallowed. There were things in the Archive that could be devastating in the wrong hands. Terror ran through her veins like ice water, those razor-sharp teeth slicing painfully into her skin. Every small movement was agony.

If she said no, she would die. The intruder would steal the key from her anyway.

Cirelle croaked out the words. "I can't reach it from here. You have to let me down." Anything to get those teeth out of her skin.

"If you or either of your friends makes a sudden movement, this creature will snap you in half before you can scream. Do you understand me?"

Cirelle nodded. As the creature lifted her from its mouth and set her on the floor, she sobbed and then gasped at the pain that lanced through her. "How?" she managed to rasp. "I'm mortal. How can they harm me?"

She didn't expect an answer, but the stranger laughed again. "The ilthys follow the Scath, but even he has a Queen." She held up the curved blade. "Which, since I just killed the last one and took her daggers, is now me. The ilthys have no consciousness. They are mere tools with no will of their own."

But if the intruder could harm her... "You're mortal," Cirelle said in sudden realization. A glance at the woman's ears proved her right.

"Enough talk. The key."

Fear scraped its way through her as she slipped a hand into a damp pocket, soaked through from her time in the mouth of that creature. Each movement sent jabs of pain through her midsection. She withdrew the key and tossed it to the ground before the stranger.

"No!" Shai shouted, taking a step forward.

The intruder picked up the key and barked a bitter laugh. "I warned you not to move." She lifted the daggers again and the eyes of every ilthys in the room followed the motion. "Kill them."

Everything exploded into motion. The ilthys behind Cirelle darted forward and she barely managed to scrabble away as Issen moved like rushing water. He drove his knives into the crease where the beast's leg met its body. With a twist and a sharp wrench, the limb came away with a sickening pop. Black ichor spilled free, and the monster screamed in rage.

Behind the creature, Shai battled the male intruder with the heavy axe, their weapons clanging fiercely together and punctuated with grunts of effort.

More ilthys swarmed, crowding on the edges of the fight.

Cirelle scrambled away and pressed herself against the wall near the open doors to the Archive's office. A howl of anguish yanked her attention back to the woman, now standing in the moonlit antechamber. The thief stared at the now-open doors to the Archive.

But tonight only an empty space stood behind those doors. Just a small, hollow closet.

The intruder swore in words Cirelle did not know, but the meaning was obvious.

Cirelle, in her shock, had stupidly moved to stand in the doorway. Growling her frustration, the intruder dashed directly toward Cirelle, those knives brandished menacingly. Instinct took over, and Cirelle leapt aside. The woman slipped past her, right into the middle of the melee taking place.

It was a scene from a nightmare.

Several ilthys twitched miserably, their legs scattered on the floor, glistening spikes dripping with dark ichor. The hulking masses made a forest of dead and dying beasts. Issen slipped between them, severing limbs and piercing eyes of beasts still standing. But there were always more of the creatures.

Nearby, Shai still faced off against the other stranger. She whooped in glee as she parried one of his attacks. The faerie grinned madly, sweat glittering on her skin. The man stumbled, and one sweep of Shai's heavy sword severed his head. Wet droplets struck Cirelle's cheek, and her stomach turned.

The female intruder stood in the middle of the chaos, blades lifted and laughing madly.

Shai shook blood from her blade and stepped over the fallen body of the man. The intruder launched herself at the sidhe. Cirelle crept around the edge of the room, breath held as she tried to avoid the attention of the ilthys. Her feet squelched on sticky, pooling blood as she watched the battle between Shai and the dagger-wielding thief. They locked weapons, Shai's sword parrying quickly as the intruder sought to pierce through Shai's guard.

A chittering echoed above, and Cirelle barely had time to leap sideways before an ilthys dropped beside her. Those teeth looked worse in the moonlight, wet and sharp as daggers.

She screamed. Before she could move, Issen was there. Quicker than any human, he scrambled up a leg to perch on the beast's back and shove a knife directly into an eye. It shrieked and scrabbled, trying to dislodge Issen.

Were Cirelle's gods looking out for her? Or was it the smallest bit of luck one of the monster's flailing limbs kicked into Shai and the stranger's battle? Shai stumbled back, nicked by the edge of a leg. The main force of the blow punched into the thief's stomach, knocking her onto her back. The knives slipped from her grasp, skidding across the floor.

One came to a halt by Cirelle's feet, the other a mere two paces away. Cirelle didn't think, she just reacted, instinct grasping for any weapon in this melee. She fumbled her first grab. The curved blade bit deeply into her palm at the base of her thumb. She yelped and reached for it again before collecting the other knife as well.

The blades were heavier than Cirelle expected, but their weight was a comfort. Where her skin touched the black hilts, all warmth leeched away, as if the knives had been sitting in a snowbank. A tremor slid through her, something cold and dreadful. The knuckle of her missing finger ached from the chill.

Cirelle hadn't the first idea how to fight. Still, she clutched them tightly in her sweating, bleeding hands. In this chaos, she would take any chance she could to survive. She held the blades up before her in an unsteady pose.

The ilthys loomed silently throughout the foyer, suddenly as still as carved stone. The intruder lurched to her feet in the midst of the beasts, holding her midsection and casting panicked glances around the room.

Cirelle stared up at the nearest ilthys, into its giant and disturbingly human face. Those eyes were onyx orbs, nearly indistinguishable from the exoskeleton plates that made up its features. Jaws of gleaming black teeth sharper than a shark's lay open, frozen mid-scream.

The thief had held this knife up before one of the ilthys while issuing orders. Cirelle lifted one of her blades, and the creature's head tilted to follow it.

The stranger jolted into motion, making a break for the outer door, scrambling through the scattered bodies and slipping on the bloody floor.

"Stop the intruder!" Cirelle demanded. The creature launched itself at the thief, and a thrill skittered through Cirelle's veins. It worked. The spider-like beasts were hers to command. In the middle of this forest of spider legs, blood, and bodies, Cirelle laughed in triumph.

Something inside her had broken.

She pointed the blades at the other ilthys lurking around the foyer. "All of you. Catch the thief."

They obeyed with stunning speed and violence. Before she could utter another word, the ilthys darted down and those teeth crunched through bone.

"No!" Cirelle screamed, but it was too late. All the ilthys froze, but black blood pooled around the thief as she collapsed, a puddle widening so quickly it was obviously hopeless. The intruder groaned weakly and tried to roll over, but flopped back down with another grunt of pain.

Without a word, Shai stepped forward. Her blade made a quick and merciful end to the stranger's misery.

Cirelle's head swam, and her skin grew unbearably hot. *I'm going to vomit.*

Even so, Cirelle kept her grip on those daggers as she pressed her knuckles into the wall for support and heaved her stomach's contents onto the floor. For one brief moment, she felt guilty about sullying that mosaic, then realized how utterly stupid that worry was, considering the gore that splattered the foyer.

When she wiped her mouth with one sleeve and turned, the sidhe stared at her with expressions ranging from pity to pride.

Cirelle wasn't sure which she deserved most.

Chapter Forty-Six

THE ILTHYS STOOD STILL, waiting for Cirelle's command. Silence held, and half a dozen spider-like corpses leaked sticky fluids onto Ellian's beautiful tile floor.

"You were told to stay in your rooms," the Scath's rustling voice came from the upper balcony.

"And you were supposed to command these things!" Cirelle snapped, pointing at the one of the dead ilthys with her blades. The rest of the creatures turned their heads in unison, eyes following the motion.

The Scath no longer faded away when she looked at him, so Cirelle stared him down. A figure wreathed in shadow, a silhouette of light-swallowing darkness. He had two pairs of eyes, one atop the other, the lower ones spread apart. They pulsed with a purplish light. Once, the sight would have made Cirelle cringe, but her fear had all boiled out of her, turning into rage. The rows of bite marks around her belly and back burned.

His reply was crisp, the scrape of dry wood on stone. "I cannot override the oaths made to the bearer of those blades." Those four dots of light narrowed to slits.

Cirelle held up the knives, her hands and arms shaking.

Some voice in the back of her mind was still screaming, crumbling apart at what she'd done. The taste of vomit coated her mouth. Still, when she lifted the daggers, the Scath backed up.

Cirelle had split in two. The cowering princess sobbed and shrieked somewhere in the deepest recesses of her soul. A new, fierce part of her rose to the surface. Faerie had made her into something new, something strong. A rush of pride and determination rippled through her. She bared her teeth in a snarl, her whole body trembling. "If I use these, can I control you as well?"

He was silent.

Cirelle gripped the blades tighter, pointing one of the knives at him. "Go. You and your beasts will do as you pledged and protect the manor."

The Scath hissed, windblown sand skating across stone, and withdrew. The ilthys followed suit, scattering up walls and down corridors.

Cirelle clutched the daggers tightly, wincing at the ache of her missing finger, the sharper pain of the new cut on her palm, and the bite marks on her stomach.

Shai approached, staring at those bared blades with something approaching admiration. Despite the blood-soaked floor, the corpses of giant spiders, and the spattered gore that covered them all, Shai gave Cirelle a flash of a grin.

Cirelle burned with questions. "So, if magic is dead, why do these knives still command the Scath and the spiders? And how did I understand what he said?"

Issen stared down at the daggers in Cirelle's white-knuckled grasp. "No magic, or lack thereof, can break the power of oaths. Not for a faerie." His eyes darted toward the empty closet on the other side of the antechamber. "As for his speech..." Issen grimaced. For a long moment, his gaze lingered on the blades

‿ırelle's grasp. "That's a mystery for another day. The manor is yet vulnerable."

Cirelle's heart fluttered. With a curt nod, she agreed. "Let's find another room to hide in."

"We'll use my parlor," Issen suggested.

With equal parts weariness and anxiety, the group picked their path around the dead ilthys. Cirelle's boots made a horrible sucking sound where they trod in half-dried blood, and she nearly lost her stomach's contents once more. The charnel-house stench was worse than anything she'd ever experienced.

As they passed the foot of the stairs, the front door crashed open. Es flapped through on his bat-like wings, something caught up in his massive talons.

No, not a thing, a *he*. Ellian hung unconscious from those clawed feet.

Es loosened his talons, letting Ellian slide to the floor more or less gently while the bat hurtled to a less graceful landing between the husks of the dead ilthys.

Someone had wrapped Ellian's torso with shredded gray silk, the edges ragged, torn from some fancy curtain or fine dress. He lay on his stomach, his face turned toward Cirelle. The pale, wan look on his face made Cirelle's already-racing pulse sputter. The makeshift bandage was rapidly soaking with a dark stain, like ink on wet paper.

Es struggled to stand with a harsh caw of a sound, and the skittering ilthys came running. Cirelle lifted her daggers and bared her teeth at the beasts. They lurked in the corners of the ceiling, their sharp teeth clacking softly.

Her head turned back to stare at Ellian's limp form. Time had stopped, and Cirelle's heart with it. She only took a single step before another person came tearing through the door.

Cirelle didn't realize she'd thrown herself between the unconscious Ellian and the intruder until they skidded to a stop before her. Cirelle crouched in front of Ellian, daggers raised despite her lack of skill in using them. Kith, the great black cat, all glares and imperious snarls, scrambled to a halt. Astride his back sat a lavender-skinned sidhe. Dirilai, the rattish one who had stared so intently at Cirelle in her sylvan disguise.

"You," the sidhe said in recognition, and Cirelle suddenly knew. This faerie had seen through Ellian's illusion at the palace, shredding it like paper.

Dirilai slid off the back of the beast, garbed only in the Unseelie court's flimsy underthings and a scrap of pale gray silk around her collar. Dirt and mud streaked her shins, knees, and hands. She grasped a small, utilitarian knife in one hand and a pack was slung over her back.

"Make yourself useful and fetch some hot water." The command was crisp as she circled to Ellian.

Cirelle gaped.

Dirilai snapped, "Do you want him to live?" She knelt and began using the knife to slice through the hastily-tied silk that matched the few shreds left around her neck. "We have nearly three hours left until magic returns, and I have to keep him alive until then. So hot water, now. Along with a second empty basin, a cup, and clean rags."

Cirelle's reply died in her throat. Her entire world had been swallowed by that one simple sentence. *Do you want him to live?*

All that dark, inky blood spilled out of Ellian, staining the fabric with a growing dark blotch. Cirelle's head spun, but her feet spurred her into motion anyway. She turned and darted down the dark hall to the brownie's wing, to the kitchen. The wounds around her torso stung fiercely, and her boots slipped on a smear of blood. She awkwardly held both dagger hilts in one hand and yanked on the handle of the door to the brownie's wing, but it rattled uselessly.

Locked.

Footsteps approached. Cirelle's head whirled to see a large silhouette limned in the moonlight spilling from the foyer.

"You can't carry all that on your own," Shai explained. "Plus, you'll need this." She held up the skeleton key, the one the intruder had stolen from Cirelle.

In the dark, they fumbled at the lock until it clicked open and then dashed through blackened corridors. Cirelle's heartbeat counted out the seconds, measuring out Ellian's lost blood with each passing moment.

In the brownie's wing, a few small doors creaked open, then closed. Cowards.

Cirelle's terror struggled to claw its way out of her throat, a scream that wouldn't come. The worst had happened. Ellian had assaulted the palace and paid the price.

You arrogant, foolish idiot. But it wasn't anger fueling the tears that sprang to Cirelle's eyes as she rushed through the halls. They burst into the kitchen, and Cirelle hissed a curse. There was no fire in Ellian's home, no kettle burning in the hearth. Everything was heated by magic. Moonlight leaked through the slats of the window shutters, but all else was dark.

"Stars go black," she spat angrily. "Cold water will have to do." Cirelle shifted the knives and gave one to Shai.

Silently, Shai helped her fill a basin from the wooden barrel in the corner. The sidhe gave Cirelle a second, empty tub, dropping a tin mug, the daggers, and several clean rags into it. The full one Shai carried herself, holding the weight easily.

It would need to be enough.

Heedless of the water they sloshed all over the floor, Shai and Cirelle dashed down the pitch-black halls, now as familiar to the princess as Palace Arraven. She truly had no need of light to navigate them. With her injuries, it hurt to carry the basin, but Cirelle didn't care. The worry pounded in her head with every step.

If Ellian dies, what then? She'd never tease him again. No more mocking smile or bright blue glint in those eyes. She wouldn't get the chance to apologize for the times she snapped at him when he didn't deserve it or chide him for the times he did.

Cirelle could never tell Ellian of those moths that fluttered in her stomach when he looked at her a certain way, never confess that maybe she really was as stupid as Kyrinna. And she'd never find out whether maybe, just perhaps, those feelings were less foolish than she feared.

That creeping despair lurking within her surged forward, but she took a long, harsh breath and shoved it down deep. Later she'd fall apart. But not now.

When they returned to the foyer, the other faeries were nowhere to be found, the hall empty save a dark puddle where Ellian had lain.

"*Pagresta,*" Es called, his soft voice carrying in the silence. The word was gibberish to Cirelle, but her head whipped around to find the doors to the Archive antechamber lying open. Es gestured inside with one leathery wing.

In the waiting room, Ellian lay on the long sofa along the back wall, still unconscious. Dirilai knelt beside him, peering at the wound. A fat, moss-colored candle flickered on the low table in the center of the seating area, and the green scent of herbs scratched Cirelle's nose.

Cirelle blinked at the tiny flame. "Where did you get that?"

"I brought it with me." Dirilai's tone did not involve further discussion as she rummaged through the rest of her pack.

Shai dropped the full basin on the table, some of the water

splashing over the edge. "I'll go keep an eye on the rest of the manor with Issen," Shai said, placing the dagger beside the basin.

With one final look back at Ellian, Shai left with Es on her heels.

Chapter Forty-Seven

Cirelle set the empty basin and its contents on the table to kneel beside Dirilai. The faerie woman had finished slicing off Ellian's shredded bandages and cut off most of his shirt as well, peeling it open like the pages of a book. Ellian's back was covered in blood, the dark, tar-colored stuff faeries bled. And from his right hip to his left shoulder, a large gash gaped open, revealing muscle and a white spot of bone at his shoulder blade.

Cirelle fought back another sudden wave of nausea and dizziness. That couldn't be Ellian. It couldn't be a person. It wasn't possible for someone be torn open like that and still be alive.

No, not torn.

This slash was perfectly clean, razor sharp. Someone at the Unseelie Court had cut him down from behind. Underneath her terror, a seething anger bubbled up.

It seemed impossible Ellian could still live, but his back rose and fell with shallow breaths that rasped out of his mouth, ragged and rough-edged. His long hair was plastered to his upper back with blood. For some reason, that was the thing she suddenly found intolerable and stretched out a hand to pull it away from the wound.

"No!" Dirilai snapped. The woman shook her head. She was pouring water over her own hands into the empty basin using the tin mug. "Wash your hands first, then you can go back to man-handling him all you want. Preferably *after* we've healed him."

Cirelle's cheeks warmed despite her fear, all the terror flipping to anger at once. "I wasn't—" she stuttered. "I mean, I'm not... we don't—"

"I don't care," the woman said. "If you want to help me, you must touch him, and that you cannot do until you've washed your hands." Dirilai opened the pack she'd brought with her and withdrew a heavy bottle of some clear liquid. When she uncorked it and poured it over her hands, the acrid smell of alcohol burnt the air.

Too afraid for Ellian's sake to complain or to be stubborn, Cirelle followed the woman's orders.

"What happened to the others that went to the castle?" she asked while Dirilai handed her the bottle of liquor and Cirelle poured a small amount over her hands. Where it coated the wound at the base of her thumb, it burned like a bee sting. She hissed sharply.

"Carid should be here soon. Ixikki and the rest will be longer."

After Cirelle washed her hands, Dirilai's eyes narrowed toward the cut on Cirelle's hand. That canny black gaze took in all of Cirelle's mess, her clothes still damp with the saliva of an ilthys and blood soaking through her shirt where she'd been bitten.

With a grimace, Dirilai found a small roll of fabric in her bag and sliced off a section. "Here," she snapped, gesturing to Cirelle's hand with her chin. "I can't have you bleeding all over him."

Reluctantly, Cirelle placed her hand into the scrap of fabric stretched between Dirilai's hands. She was painfully self-conscious of her missing finger, but Dirilai said nothing of it. The healer made short work of wrapping and tying the bandage, a weaving pattern around Cirelle's palm and the base of her thumb.

"How bad is your stomach?"

Cirelle lifted her shirt. Dirilai glanced at it and grunted. "I don't have time to bandage all that, and it's not fatal. I suppose we'll have to make do." She made the words an accusation, as if it had been Cirelle's fault she'd gotten abducted. Dirilai soaked a rag in alcohol before throwing it at Cirelle. "Clean the blood around his wound. You'll need a good grip to hold the cut together while I stitch it."

Cirelle's stomach lurched.

Dirilai retrieved other items from the bag and assembled them. She threaded a silver needle with a long and shining black strand. Cirelle tore her eyes away from it and did as she was bid, wiping away the blood around the wound. *Stars, it's bleeding even still.* She bit her lip, forced down her nausea and fear, and kept wiping gently. The fabric came away stained the color of pine needles.

After a few moments, it became painfully clear something wasn't right. Ellian's back was a mess of rumpled tissue, rough to the touch. The uneven ridges of the texture were paler gray, creating a strange contrast.

Something about the scar tugged at her memory as she continued to wipe away the sticky blood. The smell clogged her nostrils, thick and metallic. Faerie blood may have been darker than a human's, but it smelled much the same. It surrounded her, choked her, snaked down her throat as she ran the cloth over that strange texture.

Then it hit her. One of the kitchen boys at home had fallen into a hearth fire years ago, and his hands bore the scars of it still.

These were old burns.

But she'd seen Ellian's bare back at Adaleth's palace. It had been smooth and unbroken then. She paused, and Dirilai turned sharply. "What?" Her eyes flickered from Cirelle's face to Ellian's back.

"He didn't have these scars before."

"Oh, that." Dirilai cut off the end of the thread from the spool and wrapped it about her fingers to tie it. Her head tilted and she raised a single eyebrow, mouth canted into a grim, sardonic smile. "So, you *have* seen him naked."

Cirelle glared but continued cleaning up the blood. "Only without the shirt," she muttered. "And it didn't look like this."

Dirilai shrugged. "Glamour."

"How did this happen?" Cirelle asked as she finished cleaning away the blood. Despite the ripples, the texture was smooth, like polished stones.

"Not my story, human." Dirilai finished tying off the thread and poured yet more alcohol over the needle. "Now, I'm going to pour this over the wound. It will probably wake him up." She took a smaller brown bottle from the bag and handed it to Cirelle. "As soon as he does, you need to force him to drink this."

"What does it do?"

"Put him back to sleep until we're done. Nothing more, nothing less."

Cirelle uncorked the bottle and took a careful sniff. Cloying sweetness and green herbs assaulted her nostrils. She didn't know why she bothered; she could hardly have told poison from cure. And faeries could not lie, after all.

With a nod, Cirelle knelt beside Ellian's head. His face was ragged and pale, with dark circles beneath his eyes. His glamour gone, his features were less ethereal but still beautiful. His nose was slightly crooked, his jaw a bit softer. A worried furrow clung between his brows even in unconsciousness. Then Dirilai tipped the bottle over his back and those eyes snapped open. An agonized shout burst from his lips. He tried to sit up, but Dirilai held him down. "Now, girl!"

"Ellian." Cirelle's voice came out strangled. His eyes locked on her own, two bottomless silver pits.

"What?" His reply was anguished, breath panting as he tried to force himself up. He cried out with pain and flopped down again.

"We're helping, but you have to drink this." She held the bottle up to his lips.

He jerked away, and his voice quivered, thready and weak. "In… in my boot." His breath hissed sharply, face creased with agony.

"Human, do it now!" Dirilai snapped. "He's bleeding again."

"I will," Cirelle said hurriedly to Ellian. Anything if he'd just drink the concoction she held. There was so much pain written on his face, and tears sprang to Cirelle's eyes. "I promise. Just drink. *Please.*"

He did, letting Cirelle tip the bottle up and pour the potion into his mouth. With his head lying sideways, half of it spilled onto the floor, but hopefully enough of it made it into his body to work. It seemed so, for his eyelids sagged instantly. "Thank you."

Cirelle's stomach twisted. How addled was he, to forget that simple rule and utter those two words? And what did it mean now that he had?

"Human, I need your help," Dirilai barked, and Cirelle left the bottle on the table as she stood to aid the healer.

It was grisly and stomach-turning work. Cirelle pressed the edges of the gaping wound together while Dirilai stitched them with sure, even lines.

Only now did Cirelle realize she could understand Dirilai's words. The faerie was speaking the Trade tongue without a trace of accent. How many sidhe spoke the human tongue?

It didn't matter. Right now, Ellian was Cirelle's only focus. She tried not to inhale the scent of blood or to think too hard about that needle piercing his flesh. Dirilai's scent of dried herbs and dust mingled with the cloying metallic odor. Taking in deep breaths through her mouth, Cirelle made it moment by moment.

When it was done, Dirilai tied off the string and let out a sigh.

The dark zigzag of those stitches burrowing into Ellian's skin like obscene worms left Cirelle even queasier.

As Dirilai sat back on her knees and wiped her forehead with the back of a hand, Shai burst through the doors.

"Princess," she said, "Carid is ba—" Shai's voice stopped. "Oh, shit," she muttered.

Cirelle could imagine how gruesome a scene they painted. Ellian lying prone with dark stitches on his back, both women covered in his blood. More of the dark ichor had dripped onto the gray couch cushions, staining them beyond repair.

Shai's exclamation snapped something inside Cirelle, something she'd been holding tightly coiled inside her. Tears fell freely and a jagged laugh tore itself from her throat. She'd murdered a person. The Scath was hers to command. And Ellian lay in a pool of his own blood.

"Um," Shai said. "Carid and some of the others are back."

Cirelle's shoulders sagged in relief. "They're okay?"

"So far, so good. Just Ellian that was hurt."

Cirelle stared down at him, at those grotesque stitches. Abruptly, she remembered her promise to him during his brief bout of consciousness. *In a pocket in my boot.*

When she walked to the end of the couch and began tugging on Ellian's boots, the other two women stared in shock. "Can you not keep your hands off the man for more than a minute?" Dirilai asked sharply. "He's unconscious, you idiot."

Cirelle ignored her, glancing up at Shai, who still stood in the center of the room with a puzzled expression. "Shai, help me, please?"

"Er... why are you taking off his shoes?"

Cirelle sighed. "He said there was something in them. Something he told me to keep safe."

Dirilai's eyes widened and she sat up straight. "The Key?" she asked, her sharp edges vanishing under the light of hope that glimmered in her eyes.

"He didn't say," Cirelle replied. In some part of her brain, she knew she should have kept this secret, that Dirilai may not be entirely trustworthy. But the sidhe woman had saved Ellian's life.

The three of them managed to pull off Ellian's boots. The task felt like a violation, but he'd told her, *begged* her to do it. Turning the boots over and over, reaching inside them, Cirelle found a small pocket with a hard lump inside it. Her fingers plucked it out and held it up.

A key.

A literal key. It was elegant and beautiful with a whorled pattern at its head, but otherwise nothing extraordinary.

Dirilai let out a sudden sigh, dropping into a nearby chair in relief. "He got it. The fool actually managed to steal it. Even if that idiot prince finds the Lock, we have the Key."

"It doesn't feel like much," Cirelle admitted, clutching it tightly.

"In case you forgot, magic is dead right now." Dirilai's eyes were back to her emotionless cold stare. "When it awakens, tell me then if the Key feels like nothing."

Cirelle had no reply to that. She took the Key and slipped it into a pocket of her own trousers. She couldn't place it in the Archive until magic returned, anyway. She brushed away a lock of damp, sticky hair that clung to the side of Ellian's face.

Perhaps Dirilai was right; she couldn't seem to stop touching him.

It was unbearable to her that blood still matted his hair, still stuck to his ribs at the sides. She took the last clean rag and dipped it in the clear water, wringing it out and squeezing it around locks of his hair to soak up most of the blood.

So much. He'd lost so much. How much blood could a sidhe spill and survive?

Dirilai's voice was quiet, but she answered Cirelle's unspoken question. "If he can make it until magic returns, he'll live."

Still perhaps two hours yet.

"Don't you dare die on me, you ass," Cirelle muttered as she combed through Ellian's damp hair with her fingers and began to wipe off the rest of the blood on his sides. The thick coppery scent of it had dissipated as well, the sickening tang fading away. Either that, or Cirelle was becoming accustomed to the smell that stained the air.

Ellian's own aroma wafted up to her underneath the metallic odor, and she took heart from that. Smoke and honey, a scent she'd come to find soothing.

"Stop fretting," Dirilai said shortly.

Cirelle slid a hand in her pocket and clutched the cold metal. The silver teeth bit into her hand, and her empty knuckle ached. "You don't really care about him at all, do you? Why help us?"

Dirilai shrugged, still leaning back in the chair, head tilted up to look at the ceiling. "Using the Key spells doom for all of us. I gave my oath of aid to Ellian for this night, and I swore I would speak nothing of Ellian's plans to the royals. After tonight, my part will be done."

Cirelle couldn't look away from Ellian's wound, from his pallid face. She counted every rasping breath. Spiky vines of dread bound her chest, and the thorns pierced her with each inhalation. Her familiar sorrow bared its fangs once more, that sharp-edged anguish strangling her.

Out in the foyer, a cry of surprise rang out. Steel clashed, and voices rose. Cirelle's pulse increased. The clang of blades was followed by a shout from Issen outside the doors.

Shai bolted upright at the first sound. "Stay here," were her parting words as she slipped out the doors. They thudded shut behind her as Cirelle cried out her name.

Chapter Forty-Eight

ELLIAN'S DREAMS WERE FEVER-SHARP, delirious, and jagged things.

He stared into Ayre's hateful golden eyes and turned to run. Her blade bit into flesh, searing a line across his shoulders and back.

The Unseelie court laughed at him, jeering as Rhael forced Ellian to be his footstool. Humiliation burned his cheeks.

No, wait. That was an older memory, far older.

The smell of smoke, of charred flesh. Too far back. He cringed away from it.

A shift. Now he lay in the cold, stinking Unseelie dungeon, his blood pooling on the pale pearlescent stone beneath him. No rushes, no straw for this prisoner. His cheek was chilled where it rested against the cold rock, but he couldn't find the strength to rise. No one had tended his wound, and his entire back burned with it.

For one brief flicker, a softer memory, of lips yielding to his, tasting of sweet, ripe berries and the giddy flutter in his belly when they did not pull away.

Only to be replaced by a hallucination of Adaleth's burning, cruel eyes, his mouth a satisfied, languorous smile as someone nearby screamed in agony.

Hands hauling him upright off the dungeon floor, familiar voices chattering in concern and fear.

"Too much blood—"

"Don't touch it, you fool—"

"How will we—"

"Quickly—"

The scene flickered again, and he drifted up to awareness. His back still screamed in pain, but he lay on something soft, and a familiar cinnamon smell carried to him over the choking stench of blood and medicine.

His eyes fluttered and he tried to speak, but his lips were gummed shut, and he fell back into the darkness of his memories.

ᕦᕤ

CIRELLE STOOD AS ANOTHER clamor rang outside but faltered as she approached the door. She couldn't fight. She couldn't heal. The Archive was sealed off, and magic was dead.

She was useless.

Dirilai glanced from the closed doors to Ellian's unconscious form and back to Cirelle. "Watch him." She darted a glance to the curved blades on the table. Their sharpened edges gleamed yellow in the candlelight.

"I don't even know how—"

"Then sink or swim, girl," Dirilai told her, emotionless. "I'd see if I could block this door if I were you. If he wakes up, give him some of the liquor to knock him out again. The idiot needs to sleep until magic comes back."

"Wait!" Cirelle called, but the woman slipped through the doors and slammed them shut behind her.

"Blockade them!" Dirilai called through the heavy wood, and then her voice fell silent.

The manor was not quiet, however. The ring of steel on steel, shouts, and grunts of battle sounded in the front entryway. The clatter of chitinous legs echoed, the chittering of the ilthys like laughter atop the din. Cirelle's last command to the Scath had been to take the spider-like beasts and use them to protect the manor. She had to hope that yet held.

Dirilai was right. She could only stay here with Ellian, useless as she'd be in a fight.

The desk was heavy, incredibly so. Cirelle could never have lifted it more than an inch. But she didn't need to lift it, only to drag it across the floor. The woven rug beneath the desk allowed Cirelle to push it across the room, inch by grueling inch.

The claw-footed legs tore jagged holes through the fine rug, but she managed to wedge it before the doors.

Still the battle raged.

Cirelle paced circles around the room, peeking into the Archive's empty closet to see if magic had returned. A slithering anxiety ran up and down her body. With every scream outside, she was left to wonder if it was friend or foe.

Often, too often, she checked on Ellian to reassure herself he still breathed. She placed the back of a hand on his forehead to check for fever, but his skin was cooler than usual. That frightened her even more. Ellian's skin ran so hot; how badly did he have to be injured to lose that warmth?

So, she sat on the floor beside him, taking his hand in her own where it rested by his head. Her empty knuckle throbbed, and the wound on her palm soaked into Dirilai's hasty bandage. Her stomach and back still stung. But it was nothing compared to Ellian's injury, still an angry slash against his skin. "Don't you dare die," she whispered, angry at the tears welling in her eyes.

So stupid, to care so much. He was a faerie who'd made a fool of her more than once.

But he was also the man who'd had her favorite tea delivered to the Archive on long nights. He'd teased her so playfully with those summer-sky eyes. When she'd thrown his books and crumpled their pages, he'd responded with kindness rather than rage. Ellian had believed in her, pushed her to be *more* than a mere princess. And he'd kissed her; first with passion, then with tenderness. She hated those moths in her belly when he was near but couldn't deny their existence.

The thought of all that vanishing... It was too painful to even consider.

Another shout outside, Shai shouting Issen's name. Cirelle closed her eyes as panic raged through her, a prickling, stinging sensation. *There's nothing I can do,* she told herself bitterly.

Ellian's hand twitched, and he gasped.

Cirelle's heart fluttered, and she clutched his hand more tightly. His eyes snapped open, brilliant silver. He moved as if to roll over, but she caught his arm to stop him. "No, Ellian..."

A ragged breath tore through Ellian as his eyes focused on Cirelle, plain gray. Tonight, those shifting colors had fled. His brows lowered from their startled expression and he blinked. "Cirelle." The naked relief in his voice was painful to hear.

"Yes. You're home. But you shouldn't move."

He groaned, his hand clenching tightly about hers. "My back hurts."

Cirelle barked a bitter laugh. That was a gross understatement. "You were injured. Dirilai and I stitched you up, but you need to stay still." With her free hand, she reached behind her for the liquor bottle. "She told me to make you drink this for sleep."

Ellian grimaced. "I'm not going to sleep." His gaze darted to the candle on the table, eyes widening.

The battle chose that moment to erupt into sudden chaos, a clamor of weapons ringing against one another. Shai's clear voice rose above the din, and Issen's shouted reply echoed back. Ellian stared in shock at the heavy desk pressed up against the door. "I have to go out there!" he demanded, trying to make his weak voice sound imperious.

"And do what? You're hurt." Her jaw set stubbornly, and Cirelle gave him her most commanding glare. "It's my job to make sure you stay put, and Stars damn me if I fail."

With a grunt of pain, Ellian flopped back down. "The Key," he gasped.

"I have it."

"Thank Jisanti." He tried to roll over, cried out, and settled back onto his stomach with a grimace.

"Who did this to you?" she asked softly, though she already knew the answer.

"The Queen," he muttered darkly. Cirelle's knuckle gave a sudden pang.

She held the bottle up again. "You really should drink this."

"No."

"I could force you to. I've seen the stable hands dose the castle dogs."

That got a faint chuckle out of him, followed by a whimper of pain. The small, pitiful sound left Cirelle uneasy. "Are you calling me a dog?" he asked.

"I've called you worse." She smiled, but it was a half-hearted gesture.

"I suppose so." His returning grin was a feeble thing. "For what it's worth, I'm glad you and Dirilai helped me." The closest a faerie could come to saying, 'thank you.' She still didn't know what his earlier thanks implied, and whether he even remembered it. Would she remind him if he didn't?

"I'm glad, too," she said quietly, tucking a lock of hair behind his ear. It was still a little matted with blood despite her best efforts. She brushed the long hair off the nape of his neck as well. Her hands grazed the top of the scars, just above his shoulder blades, that sea of gnarled skin. Ellian flinched and tried to writhe away from her touch, hissing in pain at the motion.

"Don't." A hoarse rasp. "I... I don't want you seeing that," he added miserably, closing his eyes. "Or touching it."

Cirelle knew what he meant. The scars were awful things, but not because they were ugly. Because they told a story of unimaginable pain. "How did it happen?"

Ellian was silent a long while, and Cirelle wondered if he'd slipped back into unconsciousness.

"When my family died," he finally said.

It was enough of an answer, and the tears spilled now. Cirelle could not hold them back any longer.

What were they like?

Brave, and kind, and painfully mortal.

The scars crisscrossed his back, the only place the flames had been hot enough to burn. "Stars," Cirelle swore through the tears. "You tried to save them, didn't you?"

He swallowed hard. "I could only make it to my youngest sister." Silence fell for a time. "I tried to shield her, but the smoke... It wasn't enough to kill a sidhe, but..."

Cirelle's throat tightened. How awful would that be, to feel a loved one go limp in your arms? She'd given up her entire world to see Aidan safe. She didn't know if she could have survived watching her brother die while she held him.

That's why there's no fire in his home, why he flinched away from flames that night of the faerie revel.

"I'm so sorry, Ellian." His scent wafted toward her, stronger now, and she blinked away tears. "How cruel, then, to smell of woodsmoke. Is that Faerie's twisted humor?"

"I don't know. It's a strange mercy we can't detect our own scents."

Cirelle sighed. She'd found his fragrance cozy and comforting before, but in truth it was something else entirely. A badge of courage.

His hand found her shoulder with a gentle squeeze. Still, Cirelle didn't miss his small grunt of pain at the movement.

"The candle," she blurted. "I can put it out. If it bothers you."

"And leave us in the dark?"

Cirelle had no answer to that. She let her head tip sideways until her cheek brushed his knuckles. "You really should drink whatever's in that bottle."

"I can smell it from here, and I know what it is. I won't be drinking it."

Her heartbeat fluttered. "Poison?"

"Faerie liquor with some herbs steeped in it. It would knock me senseless, but it burns all the way down and isn't worth the headache tomorrow."

"Oh." Cirelle recalled her own experience with faerie spirits and grimaced. She placed her hand atop his where it touched her shoulder. For a moment, they sat in that tableau, until he startled and lifted her hand, staring at the bandage.

His eyes widened as he glanced down at her blood-soaked shirt. "You're hurt."

Cirelle rasped a humorless laugh. "I think if we're comparing battle wounds, that's one argument you might win."

"Battle wounds?" A darkness lingered in his question.

"It's a long story. Ask me tomorrow."

"Would that long story explain the knives sitting on the table?"

"It would."

"Who is it?" he asked. "Outside?"

"I have no idea. Dirilai and I were in here stitching you up when Shai came running in, then the clamor started and they both ran out. Dirilai told me to block the door and left."

Ellian was utterly quiet for a few moments. "Why were you even out here? Why did you leave your room?"

"There were intruders." Cirelle swallowed. "They stole control of the ilthys and broke into the parlor. Shai killed one. I—" She hesitated, that dizziness gripping her again. "I killed the other." The statement came out flat, but the memory still left a crawling sensation in Cirelle's chest. All that black blood spilling on the floor, splattered on the pale walls. The shock of seeing a head severed from a body, the horror of hearing bones shatter between the teeth of an ilthys. Another nightmare Faerie had bestowed upon her.

Ellian shifted and grunted in pain. "You...what? Cirelle..." He spoke her name softly, a worried crease between his brows and something else kindling in his eyes.

Cirelle's gut did another guilty backflip. She looked away.

After a long pause, Ellian cleared his throat. "Did Shai know who the intruders were?"

"No." She pointed to the open Archive doors, at the tiny unassuming space that now rested there. "One of them opened those doors and found only an empty closet. With magic gone, how did you move the Archive?"

"I didn't. The Archive was never here."

Cirelle was struck by the memory of the tingling she felt when she walked through it, stronger than any other door in the manor. "Stars go black," she swore. "It's somewhere else, and the door just connects to it."

"Yes."

"Why did you even bother guarding it tonight, if there's nothing here?"

"If I didn't act like it was here, someone might figure out where it really was." She got the impression he'd have shrugged if he could.

"Sly, crazy, faerie," Cirelle replied, but there was no venom in the words.

"So, you've told me before," he pointed out.

"You don't deny it."

"No."

Cirelle couldn't help but smile, couldn't help but giggle madly. Soon Ellian was laughing too, the strained sort that comes when all hope is lost.

Gasping for breath, Cirelle almost missed it. A flicker of motion out of the corner of an eye, one that could have been attributed to a gust of air disturbing the candle. But Cirelle had seen the four glowing purple dots, just for an instant. The laughter died in her throat. She darted for the knives, wrapping her fingers around the cold metal of their hilts and blurting a single word. "Stop!"

Like he'd hit a wall, the Scath froze. His spiky, shadowy hand was lifted, so close to grasping the knives himself. A surge of icy adrenaline crashed through her, leaving her snarling at the faerie.

"Cirelle." Ellian's voice was raw and laden with dread. "Tell me those knives aren't what I think they are."

Chapter Forty-Nine

THE SCATH IGNORED ELLIAN, and Cirelle didn't dare take her eyes from the shadow. "You fool human," he snapped. The sound of steel scraping on stone came from the creature, but this time Cirelle made out the words contained within. She glanced down at the blades in her grasp. Now he solidified before her, and why could she understand his speech?

"How? With magic gone—"

"The claimhte are more than merely enchanted, human," the Scath snarled. His next words were a challenge. "You must give them to me."

"What?"

"The ilthys aren't following my orders. They know the knives and their queen are near. It confuses them."

A heavy stone settled in Cirelle's stomach, only now remembering the thief's words. "Their... what?"

"Queen." Ellian's reply was ragged. "Oh, Cirelle." A world's worth of weight hung on those words.

"If you won't leave this room to lead the ilthys, your friends *will* lose this battle, human. There are too many opponents for them to handle alone." The Scath's eyes narrowed, the tendrils of shadow dancing like agitated serpents. He held out a hand. "Or you can give the blades to me, and I will command the ilthys once more."

Cirelle's grip on the daggers—the claimhte—tightened. "Making you their king."

Somehow, the shadow managed to convey a shrug. "Your choice." The clang of weapons and shouts still echoed outside. A scream rang through the foyer.

Cirelle risked a glance at Ellian. Something dark and heavy lay in those pained silver eyes, something she couldn't decipher. His mouth was set in a stern line, but he remained silent.

"You aren't going to tell me to stay?" she asked.

"Would you listen?" A bleak bit of humor colored his sigh. "The blades are yours, as is the choice."

Something churned in her belly. "What would you do?"

Ellian's eyes darted to the Scath and then back. "I'm a faerie. We don't relinquish power without equal recompense. I would not give him the knives."

The very air thrummed with silent apprehension.

Three paths lay before her.

Cirelle could give the Scath the knives, handing full control of the ilthys to him. And after? Without a doubt, the creature would turn on her. A second choice. She could stay, keep the daggers here and guard Ellian, at terrible risk to those who fought so bravely outside. Or she could abandon Ellian, plunging headlong into battle and leaving him defenseless.

Cirelle shook her head. She wasn't a soldier. She couldn't do this, couldn't go back out there into the blood and the screaming. Her hands tightened on the blades. Something about cold weight reassured her that yes, she could do this, with the ilthys under her command. She had to.

Cirelle glanced back to the Scath. Perhaps he was oathbound

to Ellian tonight, but she didn't trust him. Then again, she didn't have to. He was committed to these knives, to her.

Cirelle stood, never loosening her grip on the daggers. She straightened her spine and pointed one of the blades at the Scath. "You, Scath, will stay in this room until I tell you otherwise. You will protect Ellian and our allies from any harm even at the cost of your own life, and you will take absolutely no action that may result in harming Ellian or our allies in any way." She tossed a lock of hair out of her eyes, damp with either blood or sweat or both. She met that eerie purple stare, those four eyes set among shadow. "Is that understood?"

Again, the Scath's voice was the scratch of bare branches on a window. If Cirelle hadn't known better, she'd have said he spoke through clenched teeth. "Yes, my Queen."

The title sent a shiver down Cirelle's spine.

She turned to face Ellian's anguished gaze. "I don't like this," he said quietly. His resigned expression said it all. He too knew there was no choice.

"I know." Cirelle's heart already pounded fiercely, preparing her to join the fray outside. The chill of the daggers spread up her arms, a frenetic tingle. Quickly, she bent at the waist and pressed a small kiss to Ellian's temple. The barest brush of lips and she was gone.

Before he could say more, Cirelle ran toward the door. A few laborious moments of shoving the desk with her body's weight and she freed one door enough to squeeze through.

The din hit her immediately. Shouts of warning, cries of pain, weapons crashing together. The smell was worse. The stench of death coated the air. Everything was cast in black and white, stark shadow and slivers of illumination. The ilthys scurried along the staircases and across the ceiling, chittering their confusion.

"You," Cirelle pointed at the nearest one with her daggers as she circled the edges of the fray. "Protect me." The spider leapt over the banister, landing beside her and tilting that eerily human face. A figure drew close and the ilthys snapped its teeth at him. Issen.

"No!" Fire burned in Cirelle's lungs. "Only harm those who are not Ellian's allies." The spider took a step back.

Issen stood before her, his golden robes spattered with dark blood. At least he appeared unhurt. Narrowing his eyes, he asked, "Why are you out here?"

"The ilthys need orders." She lifted the daggers, her heart in her throat. "I left the Scath with Ellian, under a command to protect him, but—"

"I understand," the sidhe told her, face calm even in this chaos. "I'll watch him." His gaze dipped to the blades in Cirelle's grasp. "Be careful." Issen darted gracefully past her and through the doors to the antechamber. They slammed shut behind him.

It was the longest hour of Cirelle's life. She danced about the outskirts of the skirmish in the foyer, directing ilthys where needed. Their enemies were an assortment of fae, easily picked out by their black and white uniforms. Only a few of Ellian's allies fought in the entryway.

Shai held the foyer. Catching sight of Cirelle, the warrior paused in her fight to stare open-mouthed.

It almost cost the sidhe her life. One of their foes darted toward Shai's back. Without thinking, Cirelle commanded the spider at her flank, "Stop him!"

The enemy never stood a chance. Even as Shai turned, the spider-like beast scurried past her and pierced the enemy with one of those razor-sharp legs. Shai grinned widely and made a strange gesture at Cirelle that may have been a salute. Cirelle left two ilthys to help and moved on.

With her spidery escort, Cirelle dashed through the halls,

heart beating a rhythm of war drums in her ears. As she stumbled across pockets of battle, she assigned ilthys to assist before continuing onward. The windowless corridors should have been dark as midnight, but Cirelle could make out the edges of walls and floors. She wondered if the daggers held still more abilities unknown.

The Scath had not fully answered her question. When all other magic failed, how were these still functional?

She couldn't worry about that now. Cirelle ran with abandon, the knives held out to her sides, flanked by her chitinous warriors. Blood sang in her veins. The wintry cold of the shadow blades bit into her skin. She was fierce, strong. With her ilthys at her side, Cirelle was unstoppable. Her spiders cut their enemies down like weeds.

One of the enemy fae traced a jagged blade across Carid's ribs. The beast-like man stumbled, stood again, and gave a bellow to shake the rafters before slashing his attacker with his yellow claws. An ilthys bit into the enemy faerie's head from behind, and the foe crumpled. Carid gave a nod of thanks and kept moving.

So much blood, so many lives lost. Some small part of Cirelle's brain warned her she'd feel differently about this bloodshed when that ice no longer flowed through her and survival was no longer a concern. But at this moment she was fury made flesh, protecting her allies and Ellian.

Ellian.

Cirelle's heart paused and lurched back to life. She forged back through the halls, a single remaining ilthys on her tail. She returned to the foyer. Her eyes scanned the corpses for her allies but found only ilthys and the bodies of enemies.

Three fae scrabbled at the door to the antechamber. A furred beast with heavy arms and long, thick claws scraped at the wood.

He threw his weight into the door, and it splintered open. The three enemy fae spilled into the room.

Cirelle sprinted for the antechamber at once. Panic tore at her, a white-hot terror that made the rest of the world fade to gray. She burst through the door as her final ilthys lingered outside, too large to enter.

Issen already fought against the hairy intruder. He ducked under a heavy blow and slashed at the creature. The Scath blocked a second enemy's path to Ellian, lashing out with claws made of smoke and shadow.

Which only left the third, a faerie with slimy green skin like a frog's and talons of a sickly chartreuse. It scuttled toward Ellian on spindly legs, those clawed hands lifted to plunge into Ellian's flesh.

Ellian watched him come, glaring defiantly as he struggled to sit up despite his wound. Those silver eyes darted to Cirelle and widened. Her name formed on his lips.

"No!" she shrieked.

The frog-like faerie whirled.

One split second to make a choice.

Time slowed, everything but her foe fading to gray. The faerie growled, his wide mouth full of tiny, pointed teeth. Beady, golden eyes narrowed to slits. This creature had come into Ellian's home. It had tried to kill her friends. To kill Ellian.

She lifted her knives, those chill blades like slivers of moonlight cutting through shadow.

The first slash was not a clean one, Cirelle's attempt sloppy. A slice across the faerie's face left blood streaming from one eye. He stepped back with a scream like steel on glass.

Another frozen moment. Another choice.

The ice inside her cracked, filling her with a vast, frozen fury.

This moment was a precipice. If she leapt over it, she could never go back. But for Ellian's sake, for her own sake, Cirelle made her decision.

Her blade sank into the faerie's throat, her lips curled in a snarl. The blood that surged out reeked of rotting moss. Cirelle screamed her fury and terror, yanking the knife out of the creature's flesh with a sickening plop. Those talons clawed at her as he fell, scoring ragged red lines across her forearms. She cried out in pain but kept her grip on the knives.

The body fell at her feet, a wet and heavy weight. A dark puddle spread beneath him.

Over the bleeding and limp form between them, her eyes met Ellian's. An anguish and horror lay in that silver gaze, and it cracked the ice floes in her chest. Shame and disgust smote her to the core.

Issen and the Scath, having dispatched their own foes, stared in heavy silence. Cirelle stumbled to the desk on the opposite side of the room, the closest thing to escape she could manage.

Her hand left a sticky black handprint on the fine wood.

Chapter Fifty

They all stared at Cirelle aghast. The flood of energy abandoned her and her knees threatened to collapse. The enormity of what she'd done nearly dragged her into unconsciousness. The edges of her vision turned black.

Cirelle had killed. Not only the accidental death of the first intruder or commanding the ilthys, but with her own hands. The creature's sticky blood coated her, and the stench threatened to gag her.

Worse, she knew she'd do it again if it meant protecting her friends and Ellian.

Cirelle couldn't tear her gaze from his. The naked disgust on his features was like a physical blow, a wound that pierced too deeply. The moths in her stomach became hawks, screeching and violent things that raked sharpened talons against the inside of her ribcage.

The rest of the group trailed into the room in a chaos of noise, covered in the stench of battle. Kith padded casually over to a corner and licked blood from his claws with a long pink tongue. Cirelle shuddered but turned to scan the rest of the small crowd. "You're all okay."

Shai snorted. "Not entirely." Cirelle took another glance to see Shai cradling one arm against her chest with the other, her shoulder jutting at an odd angle. Cirelle's stomach turned.

"Oh, no. Shai—"

"Dislocated. I just need someone to pop it back in place."

"I'll do it," Issen offered, and gestured her over to a far corner.

Leilarie, the tiny salcha, was covered head-to-toe in blood. When Cirelle looked at her in dismay, the faerie said in trilling tones, "Don't worry, it's not mine." She grinned, revealing a mouth of shark's teeth stained with black ichor.

Cirelle's stomach curdled, and she turned aside.

The Scath stood in the corner, roiling with anger. Shadows licked around his body like flames, his silhouette swallowing the light. Violet eyes burned in his featureless face. "You are dismissed," Cirelle told him. "Leave this manor and do not enter it again unless I summon you."

With a growl like shifting sand, he slithered directly through the wall.

Everyone else rushed to Ellian's side.

Dirilai, one long smear of blood on her cheek, glared at Cirelle while she pointed at the liquor bottle. "I told you he should drink this."

Cirelle's mind screamed a litany of tonight's awfulness. The room reeked of faerie blood. *Cirelle* stank of it. The taste of vomit still lingered on her tongue. How many deaths were on her conscience now? Ellian was still wounded, those black stitches drawing stark lines on his skin. And now Dirilai was scolding her like a child.

"Well," Cirelle spat, "if you can get him to drink it, go right ahead."

The faerie woman scowled in silence for a few moments. "Fine," she barked, but it was directed toward Ellian. "If you insist on being awake, you will feel every step on the way up to the rooftop. Magic will return in minutes, and we need to get you to the garden before dawn."

Ellian glared at Dirilai, but the gesture was ruined while he lay on his stomach.

Cirelle glanced around at the group. Part of the attack party was still noticeably missing. "Ixikki—"

"Is fine," Carid cut her off. "He's just slow. Agdarr is with him." The wolf-man crossed over to Ellian, as did Vilitte and Shai, the latter rolling her shoulder experimentally. She nodded at Carid, and the three of them slid their arms under Ellian and lifted. The slash to Carid's ribs split wider, spilling more dark blood onto his white fur, but he didn't seem to notice.

Ellian cried out at the sudden pain, and something inside Cirelle echoed the sound. She continued to clutch the knives as they left the room.

The grisly scene in the foyer was made all the worse by the stillness and silence, lit only by sharp moonlight falling through the skylight above.

A clicking sound came from nearby. Cirelle turned to find one of the ilthys only a few feet away, its face buried in a limp torso with no legs. It lifted its head and made a warning hiss that froze Cirelle's heartbeat for a few moments. Her allies, her subjects, but her veins still ran cold at the sight of it.

She had dismissed the Scath, but not the spiders.

"Go," she said to the one she faced, a bit of gore hanging from its sharp teeth. With a shudder, she raised her voice, shouting to echo through the halls. "All the ilthys, leave here and do not come back unless your Queen commands it!"

Perhaps the others heard the tremor in her cry. They all halted to stare at her. Cirelle returned their surprise with a glower as the spider-like creatures scuttled past in their exodus.

As one, the group's gazes slid away from Cirelle without a word and the procession continued. Dirilai trailed after the faeries carrying Ellian, followed by Cirelle, then the rest. Why they needed to be on the roof, Cirelle had no idea, but she was beyond asking questions.

They emerged out onto the rooftop, bathed in the light of the moons, one full and silver, the other waning at half-full.

Dirilai cast her face up to the sky, eyes closed as if she could feel the moonlight beating against her skin. She opened them, glanced around the garden, and pointed. "There."

The three carrying Ellian hurried over to the spot, a flat bit of grass far away from any tall plants or sculptures and untouched by shadow. They set Ellian down as gently as possible, but he panted with pain nonetheless. His face had gone pale and sallow again.

"Now we wait for magic to return," Dirilai told Cirelle before she could ask, her tone inviting no further questions.

The group murmured as they nursed their wounds. Cirelle set her blades beside her as she sat cross-legged on the grass next to Ellian. Her fingers itched to reach out to him, to brush his hair away from the injury, to touch his face, but she hesitated. Her hands clasped one another tightly in her lap. The wound must be agonizing, but he held onto consciousness tenaciously.

She told him everything that had happened, starting with the false mimicry of his voice and ending with his startling arrival in Es's talons. She left out nothing, not even how the ilthys had killed the first intruder at her command.

After she'd finished, Ellian was silent for so long it seemed he had fallen asleep. But no, when she met his eyes, they were clear, if furrowed in pain.

"Everyone stand back," Dirilai suddenly snapped at the

whole group, but cast a pointed glare at Cirelle. "If you want him to be healed, that is."

The group—including Cirelle—scattered a distance, their backs against a hedge covered in tiny pink blossoms. Dirilai stood beside Ellian, her arms hanging at her sides and her face turned up to the moons.

When the magic returned, it felt like the earth itself took a shuddering breath and exhaled. The night was *alive* again, as if the very air held a conscience. It tingled against Cirelle's skin like a fine misting rain. She glanced down at her hand, and her illusory finger was back.

The moment the magic fell upon them, Dirilai raised her hands and began a beautiful, sinuous dance, marking a circle around Ellian. Her hands kept lifting and dipping, twirling as they did. It was almost as if she were reeling in a rope, or winding yarn about her wrists.

After a few moments, Cirelle was certain her eyes weren't deceiving her. Trails of light were indeed spooling around Dirilai's hands, spiraling around her arms down to her chest. It cast a silvery glow on the scant undergarments she still wore and the silken tatters about her throat.

When the light had grown so bright Cirelle squinted, Dirilai knelt beside Ellian and brushed her hands lightly along his wound. Ellian gave a sharp, sudden cry of pain, then screwed his eyes shut and was silent. Agony was evident on his face, and a lump formed in Cirelle's throat.

Faerie magic. Dirilai was a healer in more than herbs and stitches.

"Moonweaver," Issen said softly at Cirelle's side, and she glanced sharply at him. He nodded in Dirilai's direction, a grimace on his lips. "That's her talent. Harnessing moonlight to heal. If rumor is to be believed, she can do a few other things with it as well." He shook his head. "Don't trust her, Cirelle. She helps this evening only because she's oathbound."

Cirelle didn't respond. Right now, she didn't care. The light surrounding Dirilai was fading, and Cirelle's eyes returned to Ellian, glued to the scene unfolding in the garden. The moon-weaver sagged to the ground, staying upright only by propping herself up on her arms. Her head hung low, that black curtain of hair hiding her face. Her chest rose and fell in labored breaths.

And Ellian...

The cut was gone, and the black zigzag of stitches, vanished. Only pale scar tissue revealed where the wound had even been, a harsh line that bisected the burn scars on his back. A band of tightness clutched at Cirelle's chest.

Ellian shuddered, coughed once, and pushed himself up onto his arms. In a few stiff motions he stood, the tattered remains of his fine shirt hanging from him. His eyes unerringly sought out Cirelle, a wan smile touching his lips when their gazes met. The night's events had shredded his glamour, and those eyes swirled with colors. A light fawn-colored brown, rosy pink, pine green.

He still looked pale and held himself gingerly. "You've all done well this evening. You're welcome to stay as guests, but tonight, I have to rest." His breath grew thin by the end of the statement, as if it took all his energy to utter the words. "Shai, could you find them each a place to sleep? Cirelle, help me to my room."

That gave Cirelle the excuse she needed to hasten to his side. He leaned part of his weight on her, an arm around a shoulder, and her spirit lifted to feel his skin once again warm against hers.

"My part in this is over, Ellian," Dirilai said from the ground. She tossed her head back and stood wearily. "My bargains paid, my oaths kept. I'm done here." With those words, her form misted and vanished.

The sky was lightening, dawn rapidly approaching.

Shai yawned. "I so need a bath and a good night's sleep. Well, day's sleep. Or three." She turned to the gathered faeries, gesturing. "Any of you wanting rooms, follow me."

Most of them chose to stay, only Kith and Carid declining. Vilitte, silent this entire time and her crystalline body looking so obscene splattered with blood, gave Cirelle a long, thoughtful stare before turning to follow.

As Issen passed Cirelle, he murmured. "Do you want me to keep the knives until you can put them in the Archive? I swear I will return them to you when we awaken later today, and will not use their powers. Nor will I let anyone else touch them. My oath."

Cirelle stared down at the blades in her grasp. Though her fingers were reluctant to uncurl themselves from the hilts, Cirelle nodded. She couldn't carry both the knives and help Ellian. Issen coaxed the blades from her grasp and followed the strange parade that left the garden.

With each step toward his rooms, Ellian's movements grew more leaden. As they approached his private wing, Cirelle's heartbeat quickened.

She entered, ignoring the angry buzz of the doorknob against her hand.

"Second door on the right," Ellian mumbled. She already knew that but didn't comment as she helped him to his chamber. With a yawn, he cast a weary stare at the bed and its glorious golden sheets. He glanced down at his blood-soaked form and shuddered.

"I can draw a bath for you," she offered.

"I fear I lack even the energy for that," Ellian admitted in a rasp. He tugged off the torn and bloody remnants of his shirt and discarded them with a shudder. They fell to the floor in a heap, puddling heavily on the stone. With another deep yawn, he sagged into a wooden chair at a small writing desk.

He hadn't bothered replacing the glamour over his back again to hide the scars. Too tired, or did he no longer care if Cirelle saw them?

He leaned his head back and his eyes drooped shut. Within seconds, his breathing slowed. Cirelle considered leaving, but he'd collapsed in that chair still smudged with blood and his hair still matted with it despite her feeble attempts earlier to clean it.

He'd hate to wake up like this.

Cirelle bit her lip, her heart beating a rapid staccato rhythm in her chest. Maybe it was the strange, surreal quality of the evening leaving her bold enough to even consider an action like this. She ventured into the bathing chamber and found a washbasin. After scrubbing the blood from her own hands, she filled it with warm water, selected a fluffy washcloth from a cabinet, and put a small dash of scented oil in the water. Cedar and vanilla.

As Cirelle set the washbasin on the writing desk and soaked the towel, another aroma mingled with Ellian's. She leaned closer and sniffed. Something crisp, something cold. Running water and soil. No, wait. Rain-soaked leaves. It was in Ellian's hair, heavy and tangled in the strands.

With a sickening lurch, she recognized that smell. The memory of Adaleth's steely fingers grasping her wrists as he snarled in her face would never leave her. Had Ellian searched the prince's room for the Key, in closets and under beds? Or donned a cloak belonging to the prince as part of his attempt to sneak out? It certainly made more sense than her first wrenching thought.

She squeezed the damp cloth around a lock of hair and tried to steady her shaking hands. Ellian didn't even wake up as she repeated the process a couple dozen times, working the tangles loose with a comb she'd found in the vanity. It took a lot of passes before she was convinced the blood was mostly gone.

With gentle strokes, she began washing away the last of the blood on his chest and arms. He'd have to clean his own trousers later. There was at least one line she would not cross.

Cirelle tried hard not to think about the smell of Adaleth on his skin as well. Or the faint, muskier scent that left her stomach in knots.

She didn't hear him awaken. Nor did she see the hand move before it latched gently around her wrist. "Cirelle," his voice purred in her ear, hoarse with sleep. That sound, both smooth and rough, with his warm breath caressing her earlobe, made her shiver. "What are you doing?"

"Cleaning off the blood," she replied.

"While I sleep."

"Well, yes." Neither of them moved.

"And are you enjoying the task?"

How does he lack the energy to bathe, but still has enough to mock me? "I'd enjoy it more if you didn't smell like the prince," she muttered, pulling away.

The look in Ellian's eyes froze her in place. Dark, they were so terribly dark. Black and emerald ringed with a sicklier green she'd only seen once or twice before. Something in that expression turned her blood to ice. "Ellian." Her voice broke. "What did you do to get the Key?"

His lips set in a firm line. He lifted the rag from her hand and threw it back in the basin. "I'm going to bed."

It hadn't been a dismissal, not really. So, she pressed him. "I helped save your life tonight. I held your flesh together to be stitched. I kept the Key safe when you made me promise to. I blockaded the door that separated you from our enemies. I stood watch over you, over every breath to make sure you didn't stop." She panted raggedly, her eyes wild and swimming with tears once more. "And I want to know how you got that Key."

"No, you don't." Ellian's voice was brittle as he made his way wearily to a wardrobe in the corner. He withdrew a long nightshirt and draped it on the foot of the bed as he began to unlace his trousers.

Cirelle turned away, skin burning hot. But still she replied. "I'm owed something in exchange for what I did tonight. You *thanked me.*"

He sucked in a sharp breath.

"Balance, Ellian." She spoke toward the wall. "Tell me."

The flop of leather hitting the ground made her flush even more deeply. Cotton rustled as he donned the shirt, followed by the tread of three quick footsteps. "If you really want to know, I'll do better than tell you." The voice came from directly behind her. Ellian reached past Cirelle to a silver box on the table and flipped it open. It was full of his usual assortment of rings. "Or *worse* than, more accurately. Then maybe you'll learn to stop asking questions you don't really want the answers to."

She turned her head to look at Ellian. His eyes had taken on a frenzied, pained light, swirling with pale green, his teeth bared in something neither grimace nor snarl. He selected a ring from the pile, a heavy silver one with a large blue-black stone, dotted with tiny flecks of silver. It looked like the night sky.

There was a small catch on the side, and he flipped it open to reveal a hollow space. Ellian plucked a strand of hair from his head and curled it up inside the locket, then clasped it shut again. "Put this on and sleep while wearing it. You'll have your answer." His voice grew icy cold. "If you still want it."

Cirelle knew, then. She really knew. But his words held a challenge, and she wouldn't back down. She took the ring and slipped it on a thumb, glaring up at him. "Now go to bed."

"After you, Princess." His words were sharp-edged as he pointed to the door.

She tossed him a vicious little smile and left. It took all her strength to stop by the Archive and drop off the Key safely.

The walk back to her rooms was longer than ever, weary step after weary step. Once there, Cirelle stripped off her clothes, wiped the dried blood from her skin, and washed her wounds. She fell asleep the moment her head hit the pillow and slipped into the most vivid of dreams.

Chapter Fifty-One

Ellian breathed slowly, in, out, in, out. His heart hammered in his ribcage as the blinding whiteness of the Unseelie palace walls mocked him.

Why did I ever think I could do this?

The sound of battle still echoed down the corridors, Ixikki and Carid and Kith executing their task perfectly.

If his allies could all do their part, so could he. Even if none of them knew about this particular aspect of the plan. Ellian choked back his nausea and fear and moved onward. As he neared the hall outside the prince's chambers, he peered around the corner and withdrew quickly.

No guards. Of course not. Why would there be? Who would be foolish enough to breach the prince's very chambers?

Ellian paused at Adaleth's door, legs trembling. In his mind's eye, Cirelle's disapproving face glared. A sharp stab of remorse consumed him for what he'd done to her to get here.

For what I'm about to do to her.

He gritted his teeth. The Key. This was all for the Key. Of every sacrifice that got them here, his would be the final one. All he had to do was carve another chunk of his humanity away.

A deep breath steadied Ellian's nerves. All too aware of his unkempt appearance, he straightened his spine, plastered his most sardonic smile on his face, and knocked lightly.

"What is it?" Adaleth's irritated voice muffled through the wooden door. Not even a hint of fear threaded into that cold, crystalline tenor.

"It's Ellian."

There was a long pause, then the door opened a crack, a yellow-green eye peering through the threshold. Ellian kept his smile on, his eyes hooded. What would he do if Adaleth slammed the door in his face or called guards?

The tense silence held for several heartbeats before the prince opened the door wider. "So, this is what you choose to do on Thieves' Night?" Adaleth asked, his tone as imperious as usual.

Ellian let his smile widen, tilting his head to sweep his gaze over Adaleth slowly. The prince was fully dressed in typical Unseelie attire. An elegant, perfectly tailored coat in alabaster white emphasized the lithe slimness of his figure, black trousers practically painted onto his skin.

Ellian rested casually against the door frame. If magic still flowed, he knew his eyes would gleam crimson red, the color of hatred, of human blood. But tonight, they would remain colorless. He locked that gaze onto the prince's face as he smiled a fox's grin. "It killed you, didn't it? Watching her hands all over me, her lips on my skin?"

The prince's eyes grew hard, cold. "Wasn't that the point?"

"And it worked beautifully," Ellian gloated. He leaned in closer. It was hard to keep the anger from his voice, his hand shaking with fury where it pressed into the door frame. "You didn't take her finger because she destroyed the poison. You did it because a lowly sylvan stole what had been yours."

Adaleth's mouth was a perfect little frown, but those eyes could have melted steel. "Did you come here just to boast?"

"No," Ellian whispered, gathered his courage, and kissed the prince.

Those stone-hard lips grew soft beneath his own and the prince pulled him into the room, shutting the door and pressing Ellian against it. "You have a strange choice of activities for Thieves' Night," he said against Ellian's throat. "I'm sure you have no shortage of enemies to assault, given your behavior over the years. Especially recently."

"Like you don't love it." Ellian laughed, grasping a fistful of that snow-white hair and yanking Adaleth's head back to kiss him again, possessive and nowhere near gentle. "You'd tire of a dull lover."

Adaleth rasped out a brittle laugh between gasps, between kisses. "I don't think you count as a lover if you've been absent from my bed for two decades."

"I'll make up for it," Ellian growled, pulling the prince's head back farther to run a line of kisses down his throat. Something inside him recoiled at what he was doing, his disgust growing with every brush of his lips, his tongue.

Necessary, Ellian reminded himself as his stomach churned. This was necessary. He felt no compunction about Adaleth's feelings, only an overwhelming shame for his need to resort to this, for even entering this room again. Outwardly, he let none of his self-loathing show, but it was a monumental effort. "One night for old times' sake."

"Why now? Why Thieves' Night?"

So I can take back what you tricked from me.

Instead he whispered in Adaleth's ear before nipping on his earlobe. "Would your guards have let me into the palace any other night?"

"That crash I heard... that was you."

"A distraction, yes." Ellian drew back, leaving the prince's breath shallow and panting. Adaleth's pupils were wide and dark. "How else was I to convince you to let me in?"

The prince's lips twisted into a wry smile. "A message is often the accepted way to request a visit."

"Would you have even opened a letter from me, or let in a messenger? You did just try to poison me."

The prince laughed, placing those pale blue hands, the color of winter clouds, against Ellian's bare chest and sliding them up under the edges of his open shirt. "Probably not."

"Then tonight was my best bet, wasn't it?" Ellian kept one hand fisted in the prince's hair, but let the other wander lower, stroking a line along the hardness pinned beneath the prince's trousers. Adaleth groaned, and Ellian leaned in to whisper in his ear. "Don't even pretend you don't love it. You absolutely relish that I'd destroy part of your own castle to get to you. And that I made such a scene at the festival." His voice grew darker. "You even enjoyed it when I tormented you with that woman."

"With that *sylvan*," Adaleth hissed, his nails digging into Ellian's flesh as his grasp tightened.

"You didn't deny you liked it."

Adaleth's reply was low, voice dripping with molasses. "No, I didn't. You vicious creature."

"Which, if I recall correctly, is why you kept me around in the first place."

"*And* why you left."

"I'm here now." Ellian purred the words against the base of Adaleth's neck, teeth scraping the prince's skin. A dark, feral part of him wanted to bite down hard, to tear open the man's throat. He forced the urge back and only nipped lightly, teasing.

"Yes, you are." Adaleth's eyes darkened, the green glow dimming. "And as I've been ordered by my mother to remain in this room for the duration of the evening, so will you."

Ellian squashed down his anger and pushed away from the door, shoving the prince backward toward the bed that rested in the middle of the lavish chamber. A growl entered his reply, "I think that was the idea."

After their session, Ellian felt as if insects had burrowed beneath his skin, as if a merciless vise of red-hot steel squeezed him. Adaleth peered at him through the disheveled curtain of that opalescent hair. A fine sheen of sweat misted his skin.

It was an effort not to cringe as Ellian inhaled and tasted Adaleth's scent on his tongue, ice and withered leaves.

The old, familiar smell made his stomach twist into queasy knots. When he'd left the palace, he swore he'd never return. Would never again become the heartless and wicked thing Adaleth had made of him.

Ellian was one of the few people to know the prince's darkest secret. Many fae liked to mingle games of power with sex. That was nothing unusual in faerie society. But the prince of all the sidhe, someday to be the king, wanted to be subjugated in the extreme. He savored helplessness, and shame devoured him over it.

Even more scandalous was the prince's dalliance with Ellian, so loathed by his mother and many of those immaculate faerie courtiers. This dirty secret had kept Ellian alive in his early days at the Unseelie Court. He'd been bitter and hollow then, terrified of this new world and still grieving his old one.

They'd made a fitting pair.

In public, the prince derided and laughed at Ellian alongside his court. Nights were spent in Adaleth's bedroom, and Ellian took his payment for every humiliation. Ellian had wanted to see something, *anything*, suffer as he had. And Adaleth was all too eager to find someone who would bring him both pain and pleasure.

Adaleth discovered Ellian held the Key, part of the Urisk's fortune. The prince tricked the Key from him, and only much later did Ellian discover what he'd lost.

When he tired of their bedroom games, Ellian fled without so much as a goodbye.

Right now, it was a painful chore for Ellian to keep his eyes from lingering on the black, rune-carved box on Adaleth's mantel. So instead he focused on the pale blue skin of the man beside him. A corpse's color, cold and lifeless.

Adaleth watched him with a glazed look in those sickly green eyes, mouth parted as he panted softly. Ellian had a role to play here, so he did. His hands carded through the prince's fine hair, loosening tangles and soothing with a touch. It was always so after their sessions. Pain and humiliation, followed by soft caresses and gentle words.

Once, it had all been a welcome part of the games they played. Now, his stomach curdled painfully.

For the Key.

For that, he'd do so much worse. To maintain the ties between their worlds, keep the magic flowing between them, he'd do far more awful things than this. And he had. Orwe had not been the first of his little rebellion to perish for the cause. Someday he would become a hollow, vicious thing forever. Empty of all that had ever made him human.

Maybe it would destroy him, but Ellian could think of worse reasons to become a monster like the man beside him.

The prince's hand drew idle patterns on Ellian's stomach and chest with a single teasing fingertip, and Ellian couldn't stop the shudder of revulsion that rippled through the muscles there. Adaleth only smiled, mistaking disgust for arousal. The prince's lips found his neck, and Ellian forced out a small sound of pleasure.

"Again," the prince demanded, and Ellian could not refuse without this whole house of cards tumbling down. He wound up his resolve and tightened his grip on Adaleth's waist, letting his fingers bite in deeply enough to bruise. The prince laughed, gasping. "Yes," he smiled up at Ellian with languid, indulgent eyes.

Choking back his disgust, Ellian painted a similar smile on his own face and pulled the prince closer.

After their second bout , Adaleth had wearied enough to sleep and Ellian felt as if he'd rolled in muck.

The prince was always a heavy sleeper afterward, and tonight was no exception. Ellian slipped out of the bed, quietly dressing, and pulled an exact twin of the Key from an inner pocket of one tall boot. It had even been enchanted to give off a steady thrum of magical energy, though it was dead in his palm tonight. He opened the black box, any protection wards now absent, and swapped the two items.

Closing the tiny chest, Ellian cast one last, angry glance at the prince where he slept. He crept out of the room and pulled the door shut as softly as possible before turning to make his escape.

Only to find himself face-to-face with Queen Ayre.

"I do hope you enjoyed yourself." That voice. High and incongruously sweet, but he'd forgotten how awful and terribly heartless it could sound. It was as if the night wind itself spoke. Ayre did not wear her finery tonight, but armor in an overlapping design of flower blossoms. Such a simple, harmless thing to adorn a viper.

Two of her knives were already in her hands. "I suppose you can taste my blades while you think about all your companions felled beneath my minion's weapons tonight. A lovely bit of symmetry, that."

Ellian's feet were already stepping backward. He turned to flee, but a scorching line of fire sliced its way down his back. Too deep. The metal scraped his shoulder blade.

A little voice inside him laughed bitterly. How inelegant to die like this, so close to success. But it was Thieves' Night, and the queen had caught him where he shouldn't be. She would murder him, sure as dawn would come tomorrow.

Ellian stumbled and fell, feeling the warmth of the blood seeping through the back of his shirt, a spreading cold sensation around the wound. He tried to get up, to run again, but his arms collapsed beneath him, his back screaming in agony.

I've failed. It was his last thought before his consciousness fled. *I failed them all.*

Chapter Fifty-Two

Cirelle awoke gasping, her stomach churning from the dream. She rolled out of bed to hunch over the small waste bin in the chamber, heaving up bile and little else. When the wave of retching abated, Cirelle was left shaking in a cold sweat. She wrenched the ring off her finger and hurled it across the room where it clattered on the stone floor.

Ellian had warned her. He'd told her she didn't want to know. And now she'd never be able to unsee what he'd done.

Worse, she'd relived the scene as if she inhabited Ellian's skin, felt every surge of revulsion and every thread of anger. She now knew why the prince had stared at Ibrafel the sylvan with such cold hatred.

The man she'd seen in that vision was the same one who'd looked out of Ellian's eyes when he gave her the ring yesterday, someone cold and viciously cruel. But there had been something else in his gaze, a mad desperation. That new color had lingered there, a wan green, and now she knew what it meant.

Shame.

She leaned panting over the refuse bin for a while longer.

Adaleth, icy as his aroma and utterly heartless, the man who'd so casually taken her finger. Ellian had bedded him. Not just last night, but willingly and for years.

Her knees were still weak when she stood, and her hands trembled when she went to unlock her door, but she strode across the hall anyway.

Cirelle rinsed out her mouth and drank mint tea to cleanse her tongue. Her bath lasted an hour before she was convinced she'd scrubbed out every last bit of blood and gore clinging to her. The wounds on her belly and scratches on her arm glared an angry red, a stinging reminder of last night.

After she was dressed, Cirelle let the misery wash over her as she curled on her parlor sofa and the truth settled in. She'd been nothing but a pawn from day one. Ellian's little glances and smiles, their banter and teasing and games, all a ploy. Weeks of grooming, preparing her to be paraded about in front of the prince as a foolish, besotted sycophant. How many years had he plotted, only to have the perfect idiot fall into his lap just when he needed one?

Worse, he'd given her every warning, and she'd ignored them all. Her old faerie books had been right all along. Cirelle had tumbled willingly into the embrace of a monster, welcoming his snare with open arms. She'd been blinded by a pretty face and that voice that felt like wrapping herself in plush furs.

There had been a single moment in Ellian's memory, one small stab of guilt for what he'd done to her. Yet he'd known he was using her all along, and still had continued to do it. Feeling bad about it now didn't excuse all his deception, his manipulations. How thoroughly he'd duped her. All she merited was a brief flicker of doubt before he tumbled the prince anyway.

Stupid. She'd been so very, very stupid.

Her sorrow and fury built with each moment, until she could

stand it no longer. She rose, collected the ring once more, and prepared to face the beast that held her captive.

Cirelle stalked down the hall. It was early in the evening, and she passed only Vilitte in the hallway. The woman raised one glittering silver brow at Cirelle's glower but did not speak. The foyer was spotlessly clean, no sign of the battle last night nor of the body Cirelle had left there. Her victim. She closed her eyes and took a long slow breath as the panic threatened again. When she opened them, Cirelle was greeted with the sparkling cleanliness that made last night merely a bad dream.

Whatever the brownies were being paid for their labor, it wasn't enough.

Collecting her courage, Cirelle ascended the steps and pounded on the door to Ellian's wing, loud enough for him to hear even from his room.

Eventually, he answered. Ellian did not look bleary with sleep, nor was he garbed in his night shirt. He stood before her fully dressed, in one of his chest-baring shirts of cream-colored suede, his usual jewelry back in place. He'd even donned the filigreed boots once again. His hair was brushed, and the scent that wafted toward her was entirely his own smoky aroma.

"Cirelle," he greeted her, his eyes flat silver, the skin around them tight.

She hurled the ring at him. It hit his chest and clattered to the floor. The raging tempest inside her could not be quelled, hurt and anger all tangled together.

Her hands stretched into claws. The urge to scratch at that cold, impassive face overwhelmed her. His betrayal tore her to pieces inside, ripping her apart like paper. Cirelle wanted to fling that pain back at him, tenfold.

Her breaths were scratchy, jagged things, but with an effort, she held herself back. "You used me."

"You knew what I was, what I am." Ellian's eyes flickered with something dark. He bent to collect the ring. Then his cold mask fell, and he walked past her.

$$\wp$$

BY LAW, THEIR ALLIES could have claimed guest rights and stayed longer, but everyone bore the weight of last night and agreed to leave after breakfast.

Wounds were tended before they ate, their remaining supply of healing elixir distributed where it was needed. It seemed Shai had helped them with a soldier's knowledge of first aid last night, binding the injuries as best she could. True to his word, Issen had returned the icy daggers to Cirelle this morning, and they now lay tucked securely in the Archive.

Cirelle prodded at the cut on her left hand and winced at the half-circle of holes around her middle. Minor wounds. Shai had merely washed and bound them after Cirelle's confrontation with Ellian that morning. The claw marks on Cirelle's forearms had been doused with elixir, though, starting to fester from whatever toxin those talons had borne. Now they were angry scars, white against the gold of her skin.

Would they fade with time, or remain as eternal reminders of what she'd done?

Ixikki and Agdarr had arrived later in the night, allowed in by the brownies at Ellian's previous permission. They now breakfasted with the rest in Ellian's largest dining room. Even here, the top of Ixikki's head threatened to scrape the ceiling.

The meal was a somber affair, a chorus of determined chewing punctuated only by stilted bits of conversation. The puzzle of those first two intruders remained unsolved. They had both been human, a fact that left Cirelle with little appetite. Ellian was not the only faerie to bargain with mortals. Many of the less scrupulous fae did not balk at bewitching Cirelle's kind.

That was bad enough. Worse was Cirelle's new suspicion. The first intruders had known the ilthys guarded Ellian's manor, had known Cirelle held the Archive's key for the evening.

Someone had told them.

It wasn't information from Orwe before he died. The small faerie had never known Cirelle existed, much less that she would hold the Archive's skeleton key.

Cirelle glanced around the table. A traitor broke bread with them. Who had sent a human to steal the claimhte from the queen of a shadowy spider race before coming here? While everything about their first round of thieves was a mystery, the second batch of intruders were no secret. The queen's hired soldiers in her monochromatic livery. A bit of vengeance for Ellian's display at the Unseelie festival. It seemed such an unnecessary and intolerable loss of life. So much bloodshed, and not a small amount of it on her own hands.

As if dealing with her own actions last night wasn't enough, there were other memories now etched in Cirelle's mind, recollections that should never have belonged to her. She'd never wanted to know how Adaleth's skin tasted or exactly where he liked to be bitten.

Her stomach doing somersaults, Cirelle picked listlessly at her pastry.

Vilitte explained to Cirelle what happened. They'd had no luck with the treasury and hunted the corridors for Ellian. Dirilai had found them and led them to the dungeon where Ellian lay chained and bleeding. They took care of the guards, a fact Vilitte conveyed with no remorse. Agdarr's lock-picking was enough to free Ellian, and they made their escape through the same tunnel they'd used to enter.

Cirelle told herself she didn't care, that he could have been left in that dungeon to rot, but she didn't believe her own lies.

Chapter Fifty-Three

"YOU JUST COULDN'T TELL HIM NO," the queen growled as she kicked at the open shackles, her pale gray boots carelessly trodding in the pool of dark, half-dried blood.

"He was already in the palace," Adaleth shrugged, tugging a sleeve smooth.

"You could have called the guards." Ayre's frown was deeper than usual, though not a single crease marred her snowy-white face.

"The guards that were busy at the front gate?" Adaleth sneered. "The ones that were knocked down by a stone giant?"

The queen paced back and forth across the dungeon cell, leaving sticky footprints in her wake. "How did he even get free?"

The prince knelt, poking at the manacles. "It's not like Thresk to be careless in locking up a prisoner."

"He wasn't," Queen Ayre said. "And now he's dead, along with the other three guards that were at this post tonight. The chief of staff is rounding up all the servants. We have a snake in our midst, my son."

"Ellian's serpent," Adaleth mused, thinking of the pin his sometimes-paramour often wore.

"Don't sound so pleased," his mother spat. "It will take weeks to repair the damage, all for a single night's tumble. I hope it was worth it."

Adaleth shivered, remembering hard teeth bruising skin, a booted foot pressed to his back as he crawled on the floor. Flesh on flesh, steel and leather and sweet degradation.

It was.

Until his mother had cut Ellian down, imprisoned him, and forced him to flee. Would another twenty years pass before the fickle sidhe sought Adaleth's bed once more?

The prince had thought Ellian had long since discarded the Unseelie ways, too high and mighty and mortal for their sins. But then he'd arrived with that sylvan in tow, teasing Adaleth mercilessly with his eyes while the woman claimed him with her hands and mouth. Playing their old games and mastering them oh so well. Ellian had returned to Adaleth's bedroom as deliciously wicked as he'd ever been.

If Ayre had not assaulted Ellian this night, would he have returned to dominate Adaleth in secret whenever he wished? Ellian had pledged never to rejoin the Unseelie court proper but had made no promises about the prince's bedchamber.

The phantom memory of those demanding, cruel fingertips left Adaleth's breathing shallow. He made an effort to steady it and ensured his voice was clear as he said, "He offered. I accepted." He could feel the glint in his eyes as he stared at his mother. "Why? Are you wishing you could do to my lover what I did to yours?"

The queen's voice dropped from her usual crystal soprano into something harsher, deeper. "To your own father?"

He shrugged. "A sire, maybe. Never a father." Adaleth stared at the spot where his bleeding lover had lain only hours before.

Her face impassively cold, Ayre turned to lead the way out

of the room. "Come, we've a story to weave, something to tell the court that doesn't involve my son—their future king—being blinded by lust for a mongrel."

Adaleth cast his mother a cold, defiant grin. "After you, my Queen."

&

ELLIAN STRAIGHTENED HIS JACKET, realized it was the fourth time he'd done so in as many minutes, and forced his hands into stillness at his sides.

It was a struggle not to pace the ballroom as soft music floated up from the enchanted instrument in the corner. An astralir, something rather like an overgrown mandolin, charmed to play without a musician. With a vast repertoire, its random selection was sometimes bitterly cruel.

It was playing an appropriately melancholy dirge when the heavy doors opened. Cirelle stepped through with her head held high, her lips pressed together in determination.

The world froze as their gazes met, a hundred unspoken words flickering between them.

She'd girded herself for battle, in her own way. The gown was a rich, bloody crimson, violent and breathtaking. In a human style, it was tight in the bodice with skirts blossoming out at her waist. He didn't miss the statement, a declaration of her mortal nature.

Moreover, she'd worn war paint. Or at least her own feminine version of it. Dark, smoky eyes and garnet lips. If he'd thought of reconciliation and a stolen kiss, this squashed that faint hope.

She never painted her lips. It was a warning, a deterrent. If he kissed her tonight, he'd smear the cosmetics over them both.

Not that it wouldn't be worth it.

His eyes skated over her from head to toe, and something stuttered in his chest. But what truly made his breath seize was the defiant look in those stormy eyes. It sparked a matching fire in him, one he doused quickly.

Fool. The princess was only here because she'd lost a wager. Every inch of her posture screamed her fury at him. They'd both made this bed, but Ellian was to blame far more than she.

It's good that she hates you, an insidious little voice echoed in his mind. *Do you want another Kyrinna?*

No. The woman standing before him with her fists clenched tightly at her sides would never be a simpering, lovestruck maiden.

He held out a hand. Wordlessly, she took it, letting him pull her into position for the elegant baliterre that had just begun. A structured dance, she remained stiff and unyielding in his arms, her furious gaze aimed at his collarbone. Her steps were technically perfect but lacked the joyous fire of their previous dances.

Something withered inside Ellian, and he found his tongue. "Are you going to remain silent the full hour?"

Her reply was crisp. "I've nothing more to say to you."

They plodded through several silent dances, each as lifeless as the first. Then a new song began, a deep and resonant melody. A sidhe song, an echoing pulse of drums and a single string instrument. The last time they'd performed this dance, she'd been garbed as a golden serpent and they'd both ended up drowning in their own desire.

Cirelle shoved him away, snarling. "You arrogant, hateful ass," she hissed.

Ellian swallowed back the sharp, stabbing pain inside his

ribcage and kept his gaze carefully gray. "I don't control the astralir's song choice. The bargain was struck fairly; an hour of dancing. You didn't specify the dances."

"Neither did you."

He stared at her and held out his hand once more. A tiny, dark tendril of something cruel sprouted within him. His sidhe nature, the one he tried so hard to smother. But tonight, he was tired of fighting. If he unmasked his gaze, would it flicker faintly red beneath the violet?

Or would it burn with the rosy pink he tried so hard to keep hidden? Even seeing her spitting and growling at him left a slow trickle of warmth inside, and Ellian hated it. So, he let that self-loathing harden into something vicious. "An hour, Princess."

She sucked in a long breath, her breasts pressing against the restraint of her scooped neckline. Despite himself, Ellian's eyes flickered down and back up again.

Cirelle's eyes widened, and Ellian realized his glamour had faltered once more. Why did this mortal rattle him so?

"Purple," she murmured, tilting her head at him as she put together the pieces. "You said your eyes can't lie."

He frowned. "They can't."

Her grin turned wicked. Ellian could practically read her thoughts. His shifting gaze had betrayed him, and she now realized his desires ran true, despite everything else he'd done. That they always had.

The princess's voice dipped low, a barb poisoned by her sugary tone. "Fine. You want dances, you shall have them. But that is all you will ever have of me."

Ellian's tongue went dry as she took his hand and wrapped herself in his arms, her body growing pliant and soft against his. He sucked in a breath. She laughed with a roll of her hips that sparked desire through him like lightning.

Cirelle's hands guided his grasp lower on her sides. His fingertips dug into her skin through the silk of her skirt. He bent his head and breathed in the scent of her hair. Cinnamon and amber, the fiery fragrance she wore when she was upset with him.

"You truly do desire me, don't you?" she asked sweetly.

He could not lie. "Yes." The word came out half-croak, half-whisper.

She turned in his arms, pressing herself to him, chest to chest. Her breath warmed his throat. "Does it hurt? Knowing this is all you will ever have of me?"

Ellian's hands tightened on her hips, stifling a small, animal sound at the way they moved against his own. False. He'd stolen this. She only teased him for cruelty's sake.

Yet he would give her the satisfaction she so craved. The truth. "It feels like iron in my blood," he whispered as her spicy scent drowned him. "But I'll gladly drink any poison, as long as it's yours."

Her returning laugh was almost sidhe in its viciousness. "I know."

Ellian had chosen too well with this human, one who could match any faerie in cold-hearted wickedness. For too many long minutes, she tormented him with her touch. He took it all, though it stung worse than any thorns. She was the picture of a sidhe, masking pain as pleasure and relishing in her mastery of him.

The agony built and crested until he could bear it no longer. The words spilled from his lips before he could stop them. "So, this is to be our fate, every fortnight?"

She replied without hesitation, without gentleness. Her teeth grazed his throat, turning his knees to water. The words were honeyed, heartless. "You used me like a toy. So now you are mine to play with. You earned this punishment. You've taught me oh so much about balance, after all."

A groan seeped from him as the song ended and she slipped out of his arms. He carefully constructed his mask once more and asked stiffly, "And how long will my penance last?"

"You'll find, faerie, that human memories can be long, and our hatred runs hotter than any sidhe's." Only anger burned in those eyes as she turned and left with swaying hips. At the door, she paused. "Did it even once occur to you that I'd still have helped, had you told me everything?"

And then she was gone. On shaking legs, Ellian strode over to the astralir and silenced it.

Chapter Fifty-Four

CIRELLE STOPPED SPEAKING TO ELLIAN after that, save when
forced to attend a summons. She followed silently and stalked
away the moment they returned.

In a fortnight, Ellian would claim her for another hour of
dance, another evening of his own torment, and she would relish
every moment of it. Until then, she had nothing to say.

It still felt like breathing glass to be near him. Cirelle wondered how long that would last.

Ellian had told her himself. *Give a faerie an inch, and we'll
take everything.* But she hadn't listened. Now she had to share
a home with a man who had made her nothing but a pawn in
his games.

Worse, every night in her dreams, Cirelle lived her victims'
last moments as if they were her own memories. The snap of
bone, blood clogging her throat and nostrils as that ilthys loomed
over her. In other nightmares, Cirelle's hands grew wet and
sticky with faerie blood that would not wash off, the frog-like
man's throat slashed open and gaping wider, ever wider until
it swallowed her whole. It was a river of gore, a fountain that
drowned her. She was suffocated under the pile of bodies that

she'd created, her ilthys tossing them upon her until the weight crushed her bones.

Cirelle ate little and slept less.

As she did most evenings, Cirelle now stood in the Archive, staring at the tiny, separate shelf she'd made for herself. Ellian had said nothing when she set it apart from his, marking it as her own. The two curved daggers of the ilthys sat upon it. Claimhte, the Scath had called them. *Swords*, her earring translated. Too short to be true swords, it was merely a name.

Hers and hers alone. Ellian had not won these.

She caressed the flat of one blade with a fingertip, enjoying its cool smoothness against her skin, the way the white metal gleamed in iridescent shades like mother of pearl. They sang to her, a lullaby of darkness and whispers. The knives spoke of moonless nights best for stalking, for hunting. Of power.

A hard lump congealed in Cirelle's chest, something cold, something hollow. Thieves' Night had been her forge, making of her something else, something indomitable. She would not let Ellian's betrayal break her. She would neither weep nor sulk anymore. Not for his sake. Even if she was pledged to dance with him.

There was work still left to do, and Stars help her, she would see it done. They had a traitor to ferret out. Cirelle would not let that go unanswered, even if it meant wielding the dark power of these blades.

Her hand tightened around a black hilt. Perhaps Cirelle was never meant to be a princess, but here in Faerie, she would claim her place as a queen.

Acknowledgments

FIRST AND FOREMOST, my largest thanks go out to my husband, Nathan. There were many long nights of writing and many emotional breakdowns; he saw me through all of them with compassion and never complained once.

Another enormous thank you to Pascalle Ballard. Their constant encouragement throughout the entire process often kept me going when I wanted to throw up my hands and quit.

All my gratitude to Laurie, my very first fan. She's been reading my work since I could hold a crayon, and I wouldn't have become the writer I am today without her friendship and support.

Thank you to Kita, my writing-night confidant and a patient listener to many book-related rants.

My editor Charlie Knight's keen eye helped develop the final product you see here and caught so many of those pesky stray commas. Any mistakes that remain are mine alone.

So many thanks to D.C. McNaughton for breathing such beautiful life into Cirelle, Ellian, and other members of the book's cast on that gorgeous cover.

A big shout-out to my critique partner Amren and all of the

beta readers who gave feedback on Cambiare. Their assistance shaped this story into something so much better than I could have created alone.

I couldn't have done this without my online writing group, the Teamiest Team. Alicia Hawks, D.C. McNaughton, Renee Brown, Elina Pilar, and Ann. They kept me sane when I needed it most. I'm so grateful NaNoWriMo and RevPit connected me with such wonderful people.

Speaking of which, thanks to National Novel Writing Month for showing me that I could finish a novel way back in 2006. My local NaNoWriMo group has taught me so much, and November is a highlight of my year thanks to all of you. (Especially the Hemingway Party group. You know who you are.)

Thanks to the Wichita Public Library for giving me a peaceful place to work, for supporting local writers, and for being an awesome resource in our community.

To everyone who touched this book or helped me along this journey, I can never thank you enough.

About the Author

AVERY AMES is a graphic designer currently residing in Wichita, Kansas. A lifelong lover of lush fantasy, she was introduced to Ridley Scott's film Legend as a child, and it was all downhill from there. She writes novels that toe the line between glittery and dark, for lovers of fairy tales and everything gothic. When not writing, she can be found playing video games, making candles, or concocting new tea blends.

Twitter: @AveryAmes
www.averyames.com